PUNCHING OUT

Praise for *Punching Out*

"A book written from the inside; soldiers' stories butting up against civilian realities; British lives as they are lived. I read Punching Out *with admiration."*

Rachel Seiffert, author of *The Dark Room* (2001 and short-listed for the Booker Prize); *Afterwards* (2007 and long-listed for the Orange Prize for Fiction); *The Walk Home* (2014); and *A Boy in Winter* (2017).

*"*Punching Out *offers the braided stories of five men, from a single regiment, as each navigates the transition from soldier to veteran to civilian. They come up against indifference, the complexity of civilian life, the unfamiliar ambiguities that surround how decisions get made, how a man is valued, about what matters. Each of these brothers in arms adjusts to a new life – or doesn't. Smith's gift here, as in his previous works of fiction, is his ability to present and embody, with delicate, ruthless, and heart-breaking precision, the hearts and minds and lives of unique individuals about whom we come to care deeply. Beyond this,* Punching Out *is also, without polemic, a portrait of the Britain they come "home" to: a country, and its politicians, stumbling through Brexit, navigating – like the soldiers – the uncertain debris of empire."*

Elizabeth T. Gray Jr is the author of *Salient* (2020), *Series|India* (2015), and *After the Operation* (2025). She is a translator of Persian and Tibetan literature and an expert in complex negotiations and inter-organizational collaboration.

Also by Fergus Smith

In the Shadow of the Mountain, published by Headsail Books 2013. Paul Illingworth, a dedicated and ambitious young officer at the threshold of life's great adventure, comes face to face with the realities of military command. Set against the collapse of the IRA ceasefire in the mid 1990s, this is a compelling story of leadership and the tough decisions it requires. This novel creates a beautiful political allusion of Tony Blair and New Labour coming to power.

> *"The British public sympathises with its army, but does not empathise with it... The army trumpets the ideals of leadership; this book explains what they are, and how they operate."*
>
> **Professor Sir Hew Strachan**, Chichele Professor of the History of War at All Souls College Oxford

> *"...as thought-provoking as it is enthralling."*
>
> **James Clark**, former Defence Editor, *The Sunday Times*

> *"Anyone with ambitions to lead should read this book."*
>
> **Professor Chris Ivory**, Deputy Director, Institute of International Management Practice, Anglia Ruskin University

Sunrise in the Valley, published by Headsail Books, 2016. As the new millennium dawns, NATO is protecting a fragile peace between the Albanians and Serbians in the Balkan region of Kosovo. British Army spokesman Major Paul Illingworth must win hearts and minds to build peace and stability. But all factions are suspicious and volatile, and veteran war reporters deeply cynical of what he is trying to do. Can he trust Roza, his young Albanian interpreter? Which version of the truth does he believe? He who controls the message, controls perception. And he who controls perception, controls behaviour. The sequel to *In the Shadow of the Mountain*, this novel brilliantly highlights the vanity at the heart of New Labour.

> *"Explores the power relationships between the media, the government, and the civilian population."*
>
> **Professor Catherine O'Connor,**
> Leeds Trinity University

> *"Captures the intense complexities, personal as well as military, of the Kosovo war."*
>
> **War photographer,** Associated Press

Along the Swift River, published by Headsail Books, 2016. After the 2001 attack on the World Trade Centre and other targets, a multifaceted global war is fought between Western, Christian countries and various Islamic forces in Syria, Libya, Iraq, and Afghanistan. Keen to protect and enhance its reputation, the British Army supports all American led overseas operations, including those into Iraq and Afghanistan. For Lieutenant Colonel Rolly Rawlins, the frequent deployment offers the opportunity for advancement and to demonstrate his growing confidence. Being offered command of an operational parachute battalion on a tour of Helmand province is not something he would ever miss. It is the high point of his career to date and the culmination of everything he has worked for. But we should always be wary of the things we crave and the costs we must bear to get them.

Along the Swift River is a searing study of arrogance and wilful self-deception at the personal, organisational, and national level. It summarises the heroism, tragedy, and lunacy of Operation Herrick in a way no other writer has dared to do.

The sequel to *In the Shadow of the Mountain* and *Along the Swift River*, this novel brilliantly mirrors the collapse of moral authority at the end of New Labour's term in government.

PUNCHING OUT

Fergus Smith

Published by Headsail Books

© Fergus Smith, 2025

Published by Headsail Books, 55 Westgate, LEEDS, LS20 8HH
www.headsailbooks.com

First published in the United Kingdom 2025 by Headsail Books.
All rights reserved. Reproduction of short sections of the text
of this book (but not the cover) for non-commercial purposes
is allowed. Where commercial exchange is involved, no part of
this book may be reproduced, adapted, or stored without prior
permission in writing from the author, contacted through the
publisher at books@headsailbooks.com

The rights of Fergus Smith to be identified as the author of
this work have been asserted in accordance with the Copyright
Designs and Patent Act 1988.

ISBN 978-1-8381285-2-4 (paperback)
ISBN 978-1-8381285-3-1 (ePub)

Cover design: Claire Simpson claire@clairesimpsondesigns.co.uk

Cover photo: Fergus Smith

Cover portrait: Faye Kenny-Broom fkbphotography@gmail.com

Typeset by Clare Brayshaw

Manufacturer: York Publishing Services Ltd
64 Hallfield Road, Layerthorpe, York YO31 7ZQ
Tel: 01904 431213 | Email: enquiries@yps-publishing.co.uk
Website: www.yps-publishing.co.uk

Represented by: Authorised Rep Compliance Ltd.
Ground Floor, 71 Lower Baggot Street, Dublin D02 P593, Ireland
www.arccompliance.com

For those who have Served

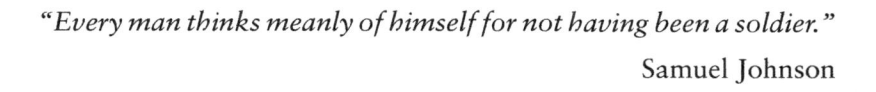

"Every man thinks meanly of himself for not having been a soldier."
Samuel Johnson

"We aren't no thin red 'eroes, nor we aren't no blackguards too,
But single men in barricks, most remarkable like you;
An' if sometimes our conduck isn't all your fancy paints,
Why, single men in barricks don't grow into plaster saints;

Rudyard Kipling, *Tommy*

Dean, June 2016

Once he'd finally cleared immigration at Manchester airport, Dean stood at the top of the steps looking down on the baggage hall. The collection belts protruded like steel ribs from the wall below him. He descended the stairs, took a piss, then took up a position close to the rubber curtain where his case would appear. Because he'd already spent an hour in the tedious snake weaving towards the automatic gates, he did not have to wait long. He spotted it, extended the handle, and barged through the crowd towards customs. Having spent the previous two months in Baghdad he sensed fresh English air just beyond the exit gates.

"Excuse me, coming through."

The arrivals area was dirty, crowded, and dark. Drab figures slouched along the railing waiting for family members. Taxi drivers held tablets with names in large letters but didn't make eye contact. Dean scanned the concourse from left to right quelling a sense of panic but his frustration vanished when he heard Michelle's excited calling.

"Deano! Deano!"

She was by the newsagent, waving, one hand on the bar of an empty trolley. She was tanned and had just had her hair done; long blonde curls tumbling over her boobs. Dean smiled as he walked into her arms and kissed her cheek.

"Aw, my hunky man. Welcome home, love."

"Thanks for coming, great to be home."

They kissed a second time and Dean swung the holdall onto the trolley. He wanted to ask about the girls but knew she'd say in due course.

"Two pound I paid for that! Two bloody pound!" she said. "Let's get out of here."

It was refreshing to feel the wind whipping through the entrance. The dry heat of Baghdad still clung to his stubble but his clothes were tacky and stinking. He'd been in them for forty-eight hours. He was exhausted but the thought of a long, cold wife-beater sat just on the edge of his tongue.

"I know what you're thinking," laughed Michelle as they crossed the pelican crossing to the meet and greet. "Now where's the car?"

He absorbed the greens, greys, and blues of the English afternoon. They were so refreshing after the monochrome desert. He wanted to be home and nothing could move fast enough, even Michelle. He wanted to drive but had had a few free ones in the lounge at Heathrow while waiting for the Manchester flight, so he pushed the trolley out of the way and got in the passenger side.

Michelle chose the motorway rather than the cross-country route to Rotherham. A good decision, he thought. She was full of smiles but Dean was too tired to converse. He dropped his seat back, folded his arms, and fell asleep, waking fifty minutes later thick-tongued and drooling. The light was fading and they were making good time.

"You ok, love?" Michelle said. "Reach behind me, in the bag. There's a Greggs and a Stella. I stopped for petrol but you were sparko."

Dean chuckled. "You're a star."

He cracked the beer, sipped the foam, then lifted the seat upright. The bacon bake in the paper bag left flakes of brittle pastry on his fingers and dropped on his trousers. He brushed himself with flicks of his hand while simultaneously stuffing the second one in his mouth.

"The girls should have got a curry in," Michelle said. "They can't wait to see you."

Dean smiled. He imagined them gleefully bobbing up and down behind the kitchen table with a meal laid out. Even though he hated being separated from them he was used to the month-on, month-off routine. It was the cost he paid for providing them with the opportunities he never had. He was proud, so proud, of the way they talked about A levels and university places; things that had never been within his reach.

Passing a road sign, he realised where he was. The next junction would be Wakefield, then Barnsley. They still had forty minutes to go.

"How was it this time?" Michelle said.

Dean told her. Mundane, really. One bomb in the city centre but nothing too messy. Nothing in the Green Zone. Global Risks still had a reputation as the best security contactor. If the Sunni militias wanted to kidnap for ransom, there were easier targets than his clients.

"Are you still thinking about leaving?" Michelle asked, glancing at him out of the corner of her eye.

Dean nodded. "They've hired a new guy to beef up the roster. So I might not have to do a back-to-back next rotation."

"Do you know him?"

Dean shook his head. "Haven't met him. Harry, the new boss, says he's ex 2REP, French Foreign Legion. We'll see what he's like."

Now he was back in England he didn't want to think about Iraq until the last possible moment. He took long drafts of the lager and burped. "How's the conservatory? Is it done yet? I want to get some mates round for the Iceland game."

Michelle said nothing. It looked like she was deciding how to answer.

"Tell me."

She pulled out round a lorry, checking the rear-view mirror. "I spoke to Mahmud. It'll be a couple of weeks more. He's had another job on that he said was urgent. An uncle or something, for a wedding."

"So it's not done?" He was frustrated more than angry but knew it wasn't her fault. The builder had always been slippery and Dean had known he'd pull a fast one as soon as he'd gone back to Iraq. "Don't worry, love. I'll speak to him."

"You sure?"

"Yeah, I'm sure. It's not your fault."

"Thanks, Deano. That would be great."

Her fingers played with the indicator. She was driving as fast as she dared through the roadworks, the yellow gantry cameras watching over them like vultures. And then, out of the fog of his fatigue, Dean noticed an Audi with Union Jack window flags flapping above the rear doors. He drummed his feet on the floor.

"But at least we're out! We told those fucking Europeans to fuck themselves! What a cracker, eh?"

Michelle smiled, pleased to change the subject. "There was a tent by the town hall this morning; people giving out flags and stuff. There's bunting all over town…"

Dean grunted as he squashed the beer can in his hands. "Fucking sick of being told what to do by Germans. Take back control! That's what we need."

He reached behind his wife for the second can. He'd heard the news at Heathrow that morning. It had been all over the televisions in the lounges. Some people had cheered. But he had also noticed the dark mood among the business travellers, the men with suits and briefcases. Why didn't they cheer, he wondered? If they lived in Rotherham, they'd be overjoyed!

"Can we get the neighbours round? Celebrate?"

Michelle nodded. She said nothing for a few miles then chirped up, "Oh, Pete rang!"

"Pete McCardle?"

"Yeah, Pete. Your Pete. Scottish Pete. Rang the house phone."

"Yeah. My mobile's died. What did he want?"

She shook her head. "He said did you remember a kid called Kyle? One of your recruits from when you was up at Catterick?"

Dean frowned while the memories seeped back into view. Yes. Nice kid. In fact, for a TA soldier, he was really good. Boxer. Horny sister too, although that was another matter. "He was known as Smiler. Smiler Hutton. Kyle. That was it. What about him?"

Michelle pursed her lips.

"What's happened?"

"He's dead, Deano. Hung himself."

"What?"

The absurdity hit Dean hard. "He only joined a few years ago."

"Pete said he'll ring again when you're back. You should go see him."

Dean was still shocked. "Hutton was one of my Joes. I took him through training." The joy of being home and the shock of the news moved unevenly in his head. The kid was the best recruit on his course. After Catterick he'd gone straight out to Afghan. That's where the demons came from, no doubt about it. "What a fucking bummer. And today of all days."

Alexander, June 2016

On 23rd June 2016, the United Kingdom held a referendum on whether to leave or remain in the European Union. The Union was a trading bloc with its roots in the international structures established after the Second World War to deter nationalist excess and provide a platform for intergovernmental dialogue. The vote was tight but sufficient: 52% supported the Leave campaign, while 48% wished to Remain.

The Prime Minister, David Cameron, resigned the following day citing the fact that the country needed a new captain to steer it. What could have been a rich debate about the sort of leader required at such times became, through the perversities of the British political system, a one-horse race. Teresa May was appointed Prime Minister a month later. Although she had personally supported the Remain campaign she recognised that the public had spoken.

"Brexit means Brexit," she said.

Alexander Johnson MP, *Al* to his friends and *Boris* to the press, did not run against her. Studiously unkempt, flamboyant, and brilliantly witty, he knew instinctively to wait until May had tried to untangle and negotiate the commercial and political deal through which the UK could leave the Union. Given the complexity of the task and the sheer number of competing interests, it was unlikely she would be successful, thus leaving the door open for him to step in as the saviour of the national interest.

In the wake of the referendum, international markets plummeted and interest rates rose. The political establishment was rattled by the vehemence of opinion. Two weeks prior to the referendum, the Labour MP for the Yorkshire town of Batley, Jo Cox, had been shot and hacked to death during a constituency surgery. She had been a Remainer advocating that people were always 'better together'. Her murderer was not.

Since Alexander held the safe seat of Uxbridge and South Ruislip, he did not have to bother with frontline surgeries. He was popular and recognisable. His decision to back the Leave campaign in the February of 2016 was a masterly act of political theatre. May, however, was suspicious of his motives and so appointed him Foreign Secretary, forcing him to champion British interests to a cynical world.

European leaders considered his appointment beyond parody but they failed to grasp that politics was changing. Truth no longer mattered. What attracted voter support was charisma, and what communicated charisma was either money or a penetrating wit.

While he was Foreign Secretary, *The Spectator* ran a competition in which people were invited to lampoon European leaders. Alexander won with a limerick about President Erdoğan of Turkey:

There was a young fellow from Ankara,
Who was a terrific wankerer.
Till he sowed his wild oats,
With the help of a goat,
But he didn't even stop to thankera.

Kyle, previously

I've just punched out of the army and Mum's died. I were discharged Friday and the lads said to stay because they wanted to send me off proper. I'd been in since 2012 and had done two year including the last tour of Afghan, and that's about as long as a regular does.

The lads said it didn't matter I was a STAB, For a reservist, I was a good lad. They took me down the nightclubs in Colchester, Collie to the blokes, and got me pissed. Gave me a statue, the twelve-inch bronze one of a GPMG gunner with a beret on his head and a bergen on his back. And on the brass plaque there's this inscription: To Smiler, All the best, from the Blokes, MMG Platoon.

I didn't get the message that Mum was slipping away till Saturday morning. I'd crashed in the block kipping in my buckshee dossbag. I didn't hear my phone till Gaz shook me. It were nearly nine and we'd missed breakfast, not that it mattered. I was out. But there was about a hundred messages from Charlotte, my big sister, saying to get myself up to Royal Stoke ASAP. Mum was poorly, she said, and you could hear she was a bit mad at me.

Gaz gave me a lift to the station in double time and I got the train to London then belted over to Euston on the underground. Got to the platform just as the guy was blowing his whistle. I got through to Char on the train. She said Mum's cancer'd gone spastic. She didn't want me to know, that's why she'd never said fuck all. But I knew when I called her from Collie that her breathing was heavy and I could hear the air tube getting in the way. She had one of those bottles on a trolley. But I didn't know she was dying.

I said to Char I'd be there 13.52 and would leg it from the station. Char said to get a taxi but I didn't have any cash. She said I had to be quick. Mum was conscious but in a lot of pain. They'd given her morphine but just get there.

So when the train pulled in I was number one in the door and banging on the yellow button going open, open, open. And then out and vaulting the barriers to get to the cab rank.

There were none there so I ran over the Queensway, through the park. Then I got lost in all those red brick streets that run down to Prince's Road. I figured it would be quickest through the cemetery but ended up getting lost there as well. I had to jump through some allotments with old gadgies shouting at me and then I had to leap this bastard fence and my jeans got cut on the top of it. I had my bergen on my back and was tabbing away, hands swinging across the body like I was in training. A van beeped as I ran across Hilton Road but I just gave him the finger and ran on. I was sweating like a fat lass at a disco by the time I got to the hospital and the woman at the desk said something about you can't bring that rucksack in here but I said Mum was dying, which ward was she in? The woman's face changed and she looked it up on the computer and pointed down the corridor with her pen. Follow signs for Oncology, she said. Then go up two levels.

I legged it, dodging the old fogeys and the wheelchairs. I felt proper guilty for staying down on the piss. I just didn't think she was that bad. And when I got to the ward, chest heaving, the nurse in blue said to follow her to the family room and this was down the back stairs. I was gutted as I was sucking air from Guildford having bolted up the main steps two at a time. The nurse's phone rang as she was leading me down and you could tell she was getting dicked in all directions. I said where is it? I'll find it. She said to go down to the next floor, through the double doors, and the family room was on the right.

So I'm going down these wide concrete steps with a blue line down the side and it bends round by this window that's made of glass bricks. It's cloudy so it lets light in but you can't see out clearly. And as I start the next flight of steps there's Char halfway down, leaning on the banister, crying her eyes out.

"Char..."

I drop my bergen on the landing and go down to her. She says: "Oh Kyle, Mum's just gone. She went ten minutes ago." She puts her arms up to hug me but I'm like way taller than her so I go down to the step below and that way we're even.

Her cheeks are wet and she looks like she's been there all night. I must smell awful because I didn't shower and have just been legging it from the train.

"I'm sorry..." I say, but she shakes her head and puts her arms round my neck again. "I came as fast as I could."

She nods, holding my shoulders. "She was asking after you right to the end. I said you'd be here any moment. And she tried, Kyle, she really tried...."

Then Char coughs a bit and there's snot on the back of her hand and tears running down her cheeks. She pulls out a hanky and blows her nose. "She couldn't hold on..." she said at last.

And I'm like hollowed out. I hang my head and Charlotte puts her hand on my chest. "It's not your fault, Kyle. There's nothing you could have done..."

And then there's a gaggle of people scuttling down the stairs: a woman in a white coat followed by several nurses. On the landing the woman points at my bergen and says, "Could we remove this obstacle before we have

*an accident." It's an order, but I don't move. Just look up
at her with a blank face. Then she sweeps on by, the nurses
following, some in blue, some in green. I wonder what the
colours mean, if they are ranks or teams or what.*

*Char sniggers, despite herself. Then she shakes her head
and wipes her nose on the back of her hand. I'm laughing
too.*

*I say, "Who does she think she is? Do you know what
I mean?"*

*Char looks up at me. "Are you finished now or do you
have to go back?"*

I shake my head. "I'm done. A civvy."

*There are people down the stairwell coming up, the
footsteps and voices echoing and we think we should move.
I climb to the landing, lift my bergen upright, and brace
it out of the way with my leg. Char looks out through
the glass bricks. Her eyes are red round the edges and her
hands are shaking. She puts them flat on the glass.*

*I'm thinking of Gaz's face after Johno got slotted in
the ambush, how gutted he was. Gaz and Johno were like
brothers. When Johno took one, Gaz was there, applying
pressure to the wound, shouting to stay awake. Later,
when we were packing Johno's kit after the chopper picked
up his body, Gaz was trying not to look like he was upset.
I just felt cold then. Unemotional. You couldn't let it get
to you as that would mean you took your eye off the ball
and someone else might get slotted. You had to stay sharp,
stay focused.*

*So I'm looking at Charlotte and I'm like trying to protect
her from the pain. I want to lift it out from around her
and carry it away. This is something I can do. Something I
learned in Afghan.*

*"Where are you staying?" she asks. The light that falls
across one side of her face turns grey as a cloud covers the
sun.*

"I'll crash at Mum's," I say. "I've a key."

Char nods. She tells me to wait downstairs by the main entrance while she does the paperwork with the ward nurses. I bum a fag off this old guy who walks with a zimmer frame and is wearing a paper robe that's open at the back. I joke with him that he should think about a dressing gown but he shakes his head and lights up then passes me the lighter.

Char's car is at the far end of the carpark. There's a ticket on the window but she doesn't get riled. I spot the guy with the machine on the next row down. Black guy, high-vis vest with 'Parking Enforcement' on the back. I'm about to kick off when Char says, "No, Kyle, leave it. It doesn't matter." I'm like snapping and glaring at him. I could knock his fucking head off with a good right hook but he's not looking this way. Char says, "Kyle, it's fine. I'll challenge it. I know how to do this. Let's just go."

So I'm seething and dripping with sweat and all bent up in her little Micra. She asks if I'm hungry and I realise I haven't eaten since last night. I'm chin-strapped, snapping, and hank marvin. She takes me to Maccy D's and gets me a meal deal from the drive through and a coffee for herself. We sit in the carpark scoffing. Well, I'm scoffing, and she takes one sip of the coffee then pours the rest out of the window pulling a face. I scoff the BigMac and offer her some chips. She takes a couple and nibbles on them while I dip the rest in barby sauce and cram them down my gregory.

We say nothing. There's nothing we can say. Mum's dead. Char doesn't see her father anymore. My Dad died in Iraq. There's just us. And her husband Danny, of course, who's out on site. And little Dan, who's at school.

Char gets me some food from the Co-Op then drops me off at Mum's and I go to the door and put the key in the lock. Char's leaning down from the driver's seat so she can shout at me. "Will you be alright? It's really ok if you want to stay with us."

But I shake my head and give her a thumbs up. Mrs Opatha is at the window opposite, peeking through the lace curtain and I wave at her before realising that I shouldn't really be smiling. My Mum's died. So I shout at Char that it'll all be fine and maybe I shout a little too loud. I don't mean it the way it comes out. Char looks down and then drives off, making me feel worse.

I don't want to talk to Mrs Opatha so I turn the key, push the door, and pull my bergen in. The Co-Op bag bangs against my arm. Once inside, I push the door shut and I'm thinking that's the smell of home, that is: fags and floor cleaner. I put the food on the floor before the bag breaks and untie the laces in my desert boots, then pull each of them off using the other foot. I go to place them on the rack but Mum's not here so I leave them side by side on the mat.

And that's when I remember the visiting officer. He was grey haired. Old guy. I know now he was a Late Entry officer, commissioned from the ranks. He had a blue-red-blue watch strap and a leek badge on the lapel of his blazer. The sleeves had five buttons on the cuff to show it was proper Welsh Guards.

Mum was shaking. She knew why he was here; she just knew. And this officer was all smart and done up when he stepped in the doorway. But he bent over and took his shoes off because he could see that's what Mum made us do. Proper shiny dark brown they were, so shiny they were almost black. I was sitting on the bottom step, watching his face turn red as he placed his shoes on the rack next to Mum's slippers. I was twelve. He looked right into my face. Then he stood up, the full height of him like a giant. He stepped into the living room and said to Mum that maybe they should go into the kitchen. Mum's mouth hung open. Her eyes were wide. She looked at me and shook her head.

"No," *she said.* "They can hear this. Kyle, come here," *and beckoned me with her arm. Then she shouted,* "Charlotte, get down here. It's about your dad!"

So we're there, all three of us, Mum in the middle with her arms around us and the guy in his socks on the hard bit of the floor, straight as a ramrod. He clears his throat.

"*I regret to tell you, Mrs Hutton, that Micky was killed in Al Amarra yesterday afternoon. The battalion had been on an operation to clear insurgents from...*"

But that's all I remember. The rest is a blur.

Malcolm, July 2016

As they followed the wooden walkway down to Bamburgh beach, Malcolm felt torn. Bonkers, his black cocker spaniel, pulled at the full extent of the lead, tail wagging, expectantly glancing from side to side. The dog's powerful legs hauled him forwards. His wife, Penny, lagged behind, walking with heavy steps. They'd left little Luca with Malcolm's parents in the café at the castle.

"He'll be fine, pet. It's not like they'll feed him peanuts."

When they got to the steps he bent to unclip the lead. Bonkers bolted off, exuberantly barking at the wind. The tide was coming in. Waves rolled and crashed along the arc of sand. The wind whipped his cheek and sand in the air made him blink. Penny lifted her chin, eyes watering.

Bonkers ran back to bark insistently. The ball was in Malcolm's cagoule pocket. The dog had been patient all day and was now desperate for a run.

"Look, I have to..."

"You go..."

Malcolm left her by the safety sign wishing she'd stayed in the café. Whatever he did would be wrong. He pulled the ball from his pocket and Bonkers leaped up at him, thumping against his jeans. The impact jarred his injured knee.

"Down!" he yelled, then threw the ball. It didn't go as far as he wanted and he jammed his hands into the pockets of his jeans as he pushed through the powdery, pockmarked sand. The effort was strenuous. The dog ran back with the ball triumphantly high. He dropped it at Malcolm's feet and shuffled back, vigilant and eager. Malcolm picked it up and kept hold until he was on the smooth wet sand.

Far off, a man walked an Alsatian along the water's edge. He was throwing a ball into the waves for the dog to collect. Bonkers wouldn't do that. He was the only spaniel ever to be afraid of water.

Malcolm walked fast with his head down. He was angry and conflicted at the outcome of the referendum, tired from work, and frustrated by the tensions between Penny and his parents. He glanced round but she was some way behind and walking with a deliberately slow pace. He was in no mind to wait. The wind penetrated his cagoule. He ran a few yards, yelling and waving his arms at the dog. Bonkers skipped nimbly from one side to the other then darted off to scatter a group of gulls. The birds launched, sailed, descended, then did so again.

Malcolm shivered. He blamed Penny for distracting him when he was going in to get his Barbour as they were leaving. She'd asked him to get milk from the fridge if he was going back inside and that had made him forget the coat. He watched the dog for some minutes. Penny came up beside him. He feared she was angry for walking ahead but didn't feel in the mood for admonition.

"You ok?"

"Yes, you?"

"Dog had enough?"

"No, but I'm cold."

"Me too. Let's go back."

They turned, putting the wind behind them. The dog raced by and dropped the ball at his feet but it rolled downhill, towards the waves. When Malcolm scooped it up, it was wet and gritty. He rubbed it as clean as he could on the sleeve of the cagoule and put it back in his pocket. He wanted to be with his wife since they got so little time together. The dog ran to him, tongue out, but he waved it off.

"Away. Go play."

He glanced at her. She was looking at their footprints going the other way. Her family were from the Mourne Mountains. It was her accent he had first noticed when they met. *Kinety Dine, Norn Iron.*

Her hair hid her face. She blinked and shook her head then grabbed his elbow and pulled him closer. They walked slowly arm in arm, the dog running between them and the incoming waves. She gripped his elbow tightly and he glanced at her again. He was relieved to see in her face that it wasn't him angering her.

"Daddy thinks it'll be alright, so he does. But I think those bastards in Westminster will sell us out."

Dean, August 2016

The young journalist had been excitable and chatty on the way to filming the interview at the old army barracks south of Baghdad. Was the Iraqi army professional? How did corruption impact their daily lives?

After the interview, in the heat and tedium of the slog back along the long, straight highway, she was more subdued. As he drove, Dean glanced at her through the rear-view mirror. She'd removed her helmet and placed it on the seat. The next time he looked she had folded her arms across the outsized blue body armour and drifted off to sleep, her head lolling sideways.

Cleggy, the Convoy Commander, sat in the passenger seat with the VHF radio in his hand. The cameraman, Mike, sat behind Dean. He had been out to Iraq many times accompanying every journalist anyone could name. The security teams enjoyed his company over a few beers in the evening, standing round the fire pit in the back yard of the company compound. He was a bulky, big chested South African with rounded shoulders and a belly full of stories about police raids in the townships. He never asked why they didn't stop at traffic lights.

"Is she out?" Dean asked in a hushed tone.

Mike glanced at his young colleague as he took a sip of water from a small plastic bottle. "Yep. She was up till three talking to London, so it's not surprising."

Cleggy chuckled. "Did you get what you needed?"

Mike nodded. "Yah. Really great interview. They have, like, thousands of fake soldiers all drawing pay. 'Ghost soldiers' they call them. The commanders pocket the money. Which all comes from the Americans and the Brits."

Cleggy shook his head. "Greedy wankers, the lot of them."

Dean turned up the aircon and the three men sat in comfortable silence. The sand on the tarmac had been sculpted into ridges by the hot desert wind. Plastic bottles skittered across the road. The second vehicle was fifty yards behind, lights on. Stan was the Vehicle Commander and the new guy, Shaun, the ex-Legionnaire, was driving. In the back was Lou, the sound recorder, with all his equipment.

Cleggy and Dean were not convinced by Shaun's supposed military experience. He didn't walk right, didn't talk right. He spoke French but so what? Between themselves, they called him Elmer Fudd because that was who he reminded them of.

Twenty miles out, the low-rise city was still a shimmer in the heat but they could smell the repellent whiff of sewage and overripe fruit though the aircon. They swept beneath a gantry with road signs in English and Arabic. Dean calculated they would be home in an hour provided the traffic wasn't too dense. He felt content even though he had clocked the motorbikes that were trailing them. On two occasions they had overtaken, ridden on, then stopped to watch them pass. The second time it happened, Dean slowed slightly to take a look as he passed them. Two bikes, three men. The one in the white shirt was on the phone. Five minutes later, the bikes were behind Stan's vehicle and keeping back.

"Cleggy," Dean whispered, nodding to the offside mirror.

The team had seen this activity before and practised what to do. Gradually, Dean pressed his toe down and the heavy Landcruiser accelerated.

Cleggy lifted the radio and clicked the pressel switch. "Bravo, this is Alpha. Two bikes behind you. Increase to sixty, stay tight, over."

Stan replied after a hiss of static, "Seen. Roger ack."

Dean smiled. This is what made the job fun. After a kilometre the bikes were still with them so he pressed his toe down again. Cleggy felt the acceleration. "Seventy," he said into the radio then hunched down to look into the wing mirror.

Behind them, the second vehicle dropped some distance behind then accelerated to catch up.

"Wake up, Elmer," Dean said under his breath.

Once the correct distance had been re-established, the two bikes overtook Stan to settle behind Dean. One held the centre of the road, the other followed the white line along the edge.

"Come on, sweet cheeks, have a go!" Dean muttered.

The bike in his right mirror was ridden by a young lad on his own. His clothing puffed out in the wind making him look comically muscular. The other, in the middle of the road, was a much larger bike. The pillion rider was concealing something in his clothing.

The radio sputtered but they couldn't make out what Stan saying.

"He's armed," Dean whispered to Cleggy, who looked back over his shoulder. Mike leaned out of the way so he could see.

"Yeah. Pistol."

The Landcruisers were marked with the Global Risks logo and there was an additional sign in the front windscreen with the word 'PRESS' in blocky white script in both languages. Nobody knew why these militia groups tried to take them on but every now and then they did.

The bigger bike drifted level with Dean's door. The pillion raised his pistol and took aim at the tyres. Dean snorted. He edged the steering wheel to the left, forcing the bike into the oncoming lane. The rider didn't panic. The pillion fired two shots at the front tyre and another at the rear. The gun was small bore. Having fired, the gunman started wrestling with the magazine housing.

"Makarov," said Dean. "It's jammed."

Cleggy laughed, looking across the back of his head. "Just pull away mate. See him off."

Dean shook his head. "Nah. Let's have some fun."

He braked sharply before accelerating again. The smaller bike made a sudden swerve to avoid running into the back of him and was forced to steer wildly into the desert, churning up clouds of sand.

The bigger bike was then in front of them, slicing across the lane from one side to the other. Dean stuck behind it, keeping his bumper close to the rear wheel. The pillion rider looked frantically over one shoulder and then the other. He twisted to fire at the windscreen but the bulletproof glass registered no more than a tiny spider's web of a shatter pattern.

"He cleared that stoppage quickly!" Cleggy chuckled.

Dean leaned forward to tap the windscreen and point at the pillion rider. "Do that again and I'll run you over."

Cleggy folded his arms and laughed. "Fools don't know how armoured these cars are."

Suddenly, the bike peeled off to the side and Dean sped past him. "Why do they even bother?"

Cleggy shook his head. "Buggered if I know. Is Bravo ok?"

There was a sudden rush of noise as the second Landcruiser overtook them.

"Has Elmer seen something?" Dean wondered, checking his mirrors.

Cleggy looked out the back window. The journalist's head now rested on Mike's brawny shoulder; her mouth open. As Mike shuffled aside to allow Cleggy to see, she woke up, blinked, and wiped her mouth. "What's... where are we?"

Dean smiled at her in the rear-view mirror. "Nothing, Petra. We'll be back in the Green Zone soon."

Petra looked out of the window. "Did I hear shooting?"

Cleggy shook his head. "Nah, love. Have a good kip?"

The woman blushed and then nodded. She was tough and the men liked that. She had stuffed a plastic bottle of water into the door pocket which made a crunching sound as she pulled it out. In the late afternoon sun, the colour of the sand had softened. The roadside was littered with tyres, plastic bags, rubbish, rusting cars. A hobbled camel stood next to a thorn bush, head high, the owner unseen. Near the outskirts of the city they crossed a wide concrete bridge spanning a dry wadi.

"It's beautiful, really," Petra said.

Dean glanced sideways at Cleggy. "Are you going to speak to Harry about Elmer? If that had been real we'd be left on our own."

Cleggy shrugged. "I'll speak to Stan first. There may be a reason."

Dean shook his head. "Mate. I tell you. We're scraping the bottom of the barrel. Giving guns to nightclub bouncers and pretending they're qualified..."

Cleggy shook his head. "Not here, mate. Later."

Dean gritted his teeth. "Legion, my fucking arse," he muttered. "He's a fucking walt."

Dean, Late August 2016

In the back yard of the compound, stripped to his shorts and desert boots, Dean was sitting on the weights bench. It was arms and chest day and he'd managed to score some juicing pills from one of the ex-Rangers working for Apollo in the compound up the road. He'd just measured himself and fifteen inches round the bicep was on the way to where he wanted to be. After two hours, his arms shook with effort but the steroids dulled the pain. The left one, dislocated during a parachute jump when he was at depot, was particularly sore.

It was late in the afternoon. The sun had moved round to put the whole yard in shade. Stan had been training too, knocking out ten miles on the treadmill in just over an hour. When he finished, he wiped down the machine with a towel and went inside.

"See you in a bit," Dean said, not expecting a reply. Later, they'd probably watch a DVD. It must have been at least a week since they'd watched *Bladerunner* or *The Man Who Would be King*. Maybe tonight it would be the other big favourite, *Cross of Iron*.

Cleggy was in the twenty-metre range in the basement with Elmer. The men had reached a consensus that he might have had some military training at some stage but it certainly wasn't in France's finest. He'd probably been in the TA and read a load of books. When he told stories they sounded second-hand and he didn't swear like a soldier. He swore like the words were painful. But they needed drivers so Cleggy had decided to see if he could be trained. In the basement the sound of gunfire was muffled so they could practice their pistol drills live firing. In the back yard, Dean had his headphones on and *Iron Maiden* blasting, so didn't hear the shouts until Cleggy appeared up the steps, hopping across the sand with blood seeping out of his lifted foot.

Dean threw the dumbbells down and ripped his headphones off. "What the fuck?" He ran to take Cleggy's weight under one arm. "What happened?"

"Twat had a negligent unloading," Cleggy hissed. "Shot me in the fucking foot." He bent to grip his knee with both hands. "Fuck that hurts!"

Stan appeared at the back door and immediately took Cleggy's other arm. They lifted him up the steps into the kitchen. Dean pushed the piles of clean laundry off the table with a long sweep of his arm so they could hoist Cleggy on to it. He was gritting his teeth and making angry, painful gasps. Stan ran to get his med kit and gave him a quick shot of morphine. Cleggy sighed as his mouth fell open and his head fell back. Dean supported his weight as he went limp.

While he was out, Stan untied his laces and pulled off the blood-stained trainer, then the sock. The wound was bleeding heavily so he got a fresh bottle of water from the fridge to wash it out.

"It's not bad. Just a nick down the side."

Cleggy came round as they were applying pressure to the wound.

"Ahhhh! you fucker," he said, lifting himself up to grip his thigh. "Fucking burns."

"Where's Elmer?" Dean asked suddenly.

"Down in the range," Cleggy grimaced. "Still got the nine millie."

Dean checked Stan had the wound under control then ran into the yard. He didn't know what he would do but the weapon had to be secured. Swoops and swirls of blood on the tiled steps led him down to the concrete floor of the cellar where a dark pool lay next to the unloading bay. An unmistakable stink of cordite, pheromones, blood. The pistol sat on the ammunition box with an empty magazine beside it. Elmer was nowhere to be seen.

"Fucking coward," Dean muttered as he checked and pocketed the pistol. He'd have to come back with the mop as soon as they'd got Cleggy to the military hospital.

In the kitchen, Cleggy was gripping the edges of the table with white fingers. His legs hung over the side and he winced while Stan wrapped a crepe bandage round his foot, the lumpy outline of a field dressing underneath it.

By the doorway stood Harry Campbell. A former captain in the Scots Guards, he was broad chested and brushed his black hair upwards in a huge bouffant sweep.

Dean folded his arms. "I fucking told you."

Harry put his hands into the back of his belt. "Dean, I know. I told London we didn't believe his background..."

Dean shook his head. "No."

He shoved chairs out of the way to get round the table. He placed a thick forefinger on Campbell's chest and poked him rhythmically as he spoke. "Not good enough. I've said it before. Professional fucking standards. You're the country manager. Fucking sort it."

Campbell raised a placatory hand. "Look, Dean, calm down, it's..."

"Don't fucking tell me to calm down, *Harry*." He jabbed his finger hard into Campbell's pectoral muscle. "As far as I'm concerned, *Sir*, you are responsible for this."

The two men stared at each other. One of them was a former Colour-Sergeant who had been in Iraq since leaving the army after twenty-four years. The other was a former officer who had done six years and was now on his second rotation as the Country Manager.

Harry said, "Dean, this was an accident. It needs to be investigated..."

Dean's jaw tightened. He recognised Harry's officer-like manner. He might even have been a good one; educated, polished, and plummy as he was. But Cleggy had been shot and, since Elmer had done a runner, he wanted to hit something. They weren't in the army any more and Harry's authority no longer had the backing of Queen's Regulations. In fact, the fabric of his position was tissue thin and it wouldn't be the first time Dean had broken an officer's jaw.

He glanced at Cleggy, whose head was craned backwards while Stan fitted an inflatable splint to immobilise the ankle. This would not be the end of his career. Global Risks was huge and would doubtless look after him. But the moment crystallised something in Dean that had been brewing for months. With one splayed hand he shoved Harry backwards to clatter into the broom cupboard, knocking over the mop and bucket.

At the table, Dean gripped Cleggy's upper arm. "Hold on, mate, we'll get you sorted."

Cleggy looked at him, sinews strained. Sweat ran down his cheeks. They'd been on this gig since the beginning. They'd won all these clients, the three of them. Not the likes of Harry Campbell or those wankers in the glass tower in London. And before this, they'd all served in the same battalion for what, fifteen years?

"Mate, this is it. I'm out," Dean said.

Cleggy looked at his foot, at Stan, then back at Dean. "See you back home," he said.

Kyle, previously

It's Wednesday and I'm at Char's by Naafi break, the letter from the solicitor in my hand. It's proper nice where she is. Danny must be coining it to live in Ash Grove. The gate clatters against the brick wall as I close it behind me.

Danny's van's not on the street and there's only Char's little Micra nose in on the driveway. I press the doorbell and she appears as a mottled image behind the internal door which opens with a sucking sound. Then she fumbles with a ring of keys and opens the main door before reaching up to give me a hug. She's smiling and her eyes are kind.

"Thanks for coming love. Come in. I've put the kettle on."

I take my shoes off and go through. The kitchen is white and very clean as Danny's just refitted it. The sunlight from the window falls in bars through the blind. They lie at an angle across the worktop and down the front of the cupboards. There's salt and pepper next to the kettle but nothing else on the counter. The room smells faintly of chip shop vinegar and the only thing out of place is a tea towel on the table by the door. I take a seat and pull my legs in so Char can get past. She goes to the kettle and clicks it. The water immediately bubbles.

"Tea?"

I say that would be great. She stands with her back to me, one hand on the counter. The bars of sunlight wrap round her arm. She's wearing crocs and the pale blue scrubs of the care home where she works. It's like a nurse's uniform but the colours are paler and she doesn't have pens in the pockets or identity cards round her neck.

"You'll have a biscuit, Kyle? I got these in as I know you like them."

I say thanks, that's great. I haven't eaten at all so scoff three gingernuts while she's got her back turned. They're cheapo ones from Lidl but I'm not fussy.

"You must be glad you're out of the army now," Char says over her shoulder, "with them going to Sierra Leone for the ebola outbreak?"

I shrug. I texted the blokes when I heard and one of them got back to me.

"It's not an infantry task," I say. "They're sending medics, not the battalions."

She nods that she understands. She's right clever is Char. I haven't been watching the news anyway, just the football. England are playing shit at the moment. They didn't even get out of the pool stages of the World Cup and got beat by everyone, even Costa fucking Rica. I'm about to kick off on the subject but Char puts a brew down on a mat and pulls out the other chair.

"So you're genuinely ok if we don't take the solicitor's advice, Kyle?" she asks, leaning on her elbows.

I nod. "Yeah." I don't see how it's going to help anything. Lawyers just stir shit for the sake of it and it feels important I can make this decision. It's not like I didn't love my mother. Of course I did. But she had cancer. She smoked. And it's not like the hospital could do anything about that.

Char continues. "He said there's a class action, whatever that is. Apparently, the faults identified after the thing when all those babies died have not been rectified. He said there's a good chance we could get compensation."

She sits back in her chair, one hand on the mug handle, one on her lap. She shakes hair out of her eyes when she's being serious. I can tell by her voice that she doesn't want to do this.

"Nah," I say, but suddenly it's like there's this boiling liquid inside me and it's bubbling up. I feel trapped. My ears start to sweat and I can hear Gaz's voice telling me to calm down, keep focused. Shit happens. People get slotted. Just keep focused. Don't think about the hot splatter of blood on the walls, your boots, your face. Just get yourself in a fire position and give Terry Taliban a free ticket to paradise.

I'm silent then, looking at the ripples in my brew, hands opening and closing. Char puts her little hand on my arm.

"I'm so proud of you," she says, tears appearing in her eyes. "Mum would be too: the man you have become."

I'm flushed then, not knowing quite what I've said that makes her think that, but I smile. "You don't know when today's going to be your last day or not. Just stay focused. Stay sharp."

Char's lips quiver a bit. She rubs my arm again and throws a quick glance at the kettle. "I'll tell them we're not interested," she says. "For me, it's the cuts the government keep making. In Bellevue we're down three nurses and two care workers. No one will work for that money. And it's the same at the hospital."

She falls silent then, and we sit at the table holding our brews, looking at the laminate. On the side of the cupboard there's a shopping list on a cork board. Cornflakes. Milk. Bread. Fruit shoots. Sugar. Jam. I think about offering to go while she's at work but I'd buy the wrong type of jam as little Dan's proper fussy. I take another three biscuits but put one back and just eat two.

I turn my chair round and sit with my back to the wall. Char makes us another brew and looks at her watch. She should be going soon and that's ok.

"You know you've only got to the end of September, don't you, Kyle?" she says. "The landlord gave us an extra month to clear the place as Mum was there so long, but after that it's to be vacant."

"I know," I say. "He put a letter through the door."

Char looks at the tube of biscuits and the crumbs on the table and tells me to help myself. She got them for me, it's fine. So I take a couple more and fold the plastic over the end, then hold it up for her to put back in the cupboard. She does so, picking up my mug at the same time.

By the back door there's a little red trolley with potatoes on the bottom shelf and greens on the top. The veg sit on newspaper that's faded. Underneath the trolley, between the wheels, are two little football boots, side by side. The laces are undone and she's polished the uppers like Dad would have done. Little Dan will always have clean boots and no mud round the studs.

"What are you going to do, Kyle?" Char says. "For money, I mean?"

I shrug. "Plumbing, I guess. I did that apprenticeship with Uncle Ben in London before I joined up, remember?. There must be work round here. If I say I'm a veteran there'll be people falling over to hire me. They'll know what they're getting: reliability, graft, that sort of thing."

Char looks uncertain. "It would be good if you start looking," she says. "It might take a bit longer than you think, if you stay round here, that is."

"Oh, I'm staying," I say. "Stoke's my home."

She smiles. I stare at little Dan's football boots with the laces out to the side and see a dirty smear in the lino that she's missed. Char looks at her watch and takes a rapid drink. It's too hot, so she puts the mug by the sink and leaves it. "I've got to dash, Kyle. I'm really sorry. Can I give you a lift anywhere?"

I say no, I like the walk.

I want to tell her about the box of Dad's photos I found at Mum's. They're of him with his mates from the Welsh Guards and you could see him doing the same things I did in the Machine Guns except the pictures are older and the faces are different. There he is in the jungle in Belize with a tracker holding an AK47. There he is in Kenya, stripped down to his Union Jack shorts, standing at this big sign that says, 'The Equator', all of them cropped hair, muscular, tatts, moustaches.

And then there's him and Mum getting married. He's a sergeant at the time, proper smart in his blues. I wasn't born but Char was in a bridesmaid's dress. Dad properly leathered her father for hurting her. Told him never to come back and he didn't. Then there's some of him in what looks like Kosovo. Then there's some in Iraq, him and his mates in a stripped-down Snatch looking exactly like David Stirling from the SAS in the desert. He must have been Recce platoon.

I went through them all but never found one of him with me and I wondered why that was. We used to spend hours in the living room, him jabbing at me, telling me to keep my guard up. I had these eight-ounce gloves, way too heavy for me. And when Mum shouted him from the kitchen to cut the turkey I properly swung for him and clocked him on the chin. He fell back into the tree and knocked it against the telly which dislodged the ash tray. Char started shouting Mum! Mum! and Dad proper panicked, rushing into the kitchen to get a dustpan before Mum found out.

"Fuck sake, Kyle! Are you trying to get me killed or what!"

The memory made me smile. We proper laughed at the time. But I still never found a picture of the two of us.

Steve, September 2016

The queue at the food counter was growing fast so Steve chose to keep watching the midday news on the wall-mounted TV. He was sitting in the sofa at the back of the canteen area, knees crossed, his good hand resting on his thigh and his prosthetic lying to the side, palm upwards. His stump itched where the cup was rubbing and he was tired of the hook catching on his jeans.

It took the WIS, the wounded, injured, and sick, much longer than able-bodied people to slide their trays along the rail, especially if they only had one arm. And if they only had one leg, or were double amps, they needed time to joggle their crutches before looking for a table.

Orpheus House North was an immaculately refurbished sandstone mansion on the edge of Catterick Garrison owned and run by the charity *Save Our Heroes*. It fronted onto the steep road down into Richmond and butted up against a row of colonels' quarters to one side and the Royal Signals barracks to the other.

When Steve had first come, shortly after being medically discharged, the lady behind the canteen counter, Mary, would carry trays for 'her poor boys' to their tables. But very soon the WIS indicated they preferred to manage themselves even if it meant spilled tea, broken plates, and dusty sausage rolls.

On the news, the presenter was talking about female genital mutilation, or FGM. That meant cutting out bits of a girl's vadge so they can't enjoy sex and often weed themselves. It angered Steve that they were allowed to do such things but thankfully it was mainly Muslims in Africa and Pakistan. They didn't do it in Carlisle, anyway.

That's why they went to Afghan, or one of the reasons: to liberate women so they didn't have to wear the burka and get their vadges cut.

Steve wanted to nudge Fib as he was asleep on the other end of the sofa. The staff would wake the WIS if they fell asleep in the public areas and encourage them back to their rooms but Fib was too far gone. He was a druggy. Everyone knew it and it was against Charity Standing Orders yet no one ever bubbled him. It just wasn't what you did. Steve was worried that the staff would see the hook scars on his thighs and think he was either cutting himself, like Matty, or a druggy, like Fib.

He was neither. He was Wounded, sure. Injured, of course. But he wasn't Sick. Apart from the missing forearm and the metal plate in his head, he was almost able-bodied. He had learned to manage the tinnitus and would tilt his head to counter the loss of vision in his right eye. He could drive again and since he was on the list to get one of the new prosthetics, one with a hand that looked real and could be shaped to hold things, he should be able to get a job any time soon.

Most of all, Steve wanted to help other veterans. It didn't matter what regiment they were from, or what sex they were, or where they lived. He just wanted to help veterans come through that dark place when they realised their army career was over and they had to adapt to being both civvies and WIS. He knew how hard that was. He knew men who'd struggled. He even knew one, knew him really well, who'd taken his life. That's what it meant to him to get this job. There'd be no more men like Kyle.

Steve had applied for a case worker's post hoping that *Save Our Heroes* would be the vehicle to answer his dreams. He expected to be in with a good chance even though the interview had been really difficult. They'd spoken clearly and allowed him time to respond but they'd also asked questions like 'why do you want to be a case worker' and 'what do you think you bring to the table'. For him, the answers were self-evident: he was a veteran; he had been injured on operations, and he wanted to help other veterans adapt to life outside the military. It was hard leaving the army if that was all you ever knew and although he wasn't an expert, he had been through both the recovery and the rehabilitation phases. He had done all the programmes *Save Our Heroes* had on offer. In fact, they didn't have any programmes he hadn't done. So it was natural that he should be qualified as staff.

He glanced again at the scoff queue and noted it was still quite long. There was a course on – Basic Employability Skills – so there were a lot of unfamiliar faces. As he counted the number of people with missing limbs, he saw Clive approaching from the main hallway and its slanting, cheerful light.

Clive was low set, and broad shouldered. He was dressed casually in jeans and a tattersall check shirt over which he wore a maroon *Save Our Heroes* gilet. He'd been in the PT Corps, finishing as a Warrant Officer Class One. He'd not been commissioned. Steve liked him because he always had a cheerful and engaging manner.

"Hi Steve, you alright?"

"Yes, Clive, thanks. How are you?"

"I'm good, mate, good."

Clive was Director of Programmes. Steve really wanted to be Director of Programmes in due course. After all, he'd done all the courses *Save Our Heroes* had on offer. He'd done both employability skills courses, the sleep hygiene course, the coping with stress course, the interview skills. And whereas Clive was able bodied, Steve was WIS and that gave him a perspective that Clive could never have. So he was hopeful that one day he would be Director of Programmes and the route into that position would start with him doing a few months as a case worker.

Clive knelt by Steve's chair, his identity card swinging on a branded lanyard. He had two rubber wristbands round his arm: one in the *Save Our Heroes* colours and the other one black with *Royal British Legion* written in red.

"Steve, could we have a chat about your application to be a case worker?" Clive said.

"Yes, mate," Steve said. "Did I get it or what? I can start now, you know. Well, Monday, if you give me a few days to get me admin squared away."

Clive looked round. There was no one in immediate earshot apart from Fib, and he was stirring. People were taking places at the dining tables. The chairs scraped on the floor.

"Let's talk in the office," Clive said. "Quieter."

Steve followed him to the front of the building. There was a simplex lock on the office door which Clive shielded from view but Steve knew the number as he'd been here so often: C1245X. The office was a dark, open-plan room with the case worker desks in a row facing each other. Steve waved at Bronagh, the Irish woman who'd looked after him when he got released from hospital. She was on the phone but smiled at him and winked.

Clive led him to a small meeting room with a glass door. Inside was a table with two chairs and Steve immediately sat down. His heart started to race and his throat felt constricted. Clive didn't look at him and that meant something, though Steve was not sure what.

"Steve, look, I'm sorry, but you didn't get it."

Clive sat forward with his knees wide apart and his hands together. His voice was gentle. Steve wanted to be upset but he'd known Clive for ages and couldn't be angry at him. He was just the messenger.

"Why not…"

It came out harsher than Steve intended but that was what he felt. He was uniquely placed to be a case worker because he would be the only one who had themselves been WIS. Didn't they see that?

Clive had this way of looking at him with his chin tucked in, like a boxer. He started counting on his fingers.

"First, we all think you're a really great guy. You're part of the furniture and a real help to other veterans as they come in. You've come a long way since you first came through the doors."

Steve listened. It was part of the employability skills course, the basic one, that you listened to understand and not to respond.

"Second, we think you'd be a wonderful asset to any team you felt comfortable with. You have a lot to offer and are a great team player."

He sounded meaningful, did Clive. He was quite old, in his late forties, so Steve naturally deferred to his assessment and he was happy that they'd seen his key skills.

"But we're looking for other things as well, Steve. We found other people who did better at some of the tests. For instance, your cognitive processing is still impaired. We know that you can drive, which is great, but some of your problem solving still needs a lot of work."

"How do you mean, Clive? I think that's one of..."

Clive raised his fingers to stop him talking even though he was bubbling over with questions.

"We also don't think you yet have the fitness to undertake a full day's work. You still need to rest every few hours and our case load is growing day by day. We can't afford to have someone on the team who can't do as much as others. It's unfair on them, see?"

Steve blushed. There was nothing worse than someone who didn't pull their weight, someone *jack*. That was the first thing they weeded out during basic training.

"Can't you give me a while to get into it? A few weeks maybe? I don't mind working nights if I can stay here in the accommodation. I can work nights to make up the hours."

Clive took a breath then raised his deep blue eyes.

"The accommodation is for the WIS, Steve, not for staff. That's the point, you see? We need someone who can do a full shift and also work nights if necessary."

Steve felt hot. His brain buzzed. He had really wanted this job and had not thought about anything else since the interviews.

"So who got it?" he said. "Were it that guy in a tweed jacket? Royal Anglian?"

Clive shook his head. "I can't say, mate. But you'll find out. He's a great fit..."

"Was he WIS?"

Clive looked at him calmly, his eyes quiet. "He's not injured, Steve, no. But he has a lot of other skills to bring. He's a really great guy. You'll like him. You'll see."

"It's just I had..."

"I know, Steve. But we felt you're not quite ready yet. You still need to develop cognitive processing skills and your employment fitness."

He was talking quietly, repeating what he'd said before. His eyes were strong but peaceful. Steve trusted him.

"I just want to help other veterans, Clive. That's all..."

"I know, Steve, I know," said Clive. "We all do."

He was silent then, watching Steve's reactions. Steve felt hemmed in. He was embarrassed to have to tell others he hadn't got it when he'd already told them how much he wanted it.

"I don't know what to do, Clive," Steve mumbled.

Clive sucked his lips. He tapped Steve lightly on the knee and his voice changed. "There's nothing you need do differently. It's just there was a better candidate this time."

"I know," Steve said. "But that were the same last time and the time before that..." He glanced through the glass doors to the bank of desks. Luckily, Bronagh was not looking his way. "How do I get better?" he said. "How do I get so I can help veterans?"

Clive leaned back in his chair. He put his hand over his mouth and stroked his chin. "Let me have a think, Steve," he said. "There might be something coming up that would help you."

Malcolm, October 2016

The bid room was on the fifth floor of the Delaine offices, a glass tower at the heart of London's financial district. A flip chart was stuck to the door with masking tape and someone had written *Booked for Project Firefly* in a blue marker. They had it for two weeks, which itself showed how important the bid was. Normally, it was impossible to get a room on this floor.

"Morning, everyone."

Malcolm's team were already seated with their laptops open. They should be, too, since they lived in London and were at the Analyst or Consultant grades. Delaine was a company where advancement required effort. He was newly promoted himself and knew the team thought of him as some sort of favourite. One or two smiled at him then returned to their work. He didn't disturb them as he would find out what was happening at the midday update. He'd just arrived from Newcastle and had to clear the emails he didn't manage to do on the train.

Jenny, one of the analysts, had brought in a plastic box of home-made cookies. He took one and ate it quickly.

"Mmmm! Wow, thank you, Jenny."

She blushed and smiled at the recognition.

The pale grey curtains had been pulled back. The room faced north-east so the sun was reflected off a green tower on the other side of the Plaza. His team had left him the chair at the end of the table. He put his partially open laptop down, dropped his suitcase under the window and folded his trench coat on top of it. His phone buzzed. It was Alicia, the Bid Partner, calling. The spreadsheet she sent him on Friday took most of Sunday to finish.

"Alicia, good morning."

"Good morning, Malcolm. How was your weekend?"

He thought about a sarcastic response. What with Luca and Penny, and the time he spent on the figures, all he had to himself was two hours in the gym on Saturday morning. On Sunday, before the boy woke, he'd been hopeful of sex but Penny had made it clear by rolling over she was not in the mood. He'd got her a cup of tea and worked until everything was done; just in time for a beer and a curry in the evening.

"I hope you didn't work *all* the time," Alicia said.

"Not all of it," he responded, knowing she didn't mean what she said. "What about you? Anything good?"

"I worked all of Saturday. Well, you do, don't you, in this business? Then my husband took me to the Yvonne Arnaud in Guildford. We went to see *Waiting for Godot*."

"Nice," Malcolm said. "I got your emails this morning. Read them on the train but didn't respond. I will do so by six this evening."

"That's good, Malcolm. I trust you. You are the perfect candidate to lead this bid. Not just because of your background. It's your manner. If we win, which we should, you'll be well placed to lead the project and that'll look great on your appraisal."

Malcolm said nothing. He didn't like people trying to motivate him that way. He looked down the table. They knew who he was talking to.

"But the reason for the call, Malcolm, is to say Sian double booked me. Triple booked me, actually. So I won't be at the midday update."

"That's no problem. I need to spend time with the team. There's an issue I would like to... nothing serious, just something that requires... it would be easier if you..."

"You need team collaboration time and it would be better if I didn't constrain your thinking?"

"Yes," he said, flushed at being tongue-tied when she was so sharp.

"That's kind of you, Malcolm. I'll let you have the space and you can update me later by voice message."

"Roger ack," he said automatically. "I mean, I'll do that."

He looked at his phone but she had already gone. Down the table, his team were focused on their screens. The Dutch girl, Veerle, sat closest to him again, her long blonde hair falling straight beside her face. The tip of an ear was just visible. She glanced at him out of the corner of her eye and smiled.

He hoped she would engineer it that they ate together in the canteen after the update.

Kyle, previously

I've been watching The Invictus Games. Proper moving it is, all these veterans thrashing it out and there's, like, the media, and massive crowds, and Prince Harry all watching. Blokes with single amp, below the knee. Blokes with double amp above the knee running with their legs out sideways. Some are on blades, some on prosthetics. Some blind. It's funny the way they run as a double amp but if a civvy said that you'd properly rip him a new one.

The wheelchair rugby kills me. No quarter. Blokes smashing it. One of them fell out of his chair he was going so hard. And it wasn't just Brits. There were Yanks, and Canadians, and Germans, and Ozzies, and Kiwis. There was even Iraqis and Afghans, little skinny legs and all.

I Am. That's the logo: I Am.

And it's difficult not to get teary because there's all of these veterans, all good people, men and women, and they're giving everything. They do a lap of honour with flags round their shoulders and the crowd are all standing and clapping like they're Usain Bolt.

And you know they've given more than everything. They've been in Iraq or been in Afghan and they've stood up and been counted. They served their country. Veterans. And that means something.

So it gets to lunchtime and I know I have to go out to look for work. I don't want to miss the Games but I'm out of the house in a couple of weeks and need money for a flat. I think about taking the bus but use Mum's car instead. It's an old Saab but she never used it and I don't want to get my clothes dirty.

I know how to look good. I've ironed my trousers and shirt and have a veteran's badge on my jacket plus a little regimental cap badge. I was polishing my shoes while watching telly sitting on the sofa in a way Mum would never let me do. I've had a shave and my hair's still tidy. No piercings. No visible tatts.

So I drive to town and do a little circuit round the high street and the industrial estates south of Port Vale. I like the look of one so park up round the corner and walk in. There's a wide concrete loading area and a single-story unit at the back. The roller door's open and some blokes are loading a van. The cab has livery on the side and the blokes all wear black polo shirts with the same badge. So it feels good. There's pride and banter and you can hear them calling out to each other and laughing.

So I go in through the main door and there's a nice looking lady at the desk. She eyes me up and you can see she takes me in. As you get closer, she's maybe not as young as she dresses but it was the same in Collie. Proper lamb dressed as pig there. But this girl is alright. She says, can I help you? And I go right up and stand easy in front of her desk.

"Could I see the manager, please, Ma'am?"

She laughs. "Alan? Sure, love. Can I say what it's about?"

I don't know what to say as it should be obvious. I'm here to work. I'm strong. I'm reliable. I'm good. I have C&G. And I have experiences other blokes don't have: Army. Be the Best.

"I'm looking for work," I say.

She pulls a face as if to say, what, another one? But gets up and waves through a glass door at the back.

"Alan! Alan! There's a guy to see you. He's..."

She points at me again and I straighten, almost to attention. I can feel the blokes behind me looking and I want to stand out.

The lass takes a seat and says Alan will be with you any minute. Can I get you a coffee?

The floor's painted red and to the side of the main doorway there's a little ring of seats with a coffee machine and a rack of trade flyers. I say, thanks, it's fine. I'll sort it. I smile at her, wanting to come across right. But as I go over, Alan comes out of his office.

He's maybe fifty or something; fat in the middle, short curly hair, grey hoodie with the company name on it. It's dirty where he's wiped his hands across the pocket. He gives the woman a sheet of paper and tells her to pay it then looks at me. He smiles and I extend my hand. He takes it and you can see he likes me.

He doesn't mess about though. Can I drive? How old am I? Can I operate a forklift? What quals?

"I was an apprentice in London. But I wanted to serve my country so I enlisted in the Parachute Regiment and got mobilised to serve in Afghan. I'm out now. I live here, in Stoke, and I'm looking for work."

He pats my arm and points to the ring of chairs. "Let's take a seat," he says, and I'm glad as I don't like being interviewed in public. Some things are easier one to one.

He sits with his knees wide apart, belly hanging. I don't know whether to cross my legs or not. It looks kind of gay. So I lean forward with my elbows on my knees, clasping my hands.

"Listen, son," Alan says. "I can see you're a good one. And if things were different I'd take you in a flash. My dad was Staffs Regiment and so was my uncle. You'll know the South Staffs were at Arnhem with your mob. In the war, like. My grandad was a gunner and my great grandad was on the Arctic Convoys. So I'd always take a squaddie if I can."

He makes a flick of his head towards the racking. "One or two of the lads have done their time. But the thing is, it's difficult now. Margins are tight for all the plumbers and fitters. People are going under every year. Even in winter."

He's smiling as he's trying to help me. I lean back and nod, put my hands in my pockets. "What work is there?" I ask. I can retrain. I can do anything.

Alan laughs a bit. "Do you speak Polish?"

I shake my head.

"Well you'll be lucky round here, mate. We're one of the last English companies. They've mopped up. Literally!"

He laughs but the joke's not that funny. We stand. Shake hands. He says he'll keep my details in case a vacancy comes up but I know he's holding me off. I want to get out even though he's done what he can to let me down gentle. I nod at the lady at the desk. She says good luck, and I wink at her. I'll find something. Course I will. I'm a veteran.

Dean, November 2016

Dean was sitting at the far end of a horseshoe booth in the *Jewel of India*, his favourite restaurant. It was nearly nine on Saturday night. Every table was rammed full and at least two parties were by the bar waiting to be seated. The alternating blue and purple lighting in the window recesses, and the banging bhangra music, gave the place a boisterous, jumpy feel. If it was one thing to say for Rotherham, you could always find a good curry.

Dean was stuffed. Though it had been a staple for much of his life he now found lamb madras kept him awake at night with heartburn. Instead, he'd chosen a chicken jalf with a side of dhal and another of matar paneer. After a starter of pops and bhajis, and a few draft Kingfisher, he was looking forward to collapsing into the sofa, *Match of the Day*, and falling asleep.

Next to him, Michelle was wearing her new silk top and the girls, Elizabeth and Victoria, were to his right. The girls were doubled over Elizabeth's phone, giggling to each other and texting. Dean pulled a face at Michelle who shrugged and shook her head. She didn't know either. He leaned forward to pat her arm. "Happy birthday, love."

Michelle took a sip of wine just as Hasan, the manager, appeared carrying a small birthday cake with a sparkler on top. He was in his trademark white suit with a black shirt and white bow tie. All the other serving staff, his sons or nephews, wore white shirts with black bow ties. Hasan was bald but had a magnificent grey beard cut flat and combed in the Muslim way.

"Good evening, Mister Dean, Miss Michelle! Twenty-one today…" he beamed. "Just a little present on the house…"

Michelle smiled gracefully. "Thank you, Hasan, it was delicious, as always."

Dean patted his bulging belly. "Yes, mate. Hundred percent."

The girls both looked up with hunched shoulders, said thank you very much in unison, then returned to the phone.

"Can I get you anything else please?" Hasan smiled.

Dean looked at his wife but shook his head. "No, mate, just the bill please. That was fantastic."

The manager slid away leaving the cake on the table. Dean and Michelle watched the sparkler fizzle down then waited for it to cool.

"Want to go for a drink?" Dean said. "It's your birthday after all."

The girls sat up, deciding to be part of the conversation. "We're going out," Elizabeth said.

"We'll be back late," added Victoria.

Both of them were far too thin, wearing too little, showing too much. Victoria, nearest him, had a splatter of blemishes on her upper arm. She wasn't wearing a bra and the stubby protuberance of her nipples made Dean uncomfortable. He didn't like their fashion, their secrecy, or the thing they did with their lips when they took selfies.

"Where are you going?" he asked.

Victoria lifted her shoulders. "Owls. Meeting friends."

She wasn't old enough but Dean knew there was no point trying to stop them. He would rather they were in a club, drinking, than down the park experimenting with drugs. "Who are you meeting?" he asked as one of the junior waiters brought the bill on a plastic tray. Michelle reached over for it but Dean held out his hand. "My shout, love."

As he leaned to one side to pull his wallet from his jeans the girls shuffled sideways out of the booth without answering his question.

"Back in a minute," they said in unison, then disappeared towards the bar. Dean watched them. He thought Elizabeth needed to stand more upright and bring her shoulders back. He hadn't heard any of what they'd said all evening, only inferred it. His hearing was definitely getting worse and he wondered what was normal for someone just under fifty.

Michelle nudged him with her knee. "They'll be fine, Deano. They go out all the time when you're not here."

"I bet they do," he said but immediately realised there was a criticism implicit in the choice of words. "But I'm home now. For good. And..."

He didn't finish the sentence as she was looking at him in that way she had.

"They'll be fine," Michelle repeated. "They're good girls. And Elizabeth looks after Vics."

Dean tapped his bank card on the table. He was no one to talk. At their age he was usually so pissed he would spew up kebabs in the alleyway before going on to any bar that would let him in. But he was a boy and they were girls and he was conscious that he hadn't been there when he should have been.

"Come here," Michelle urged, pulling his chin towards her. Her perfume clashed with the curry flavours on her breath. The skin on her neck showed the fine lines of age. "Why don't we let the girls go out and you take me home for a birthday treat?"

Dean's mouth dried out. He'd been back two months and they'd only had sex once. It was the steroids, of course. Juicing meant he could train like a demon but he didn't get as excited by sex as he used to. It wasn't Michelle. Although she was getting older she still had a great figure and he could play with those puppies all night long. But he was finding it difficult to get hard and embarrassment made it worse. He needed magic pills but hadn't got round to ordering them.

Michelle kissed him on the cheek. "Come on, handsome. Take me home and give me a good time."

He smiled. At least if they went home he might be able to hear what was going on around him. And if his cock wouldn't work he could always use his fingers or his tongue. She never complained when he did that.

Alexander, November 2016

Leaving the European Union was not something the British electorate did on a whim. The roots of the decision lay in the 1995 Special Party Conference in which the New Labour leader, Tony Blair, repealed Clause IV of the Labour Party Constitution. This enabled him to reposition his Party from the political left into the busy centre ground where he could compete with the Liberals and the socially conscious elements of the Conservatives.

The move was skilfully timed. The country was open to any alternative following two decades of sleaze ridden Conservative rule. Blair became Prime Minister in 1997 and although he gained significantly in the centre, he failed to appreciate the needs of Old Labour. They felt their political voice slipping away. The era of Cool Britannia and Britpop did not pay their mortgages or address simmering concerns about immigration in traditionally white working-class towns.

Because New Labour had successfully nibbled into the centre ground, the Conservative Party stepped visibly to the right. This repositioning fenced in right-of-centre voters and sought to combat the emerging Eurosceptic parties, of which UKIP became the most resonant voice. In order to be defined as the party of the right, the Conservatives had to span a broad spectrum of agendas or risk losing support on both wings. In so doing, a significant proportion of 'small c' conservatives also lost their political voice. Although they would not demean themselves with a charge of racism, they did respond to the UKIP messaging that the European Union exerted an unwelcome influence on British sovereignty.

As such, large swathes of both traditional labour and traditional conservative voters were open to suggestions as to how their concerns could be addressed.

New Labour made matters worse by following the United States into a messy regime change war in Iraq. The hanging of the head of state, Saddam Hussein, created a power vacuum in a country where social and political stability had always required force. The American puppet government enjoyed a sparse mandate from the Shia community and none from the Sunni. The absurd decision to remove the Ba'ath Party from the institutions of state led to huge swathes of educated, managerial Sunni males being unemployed. They formed an easy recruiting pool for the militarised insurgency that took various forms before settling as the Islamic State. This institution was avowedly theocratic and held primitive views about education, women, and facial hair. Its intention was to construct a caliphate superseding the patchwork of Sunni and Shia states created by the British and French after the First World War. The ensuing violence spread across Iraq and Syria and led to thirteen million refugees fleeing in the only direction they could: through Turkey into Europe.

As this was happening, the European Council, the guiding force of the Union, made a further mistake. Although David Cameron had persuaded them to make limited changes to Britain's relationship, it then proved itself to be inflexible and authoritarian. A solvency crisis in the poorly managed Greek economy was easily portrayed by the British press as Germany exerting dominance over the entire continent, as it had sought to do since the 1930s. On top of this, the influx of refugees from Iraq and Syria was met by confused, uncoordinated policies from different states. Some borders were opened while others were reinforced with wire. The ensuing turmoil clearly indicated to the British press the sheer absurdity of a pan-European administration.

Capitalising on this chaos, the astute UKIP figurehead, Nigel Farage, realised that repeating simple phrases would attract the voters disenfranchised by both New Labour and the Conservatives. The way in which the European Union was manging both the Greek economy and the migrant crisis was an existential threat to the British way of life. It was time that we should 'Take Back Control'.

Farage was not alone. The rise of isolationist, internally focused populism was a global event driven by, ironically, the forces of global commercialism. India elected an increasingly zealous Hindu government in 2014; China became more overt in its repression of Uyghur Muslims in Xinjian Province as well as the separatists in both Hong Kong and Tibet; Brazil brought in a populist leader who openly reneged on previous commitments to protect the Amazon rainforest. The Russian leader, Vladimir Putin, invaded Ukraine in order to seize Crimea and its cold-water ports. And in November 2016, The United States of America elected Donald Trump as President.

Trump was the son of a property tycoon who tapped into the growing national mood that the traditional liberal elites should be drained from the swamp of Washington politics to allow for a new era of American greatness. Like Alexander and Farage, he instinctively recognised that people were no longer socially liberal and fiscally conservative, as they had been throughout the latter end of the 20th Century. Since 2001, nations had become fiscally liberal and socially conservative, meaning we wanted cheap credit and high walls along the borders.

Speaking about the United States' relationship with Great Britain, Trump stated that Alexander would make an excellent Prime Minister. In return, Alexander said that Trump would probably drive a better deal with the European Union than Teresa May, his own Prime Minister.

Kyle, previously

I'm sitting on my bergen, back against the wall, smoking. There's nothing else in the room. There's nothing else in the house. Everything's gone to Char's, or charity, or the skip. Tomorrow I'll pull the door behind me, stick the keys through the letterbox and that will be it.

Funny to think about it. This was the house I were raised in. Where Mum held us together after Dad got killed.

Where I brought a bird home and Mum told her not to come back. Where we had Christmas. All those birthdays.

And now I'm leaving.

I'm a bit pissed. I had a few beers and that got me thinking about Afghan and the blokes and how I miss it. Miss them. I think of the rush of it all, the pressure, the need to be properly switched on all the fucking time. Never known anything like it. Never will again.

I'm snapping too. I've been all over town looking for work as a plumber, a fitter, even as a labourer. There's nothing. Everyone says the Poles have cornered it, the Romanians run it, but I didn't speak to them, just the English. I go in proper smart: creases in my trousers, regimental tie, sports jacket. I'm tall. I look the part. I'm reliable, hard-working, not afraid of graft. I look them in the eye and shake their hands and smile. I know how to read people. And I want to say, I can do all the basics, I've got the quals and done two years. But I can also talk to people. Set them at ease. Assess the situation. Keep a cool head under pressure. Tell a joke when things go pear-shaped. I don't flap like a ten-ton budgie.

But they don't get it, civvies. They don't get half of it. They've never been on stag so their mates can get their heads down. They've never driven in convoy, keeping the distance between vehicles for hours and yet been sharp-eyed for an attack. They've never had to clear a market square after a suicide attack, triage the wounded, push the survivors aside, scoop the minced-up bodies of children into body bags.

That was a day, that was.

The woman just wouldn't stop screaming, her face all pulled round and her hands clawed and knotty. Couldn't make out what she was saying because the blast made me deaf in one ear. Sergeant-Major McCardle was shouting, arm extended, and one of our officers, Captain Willmott, was sitting against the wall trying to get the tourniquet round his lower leg. There was muscle and shit hanging from where his foot had been blown off and he hadn't gone into shock. Proper nails, self-administering first aid.

And I'm suddenly cold. Hard as tungsten. Tight.

Last time I felt like this I was in court for taking cars. I was a minor then. Dad was away. Mum was having one of her spells. I'd fallen in with a bad crowd and we were bored. Not bad, just fucking about. We took a car from B&M and drove up the motorway the wrong way. Man that was a laugh. Luckily no one coming as it was proper stupid and the rozzers were at the exit ramp so we did a J turn and legged it back, them chasing after us with blue lights on.

Proper race that was. Luke driving. Me in the passenger seat heart nearly bouncing out my chest.

In court, they pulled me aside as a minor. I was sitting there, waiting for Mrs Opatha to come and get me, and all these stuck-up women were whispering to each other, glancing at me sideways, saying parental absence this, abandoned that.

Abandoned my arse. Dad was on Public Duties in London. Mum was ill. It was Dad who picked me up. Gave me a proper punch in the ribs when we got home.

"Never do that again, Kyle," he said, finger in my face, and I never did. Not long after that he arranged for me to stay with Uncle Ben and learn a trade.

It were good, like, working with Uncle Ben. Got to go into town and see Dad at Wellington Barracks. It's when I properly got into boxing. But we did this job in White City, right close to where the Paras were, the Reserve Paras. And I knew that the Reserve Paras were as good as any regular unit so I thought I'd have a go. Do the training. Weekends. Get some extra dosh.

And that's when Sergeant Malone, the PSI, said I should go regular. Or at least get mobilised and do a Herrick tour. Get a medal. It's easy. Just tell him and he'd take me to see the OC.

My statue from the blokes is on the fireplace, in the middle, where the clock used to be. I'm sitting in my grot, smoking, drinking a can, looking up at it. I get up to hold it in my hand and look at it in detail. It's mega, it really is. You can make out the wings, the flash, the detail of the gun. But just as I place it back, I miss the edge of the mantel and it falls on the marble hearth. It breaks clean in half and the head spins off like he's been decapitated.

"Wanker!"

So I'm sitting with this broken statue in my hands wondering why the bronze is so thin and inside it's just wax. It's too fucked to be repaired and even if I try to melt the wax with my lighter it won't stick. The bronze gets too hot to touch and then goes a funny colour. The fire alarm goes off.

"Fucking wanker. Fucking, fucking wanker."

Dean, November 2016

Dean's bedroom window overlooked his small hexagonal garden, the shape a result of the house being in the acute corner between two roads. The fence was made of concrete framing and larch-lap panels. Mister T, Dean's black staffy, sniffed along the base, shuffling with an off-centre waddle. What had once been a patio paved with council slabs was now the foundation for the conservatory. The ground works were complete but the actual building, really only glass panels and aluminium posts, lay on pallets on the uncut lawn wrapped in blue industrial cling film. Dean had rung the builder twice but he hadn't replied. If he didn't hear back by Sunday he'd drive round town until he found him.

Looking at himself in the mirror on the fitted wardrobe, he flexed his shoulder muscles and puffed out his lats. His left shoulder didn't hurt too much as he'd taken a shit load of brufen. There were four wardrobes along the wall. His stuff was all in the right-hand one while Michelle used the other three. His wardrobe lay open with shelves on the left and hanging space on the right. On the shelves, his tee-shirts were folded, tidy edge facing out, stacked according to their colouring: maroon at the bottom, then dark blue, then dark green. Below this was his training kit and below that, footwear. In the hanging space, four shirts stood at ease on yellow hangers, facing to the right, a sharp crease down the outer sleeve. Michelle always offered to do his ironing but he still preferred to do it himself. To the right of the shirts hung a tweed jacket on a wooden hanger, a pair of 34-33 twill trousers, and his working jeans. His Iraq gear was stuffed into a sports bag on the top shelf. He didn't think he'd be needing it again though he did miss the informality and comfort.

He was dressing for a job interview. Grey shirt, regimental tie, good blue jeans, brown shoes, tweed jacket. Victoria had clipped what was left of his hair into a tight number one. He'd had a scrape and given himself a good lathering of aftershave. If there was one thing he learned from the Iraqis it was not being afraid of using scent. With the veteran's badge on his lapel he thought he looked the part. All he had to do was remember those fancy words about what he'd done in the army.

Mick T had given him a ring about a month after he'd put in his notice with Global Risks. It was a long story but, in short, this guy who ran a transport company on the south side of Rotherham needed someone to manage the drivers and vehicles.

"He wants an MTWO? Someone to look after the fleet?"

"That's it," Mick said over the phone. "He's got six 8-tonners and a few grabs. And a couple of loaders."

"That all?"

"Yes mate."

And that was it: an interview for a job in his hometown, starting when he wanted. Thirty grand. It was much less than he used to get as a Colour-Sergeant but given that he had a full pension, and Michelle did hair for private clients, it was alright. In fact, if he earned more he'd have to pay more tax and that would make him worse off to the tune of a hundred and fifty a month.

A year before leaving the army he'd done the resettlement course: how to write a CV, how to do an interview, what a life plan looked like. He'd known it would be important and kept everything in a yellow folder. Last night he'd pulled out a four-page document titled *Curriculum Vitae* and read it. He could remember writing it but couldn't recall why it was necessary to say he was a *'motivated team leader with developed poeple skills'*. Surely that was self-evident. He'd spent more than twenty years in Her Majesty's finest.

Mitch Bolton, the bloke who owned the business, obviously respected what Dean had done and offered him the job on Mick T's recommendation. He made it sound like the drivers were a bunch of gypsies. That was fine. Dean wasn't afraid to get his hands dirty and if they needed a quiet word in their shell-like, he'd give it.

Ideas played in his mind. But otherwise he was hopeful. They'd meet today, agree terms, and he'd start on Monday. Piece of piss, really, this civvy thing.

Dean, December 2016

A month later, at the end of his second week at Bolton's, Dean was whistling *The Boys are Back in Town* as he drove home from the Canklow industrial estate to East Dene, where he lived. He was happy. That week he'd sacked one of the drivers for swapping new tyres for old and that had brought the others into line. He also made it clear, when they played darts in the portacabin office, that if he needed to leather any of them, he would. Stripped down to a vest, he showed off his arms, his chest, his tattoos. The drivers glanced at his biceps then looked away.

But on the whole, he liked them. They were simple men with limited ambition; poorly built, untidy, slovenly. But he understood them as men. They had expensive daughters they didn't understand, wives who spent most of their money and mistresses who spent the rest. They didn't have much of a sense of humour and Dean's story about the Iraqi with his head crushed by a tank track only drew nervous glances and a deal of fidgeting, so he didn't tell it again, or any other story that might have filled an evening in the Sergeants' Mess.

It was actually Mitch, the boss, who troubled him the most. He was always complaining, always imagining things were worse than they were and throwing the problem at Dean. At first this made Dean feel valuable but he was coming to think that Mitch might be setting him up. If he was given a problem he couldn't fix, Mitch would lay the blame on him and sack him. He'd never had to navigate an environment as political as this and he felt uncomfortable and disloyal thinking about it. He liked things simple; he liked things straight.

He planned to go back to the office over the weekend to check the vehicles were ready for Monday. There was an issue with MOTs for two of them and they needed work on the clutches. Mitch owed money to the mechanic, Sam Johnson, and Dean was going to see him to beg for more time. He didn't know why Mitch hadn't paid him and was even thinking of paying the bill himself. Anything to keep the wagons rolling. But there was a niggle in the back of his mind that Mitch was not a straight shooter. If Dean could persuade Sam to do the work and put the payment on his word, then he would do it. And if Mitch didn't pay up they would be down two wagons, which would be Mitch's fault. Dean had told Mitch what he had to do, standing in front of his desk with a pen and notebook in his hand just as he had many times as a Colour-Sergeant briefing the Company Commander.

He was certain no-one else went in on a Saturday. But that was what the job needed and he was a professional. It was all about standards. Professional fucking standards.

Absent minded, listening to the drive-time show on Radio Two, he found himself squeezed by a bus into the wrong lane and forced off at a junction. This didn't make a big difference to his route so he drove on, following his nose along the Herringthorpe playing fields, noting there were fewer cameras this way. Approaching a speed bump, Dean glanced up a road to the right and saw a van with livery he recognised. He drove on, turned round at the next junction, and came back to confirm.

Yes, it was the same van. Shakir Fucking Mahmud.

The conservatory had been erected, so to speak, meaning the panels and posts had been assembled, but the structure had not been bolted to the house. It clattered against the brickwork in the wind. One of the glass panels had cracked and the noise, right outside his bedroom, kept him awake. He'd called Mahmud three times that week but the fucker never picked up. He'd left messages but they were never returned. Why did civvies never do what they said?

Mahmud's van was parked between the lamp posts with two wheels on the grass verge. A young man, dark haired and skinny, was throwing a shovel and a yard brush into the back. A cement mixer was tied to the frame behind the cab. Dean parked up, watched him for a while, then got out.

"Hello mate. I'm looking for Shaky. Is he here?"

He was polite but firm. The skinny kid looked like a nephew. He didn't meet Dean's eyes and mumbled something about Shakir being inside with a client. The nearest building was a semi with scaffolding down the side alley and a vast blue tarpaulin across the hipped roof.

"I'll wait," Dean said, taking a position by the door of the cab with his arms folded.

The young man lifted the drop side of the van and locked the panel in place. With everything loaded, he pulled out his phone to text someone. Dean hoped he was telling Shaky to come out.

After ten minutes, Dean leaned against the door of Mahmud's van. The young man started to say something but a glance from Dean silenced him. At that point, Mahmud appeared from the side alley. He spotted Dean and his face betrayed annoyance and then panic. Then his mouth widened into a smile. "Dean!" he said, extending a hand to shake. "How are you? Didn't know you come round this area."

Dean gripped his hand tightly and shook it hard. "Skip it, Shaky. You said November. It's now December. Well, originally, you said July. And it's now December..."

His voice rose. He knew it was no good losing his temper with Mahmud. He was a master bullshitter. But Dean couldn't help it. He'd gone to great lengths to find someone good. He'd interviewed them, got references, and the conservatory was a very simple job. It should have taken a week at the most.

It had been Michelle's project to manage while he was away but as the weeks had dragged by she had become evasive on the phone. She was embarrassed that she hadn't managed it and this made Dean bitter. When he had offered to take the job off her she was delighted. "Be careful of that slimy bastard," she'd said.

Mahmud read Dean's face. "I know, I know. Look, your wife said it was ok to do a job for my uncle..."

"That was months ago. Shaky, this isn't fucking good enough..."

At the swearing, Mahmud pulled an innocent face and put a hand over his heart. It was a game he played: the good Muslim. This grated. Dean hated people lying.

"I don't fucking care if you don't like the way I talk. The job's not fucking finished. The glass is cracking. The aluminium is splitting. It's not fixed to the wall. And we fucking paid you in full!"

Dean stepped forward. Mahmud was big chested but not as big as Dean. He had managed the subcontractors, the ground workers, the brickies, the labourers, the first fixers, the second fixers, the glazers, the tiler, the drivers. Dean had watched him, admired him, even. But the guy was fundamentally dishonest and it wasn't that he was a Paki. Well, that wasn't true. It *was* that he was a Paki. It absolutely was. They were untrustworthy. And he had this obscenely stupid haircut, shaven at the sides with zig zag lines, that made Dean want to punch him.

Mahmud kept his cool. "I had other work needed done before the winter. You understand, Dean, don't you?" He turned to indicate the tarpaulin behind him.

"You took this on after you started mine. I want the work done by Christmas. I've got family coming. You understand? If not, I'll take you to court."

Dean had never taken anyone to court but it seemed a reasonable threat. At a rough guess there was ten grand's worth of work to finish. It would easily cost that to get someone else to complete the job and he might have to replace the conservatory.

"Well, if you do that you'll have to pay costs and court time. Do you really want to do that, Dean? I mean..."

Dean tensed. The veins in his neck throbbed. He took another step forward. With his adrenalin pumping he didn't worry about his injured shoulder. The problem with people like Mahmud is they had no sense of duty.

How had Dean learned these things? From Corporal Harrison at Juniors and Corporal McEachin at depot. Be jack with them and you got smashed round the lughole with a black plastic mug.

Since coming back from Iraq he'd felt free. It was as though the world was open and he had an unlimited choice on what he could wear, what he could say, what he could do. But fuckers like Mahmud anchored his feet in wet cement. They made him feel constrained and this made him seethe. He growled deep in his throat as he clenched both fists.

"Ok, ok, look," Mahmud said, both hands in from of him. "Look. I understand, ok? I'll send two guys on Monday. It'll be done by Friday."

"Why not tomorrow?"

Mahmud again looked over his shoulder at the house behind him. "Look, I need to get this watertight. I have roofers coming. But Monday, I'll come to yours and I'll personally supervise it, ok? It'll be done by Friday."

"It fucking better be," Dean said.

Steve, December 2016

The theatre stage was lit from above by three powerful lamps that cast strong beams across each other creating multiple shadows of different shapes and gradations. Steve had never been on a stage and had only once been to the theatre, a school trip to *Peter Pan*. He was fascinated by the rows of seats disappearing into the darkness and wondered if anyone was out there.

He was here for a presentation skills course. This wasn't the same as the interview skills, or the basic instructional techniques he'd done as a Lance-jack. This was about how to make a mark on people. It was run by a theatre company and paid for by *Save Our Heroes*. Clive said it would help him and had squared away the funding, including enough for his train ticket and the hotel in Shepherd's Bush.

There were eight people on the course. They had all arrived on time and been invited to find a chair on the stage. Tanner was a double amp in a wheelchair, so a flat chested woman dressed entirely in black silently pulled one chair out of the circle to make room for him. He was from the Yorkshire Regiment and Steve guessed by his accent that he was from Dewsbury or Huddersfield. They'd met in the hotel bar the night before and Tanner had wanted to stay late but Steve had gone to bed. He didn't drink since it messed with the epilepsy drugs and getting dehydrated could damage his kidney.

Opposite Tanner was Sue, a corporal from the RAF who sat on her hands and had neat black hair tucked behind her ears. Next to her was Mick from the Royal Engineers, severely burned in the face after his vehicle got hit in Iraq. He had a wicked sense of humour and kept pretending the lights were alien space craft coming to take him. Jock was infantry, 4 Scots, and Steve had trouble understanding what he said. Dusty Miller was a loggie from London. There was one empty chair for a bloke who had not turned up and the other two Steve had not yet met. One was single amp below the knee. He sat with his good leg folded back under the chair and his prosthetic stuck out. The other was able-bodied but said nothing. He had the hollow cheeks and hollow eyes of someone who'd lived rough. He constantly scanned the room.

Steve rubbed his upper arm. The new prosthetic was lighter than the old one and his stump fitted beautifully into the cup. He was delighted with it. It was just a shame that the one that fitted best was intended for a black person. The artificial skin was amazing. It had the fine lines at the back of the knuckles, realistic fingernails, and palms a different shade. He was conscious of it when people noticed it on the train, then looked at his face, then looked away. Their uncertainty made him chuckle.

A man walked onto the stage having whispered something to the flat chested girl in black. He strode into the centre of the circle and introduced himself, his voice rich, full, and as clear as a bell. "Hello everyone. I'm Casper. I will be running the workshop today with Lauretta's help." He walked silently, extending his toes in a slow march, and took the chair with its back towards the darkness beyond the stage. Lauretta, the woman in black, bowed to them from the side of the stage and disappeared behind the curtains.

"This is the first of these workshops I have done so it's incredibly exciting for me. I look forward to working with you all and seeing what energies we can create. Where they will lead us."

Steve thought it odd that he should introduce himself by saying this was his first course. He made a mental note to tell him at the end: as an instructor you should convey authority. But it was soon very clear that Casper did not lack any of that.

"I haven't been on the telly. I've not played a slug from outer space in *Doctor Who*, or a stallholder on *Enders*. I'm a stage actor. I love interacting with the audience." As he spoke, he looked round all of them, his eyes stopping on each face in turn. "That is where the magic happens."

He paused. They all looked at him.

"So, why don't we start with introductions? I know some of you met last night at the Ibis. But I'd like to allow us all the space to bring ourselves into the room. What I'd invite you to do is tell us who you really are: tell us your background, where you come from and what your childhood was like; tell us where you are going. What are your goals and hopes for the future? And lastly, if you had a motto, a saying, what would that be?"

Steve patted the pocket of his trousers. His notebook was in the daysack in the pile on the far side of the stage. There was no way he could remember all those instructions. He needed to write such things down as if he was being given a set of orders. He wasn't the only one to start looking for a pen, either. In fact, all the others had either risen or looked to the pile of bags. Only Sue had thought ahead and had hers open on her thigh.

"It's ok. You don't need notes. Just take a seat everyone. I'll keep this simple, ok. Where are you from? Where are you going? And what road signs will guide you? It's like that, ok? There's no need to be formal. Just tell it as it comes. But be rich! Let yourselves out! Who wants to go first?"

There was a pause, then half the hands went up at the same time.

"Wow. We're keen. That's so great," said Casper. "How about you," he said, indicating Tanner with his head. "Where are you from, where are you going, and what is your motto for life, my friend?"

Tanner slouched in his chair. His stumps were strapped down so he wouldn't fall out of his chair but this made his legs invisible so it looked like he was just a torso. He'd spent an hour in the hotel telling Steve and Mick that he could no longer fuck in missionary position. When he had legs he could push off the footboard but since he'd lost them he had nothing to gain purchase. So he sat on a little chair with no arms and his wife would do it cowgirl. She had great tits so he was doubly happy.

"Mark Tannenbaum. Tanner. I'm from Swansea originally but my dad was Navy so I was brought up in Cyprus. Moved to Huddersfield. Don't know why, it's a shithole. Joined up aged seventeen. Wanted to join the Royal Welsh but they put me in the Yorkshire Regiment, which was fine."

He paused, then continued. "I was a platoon sergeant. This happened in Sangin. Where am I going? Back to Huddersfield. I'm married, two kids."

He then answered the question that always came up. "She stayed with me. The kids found it difficult as they're now taller than me. But they're learning."

Sue smiled as she nodded. She put her hands under her thighs and her hair unhooked itself from her ear and hung to the side. Casper was making notes on a pad which he supported with one leg.

"My motto: if it don't kill you, it makes you stronger."

Steve nodded. He sensed Casper wanted something more but what Tanner had said was short and to the point. Casper started to clap and everyone joined in. Steve slapped his good hand against his leg.

"That was really powerful, Tanner, thank you. I think it's great that you shared something about your personal life and challenges. It's a very courageous thing to do."

Steve looked at him. That wasn't his definition of courage but if that's what Casper thought, crack on. Fuck knows what he would think if he had to go out on patrol knowing the last month had cost three men their legs.

"So, who wants to go next? I know! Let's do this like the ice bucket challenge! Tanner. Why don't you nominate someone."

Tanner looked like he hadn't heard a word Casper had said until his name was mentioned. He pointed at Steve. "I nominate him," he said.

Steve's mind went blank. Casper wanted them to say something personal. There was a structure to follow that made a lot of sense but he couldn't remember what it was. They were all looking at him and his mouth dried up. The edges of the plate in his head ached. Sue had nice eyes and when she sat forward, her shirt filled out heavily.

"Hello. I'm Steve. Carlisle. Well, Bootle originally, but my dad left us so me and Mum went to live in Carlisle as that's where she's from. Originally."

He wanted to be funny. Most of all, he liked making people laugh.

"I could have supported Carlisle but I'm an Everton man. True blue." He looked at the worn boards of the stage. An idea came to him. He lifted his prosthetic to wave at people, a bright smile on his face.

"Well, as you can see, that's not entirely true."

A wave of chuckles spread across the room but it wasn't as much as he wanted.

"So, I've got a black man's arm but sadly I don't have a black man's cock…"

He smiled, laughing at his own joke. There was a second rustle of titters but the joke seemed to have fallen flat. Casper forced a smile, his eyes scanning the room as he did so.

"And what would you like to achieve, Steve?" he said. "What fires you up? What launches your rockets? What presses all your buttons all at the same time? What would you like to say you have done when you look back on a rich, varied, and purposeful life?"

The question sounded odd. He was from Carlisle. Did people from Cumbria live rich and varied lives? He'd been a Lance-corporal in an infantry regiment. He'd punched out and re-joined, this time into the Parachute Regiment. He hadn't been promoted. He'd got injured in a market square suicide bombing. His fiancée had left him. What else could he say?

"All I want to do, really, is help other veterans," he said. "That's all that I really think about. Nil satis. Nisi optimum"

Three of the others started clapping, led by Tanner. Then the others joined in. Casper scribbled something, lifting his knee to do so.

"What was that? Nil satis... You'll have to help me with that..."

"Nothing but the best is good enough, Casper. You should know that, an educated man like yourself. It's the Everton motto."

The room fell silent. He'd said his intro and it was someone else's turn. His collar was becoming uncomfortable and he tugged at the front of his shirt with his good hand to air his body. He hadn't expected to be sweating this much. He thought they'd just be reading stuff and he'd have time to close his bad eye. Everyone look at Casper, who lowered his knee.

"That was great, thank you, Steve. But just a word as we go forward. A lot of presentation is about knowing what is, and what is not, acceptable to an audience. We're going to cover this later but I'm going to mention it now so we get a feel for one of the key points of the day. It's fine to make jokes about your body. In fact, in the right context, it's a very healthy thing to do. But there are always going to be questions of appropriateness. And when we introduce ourselves, we should always be asking what sort of introduction do they want to hear?"

He was looking round the room, stopping on each person in turn. He didn't look at Steve, which meant he was saying it to him.

Steve felt his shoulders sink. All he wanted was to make people like him. He wanted to nominate Sue but was afraid to do so in case everyone thought he fancied her, which he did.

"So, thank you, Steve. That was great. Who would you like to go next."

Steve was conscious of Sue's large brown eyes looking at him but he ignored her and nodded at Jock.

"Yourself," he said in a flat voice.

Kyle, previously

I'm sitting on the sofa at Char's watching daytime TV. I'm keeping out of the way to be honest. In the mornings, Danny's out early to get to site and Char has to get little Dan up and washed and dressed and fed and off to school.

Sometimes little Dan can hear the telly so he opens the door and pokes his little face round. "Hi Uncle Kyle," he says and he has these bright little cheeks and dark eyelashes. He's a cute little man so I say to him to go into the kitchen and do what his mother says. When he comes home after school I'll play with him.

Later, about eight, Char has pushed little Dan out the door and one of her neighbours is walking the kids to school. I've rolled up my dossbag and stuffed it into my bergen round the back of the big chair where Danny sits. I'm tidy because I don't want to be a burden. They took me in after the flat fell through and I said it would just be a couple of weeks. It's been three now but Char says they really don't mind. I look after little Dan when he comes back from school. I feed him, sort out his kit for the following day, put his clothes on the chair and his sports kit in the bag. I even clean his footie boots and untie the laces. This way Char can do longer shifts at Bellevue and Danny can do longer hours on site. They can go out, too, of an evening.

First time, Danny was like, are you sure Kyle? You don't want a pint down the Grapes? I said no, it's fine. Just didn't feel like it, really. Didn't fancy the walk, the dark, the rain. I said I'd stay in and they could have fun. It's great for me to play with little Dan, anyway. Good for him, too.

Danny and Char had a proper good night. She kept texting to say is everything alright and it was. I read The Hungry Caterpillar with little Dan as there was nothing else. We watched the Spurs game. But I just liked being in the living room. The sofa was comfy. The walls were good. It felt safe and I could keep little Dan safe too, asleep beside me, his little head on my leg.

So anyway, it's morning, and Char opens the door and asks me through to the kitchen. She's had another letter from the solicitor, a different one. We get a brew and sit at the table. Char opens the envelope with a knife, slicing along the edge in a sawing motion. She puts the knife on the table, pulls out the letter, unfolds it, and turns it the right way up. She reads it to herself and then bits of it to me.

"We got just short of ten grand each from Mum's estate," she says.

"You're joking! Ten grand!" I say.

She nods. "Yes, ten grand." She puts the letter on the table and flattens it out with one hand to read again. I turn the light on so she can see better. Her hair falls over her face. She needs new glasses.

Ten grand! It's a ton of money. I'm still living on my pay from the tour. I'm hardly spending any as I don't go out. I give some to Char as rent like. But I'm just drinking cans from Lidl; the ones that look like Stella but they're not. I buy things for little Dan or give him money to get them himself as I don't like going to the shops. I don't tell Char that he's going out on his own but it's fine. He's a good lad.

Then Char says, "Kyle, this is really useful. You should use this to put a deposit down on a flat. It won't be like last time. But you'll need a job as well. To pay off a mortgage."

I nod and shrug at the same time. She's never put pressure on me but I know when she's worried. I went into town last week but had a nightmare trying to register for benefits.

"I'll go see them again," I say. "It was just I didn't have a permanent address. I put Mum's down but they said I don't live there anymore, do I?"

Char pulls a face. "I don't know where they think you'll stay when you get out of the army. You can use this address for now. It won't affect us and if you get a place of your own, you can change it then. It will also boost your credit rating to have a flat..."

"But my credit rating must be good if I've got ten grand! They're sure to boost my rating if they know that. Then I can get a place and job's a good un."

"It doesn't work quite like that, Kyle," Char says. "You need to invest this money into something for the future. A training course. A flat..."

"A car? If I had a car, I could get about the place ..."

She nods but pulls a face. I don't know what she's worried about. I don't worry about anything. I just like being in the house. That way I can keep them all safe, keep little Dan from harm.

Pete, December 2016

Pete tried to ignore the stench of boiled sugar emanating from the factory but it reminded him too much of his childhood and the nagging urge that there was something better for him as soon as he was old enough to leave Arbroath, the semi-dormant coastal village where he was raised.

The factory hadn't changed since his father's time and he might not be Steve Jobs but even he could see that all the other businesses had long since abandoned the sandstone flax mills by the rail track for the spacious, well-lit prefabs on the other side of the Westway. His two older brothers didn't agree. McCardle's (*As Fresh as The Glens!*) was a Scottish institution no less famous in discerning circles than Irn Brew, Tennent's, or Buckfast. The business would remain where it was, where it had always been, where it always would be. It relied on the town for women workers and the town relied on the factory as an outlet for late-season, over-ripe fruit and the annual giveaway to the children.

His brothers didn't trust Pete with managing production as he hadn't served his time and didn't know the processes. But he'd been a sergeant-major in the army and therefore would know a thing or two about logistics. They had invented the role of Distribution Manager and allocated him the shabby shipping container office at the far end of the carpark. This he liked. He was close to the smoking shed and it spared him having to deal with the sugar syrup and the women who peeled the ginger by hand. He was much happier alongside the lubricant cages and the sausage-fingered, bow-legged men who heaved the kegs of concentrate onto flatbed trucks.

The office measured 6.3 meters by 2.3. There was a single door in the middle of the front wall and a window either side. When it rained hard he couldn't hear what anyone said on the phone. He positioned his desk at an angle in the top right-hand corner so he could see across the yard. In the opposite corner he placed a u-shaped sofa and a table on which stood a kettle and a pod coffee machine. The walls were adorned with his army photographs: wide frame shots of company or battalion groups in Northern Ireland, Iraq, Afghanistan, and square ones of his recruit platoons when he was a corporal, or his officer cadets when he was at Sandhurst as a colour-sergeant. All these photos had the same formal feel; the subjects staring steely eyed at the camera, fists on knees, outside leg crossed over inside. Those were the days when he was lean and fit; before the drink, before the gambling; and before his hips locked up.

On the wall directly in front of the door, the first thing anyone saw when they entered, was a low wooden bookshelf containing his files. On top stood a chrome-plated mortar round on a wooden plinth and a manikin head on which sat his regimental beret.

At five minutes to nine, as always, Pete's oldest brother knocked and pushed open the door. He'd obviously been on the factory floor for the morning shift and was wearing a white coat and white mesh trilby over his shirt and tie. He sniffed as he entered and stood erect on the mat with the morning's mail held against his chest like a minister holding a bible.

"You alright, Sandy?" said Pete, sitting in the chair behind his desk, retying the laces of his brown shoes.

"Good morning to you, Peter," replied his brother. "There's a weight of invoices I'd be very grateful if you could see to and there's another letter from the Ministry of Defence. I'd hoped you would be free of that nonsense by now."

"Sandy, don't read my fucking mail. And yes, I'll sort the bills. Just drop them there." With a nod of his head, he indicated the plastic in-tray in the corner of his desk. "And you can always send Midge with the post. I don't need to be inspected of a morning."

His brother placed the mail carefully in the tray. He was tall, lean, and carved his way through life with a pinched, aquiline nose. "I'll do as I see fit, just as Father did, Peter. And I'm expecting you at the Board meeting at one pm, after the lunch break."

"Yep, got it. I'll give an overview of issues and solutions and I'd also like to make a couple of suggestions, things we need to do different."

"I'd prefer it if we could discuss your suggestions before anything goes to the Board. They don't like surprises," Sandy said, looking down at him.

Pete studied his brother with a disdainful scowl. "As you wish. But we can't keep depending on Fraser's. They don't have the lift capacity we need."

Sandy raised a long-fingered hand. "Our business partners are my affair, Peter. Please let me know your concerns at the appropriate juncture and I will discuss it with James and then with Martyn Fraser."

Pete stood up, pushing his chair back with his legs. He watched the fear flicker across his brother's face and kept staring at him while he pulled the mail out of the in-tray.

"Then I'll come and see you tomorrow. Was there anything else?"

Sandy said no, wished him good morning once more, and turned on his heel to leave. The automatic closer hissed as the door clicked shut. Pete listened angrily as Sandy's segs receded across the yard. He sat in thought for a while, pondering how to get his brother to see the reality of their position. The reason sales were falling was distribution, not demand, and this was because they relied on another ancient Arbroath firm run by a set of brothers with old fashioned views. He shook his head. At least he had a job.

The letter from the MOD was in a plush white envelope franked two days before. Sandy hadn't opened it but had clearly noticed the OHMS stamp across the flap. Pete sliced along the top with a miniature brass kukri he kept on his desk and sat down to read.

"What the very fuck?" he said, the anger thick at the back of his throat.

The letter informed him that the family of Mr Seamus O'Hare, a lawyer with republican sympathies shot and killed by the British Army during a cordon and search operation in Country Tyrone in 1993, was suing the Ministry of Defence for unlawful killing. The Ministry was obliged, in support of the policies promoted by Her majesty's Government, and as a pivotal element of the Good-Friday Agreement (1998), to inform the Historic Enquiries Team (HET) that they should allocate resource to investigate this event. The letter went on to say that the Ministry recognised that the shooting of Mr O'Hare had already been investigated on three previous occasions, first by the Royal Ulster Constabulary in the immediate aftermath, by the McKay Inquiry of 1996, and by the lengthy and expensive Donaldson Inquiry of 2008 to 2010 which studied all Republican activity in County Tyrone and the police and military responses to it.

The words were busy and dense. Pete took the letter over to his seating area and got himself a coffee. He felt bitter that the noise of it all wouldn't stop. But it didn't make him regretful. It made him furious.

It was the final paragraph that really nettled him: 'In addition to the case against the Ministry, the family of Mr O'Hare intend to raise a legal case against the soldier known to the Donaldson Inquiry as 'Trooper P' who is believed to have shot Mr O'Hare. It is not known at this time what basis in law such a case might have but we wish all addressees to be aware of events as they unfold.'

Pete read the letter aloud so that his eyes, in his anger, didn't skip any meaning. He'd thought the thing had been finally put to bed after the Donaldson Inquiry but apparently not. The IRA just wouldn't let it lie.

And why should they? He'd hurt them. He was Trooper P.

Dean, January 2017

New Year's Day. The girls were upstairs with their friends. Dean could hear the pumping bass, a trashy pop song that sounded suspiciously like Bhangra, and the thump of heavy footfall. Michelle was washing up in the kitchen. His father, Jon, was in the new conservatory in the deep sofa they'd found on Facebook, with Mr T on the floor at his feet. The sofa was old and saggy but very comfortable. It fitted neatly along the wall adjacent to the external fence. From it, there was a view into the garden and the remaining lawn.

The conservatory was a shambles. Rain sprayed off the upper guttering to patter on the glass roof. Dean had piped along all the join with silicone but the wind still managed to whistle through the gaps and the room was absolutely freezing. It was only because his dad smoked that he was out there.

Dean placed a glass of ruby port next to the ashtray on the table by his father's knee. "Do you want anything else?" he asked.

Jon shook his head. He sucked on a rollie and tapped the end with his forefinger into the ashtray, dislodging a length of ash. His shoes had Velcro strapping and his legs were scrawny underneath charity shop flannel trousers. He'd shrunk since the last time he'd stayed and Dean was conscious of his decline. But his eyes still had their unforgiving hardness.

"You need to slap your builder," Jon said.

Dean sat down. He had a glass of port in one hand and the bottle in the other. He leaned forward to put the bottle on the floor then settled back against some cushions. He was close to his father but not too close. They weren't a touchy family and his father's spiky manner created a barrenness around him.

Not knowing what to say, Dean mumbled, "I left Michelle to manage it..."

"What was his name?"

"Mahmud."

His father made a shrugging gesture and grunted. "Well. There you go."

Dean edged to the end of the sofa to support his elbow on the armrest. Jon took the last drags from his fag then worked it into the ashtray with a spiral twist that made the final wisps of smoke rise and dissipate. He coughed into his fist and Dean winced at the guttural phlegm hawked up and wiped away on his trouser leg. He lifted a hand to pat his father on the back but the old man shook his head and pulled out a red hanky to wipe his hands.

"That tile's broken," he rasped.

Dean nodded, tried to change the subject. "Shitty weather, eh?" he said, nodding into the dark. In the glass opposite there was a reflection of himself and his father. Him, broad and strong, jammed into the end of the sofa; his father, taut as catgut, spread out in the middle of the cushion.

"How are you getting on with that job?" his father asked. "The driving company."

"It's good," he said. Then, after a pause, "Well, actually, Dad, it's shit. But it's not difficult and it'll do me till I find something better. I manage a fleet of vehicles. I'm learning, all the time. But also I'm not learning. None of the problems are difficult. They just need a bit of initiative to solve them. But civvies don't know how to do that."

His father nodded, glanced at him with a critical, stern face. "Sack anyone?"

Dean nodded. "Two. One was a thief. The other was late. I gave them both a warning but they kept doing it. So I fucked them off."

His father nodded again, but slower, accepting Dean's version of events. "If they're no good, get rid of them," he said. "Was always my way."

Rain pattered on the glass below the leaking gutter. The air had changed and Dean had been hoping that his father would mention his days in the police. It was the stories of his undercover work, infiltrating animal rights groups, that inspired him as a child. Although Jon was away for months at a time, Dean had doted on him when he was home.

"I want to ask about that, Dad," Dean said.

"About what?"

"About... your undercover crew."

"What about them?"

The old man was rotating a packet of Golden Virginia between thumb and forefinger. He opened it and started rolling another stick-thin cigarette.

"You know I applied to do Special Duties in the army? The Det? Undercover work in Belfast?"

His father grunted. With a yellow thumbnail he squeezed a filter from the plastic wrapping onto one end of the rizla. "Pity you didn't get in," he said. "That sounded good."

Jon filled the paper with tobacco then stuck out the tip of his tongue to moisten along the gum. "I knew people in the RUC at the time. Bronze Section. Nicked or killed more provos than most units. Army included. Even your guys."

Dean sucked his lips tight. He had really wanted to get into the Det. He had never fancied the SAS. They were good but it was being undercover in Northern Ireland that really excited him. It would have enabled him to look his father in the eye and if it hadn't been for that officer, the lazy, unprofessional cunt, he might have made it, too.

"Do you still know people in your old team? Is anyone still serving?" Dean asked. His voice was higher than he wanted so he coughed into his fist.

"Why do you ask?"

"I'd like to… I mean I'm thinking about…"

His father glanced at him, cocking an eye, then returned his gaze to the broken tile on the far side of the room. "You want to try the police?"

"Yes."

"Or undercover work? They disbanded my team after things got in the press. The investigation didn't help."

"I was thinking of basic policing. But if there's something good, I would go for it. I mean, I'm forty-nine but I'm still in good nick. I'm good with firearms. I can lead…"

His father lit the cigarette and smoked quietly, staring ahead. Dean looked up at the roof panels and saw another reflection of them both from an angle that truncated their bodies. As he did so he noticed water was seeping through between the conservatory and the house. It made the bricks shiny. Dean followed the wall down to the tiles and saw a growing puddle to the side of the French doors.

His father said, "The flashing's not been cut into the wall."

Dean's face reddened.

"But that apart. I'll make a call," his father said. "Most of them will be long gone by now. Or dead. But there might be one with a connection. His son joined and he's now an Inspector."

This was the best news Dean had heard all day. Having to look after his father was never a joyful experience and Michelle had been asking how long he would stay. But having his dad open a door for him, given how taciturn he'd always been, made it all worthwhile. "Where?"

"South Yorkshire. But let me make a call."

Dean made to tap his father on the leg but stopped himself. "Thanks, Dad, that's great."

He looked up at the kitchen window where Michelle was drying the glasses. "Look. You sit here. I'll go help Mish. And then we'll put a film on, yeah?"

His father grunted but said nothing more. Dean topped up his port glass and turned to go inside.

"You can leave the bottle," the old man said.

Steve, January 2017

Steve had suggested Erica meet him in Bar Mio, opposite Carlisle station, because it was easy to find and they could go any number of places to eat if they liked each other. The more time she spent with him the more likely it was she would see the good and not focus on his injuries.

They'd met on Tinder. The photo he'd used for his profile pic was recent, post injury, taken while he was walking the Dragon's Back in Wales as an ambassador for *Save Our Heroes*. It showed his face, the trig point, and the blue-green spread of mountains in the background. It had been a sweltering day and his bandana was soaked. He thought he looked good. Since then, his hair had grown and he no longer needed the bandana to cover the scar. That craniectomy had saved his life and one day he would find the name of the surgeon who had done the operation in the field hospital at Bagram airbase and shake his hand. With his good hand, obviously.

He'd told Erica how it had happened. In fact, it was this information that had brought them together. She was a final year paramedic student at the university. A mature student, she said, and had been in the Navy for a while. After graduation, she would be on the ambulances and he respected her sense of public service. They had never met but he was glad he'd got that part out of the way. He knew he'd at least be easy to spot as there wouldn't be that many men out in town with a black prosthetic arm.

Would he tell her his joke? He'd have to see how the introductions went.

He sat at the window watching the traffic lights change and how the cars moved in even, regular pulses from one set to the next. It was dark and raining but the people coming into the bar had a smiling, opportunistic look that he nearly shared.

It was always possible that he would see Issy in town as well. She had left Carlisle after they split but came back at weekends to see her parents. Her mother lived round the corner from his mum so it was inevitable that they'd run into each other. They'd been mates since school and got together when he joined the army. They'd split up, of course. It was difficult, him being away all the time. But then they'd met up a month after he'd got out the first time. He was working as a roofer for one of the local firms and one of the guys, Terry, had been her cousin. When they'd got back together it was like a meeting of minds. They hadn't got married but they'd bought a house and he'd promised her it would be ok when he joined up the second time, in the Paras.

When he woke in the hospital she wasn't there. His mother was. Issy came later but he watched her face change throughout his recovery. At first, joy and relief. Then sadness. Then anger. Then fear. She started visiting less often claiming she couldn't afford the days off, the travel, the hotels, even though he knew the regimental charity paid for such things.

What he found hardest was the fact he was making great strides. He learned to walk again. He had both his legs and it was only his balance that was shot away. He learned to talk, albeit slowly. He learned to use his other hand. How proud he'd been to wipe his own arse!

But she couldn't face the long, dutiful burden of it all. She wanted children. She wanted a quiet life in a small-town terrace where she knew the neighbours and the kids could play in the street. She tried to explain, her face all wet and folded over on itself, ugly and frightened. At first he'd been understanding but then he felt lower than he'd been at any stage. What was life worth if he had no one to share it with?

He'd put her Christmas card through her mother's door. But she'd not sent one back and then her mother came round in between Christmas and New Years and told his mum that her Issy was married and expecting. Could she ask her Steven to leave her alone?

The traffic lights changed again. A pulse of traffic accelerated away. Dark figures gathered on the far side, in the rain, waiting to cross. None of them looked like they might be Erica though it was difficult to tell. He'd said six. He'd been here since five-thirty. It was now twenty to seven and the barman was coming round to clear the glasses from the tables. Steve had his foot on a bar stool in addition to the one he was sitting on.

"Want another of those?" the barman said. He was tall, angular, and had a neatly cropped beard and rimless glasses. He wasn't fussing but since Steve had only had two orange juices, he knew he wasn't spending as much as the barman wanted. The other tables were full with chatting, happy groups coming out of work or off the trains.

The security guy on the door kept looking at him. He had his SIA badge strapped to his arm in a fluorescent holder and looked like he did weights. Steve didn't box after the head injury but back in the day he'd been quite handy, good enough for the company team at light heavy. This guy was too slow to be any good. Two jabs would be all it took. When he was in battalion there was this kid, a reservist who'd been mobilised. Kyle, his name was. He was a brilliant boxer. He would knock this guy out in one.

Steve's phone lay face up on the narrow strip of table along the window. It lit up. He knew what it would be. When it started buzzing, he picked it up in his good hand and used his thumb to press the answer button.

"Hello, Steve Reedman fine dining, how may I be of service to you?"

There was silence on the end of the line.

"Hello?"

"Steve, it's Erica."

"Hello Erica. How are you?"

"Steve, are you in a bar?"

She could hear the background noise. Had they not agreed to meet here?

"Yes, I'm in a bar. Did we not say we'd meet tonight..."

He listened to her breathing. She was working up to something.

"Steve, look, I can't make it tonight. I'm sorry."

Steve stared out into the darkness, the rain, the pulse of traffic. "Well. That's a shame that. Was there... I mean is there..."

They'd spoken for an hour the first time, after they'd agreed to swap numbers. They'd talked about the town and where they liked to go. He'd been careful not to probe too deeply in case she thought he was a creep. Instead, he'd asked what she liked doing and she said she was into caving. She was quite active, actually, a climber and a caver.

The second time they spoke wasn't for quite as long and the third time, just a few days ago, had been quite short. But he'd asked her to meet him and had been elated when she'd agreed.

"Listen, Steve, I think you're a really fabulous guy. Really genuine and caring. But I just don't think it's going to work between us and I don't want to mess with your emotions."

He recognised the big fuck-off when he heard it. There was no point dragging this on. "Well, I'm sorry to hear that," he said. "I don't know how..."

She raised her voice slightly. "Look, I'm sure you'll find someone. You're a really great guy…"

He didn't know how to end the conversation without hanging up and he didn't want to appear rude. "It's ok," he said. "I understand."

She said nothing so he ended the call. "Bye. Bye, Erica."

He put the phone down. He sat for a minute looking at the blue screensaver. *Nil satis nisi optimum.* Then he looked out into the darkness and rain.

Three women were shuffling between the tables to get to an empty stool at the window along from him. One of them, a black woman with bouncy, wide hair, had a lovely smile.

"You can have these two as well, love," Steve said as he got up to leave.

Malcolm, January 2017

On Tuesday night, at the end of the holiday, Malcolm put his new wheelie suitcase, a Christmas present from Penny, by the front door. He placed his leather briefcase on top of it and hung his coat from the extending handle, patting the pockets for the chink of keys. The taxi was booked for five-thirty the following morning and he had a seat on the six-ten to King's Cross.

"Got everything?"

Penny held Luca against her chest, rocking him gently up and down and patting his back softly.

"Think so, petal. I'll order, shall I?"

The holiday had been barely more than a week. He'd finished on client site on the Thursday before Christmas and worked from home on the Friday. After closing his laptop he hadn't opened it again until that morning. After deleting the administrative noise from the IT department and corporate comms there were forty emails from his team or his managers requiring action. He'd made a list of what to do on the train but noted that there were none from the client which meant the work he'd asked for had not been done. No wonder defence procurement was in such a state.

In the kitchen, Malcolm lifted the delivery brochures down from behind the blue and white milk jug on the corner shelf.

"Curry or pizza? I'll collect."

Bonkers was asleep on the backdoor mat. He lifted his head then dropped it down. Penny stared into Luca's face and stroked his temple with the side of her thumb. His hair was coming through dark rather than red. His eyes were metallic blue but Malcolm's mother said that would change. Penny shrugged in answer to his question so he replaced the curry menu and phoned for pizzas: barbecue chicken for her and a large, deep-pan meat-feast for him. He had not managed to go running over the break and had put on a stone since leaving the army. He could just about get into his suit but knew things needed to change. Less carbs, less beer.

"Are you ready to go back?" Penny asked as she sat at the other end of the kitchen table. "I don't know if you managed to get any rest."

He smiled at her. On client site he was at his desk by eight and only left after six. But at least he got two full nights' sleep. "This week should be ok. The client isn't back till next Monday."

"So why are you going in?"

Malcolm shrugged. "There's a Steering Group meeting next Tuesday. We have to prepare."

"So your team will be there?"

"Most of them. One or two are away skiing."

She smiled into Luca's eyes making cooing noises that encouraged him to chortle. Malcolm loved the timeless, maternal beauty of them together and took a picture on his phone. Out of instinct he also checked his messages.

Luca burped. Penny lifted him to her shoulder and patted his back some more with slow, steady thumps. His breath stank of milk.

Malcolm looked at the skirting below the radiator where the towels were hanging. "It is amazing how much the client pays for us."

"You're from Delaine. They bought the brand, sure they did."

He nodded. "Yes, they bought the brand. And they pay for it. Half a million for three months work."

"How much?"

"Half a million. Plus expenses, which will be another hundred thou."

"Jesus."

He realised he needed to put a spin on what he'd said, even to her. "But when we're done they should be able to control their procurement. It will save millions in the long run."

"They give you half a million and you tell them how to save procurement costs?"

He chuckled. "That's it, yeah."

She pulled a face and said, "Very good."

Her sarcasm amused him. But he liked working for one of the 'big four'. It was a natural step from one global brand as a soldier to another as a consultant. He'd always been at the cutting edge. In fact, the *bleeding* edge as they said in Delaine.

He liked the jargon, the sense of power. Working for Delaine, he was advising senior civil servants on what to do and how to do it. In fact, he kept asking himself how they managed to get where they had. Most of them couldn't lead a troop of boy scouts to a bus station.

Delaine took him on at Senior Consultant grade because he didn't have previous consulting experience. They promoted him to Managing Consultant after a year because of the way he led the first phase of the Project Firefly bid. Malcolm wanted to get to Executive Consultant but was realistic enough to know he wouldn't get it this year.

"My Partner says I should broaden my leadership style," he said.

"Who's that?"

"Alicia de Villiers. Head of Public Sector. The one I told you about."

"The one who likes expensive cars."

"Her. Likes expensive everything."

"Why'd she say that? You were an officer in the army for God's sake."

It made him feel warm that she said this, walking round the kitchen with Luca over one shoulder, the rhythm of her pats matching the dip of her hips. "There, there."

"She said I'm too much of a soldier."

Penny tutted. "What does that even mean?"

"She said I needed to soften my mind. Develop my *Intuition*. She said I was too judgemental.

Penny said nothing at this, which reinforced the fact that what Alicia told him was true. But it still grated. Too judgemental? She had never had to make the sort of decisions he had. None of the partners had ordered a man onto the compound roof only for him to get shot by a sniper. None of them carried guilt like he did, an anchor round his neck.

He thought of his last platoon. He thought of Seb Wilmott, the officer who had replaced him. He had done everything possible to ensure Seb knew the blokes and that they'd work for him. He thought of Bilge Simpson and Jed Spencer, the men killed in the market square bombing. He thought of Steve Reedman being in hospital with half his brain and half his right arm missing. He thought of Kyle Hutton and his broad, disarming smile. They hadn't crossed over for long. Hutton had arrived in battalion shortly before Malcolm left. But why did he commit suicide? Why did he have no one to go to?

Alicia had suggested Malcolm do a coaching course. Delaine would pay for it. It was about asking the right questions rather than making unilateral decisions, as he was prone to doing. It was about eliciting ownership on the part of others rather than imposing a solution.

He had clamped his mouth shut when she said this but nodded. "If you think that's best."

"I do, Malcolm. For your development. Another style of leadership will make you more rounded."

She was the same age as him and was already both a Partner and Head of Department. She was also beautiful, erudite, urbane. Her children went to Newton. She had everything.

Malcolm's phone pinged and he looked at the time. The pizzas were ready for collection so he unhooked the car keys from below the corner shelf and ran upstairs to get his new woolly hat. It was striped black and white and had a huge, funny bobble, as he had requested.

"That looks so good. Wait and I'll take a picture for Mummy," Penny said, picking up her phone.

He smiled, folding his arms for the portrait. When she was done, he kissed her. "I'll be fifteen minutes. Do we need anything else while I'm out?"

Penny nodded. "Bananas," she said. "And cream."

Kyle, previously

It's a week after New Year's. Everyone's kind of glad to be getting back to work. Char says little Dan is a right nightmare in the mornings and she just can't wait to get him through the door. The decorations have come down and I'm sitting in the big chair looking at Facebook on the phone Char got me.

It's proper sad. There's this cartoon magazine in Paris and two Muslim dudes went in and killed ten people and injured about ten more then got shot by police.

I looked at the cartoon online and it's like not that funny or anything. Kind of scratchy. You'd be hard pressed to say it's anybody but apparently you're not allowed to draw pictures of the Prophet Mohammed. It's illegal under sharry-ah law. But this Charlie bloke did it, said it was his right and the Muslims could do one. So these brothers, proper Muslims they were, shot their way into this cartoon shop and killed a load of people, shot Charlie, and got themselves slotted when they came out.

And I'm looking at Facebook and everyone's changing the profile picture to have a French flag on it. Everyone's posting this 'je suis Charlie…' thing and it keeps asking if I want to change my profile pic and I just think no, I don't.

I've only just set a profile picture of me and little Dan, the Christmas tree in the background. I had a phone before but I lost it and then someone cloned my account so I had to start again with a new phone number, new email address. Char and Danny gave me the phone saying it would help me get work. Employers would have a way to get hold of me.

One time over Christmas, I was in the living room with little Dan watching The Great Escape, *and we were at that scene where Donald Pleasance is pretending he's not blind. He puts this little pin down on the floor and counts the paces to it and then James Garner sticks his leg out and trips him up. Donald Pleasance says something like, '… take me with you… I can see perfectly…' and I'm nudging little Dan and saying the words because I know they're coming, and he span his little head to smile at me but Char and Danny were in the kitchen and their voices were getting loud so I had to put my hands over little Dan's ears.*

"You said it would be a couple of weeks," said Danny. "It's been three months."

"Danny, he needs help. What else do you expect me to do?" said Char.

"Stop him screaming at night. He's scaring the boy…"

And I know they were talking about me. They have this really nice little nut of a family and I so want to be a part of it and keep them safe and do things so they can go out. But actually I'm like sand in the working parts causing a stoppage.

And this shit in France is making everyone so angry and bitter and shouting about Pakis and Muslims and changing their faces and I don't know what to do. I don't see why I should have to change the picture of me and little Dan and the cartoon's not that funny anyway. It's just a bloke in a turban standing next to a camel. I don't understand the words. Why is everyone getting so upset about it?

And as I'm sitting there I have this sudden realisation I'm experiencing low mood. They said to watch out for it at the end of the tour. The company commander said we might have moments where things became difficult and the best thing we can do is get up and get out and go for a run.

So I think about going for a run. My PT kit's in my bergen. I'm a good runner. Easy come in the top five on a BFT. Long legs, see? But I don't want to go out. There's something about the light, the clouds over the rooftops that makes me think something bad could happen and it would be better if I stayed here.

I usually watch telly non-stop. I turned it off because it's just angry people talking about Paris and Muslims and shit like that. But normally I sit here and watch telly. And that makes me think back to one time when I watched telly nearly all day and Mum was saying I should turn it off and get out of the house. But it was Trooping the Colour and I wanted to see Dad in the Welsh Guards Contingent. He's not that tall so he'd be in the middle. So I was lying on my belly watching the TV until Mum turned it off.

"Outside," she said, pointing at the door. "Go down the corner shop and get some milk."

So I kicked off shouting I wanted to watch the parade in case my dad's on the telly for just a second. And Mum was about to clip me but Char said she'd go. Let him lie there. So she did. And I did. But I never saw Dad.

Always looked out for me Char has.

So last night she sat me down in the kitchen and said I should think about finding a place. Even a rental. I could use the money Mum left me. She was nervous because Danny was by the sink fidgeting. And I get it. It's his house and his family. Little Dan's his son. I said a few days and I've been here months, including Christmas.

Char said, "You know you can come round any time. Take little Dan to the park. He loves you, he really does. But this house isn't big enough for all of us. You're on the sofa. You really ought to be somewhere of your own..."

I know she's right. And it would be good to have my own place. I could get a console and little Dan could come round after school and we could play games. Once he's done his homework. We could play games until Char or Danny come and get him. I could feed him and everything.

Danny's leaning against the sink. He's not as tall as me and nowhere near as strong but he's real good to Char and such a grafter. He says I should think about seeing someone, a girl like. And I'm frowning because I don't know why he would say such a thing. Why would I want to see a girl? And I know he don't mean it as an insult but I just don't know what he means.

Char put her hand on my arm. "You used to be such a happy lad, Kyle," she said. "The life and soul you were. I'm really worried about you. Since you came back from Afghanistan you've been..."

"I've been what?"

I don't know why I said it, but I did. I know I'm a burden and she didn't really know how to answer and so I was making her feel bad and that's even worse. But then she said, "You used to be a great swimmer, and a runner, when you were at school. Why don't you do more sport? Get out of the house. Just take a walk up on the Heath?"

I knew she was trying to be helpful but I just don't want to go running. I don't want to be outside. There are so many things that could happen and it's better if I stay in.

So Danny said, "Why don't you get in touch with your mates from the army? You've got Facebook on your phone. Get in touch with them. Go and see them."

I thought about it but I shake my head. Of course I'd like to see Gaz and Mick and Lego-head and all the rest of them, plus the blokes from C Company, but it's like they're still in and I'm out. I don't want them to see me as a failure, someone who couldn't find work. And anyway, they'd be busy. They're still serving. Why would they want to catch up with a STAB, a Stupid TA Bastard, like me?

"It's ok, Kyle, it's ok," Char said. "It was just an idea. A suggestion..."

Danny stood up and he was frowning and folded his arms. He looked worried. Char had her hand on my arm stroking it like she does when little Dan gets proper boisterous and won't go to bed after I've been tickling him.

"You go on through and watch telly for a while, Kyle. Me and Danny have to talk about a few things."

So I went through and sat on Danny's chair but you could hear them talking clear as day.

Dean, February 2017

The Inspector said, "Take a seat, Dean, make yourself comfortable, I'll be back in a second."

Left in the glass-walled meeting room, Dean pulled out one of the steel-framed chairs and found it bounced under his weight. The test that morning had been far harder than he expected so a lot rested on this interview.

The building was brightly lit and modern, the air dry on the throat. But it also had a heavy familiarity that produced in Dean an odd feeling of confusion. He liked the idea of small teams doing good. Their names were on the doors: Child Protection, Fraud, Drugs, Scene of Crime. But he also felt the institutional bureaucracy: the obtrusive health and safety board, the sign warning people not to leave food in the fridge. Having been left to his own devices in Iraq he began to wonder if the police would actually be a good move. Could he still follow orders?

The Inspector came back with two plastic cups of water. He took the seat opposite Dean and pulled off his cap. Dean lifted himself upright feeling the give in the chair.

"So, you're Jon Chadwick's son? I'm afraid I never knew your father. But my father certainly did, back in the day. I'm very pleased to meet you. My father asked me to pass on his warmest regards to yours."

Dean cleared his throat into his fist. "Likewise," he said, noting that the Inspector had a circumspect, guarded manner.

"We no longer run that sort of deep cover operation. There are still court cases in due process. Does your father ever talk about what he did in the Service?"

Dean shook his head. "No. He's not a talker. Never was. I just remember him being away. And coming back."

The Inspector nodded. His eyes dropped and Dean wondered if he had also been raised by his mother. He cleared his throat again and pulled his jacket pockets clear of the arms of the chair.

"Well, let's talk about you since you came all the way. Easy drive?"

Dean nodded. "Yeah, fine. You know. A bit slow crossing the motorway. But it's good."

The Inspector nodded. "Yes, it has been quiet this week. No major incidents, anyway, touch wood."

Dean tapped the table with his fingers in sympathy.

The Inspector continued. "So you're interested in joining the Service as an experienced hire? You were in the Parachute Regiment?"

Dean nodded. "I was, Sir, yes. Twenty-four years. Joined up aged twenty-one..."

He paused. He'd joined up because he'd been arrested for fighting. His father had threatened to throw him out of the house. There'd been an almighty scrap between him and his mother. But maybe the Inspector didn't need to know that.

"I did twenty-four years. Rose to the rank of Colour-Sergeant. I was also a platoon commander – that's an officer's position, at the Infantry Training Centre. Catterick. I did Northern Ireland. I did the Balkans. I did Iraq and then Afghan. Plus other places, Kenya and the like."

"So you have a large amount of operational experience?"

"Yeah, hundred percent."

In Dean's mind flashed the shadow of a Chinook with a pallet of ammunition swinging below it on a cargo net. They'd discharged the static and unhooked the netting before pulling the ammunition off, two boxes at a time, the handles biting into his fingers, the down blast whipping up sand. But the blokes needed ammo and it was his job to deliver it.

"Exciting times." Dean said.

The Inspector nodded. "What sort of things did you have to do as a Colour-Sergeant?"

Dean wondered if he'd have to explain everything. "Well, obviously, as Colour-Man, I was responsible for the company stores, and ammunition supply, getting kit forward to the blokes in the FOBs. Forward Operating Bases. And scoff. And clothing. Everything, really. It was my job to make sure they had what they needed to take the fight to the enemy."

The Inspector had his hands on his lap circling his thumbs round each other. "And at Catterick?"

Dean leaned to one side to rest one elbow on the arm of the chair. "At Catterick? At Catterick I was training the Reserve, that's the TA, in basic soldiering skills. I took them through their Combat Infantryman's Course. Made soldiers of them, basically. I had a training team, a sergeant and three full screws."

"Corporals?"

"Yes, three corporals, sorry. We, they, delivered training over a number of weekends. I supervised obviously. I was the platoon commander. There wasn't enough officers to run the Reserve Courses, you see? So they picked me. I was acting as an officer."

The Inspector had the two pips of a lieutenant on his shoulder but was not in his twenties. He wasn't as old as Dean but certainly in his forties. So an Inspector must be equivalent to a major, maybe even a colonel. It was right that he'd called him 'sir', anyway.

"And what do you want to do with the police? Why do you want to join?"

"For the pension," Dean said, grinning, but quickly realised what he meant as a joke may not have been heard as one. "No, seriously. Look. It's like. I served my country. It's what I do. What I've always done. Same as my dad. Same as you and your dad. It's what we do. And I'm out now. I work as a transport manager in a small company on Rotherham that supplies industrial vehicles to the road gangs…"

"Boltons?"

"Say again?"

"Bolton's, in Canklow?"

"Yeah, that's right. Unit seven. Hundred percent. But, anyway, I do that now. It's good, but it's not… It's not…"

"It doesn't fulfil you?"

"Hundred percent. I mean, don't get me wrong. There's nothing wrong with it. It's a good job. And I've learned loads managing civvies and that. But it doesn't…" He was looking at the wall for inspiration, carving the air with one hand "It doesn't really satisfy me," he said.

The Inspector pulled his chair forward and placed his elbows on the table. "Look," he said. "Sadly, we don't have a mechanism whereby people from the Armed Services can transfer directly to the Police Service. You'd have to join as a constable and go through the same probationary process as an ordinary applicant. I know this might be a bit demeaning given your operational experience but that's what has to happen. We've spoken about developing some sort of fast-track scheme, a direct transfer into the Sergeant's Programme, but we're still working on it."

The idea of being on the beat was not an issue to Dean. He recalled foot patrols round the estates in West Belfast accompanying the guy from the RUC; the kids dicking them, the closed windows, the open windows, the platoon commander giving hand signals, the clinking of the ammunition belt folded over the feed tray. Those were some of the most enjoyable times he'd spent. "I have no problem with that," he said.

The Inspector explained more about what a policeman did. There would be opportunities for firearms work, traffic, crime scene investigations.

Dean nodded. He sensed the interview was already over and that he was getting the same spiel that might be given to school kids.

The Inspector counted on clean fingers: "What we look for is legal knowledge, the ability to negotiate, sensitivity to the nuances of different situations..."

Dean understood all of these things. He'd watched the police, often young women, handling large groups of pissed-up blokes outside the clubs when he'd picked up his daughters. But it was still nothing to handling a riot or channelling the July marches away from the Catholic areas. Or pushing crowds of scared Afghans off the barbed wire round the airport.

There was a knock on the door. The sergeant who had invigilated the test that morning dropped a folder on the table. The Inspector opened it and scanned the cover sheet.

"We have your results," he said.

Dean said nothing. There was something in his tone that told him he'd failed but he hadn't expected there to be so much maths. What did it matter if there was 14% more Zulu speakers than Afrikaans speakers, or however many people that was in 2007?

"If you are to apply, Dean, you would need to work on your mental arithmetic. But you probably know that already."

Dean smiled. "Hundred percent. Look, basically..."

"It's fine, Dean. We didn't tell you what to expect and you clearly have highly developed people and leadership skills. You're obviously a team player and these are also important in the modern policing environment..."

There was a 'but' coming.

"And we think you'd do very well in a number of more skilled roles. But you'd still need to do basic training at the Police College and the next intake is not until the summer. You'd need to apply via the website."

He pulled a booklet out of the folder and slid it across the table. The cover read '*How 2 Become a Police Officer*' and showed the face of a young officer looking insistent but not intimidating.

"We very much hope you'll apply." The Inspector put out his hand. Dean shook it. They both pushed their chairs back and stood. The Inspector lifted his cap and placed it on his head.

"Now, you must excuse me. I've got a meeting at three. Could I walk you to the lifts?"

Dean nodded. "Listen. Thanks. I appreciate everything you've done."

The Inspector smiled. "My pleasure," he said.

Kyle, previously

I'm really trying. I know I'm a burden and Char and Danny have been proper kind to me, so I'm really trying to sort myself out.

I'm at the doctors. It's the one Mum took me to when I was a kid. I got up early, like six, and had a shower before Danny was up. I stashed my kit. Then I stood in the living room preparing to go out, psyching myself up, breathing deep. The lampshade kept touching the back of my head. My hair's got long and is starting to go curly. I don't like it being touched. So I sat on the back of the sofa to look out the window onto the street trying to decide when would be a good time to go. It was pouring with rain but it wasn't that that worried me.

A Toyota flatbed drove by and stopped at every few houses for a young girl to put milk by the doors. She didn't do ours as Char gets her milk from Lidl. The flatbed and the bottles seemed genuine. The girl got in the cab and slammed the door. She had a cagoule on with the hood up.

I couldn't help thinking who would make their daughter do that?

Thing is, I know the way I'm thinking is wrong. I'm not fucking stupid. Why shouldn't the girl work and get paid? Why am I scared of going out, anticipating something going wrong when I know it probably won't? Not here. But I can't help myself.

Anyway. I'm sitting on the back on the sofa, sweating buckets, breathing like I'm in round three and it's close on points. Char said she could give me a lift after dropping off little Dan at school but I said no, I'm doing it. I really want to prove I can do it. She looked terrified, like I was about to throw myself off the multi-storey. Then little Dan came running in and he looked at me, then at his mum, and it's like he'd been told to say something.

He said, "Be brave, Uncle Kyle."

And that's it. I had to man up. So I put my coat on and went outside before I thought better of it. When it's man down you have to man up.

The air was wet and fresh. Rain is good as it means less people. I walked quickly keeping to the side of the pavement. At the lights I didn't wait for the green man. I went up the road to the back of the cars and cut across without stopping. The drivers didn't see me. I'm a dark figure on a rainy morning. I used my patrol skills and kept moving, kept alert.

Passing the mini-Tesco, the door opened and properly caught me by surprise. I put on a hard face but no one came out. I pressed on. A cyclist sped by on the wet road. I thought he was mad cycling in the rain. The tyres made this whirring sound. In fact, everything was hissing. The rain ran down the back of my neck and I got to the doctors just as they were letting the queue of people in. There was five people ahead of me and as soon as I fell into line, others got out of their cars.

I'm suddenly sharp, focused. One male. Three females, two with children. No weapons. No bags.

Inside the waiting area the people queue at the desk. They have this darkened glass above the desk. It has signs telling you to register on the thing on the wall. I don't know what I'm doing so I just stand in line. The woman in front of me is little so I don't worry about her. The one behind me has a daughter in a pink coat. She's bent over with her hand on the child's forehead saying she'll be alright. I keep my feet moving, one foot to the other, like I'm in my corner. It takes an age to get to the front.

The people in front of me have sat down on the chairs and are looking at the telly. When the little woman gets to the window she says she needs to see the nurse. Behind the window there's this other woman talking into a microphone. Everyone has to bend over to say anything or hear what she says. When I get to the window I face the glass and place both hands on the counter. They're shaking. I say I want to see the doctor.

"What's your surname, please?"

I tell her it's Hutton.

She taps away at the computer and frowns.

"Could you tell me your first name?"

I say it's Kyle. Kyle Hutton. I don't say 'Smiler'. But she taps her computer and frowns. I can only make out part of her face through the dark glass. Higher up, on my side of the window, there's a sign saying We do not accept any form of abuse either physical, verbal, or psychological to any member of our staff. Any form of threat will result in the police being called.

And I think, Fuck, what a downer. I just came here to see the doctor and yet somehow I'm being charged with abuse.

The woman says something through the glass but I don't hear it. I bend down to speak into the microphone. Say again over?

She looks at me over her glasses. "Could you confirm your address please, Mr Hutton?"

I think then. Do I say Mum's address, Foley Street, or Charlotte's in Ash Grove? They will know me from Ash so I say that but then explain that I was working away in London and then joined up. I don't say who with. They won't believe me.

There's muttering in the queue behind me. The woman with the child in a pink coat is sighing. She's holding her child back against her legs as if I'm a druggy or something. The girl is grabbing at herself, saying she needs the toilet. I want to help her but I'm afraid the woman will think I'm weird.

I want the woman behind the glass to hurry up. I just want to see the doctor to ask if he has anything for low mood. I know there's drugs. The blokes talked about it. One or two of them had already done a Herrick tour. Jim Muir, the det commander, full screw, he'd done a Telic tour too in Iraq. He'd been on the pills after his Mrs left him but then stopped.

I'm embarrassed at the same time as being angry and the same time as being nervous. The people in the queue are looking at me because they want to get to the window and I'm in the way. They might try and push in. I want to say it's not me, it's her behind the glass, but I'm afraid to.

The woman behind the glass turns to her microphone and says could I take a seat. She'll just deal with the others and come back to me. I'm like, yes, that's what I wanted all along. Why did it take so long? So I take a seat on the back row against the wall, where I can see the entrances. I make myself small in the chair.

The telly's on but the volume's off. On the screen there's this guy with a corny smile and silver hair and a blonde woman in a dress. There's a river behind them and I wonder why you'd sit with your back exposed through a plate glass window. There is a picture of Jeremy Clarkson and the team from Top Gear *but they don't show the programme even though it would be much better. Proper funny,* Top Gear *is.*

The queue of people file past the window. The woman takes the girl to the toilet then comes back. She looks at me and sits on the front rank of chairs. No one sits near me and that's good. Then the tannoy says could Mrs Castle please go to consulting room two. The old woman struggles to her feet and shuffles along the corridor and I make an assessment of how long it will take to see the doctor. I was sixth in the queue. There's a screen that says there are two doctors on duty.

I came here when I was a kid. Tonsils. Scrapes to me knee when I came off my bike. But I never had to go to the doctors when I was older. And then I was in London and didn't go then either. And in the army, if you go sick, you put on your Number-2 dress and paraded outside the Med Centre. There'd be maybe four or five blokes with sprains, twisted ankles, broken knuckles, that sort of thing. Maybe a dose from a bird a load of blokes had been through. The doc would issue some brufen and a biff chit and that would be it. Take three a day and soldier on.

But out in Afghan it were different. If you was in the Forward Operating Base, FOB Minar, you couldn't go sick. I was there for three weeks with the C Company Det and we were like in the proper ulu, way up in Amrut. The choppers only came in if they had to, for resup or casevac. We were getting probed big style by the end of the first month. Terry really wanted the high ground so he could move up and down the valley and we were the only thing stopping him. So we were getting rocketed or attacked near every day. I was number one on the gun and because it was in a sanger up on the middle roof, protected by sandbags and wriggly tin, I couldn't hear anything going on behind me or down in the compound. I just kept putting rounds down at everything that moved. Then one day Terry has a go at us with an RPG and it strikes the wall of the tower above me, knocking out this fuck-off great stone. I don't know it's happened as all I can hear is the gun and people shouting my name. I think they're giving target indications but I can see Terry in the tree line and keep blatting away. And so this fuck off big rock, about the size of my melon, falls off the wall and starts bouncing down the outside steps. If it had hit me proper it would have killed me. But it like rolled down and kind of fell over on my ankle. I screamed as I thought I'd been hit by something. But Gaz laughed as he pulled it off and I go back to putting rounds down.

Later, after Terry fucks off for the day, my ankle swells up to like twice its size. I got the boot off which was good as otherwise I'd have had to cut it off. Nothing was broken and my toes moved so I never went sick. Ginge Hartley, the medic, gave me some brufen and strapping and told the platoon commander to keep me off patrol duty till the swelling went down. And all the blokes were like, war dodger, FOB monkey, more time off than Audie Murphy's safety catch. But they were taking the piss. I'd have gone out if I could walk even though it were proper scary and I near shit myself every time we lined up by the gates.

And the next time I went out was to the market square. That was a shit day.

So I'm sitting in this waiting room wondering how long I have to sit there. There are shiny faces on the telly, big smiles. Then after about thirty minutes I've got my breathing under control and I'm just quiet and alert. The woman from behind the screen comes out of her office through a door with a simplex lock. She comes over to me and sits in the next chair. She has a sheet of paper in one hand and a biro in the other.

"Mr Hutton, we don't have records of you being registered at this practice," she says.

People start looking at me and I don't want to look a fool. I say I must be. My mum used to bring me here.

Obviously I meant when I was a kid. I just haven't had to come when I was a man.

She shakes her head. She says again there are no records on the system. So I explain that I left Stoke when I was sixteen. Went to London. Joined up.

She nods then, understanding at last. "Ah, alright. You're MOD personnel. What we need to do is register you as part of this practice."

The people in the room have all changed. The ones that were here at the beginning have all gone. New people have arrived for the booked appointments. I've been here two hours. I need to shit. There's a toilet but I'm like afraid of gassing everyone or in case someone with a wheelchair needs it.

The woman asks me for my name and address. I give Char's address on Ash Grove and she asks why I would want to come all the way over here. I say I don't. It's just where I used to come. She says do I have my national number insurance. I say no, I don't have insurance. I had it when I was in but I'm not in anymore.

"No," she says. "National Insurance Number. It's your reference number for HMRC. The tax office."

I don't know why the tax office needs to know I'm seeing the doc. I explain again that I just need to talk to someone but I don't finish the sentence. Not here with all these strangers. I just need something to calm me down. Help me sleep. The nightmares are getting fucking wicked.

"I'm really sorry," she says. "But we can't let you see a GP until you are registered. If you would like to come back with your National Insurance Number we'll be able to register you and then book you an appointment."

I realise I've been properly had. She told me to sit here to get me out of the way and then everyone else gets to see the doctor but not me. And I can't complain because she'll say I'm being abusive and call the police. And there's a guy in the front row of chairs in a dark coat who looks really dodgy and he has his back to me and I can't see what he's holding. So I get up and go to the door. The air feels warm and stuffy in the room and I want to be away from these people. But outside there's all these cars going in and out of the supermarket carpark and they're beeping at each other and driving too fast. The rain doesn't help and I shrink against the wall and think about calling Charlotte. Maybe she'll come and pick me up. And this makes me so, so ashamed.

I'm a fucking pussy.

Steve, March 2017

Steve was sitting on the couch near the entrance to Orpheus House. There'd been a meeting about putting together a team of WIS to walk the Annapurna Circuit and Bronagh, his case worker, had invited him to give his opinion. He hadn't contributed much but was proud to have been asked.

It was raining heavily. Long rivulets ran down the window, snaking and angling. The wind buffeted the enormous beech trees surrounding the colonels' quarters and Steve thought he would stay where he was until the worst had passed. Although he had recently bought an adapted Audi SUV with part of his pay-out, the weather was daunting.

There was no rush anyway. His mother would be at home and he'd call her when he set off. In the meantime he could enjoy the peaceful camaraderie that permeated Orpheus House, the sense that everyone here, both staff and WIS, were part of a shared experience.

There were a number of courses on, the basic ones he'd done years before, so there wouldn't be accommodation for him even if he needed it. He viewed himself as something of an elder statesman of the recovery process and therefore should not be dependent on the charity. There were plenty of people who were dependent, or who talked up their PTSD, or simply lied about their addictions. Fib, from the Rifles, for example, was still a resident after eight months and that was a place that could be given to someone more deserving. Fib was a thieving little shit. If he was back in battalion he would have been given a right battering. But the House wasn't a place where you said anything against another veteran. What went around came around. Life was a marathon, not a sprint.

The problem, as Steve saw it, was there weren't enough vacancies for case workers. All he needed was a job where he'd be able to help other veterans. He was financially secure; the Legion having made sure he'd got the fullest amount possible from his war pension even though the army doctor in York had tried to say he had no visual impairment. But he wanted a job to feel purposeful, to give him something he was missing even if he could not quite define what that was.

Bronagh came out of the staff office and turned towards the canteen, her passes swinging on a lanyard from her hand. He waved. She was tall for a woman, slim, and had a sashaying way of walking. In bootcut jeans she looked incredibly attractive and Steve liked the scarf round her neck. Long, auburn hair fell in curls down her back. She didn't wear a wedding ring but he knew she was married to some Sergeant-Major in the cavalry unit. Lucky bastard.

"Waiting for the weather to clear, Steve?"

"I am, Bronagh, yes. I don't fancy the A66 in this wind…"

He didn't like admitting this. It had just come out. She had this way of making him say things.

She spun on her heel and came towards him. He had a newspaper on his legs but hadn't been reading it. He placed it on the low white coffee table and blinked. Bronagh stood in front of him then squatted to sit on the coffee table as nimble as a fawn. She had a thick leather purse in one hand. Her hoop earrings caught the light.

"I'm glad you stayed. I wanted to talk to you about a new programme we're running. It's still very much a raw idea but we're finding that we need a sort of finishing course to help people back into employment. I wanted to sound you out on the idea and ask if you would like to be a test case, part of a pilot?"

Her voice was lilting and sonorous. She looked at him with dark green eyes, elbows on her knees.

"All I want to do is help other veterans, Bronagh. You know what I'm good at. I've done all the courses. I think I'm ready to be staff, here, at Orpheus..."

She turned to look out of the window. A strand of curly hair tumbled off her shoulder. He followed her gaze but she turned back to face him.

"You're the perfect person for this programme, Steve. You've done all the courses and a mentor will just help you develop the skills you need to find work."

There was a criticism implicit in this statement. He wasn't ready. He'd done all the courses. Why were they adding another one?"

"If I do this, will I be accepted for a case worker job? I'd really like to be Director of Programmes when Clive decides he's had enough."

She leaned back and laughed. "Wouldn't we all, Steve, hey! Wouldn't that job be just great! Director of Programmes!"

She put her hands between her knees. "But listen to me now. We know what you want and we think you'd be very good at it. But there are some skills you need to develop. And what we'd like to do is offer you a mentor. Someone from the private sector, a big consultancy, who could help you."

Steve frowned, then chuckled. "Is this going to be like *Dragon's Den*? Or what's his name? Sugar?" As he spoke, he extended his prosthetic arm. "You're hired."

Bronagh laughed lightly, tilting her head back. She was wearing a heavy blue sweater with patterns in the knitting. She was like a winding country stream, clear and cold, reflecting light.

"No, it's far more than that. We hope so, anyway. We're partnering with this company. They have offered consultants to mentor WIS in a trial basis. We think it would be a really wonderful opportunity for our WIS to get exposure to real world business people, to help them get jobs, like."

Steve smiled. "Will they take me on? Can I be like their bag man or something? I'd like to do that. It'd be great."

She put a hand briefly on his knee. "This is not about them employing you. It's about them helping you… it's coaching and mentoring, Steve, yeah? It's about them asking how you can solve issues for yourself."

He'd got it wrong even though he tried to pass off his comment as a joke. He didn't like getting things wrong with her.

"So will he help me get a job helping other veterans?"

"Well, like I said, we're just at the initial stages of planning. What will happen first is we'll find someone from the list of potential mentors that we think you'd get on with. Then you'll meet and you can decide if they are the person for you. Could be a man, could be a woman. Then you'll agree what your goals are."

"All I want is…"

"I know, Steve, I know. We all do, like. But my question for you today is this: would you be interested in taking part? Would you like me to see if I can find a mentor for you?"

She looked at her purse between her hands.

"Who will I get given?"

"We have a list of names. We're going through it at the minute to see if we think anyone would suit you."

"Is there one?"

She nodded slowly. "We think there might be. He's a consultant. But he also has a few years military experience. In fact, his CV says he was in your regiment."

"What's his name?"

"Well that's just the thing. We don't know whether to put you together if you already know each other. It might be better if we found you someone who didn't have military experience."

That didn't make sense. Surely someone who had been in the regiment and was now a consultant would be the best person. That way he'd understand everything Steve had been through.

"What's his name?"

"The guy with military experience is called Malcolm. He's a consultant with Delaine. He's in his thirties..."

Steve smiled. He raised his good hand and let it slap against his thigh. "Malcolm Sewell? Captain? He were my platoon commander. Excellent bloke."

Pete, March 2017

After his divorce and the loss of his house in Colchester, Pete had spent the lump sum from his pension and all his remaining savings on a downpayment for a pebble-dashed, gardenless bungalow not far from the Arbroath Monument and the caravan parks. He was happy there, close to the links, the supermarket, and the hospital. The house was spacious for one person and easy to heat. His salary from McCardle's, after alimony, just about covered the ten-year mortgage and he was always surprised by how much he got for his money. The same house in Colchester would have been twice as much.

A second letter from the Ministry of Defence informed him that he was required to make a statement under oath in respect of the legal case being raised by the family of the lawyer, Mr O'Hare. He phoned his solicitor and asked what he had to say this time that he hadn't said before?

The solicitor sounded tired. "I simply don't know. We can argue, I suppose, that you have nothing further to add on the statements you have already provided but I sense that it will not carry much weight. They will demand your presence and have the authority to do so."

Pete stood in his living room grinding his jaw. "Am I going to get fucked so they can have their peace process?"

The solicitor mumbled that it might look that way but it would be favourable if he had faith in the legal process. He had, after all, been cleared of all charges on three previous inquiries.

"So why they doing it again? Is this no double jeopardy? Is it even fucking legal?"

The lawyer replied that he thought they'd discussed such matters before and that the peace process was to be seen as being in their favour.

The call ended inconclusively with Pete unsure what he was to do and when. This was not a position he enjoyed. He liked the solidity of lists and the certainty of ticking tasks off until everything was complete and he was free for the evening. While serving, this would have meant popping up to the Sergeants' Mess for a drink, dinner, and a game of pool or a happy half-hour on the slot machines. Now, with no one to drink with, and arthritis preventing him from running, he went out on his bike – a twelve-hundred Triumph Tiger – burning round the windy coastal bends until his aggression was sated.

On the mantelpiece sat a picture of him with his daughter, Sinead, in a silver frame. She was very young then. It had been her third birthday and she'd been laughing with her open, gap-toothed mouth, flushed cheeks. Her dark eyes glowed with happiness. The picture had been taken by Sveta but he had long since removed all the images of her from his life. Regrettably, however, he needed to go through his ex-wife to speak to Sinead. It had been six months since he'd last tried as he'd been getting his head round his new job. He'd been living in a caravan and knew it wasn't suitable for a teenage girl. But now he was on top of his job and had somewhere stable with a room for her to use.

The dial tone rang for some time. He didn't have Sveta's mobile number, just a landline somewhere in Colchester. He knew she'd shacked up with a corporal from the Logistics Regiment and though he'd never met him, he thought it said a lot about her that she preferred a loggie JNCO to a Warrant Officer from Her Majesty's finest.

"Hello?"

"Sveta? It's me. Pete."

There was silence on the line save for a clicking sound.

"Hello, Peter. How are you? How is Scotland?"

Her Russian accent was heavy and guttural but there was a subtle hint of Essex creeping in.

"It's raining, Sveta. You know that. It's always raining."

She laughed, knowing he was joking. It was actually cold and crisp, the roads recently gritted in anticipation of snow.

"Look, can I speak to Sinead, please? I want to..."

Sveta was silent again. He thought she'd say she wasn't there, or was doing her homework, but she was more direct.

"Tell me please, Peter. Have you been to doctor? Have you stopped using those machines?"

It had been the justification for divorce that he'd lost all her money at the bookies. But he had been to counselling and it had been several months since he'd placed a bet. He still drank, but that was a private matter.

"I've no placed anything since May, Sveta. I told you. I'm done with it. And I've got a house now. My own place. Two bedrooms. I'd like her to come up. It's allowed, you know. I'm her dad."

"Yes, Peter, I know it's allowed. And I know you want best. But I want best too, Peter. And when she sees you she is confused and angry. Not stable. Not happy. It's not healthy option for young girl. She has examinations."

Pete's body shook.

"But that's because you stop her seeing me. That's..."

Her voice rose. "No, Peter. I never stop her seeing you. I never..."

"You do it all the time. I ring to ask..."

"No, Peter. Not true. I never stop her seeing you. I encourage it..."

"Do you fuck! You always come out with these lies, just fucking lies..."

"I never lie. I tell you truth. I think you are bad influence and you make..."

"Bad influence. How the fuck..."

The line went dead. Pete's hand shook for some minutes before he put the phone down in its cradle. He felt his daughter being ripped from his ribs, his heart crushed by a hammer.

So be it.

He knew it would have to be this way.

He had no choice but to armour himself. He needed to be clean, lean, and free from the emotional mud that sucked at his feet and anchored him in self-reproach.

Standing in the narrow hallway he was still wearing his boots and leathers. His helmet and gloves were in the kitchen. He'd bought a copy of *The Herald* at the petrol station purely so he could study the form, nothing more.

Grabbing his helmet, he turned the paper over. The front-page headline was that Martin McGuiness had died. Pete stopped. His face broadened into a smile as he lifted the paper up to eye level.

"Well I outlived you, you cunt."

Malcolm, March 2017

Following the successful completion of Phase One, the Ministry of Defence had extended Project Firefly for a further three months. This was another sell-on Malcolm could chalk up against his name and it put him so far ahead of the sales target expected of his grade that he had nearly doubled it.

When he punched out of the army he had been nervous of having to sell things. It seemed an alien skill, the preserve of spivs, scammers, deep-voiced old men. But the training he'd been given had taught him that selling consulting was just about trust. It was the same, really, as convincing his soldiers that his operational plans were sound.

To celebrate the extension Malcolm had been given a sizeable budget – one hundred per head – to take his team out to dinner. Veerle had chosen a restaurant with five-star reviews overlooking the river. As the team followed the waitress weaving through to the round table in the corner, Malcolm whispered in her ear.

"This is perfect. Great job. Thanks, V."

Her shoulders lifted as she turned to smile at him. He sat against the outside wall and his team took places round the table in the same order that they did at work. Farthest away was the youngest, Jenny, an analyst on the Graduate Development Programme. The acronym was a deliberate Delaine joke as there was a much higher margin on analysts than any other grade. The graduates were all fantastically clever, humble to the point of insecurity, and willing to work eighteen-hour days. Jenny had a First in Modern Languages from Cambridge and once played doubles with Andy Murray. She was responsible for the project communications strategy and Malcolm nurtured her as he might a young soldier. She glanced up at him, saw him looking at her, and coloured.

Veerle sat to his left, her shoulders slender in a blue jacket. She had a Master's in Business Administration and Finance from INSEAD and could switch between five languages as if picking up pencils. He liked the way she tucked her white blouse into the band at the top of her skirt. She was a little younger than him and if he wasn't married he would definitely try it on.

Of the six in the team, the only one he didn't like was Jerome. He slouched along the wall opposite Jenny. He had also joined Delaine through the GDP and had been promoted to Consultant after two years. Because he was considered the very top of his intake, he was also given one of the Business Partners as a mentor. Malcolm suspected it was Alicia because she kept asking how he was doing.

Jerome had already drunk too much and was laughing too loudly in an annoyingly high pitch. Malcolm didn't like the other diners looking over. The team's success should not be marred by mutterings of excess on social media. They represented Delaine, after all, on and off duty. He put a finger to his lips and made a 'quiet' motion with his hand. Jerome didn't see it but Jenny did and whispered across the table. Jerome scowled at him like a petulant child but lowered his voice when he continued.

Malcolm's reservations about him stemmed from the young man watching his every move. He suspected him of telling Alicia everything. There was no hard evidence for this suspicion but he could see their diaries on Outlook and knew they talked on Friday afternoons.

"How was the coaching course, Malcolm?" Veerle's knee knocked gently against his. "Sorry," she said, though he sensed it was deliberate. He moved his leg but feared she would take the action as a brush off.

"It was good. GROW model, you know?"

She nodded, leaning forward with her chin on the back of one hand.

"I enjoyed it. Common sense. But it also adds a string to one's bow."

She had very pale grey eyes and he liked her accent. "It's really inspirational what you have done," she said. "Promoted within a year. Selling so much work."

He shrugged. "It's about what we have done together."

He thought the words sounded false but she didn't pull a face. She hid her mouth behind her hand as she spoke as though ashamed of something in her teeth. She had a lovely smile when she chose to show it and he wanted to pull her hand down.

He didn't really understand these people. They were all so capable and yet nervous of everything. He wasn't nearly as clever or accomplished. He just worked hard and knew how to manage people.

"Have you thought about doing the course? I'd recommend it."

"I'm just SC. It's for ECs and above," Veerle said.

"I'm an MC. I got it because I volunteered for the coaching partnership they're pushing. The *Save Our Heroes* thing."

"The programme to support injured soldiers?" She looked worried. "I thought about doing it but didn't want to commit to something I couldn't deliver."

Malcolm nodded. "I thought the same. But because of my background I felt I should..."

"You are very brave," she said.

He didn't know what she meant. What was brave: being a soldier or volunteering to coach one? When he arrived at the coaching course he'd found he was one of only five people from across the entire company who'd accepted the offer. Why didn't they want to help soldiers? Or learn a new skill?

"So the next thing is a course at Catterick where I might get matched with a veteran."

"How will you cope with it?"

He frowned, drawing circles on the table top with his finger. "I don't know. I have a certain trepidation about it. I punched out... I mean, I left the army because I found it frustrating and turgid. It's not creative. It's *sooo* bureaucratic. But I am hoping that a veteran, even if he's injured. Sorry, even if *they* are injured. Will be able to learn from me..."

"I think it's inspirational you should do such a thing."

She'd leant towards him but he was uncertain of the signals. He glanced down the table to see if the others were watching them but they were talking amongst themselves. He thought about mingling amongst them but he liked the way Veerle looked at him and the gentle, accidental caress of her hand on his arm.

The waiter took their drinks order. He was formal, standing with one hand behind his back. He remembered everything and brought it all within a few minutes. Malcolm made certain there was a bottle of red at his end of the table.

The restaurant was full. The staff moved efficiently between the tables. One of them was taking a food order and had to bend to pick up a fork the customer had dropped. As he stood, he slipped it backhanded to one of his colleagues who was returning to the kitchen with an ice bucket. Within a minute, the fork had been replaced.

"Did you see that?" Malcolm said to Veerle, nudging her elbow. "Now that's teamwork. If only the Ministry could do something like that then our work would be done."

He glowed, proud of having brought the incident to her attention.

"Then we wouldn't have you to help them," she whispered, which took him aback and also made him smile.

He was silent for a while, unsure of what to say. The mood spread down the table. One by one, they turned to look at him. He didn't want to talk about work. It had been a rule in the Officers' Mess not to discuss work after dinner. But Jenny asked about his thoughts for the workshop the next day. He told her. They were happy and he was beginning to sense the level of camaraderie he wanted.

Veerle leant towards him. "When you were in…"

"Afghanistan?"

She nodded. "Did you ever have to…"

He knew what she was going to say. Her hand held a glass of fizzy water. He touched it gently.

"It's not a question you should ask, petal," he said.

Dean, April 2017

After watching the rugby on TV, Dean pushed Mr T into the garden and went upstairs for a shit-shower-shave and to change for the evening. Saracens had played brilliantly but there was no stopping that Exeter fullback when he got going. He commanded the game and the competition between him and the Saracens' stand-off, one captain of Scotland and the other captain of England, had a very personal feel. Not surprising since England had given Scotland a damn good drubbing in the Six Nations.

All in all, Brexit had done wonders for British sport. Before the referendum, the English football team couldn't beat Iceland, a country relying on cod and Björk to make money. After it, the United Kingdom came second in the Rio Olympics. Second in the medal table! And very soon, on Dean's birthday in fact, Anthony Joshua would fight the elder of the Klitschko brothers and that, surely, would go his way. He was twenty years younger for a start.

With the evening he had lined up Dean felt happy buttoning his grey shirt, the silk regimental tie round his shoulders. He pulled the tie off and swapped it for the battalion one. When he went to the Regimental Association meetings it was the green one he wore. The maroon one was for meetings with civvies.

Michelle was taking Elizabeth out for a driving lesson. Dean had said he would take her tomorrow but today was the monthly meeting of the Regimental Association so it would have to be in the afternoon. While he waited for the taxi he stood in the living room looking at the picture that had just come back from the framers. It was a print of a C130 Hercules aircraft flying at low level through mountainous terrain out of a red dawn. The side door was open showing a figure standing in the doorway, bergen strapped to his legs, his body braced for the red light to turn green. With a few intense brush strokes the artist had conveyed the power of that moment. At any second, the jump light would illuminate, the man would snap his hand off the stanchion, the light would turn green and he'd hurl himself into the void: *one thousand, two thousand, three thousand, check canopy.*

Thank fuck for that, Dean always thought at the tug of the canopy opening.

Below the print were replicas of Dean's medals, court mounted. The originals were upstairs on the back wall of his wardrobe. But he liked the array of them, neatly overlapping, in order, the ribbons meaningful, the metal polished. A few were celebratory, the Jubilee Medal and so on, but most were operational. And, of all of them, the one he was most proud of was the first he'd earned: on the left, a purple ribbon with green edges. The General Service Medal 1962 with a clasp reading *Northern Ireland*. In the middle of the ribbon was a small bronze oak leaf, an addition that marked him out.

Dean put one foot on the sofa to lift the picture off the wall. He would take it to show the blokes at the Association. It was *ally*, warlike, and he wanted others to enjoy it.

In the taxi, Dean placed the picture behind the front seat and sat next to the driver, who was in a shalwar kameez and had a lace cap on his head. The care smelled of spices and he was playing some shitty Muslim crap on the radio. But since he remained hunched and incommunicative, focused entirely on the road, Dean didn't bother chatting.

As usual, the Association had hired the small bar at the Royal British Legion, an oak panelled room with rows of regimental shields along the pelmet, a dining table, and a corner bar staffed by a pretty young girl about Vic's age wearing a black skirt and white blouse. They had a few beers. Andy was there, and Shane, Daz, and Red Phil. Two of the old boys were there, plus Stu, who had been Down South with the second battalion. He was the only other one wearing a tie, a blue one with a Falkland Islands outline on it.

When Dean had joined, the Falklands veterans were treated like gods. Nobody could criticise anyone who'd been *Down South*. They had set the bar for the generations that followed. But once Iraq and Afghan kicked off the dynamic changed. To Dean, the Falklands had been bloody and gritty but it was still only seventy odd days long. During his tours of Iraq and Afghan he'd been in contact, or the blokes in the FOBs had, for days on end.

Once, running off the chopper with boxes of ammunition, he'd been mortared as he ran, then sniped at, then subject to sustained machine gun fire before he'd even managed to get behind the compound wall. Inside the FOB, a young tom was firing careful, aimed shots through a hole in the wall. He wore flip flops, shorts, body armour and helmet. On his shoulder, the regimental tattoo stood out dark and fierce against sunburned skin.

"Got you, motherfucker," he said.

"Is it always like this when the chopper comes in?" Dean had said. In truth, he was a little rattled by the amount of incoming fire.

The young soldier had spat on the floor before putting his eye back to the rifle sight. He stank of sweat, dirt, sand. "All the fucking time, Colour," he muttered.

But when it came to Association gatherings, all that mattered was that you had been in the regiment. That fact alone marked men out; the steel, the banter, the slagging, the jokes. Story after story after story, no end of laughing.

After a meal of pie and chips with mushy peas, Dean picked up his picture and supported it on the table for the others to admire. "What do you think, lads, eh?"

Stu nodded in appreciation. "Ally as fuck, Dean. I've got that print. But I've no done my medals. I should, but the wife willnae let me put anything else up in the house."

The others laughed. They had the same problem. It was only Dean who was allowed to have his up in the living room, though Michelle had made it clear that was it. Nothing else, especially the one where one guy was killing another.

Nick, one of the younger guys, peered at the medals. "You've got a Mention in Dispatches Dean? From NI?"

Dean nodded as he lifted the picture off the table to place carefully with the glass against the radiator. There was no one in the room who had been on that tour so it wasn't surprising they didn't know.

"Dungannon. Ninety-three," Dean said. He pulled his chair out and sat down. The meal lay heavily in his belly and he'd had his fill of beer. He fancied a dram now. Or a gin. Just don't start on the port, he told himself, or else Michelle would be shouting at him to wake up before he pissed in the wardrobe.

"Was that when Pete McCardle shot that lawyer?" Nick asked.

Dean nodded. "Same operation. Pete's one of my best mates." He leaned back, rocking the chair on its legs. The floor was his.

"So you were there?"

"I was. It was a cordon and search on this farmhouse along the border. We knew there was an arms cache and we were chasing down two rifles that the King's Own Scottish Borderers had lost. They got taken of them in a riot in Coalisland. Int said the weapons were in the farm. But we'd put an observation post on it for three days and come up blank. Fucking freezing it was, edge of a field. So the company commander, Major Hartley it was, decided to search the place. Me and Pete were the cut offs round the back."

The others were nodding. Dean never got a chance to talk about this stuff. He'd never even told Michelle.

"Go on, what happened?"

"Well, anyway, the back door opens. We're behind this plough thing, shivering our tits off, sitting in a bunch of nettles. The cows are in this barn and they can smell us so they're mooing. And this guy opens the back door. He's silhouetted against the light, you know?"

The others nod, then shake their heads. Basics. Camouflage and concealment lesson one.

"But he's got a shotgun in his hand and he's holding it at the high port. Meant to be a lawyer but he's packing, right? And he's come out for us. Pete nudges me and we look at each other. He was senior to me so he took aim and just at that minute the guy must have clocked us. Seen the movement. So he shouts, 'Who are you?', or something like it, and that's when Pete slots him. Head shot. Down he went."

Dean chuckled. Although he'd never told this story to Michelle he'd told it many times and the telling had shaped how things were. Obviously, he stuck to what had been said in court. Only Pete and him knew what really happened. And only Pete and him ever would.

He continued. "There was a car in the yard. A red Renault 11. The shooting made it all kick off round the front and the rest of the boys went in, battering the door. They arrested the family inside, you know? We thought there might be a provo gang there too but there wasn't. But there was a few rifles, AR16s, plus the two SA80s in the boot of the car. Pete got the kill but I got the find. One of the rifles had been used against our blokes, killed Scotty the month before?"

He put all four legs of the chair on the floor. The older guys clapped.

Stu said, "You only got one chance to kill a terrorist in NI."

Others nodded.

"It's fucking shocking what they done to Pete," Stu continued, his voice bitter.

The old guy leaned forward. "Is that 'Trooper P'? The one in the newspapers?"

Dean nodded.

"Why's he being tried again? Sounds like he was perfectly entitled to shoot."

"Did he what? Say again?" Dean asked.

"I said, did he give a warning. Yellow card?"

Dean shook his head. "No. Bloke had a shotgun. I acted in self-defence. Pete did. But the family..."

"The family say he wasn't armed?" Stu said.

"Yep. And Tony Blair, cunt, set up the inquiry."

"The Donaldson Inquiry?" asked the old guy.

"Yep. Donaldson. And they interviewed Pete again and again. And me. Trying to say we were lying. But we stuck to it. We know what we saw. And we found weapons, which they couldn't argue about. It's not like we stashed them."

The men round the table nodded. They'd all been young men doing what their NCOs and officers told them to. And now, stiff from arthritis, knees replaced, spines compressed, increasingly deaf, overweight, they were being punished for it.

"It's fucking shit," Nick said. "Same in Afghan. That marine sergeant."

The men nodded, arms folded, serious.

Dean chuckled again. "But wait. After we'd found the stash, the platoon commander, some young looey who only did three years, he's running round the back of the house shouting at us to do this, do that... but he opens the wrong gate." He cracked up, the moment coming into focus. "So this fucking bull comes out the shed and..."

The men round the table broke into smiles. Dean can't talk for laughing.

".. and he starts chasing the platoon commander... who legs it down the lane..."

They're all laughing now, bent over, hands on their bellies. The girl behind the bar was smiling as she dried the glasses.

"... and then he slips and falls into an electric fence..."

They burst in gales of laughter, all of them, hands round their ribs, heads rolling back, the guffaws rich and continuous. The absurdity of it all, the madness of what they had done. How special these things had been. To have shared those moments of terror and utter insanity was what it was all about.

Civvies would never get it.

Dean, Late April 2017

There was something about the Army-Navy rugby match at Twickenham that put other annual celebrations in the shade. The whole stadium was buzzing; forty thousand people all drunk and enjoying the pale spring sunshine. It was a street party where everyone knew everyone.

Soldiers wore regimental rugby shirts. Officers with access to the hospitality tents wore blazers and regimental ties. People sat in gaggles ignoring the ticketing system.

They kept one eye on the game but as the army was winning, as it did most years, the rugby was a side show.

A male streaker raced across the field and almost succeeded in picking up the ball but the army fullback shoulder-charged him and knocked him flying. Two red caps with high-vis vests over their combats went to pick him up but he scarpered across the field, vaulted the signboard and ran up the steps on the opposite stand to huge cheers from the crowd.

There were people dressed in inflatable sumo suits which made their arms look really short when they tried to drink their beer. There were people in superhero outfits, Union Jack sweatshirts, kilts, drag. Groups were dressed in tweeds, as vegetables, as the characters from *Shawshank*, their surnames penned on zinc oxide tape above the pocket. A group of women dressed as bees, cackling away on the wine, were shepherded by a man in a full beekeeper outfit. But best of all were the two bootnecks dressed as pirates. One was double amp with a type of prosthetic Dean had never seen before. The other had one full leg inside a leather, knee-length boot and the other amputated below the knee. He had replaced the aluminium strut underneath the stump cup with a piece of broom handle, so it looked like he had a genuine wooden leg. As Dean and Pete came up the concrete steps into the stand, the pirates were already leathered, arm in arm and shouting '*Arrrgh, me hearties*' at anyone passing.

Dean burst into laughter. "That's fucking class!" he said. He had two beers in plastic glasses in each hand, squeezing them between thumb and forefinger. He placed one on the concrete wall next to the two men. "You can have that on me."

The pirates looked at each other, then at Dean, and simultaneously cheered and raised their glasses, spilling beer over their hands.

Dean shook his head in admiration as he followed Pete up the concrete steps to find a place to sit. Normally they came with a big group but neither of them had made the time to organise it. Dean had given Pete a call at the last minute and was confident they'd run into the others at the Cabbage Patch after the match.

"One of them just rowed the Atlantic," Pete shouted over his shoulder, indicating the pirates.

Dean didn't hear him but nodded and smiled. He pointed to a place beyond a party of women along a row of yellow seats. They must have been Navy judging by the look of them but the one Dean took for a lezza pinched his bottom as he went by.

"Oi, cheeky!" he laughed.

The sun wasn't strong but it was still warm enough to be in a shirt. The pair were both wearing desert boots with gillie ties, blue jeans, and black sweatshirts with the regimental logo on the breast. Dean wore sunglasses and a *Stone Roses* bucket hat branded with a slice of lemon on the front. He had put a load of brufen gel on his shoulder to stop it hurting. His broad nose was turning red. Pete had a sand-coloured regimental baseball cap pulled low over his face.

"You ok mate?" Dean said.

Pete nodded. "Aye. Been a while since I was out in public. People do a double take if they recognise me, you know?"

Dean patted his knee. "You'll be fine, mate. You'll be fine."

The pair leaned back to watch the rugby, one foot on the other knee, their thighs and shoulders touching. Pete nudged Dean to admire a woman on one of the lower levels. As she leaned over to put a coat on her seat, her cleavage created an inviting shadow.

Dean said, "Reminds me of being out in Aldershot when a battalion's just left for an Ireland tour and all the wives are down the Traff…"

"In high heels and Ron Hills."

The two laughed easily. They had so many memories between them and had known what the other was thinking from when they were in the same brick in their first tour of Northern Ireland and the same four man room in Aldershot.

"How did you get on with the police?" Pete said after a while. "Deafness trip you up?"

"Say again?"

Pete grinned. "Boom tish. Did you get in or what?"

Dean's face clouded. "Not sure, mate. Still waiting."

Pete said nothing but finished his first pint, then split the second into two glasses to give one to Dean.

"You still want to go undercover? Like your dad?"

Dean shrugged. "Maybe."

Pete looked across at him. "It's a pity you didn't get in the Det. I know it's what you wanted. I did what I could to help…"

Dean nodded. "I know, mate. I spent three years trying. It wasn't that the selection was hard. Of course it was. Harder than SAS selection."

"Didn't fail on fitness though, did you?"

"No. I failed cos I lost my rag and smashed an officer in the face."

After that attempt, the Commanding Officer had refused him permission to attempt Special Duties selection another time. He was being overtaken. Blokes who had been Corporals were now Colour-Sergeants and he was still a Sergeant. Then he was posted to the Training Wing rather than Support Company and that in itself was a career killer. Two years packing up basic lesson plans. Very soon there were men entering the Sergeants' Mess that Dean had taken through Depot as recruits.

If he'd got in to the Det it wouldn't have mattered. He would have been branded a Special Forces soldier and everything that went with that: the admiration, the pay, the pension entitlement, the jobs after the army. These would all have been secure. Plus, he could have looked his father in the eye.

"You did break his jaw," Pete said.

Dean sniggered. "He deserved it. They dropped him off the course too."

"Well you know what Special Duties is like, mate. If the face fits what the Det want, you get in. If it doesn't, you don't." Pete was silent for a second, then added. "And anyway, undercover work is all about being unrecognisable. If you walked into a bar in XMG they'd be talking about your fucking nose even now."

The two men cracked up, curling up in their seats. Dean held his beer level so as not to spill it. "Those were the days, eh?"

They leaned back with the sun on their faces, smiling. Michelle had phoned Dean that morning to say there was a letter with *South Yorkshire Police* on the envelope. Did he want her to open it? He'd been in a twin room at the Premier Inn near King's Cross. Pete was lying on his side, facing away, in the other bed. Dean had shaken his head knowing what it would say. "No love. I'll read it when I'm home."

He'd done the test as well as he could but still couldn't get his head round the maths questions. Was that what policing meant, a statistical assessment of risk?

Dean knew risk. He knew when to run and when to melt his belt buckle into the gravel behind hard cover. He knew when to shout and when to whisper. He knew when to praise and when to slap. He knew when to raise his hand and when to keep shtum. He knew when to pull the trigger and when to watch and wait. He knew when to follow instructions to the letter and when to use his initiative. He knew when to stand alone and when to ask a mate. He knew when to rush and when to idle away the long, tedious days while others flapped and panicked. He knew when to lay into the beer and when to stay focused. He knew when to laugh and when to chuckle. He knew the very moment when all else had failed and there was nothing left to do but tell those around him to fix bayonets and prepare for what must come.

And if the police didn't want that, fuckem.

Alexander, April 2017

David Cameron agreed to hold a referendum on Britain's future relationship with the European Union because he thought the vote would go his way. He had run another referendum two years earlier concerning the relationship between Scotland and the United Kingdom. He expected Britain to vote to remain in Europe just as Scotland had voted to remain in Great Britain.

But Camron lacked instinct, insight, and Alexander's populist appeal. In his political memoirs, he suggested Alexander had backed Brexit purely for his own advancement.

Alexander's response: *And?* He saw himself as the natural successor to Winston Churchill; a leader who overcame tumultuous times armed only with a sharp intellect and an eloquent tongue.

Papers found later at 10 Downing Street dated April 2017 record that:

> Today, in the House, the Right Honourable Member for Argyle and Bute, something of a nationalist, did me the immense service of stating that he had written to the Prime Minister demanding she do more to ensure the security of Yazidi women imprisoned between the Turkish border they cannot cross and the warring factions in Iraq and Syria. What he thinks she might be able to do for them remains a mystery to me. But his intervention allowed me to expound at length about the importance of such a policy and the grave nature of their treatment under the cruel hand of fate. And not only this: how Britain must retain its global position as the guardian of the international moral compass. Not simply in regard to Yazidi womenfolk

but those blighted by Sarin attacks in Syria and other such abominations. Surely the House would agree etc. etc.

Later, in the bar, May having absented herself to run through fields of corn or some such malarky, I bought Brendan a drink. I want him to invite me up for a spot of fishing. If I dangle the idea of another Scottish referendum in front of him, he may well oblige.

Dean, May 2017

Dean lounged on the sofa scrolling through Facebook. The attack on Westminster Bridge in March was being investigated formally by the Metropolitan Police. The investigation was being reported by the news media and criticised by anyone on social media who had a point of view. It was clear the Security Services knew there was going to be an attack. The security level had been increased a few days before. The attacker had been a Muslim convert who had become more radical than a radical. Dean shook his head. Frankly, he deserved to die.

The next post was a picture of a knight in full armour kneeling in prayer before his sword, the cross of Saint George emblazoned across his tabard. Below the picture in bold letters it said, 'We sleep safely because rough men stand ready in the night to visit violence on those who do us harm'. The quote was attributed to Winston Churchill.

"Fucking right," he muttered. He pressed the like button and shared the post as well.

He was still angry at the way the police had phrased the letter. He'd worked hard at the assessment and done very well at the physical tests, far outdoing younger applicants. And on the scenario tests he'd shown himself adaptable and quick to learn. He'd known how to disarm someone with a kick to the shin, a ward off, and a choke hold. And his knowledge of First Aid was exceptional. But the letter went on to say that he lacked both initiative and mathematical processing skills and though obviously in good physical shape he was not recommended for further police training.

Lacked initiative? What the fuck did that even mean?

Michelle shuffled into the room with a mug of tea in one hand. "Want one?"

Dean shook his head. "No, love. I'm off down the gym. Just catching up with the blokes."

She sat next to him on the sofa. "Anything from Pete? Did he get home ok?"

Dean smiled. The evening after the rugby match was still a blur. There were flashes of people he remembered speaking to. A brief scuffle. A burger. A seedy club. A lap dance. An expensive taxi. Pete snoring. Pete shaking him before he pissed on the kettle. On Sunday they'd got the train back to Rotherham too hungover to talk. Pete had intended to pick up his bike and get north but they both decided that fish and chips and more beer would be the better option. Pete had crashed on their sofa and left early in the morning.

"I never asked," Dean said as if it was self-evident he didn't need to.

Michelle cradled her mug in her hands. She was wearing slippers and her legs looked trim and slender. She rolled the mug between her hands.

"Deano, what are we doing about that conservatory flashing?" she asked, her tone indicating it was his job to do something. "It's leaking again and I'm not going back to Mahmud."

Dean put the phone down on his thigh with a resigned growl. Everything about that man made him feel cheated. He shook his head. He could chase the bastard down but what good would it do if the work was substandard? Having to admit that made him hot inside. If he had a sword he would gladly cleave Mahmud from shoulder to groin.

"I'm not saying speak to him," Michelle said. "We need to get someone else in, Deano. We need it fixing."

Dean grunted. He was glad she was giving him permission not to chase Mahmud even though the sense of being conned burned like a bullet wound. The conservatory was not a place of joy. The puddles of water and cracked tiles only reminded him of his failings. The room left him exhausted, sour, and uncertain.

"I was talking to Jane about it. Said what trouble we'd had. She said we should get a guy she knows. Polish. Or Roman. Something like that."

"Romanian?" Dean said, grinning.

"You know what I mean. Eastern European. Says he's cheap and very good."

"Very good was he? Was she happy with his work?"

Michelle laughed. "Yeah. Said he was very good looking too. So you be careful now, Dean Chadwick. I'm going to give him a call."

Dean shrugged and looked down at his phone. There was no point arguing and she was doing him a favour. Just this time he wasn't going to pay up front, not one penny. A brown envelope had arrived the day before from HMRC. Inside was a letter saying he needed to submit a tax return and he was dreading it. The previous year it had taken him all day, sitting at the kitchen table shuffling receipts into piles and dates, wishing he knew what he was doing. In the end, Elizabeth had put them in date order and find an accountant who could do the forms but that had cost near five hundred quid.

This year he hadn't been expecting to do a tax return. He was in full-time employment. Why did he have to do a tax return? And why were the forms so hard? Where was his *UTR*? Or his *P60*? Why wasn't this done by Bolton's? Was he going to have to pay for this too?

Michelle pushed herself up with a hand on his knee. "Anyway. I want to finish the kitchen. And you need to fill the car and wash it down. There's bird shit on the roof from the tree."

Dean growled again. "I know, love. I'll do it when I get the chips."

She touched his shoulder as she stepped over his legs. "Ok, love. No rush."

Dean smiled to himself. He knew an order when he heard it.

Malcolm, May 2017

When the boy was finally asleep, Penny joined him on the sofa to watch the news. She folded one leg under herself and leaned into him. Malcolm was usually asleep by this time. He was away to London in the early morning and felt relaxed about going after a few beers. The latter part of the week would be based at the submarine base in Barrow on the far side of Cumbria. It was closer to home geographically but would probably take longer to travel. He didn't know the route but he was excited to be going to the base.

He enjoyed Penny's softness against him. She felt precious. He was grateful that she gave herself to him that morning. It was the first time they'd had sex since his son was born and he could not recall the last time he had gone so long without.

He sat in his slippers and pyjamas, the bathrobe undone. Even though it was getting dark it was still warm and sticky when he took out the binbags. A downpour would provide a release. Penny radiated heat.

The news kept assessing the implications of Brexit. The reporter tried to summarise complex issues into digestible chunks as though feeding a child.

"They're making it up as they go along," he said, shaking his head.

Penny's head lolled against his shoulder. Her breathing deepened. He used the remote to change channel, seeking the local news from Cumbria to see if his client featured. A face he recognised made him start.

"That's, that's..."

Penny jerked awake. She muttered, eyes heavy with fatigue.

"Sorry, pet. I know him! That's Mark Simpson, my old..."

The report was about a Court Martial in Liverpool. A former army captain had been accused of dereliction of duty resulting in the loss of two lives and key military equipment to the Taliban. Malcolm sat forward with his elbows on his knees. His mouth hung open.

Penny yawned, "What happened?"

Malcolm sat back, the hand holding the remote slack against his thigh. "It was terrible. I had left the battalion before that tour, thank God. We had a fucking awful CO. I mean a real bastard. Selfish, arrogant, toxic."

He thought about what to say.

"We had a, they had a drone that could spy on the Taliban. It got shot down. This CO sent out a patrol to recover it. The patrol was led by a good officer. He wasn't from my regiment but he was very good. Looking to transfer."

Penny's eyebrows arched. "Was he killed?"

"Yes. Him and four men tried to recover this drone but they got caught in an ambush and two of them were killed. The officer and a corporal."

"When was this?"

"2009? No, 2010."

"That was ages ago."

"Yes, it was. They did an inquiry at the time. This oily little fuck called Kerry ran an investigation into what happened. He was the Intelligence Officer. He's probably CO by now."

Malcolm realised he had to explain.

"Kerry Nairac was one of the CO's stooges. He blamed the incident on the guy who was killed which was easy to say but not actually true. And now the army have run a second investigation and blamed that guy, Mark Simpson.

He was a captain at the time, the Company Second in Command."

"So why they blaming him? What did he do?"

Malcolm shook his head. "I simply don't know."

He was upset at seeing Simpson on the television. The man looked afraid in the crowd outside the courthouse. He was no longer serving so wore a dark blue suit and was being jostled along by military police escorts in uniform. Cameras flashed. People shouted. He made no comment, not even through his lawyer.

"Is he guilty?"

Malcolm shook his head. "Fuck no. In fact, he should have been given an award for that tour. His company commander was sick most of the time. Mark was running the company as a captain. It's usually a major..."

"I know."

He could see her mind working.

"So what's he accused of?"

"Cowardice, basically."

"How can they prove that?"

"I don't know. It's complicated."

She shook her head. "I don't see what the case is. Somebody was killed, right? And it was the Taliban that shot him?"

"Yep."

"Right, so they're saying this guy could have prevented his death? It was negligence?"

He nodded, uncertain of the details. He only knew what they said on the report and he hadn't been in touch with Simpson since he got out.

"But you know the guy they're charging? That man there?"

"Yep. He's a bit senior to me. He was a captain when I was a lieutenant. But he was good. We played rugby together."

"So why are they blaming him?"

Malcolm shook his head. "Don't know. Probably covering the arse of that colonel."

"The one you said…"

"Yep, him. He's still serving. As is his toady Intelligence Officer. I tell you, I'm so glad I'm out of it all."

He placed his free hand on his head. He flicked the remote and turned the television off. He was tired.

Penny placed a hand on his leg.

"Are you?"

"Oh God yes. I mean, I did some amazing things. And I served with some amazing blokes. But when I see shit like this, how the army treats you…"

He shook his head slowly. He recalled the night he spent with Mark Simpson in Mirabel after a day's skiing. The memory made him smile but he wasn't going to admit why.

"I'm going to give him a call tomorrow," Malcolm said.

Alexander, June 2017

Theresa May knew her term as Prime Minister would be characterised by delicate manoeuvring between competing agendas rather than boasting a few broad principles. Her job was to guide a divided, fearful, and angry country through a crisis she did not believe in, while most of her colleagues sat gleefully on the side-lines waiting for her to crash.

Believing she would benefit from shoring up her mandate, she called a General Election. Her intention was to establish a convincing Conservative majority while also preventing her critics from replacing her. She thought the leader of the Labour Party, Jeremy Corbyn, was too far to the left for most centre-ground voters and she expected to win back the Conservative vote lost to Tony Blair in 1997.

Sadly, her plan failed. The Conservatives won the election but only just. The left coalesced around Corbyn. The far right had already been lost to the brilliant strategist Nigel Farage. The centre ground was confused and divided. In order to assure even a semblance of functioning government the enfeebled May had to grovel for support from the Democratic Unionist Party (DUP), the dominant voice of Ulster Protestantism. Although they represented only a limited proportion of the Northern Ireland population, there was always an ill-informed perception in the Conservative Party that loyalism was intrinsically conservative by nature.

Throughout this fiasco Alexander comfortably retained his seat. With May looking hapless, the media turned to him for comment on the DUP support agreement. His response was to deny he would challenge May for the leadership role, which quickly ignited speculation that he would. He then repeated the Brexit campaign slogan that the UK was giving £350 million every week to the European Union and this money would be better spent on the NHS.

When the Chair of the UK Statistics Authority, Sir David Norgrove, stated that the assertion was utterly untrue and 'a clear misuse of official statistics', Alexander dismissed his comments with a wave of his hand. Truth no longer mattered. What mattered was power. Only in power could he give the people what they wanted. Papers found later at 10 Downing Street dated June 2017 record that:

> I am starting to see who will be in my cabinet when the time comes: who will open the batting, and who will remain in the far reaches of the outfield.

Dean, July 2017

From his portacabin office Dean watched the delivery driver turn into the yard and circle round in a wide arc, the tyres skidding to a halt on the baked mud. He drove in a jerky, clutch intensive way, which was funny since he worked for a parts business. The mechanic, Sam Johnson, was now owed nearly twelve thousand pounds and had refused to do more work until the bill was settled. Bolton had offered to pay an instalment but the mechanic refused. "Pay up or fuck off," had been his words. He had apologised to Dean, saying it wasn't him, it was Bolton.

Dean had been equally sorry. "Mate, I'm gutted. Honest. If it was me, I'd pay out my own pocket...."

But with the impasse, and the need to keep the vehicles on the road, someone had to do the maintenance. One of the wagons needed a timing belt and Aiden, one of the drivers, said he would do it for cash up front providing Bolton got the parts. And so the delivery driver was standing by the back doors of his van scanning a barcode with a handheld machine. After tucking a box under one arm he slammed the van doors and jauntily entered the office without knocking.

Dean thought he recognised him. He looked like the little half-caste kid who followed him round after Dean had stopped him getting filled in by skinheads. But he was now a man. He was short, squat, and wore his hair cut high and tight. He'd put on a bit of beef but Dean knew a weakling when he saw one. Big arms didn't make you hard. He still had the eyes of a scared child.

There was no one else in the office. The drivers were out, Maggie was away to the shops, and Bolton hadn't been seen for two days.

"Hello, mate. Car parts. Anyone sign for it?" the man said. He was chewing gum and had a presumptive air. Dean stood up from his desk puffing out his shoulders and elbows. He wasn't much taller but was considerably broader.

The man's face immediately changed. "Dean? Dean Chadwick?"

"Yes, mate. Your face is familiar too. Is it Dillon?"

He shook his head. He didn't have earrings, a thing Dean thought as gay as they come, unless you're a pirate. But he wore a gold block chain necklace that looked cheap. "Billy. Billy Atkins. You was a couple of years older than me at school."

Dean frowned. Atkins? No, he was sure. It was Dillon. His dad was Indian. That's why the skinheads were giving him a kicking. In fact, it was *Dhillon*. He'd only spelled it *Dillon* so it looked more English. All Dean could remember was a gawky, skinny-legged kid with a lopsided walk trailing him home at a safe but respectful distance.

"Atkins?"

"Yes, mate. Billy. How are you? Are you... you must be out of the army now?"

He had a missing eye tooth that was obvious when he smiled. He seemed straight enough. He obviously knew who Dean was.

"Yeah. A few years now. I did..."

"You were in the Paras, weren't you?"

"Yeah, I was." It seemed an odd thing to say. Dean sometimes felt as if he wouldn't be believed when he told people what he'd done in the army. And he was not a walt. He was gen.

Atkins kept nodding, smiling, the gum in his cheek. "Fucking great, mate." He extended a hand. "May I congratulate you on your service to the country."

Dean shook his hand. He had a tight grip that made Dean tense his shoulder. It was a meaningful compliment but, coming from a man wearing jewellery, he was unmoved. He withdrew his hand and folded his arms.

"Thanks. Now, what can I do for you, Billy?"

Still staring at him, Atkins remembered the box under his arm. He handed it over with the electronic tablet. "Just put your squiggle in that box with your finger," he said.

Dean did so conscious of Atkins' continuing gaze.

"So how long have you been here? I heard you was in Iraq. Mercenary work, yeah? On the circuit?"

Dean had heard this patter before. "I was in Baghdad, yeah. With Global Risks."

"CP work?"

"It was close protection, yeah. Why do you ask?"

"Wow. And how long have you been back in town? I didn't know. I'd have come to see you otherwise."

There was something about him that was getting on Dean's tits. He put his hands deep into his pockets and flexed his triceps as he did so. "A year, maybe. What you up to, then? Deliveries?"

He hadn't meant it as a dig but some might have taken it as such. Not Atkins.

"Oh, this is just a side job. For money. I do other things as well."

He looked round the office: the coat racks, the electric fans, the desks covered in paperwork. The windows were open to allow the wind through. He took a step closer and dropped his voice.

"Are you a patriot, Dean?"

"Of course."

"I bet you are. A man who served Queen and Country! Of course you're a patriot!" He was smiling again and chewed as he spoke. "Listen, I'm connected to... I run an organisation of like-minded people. People who want the best for Rotherham. Do you get my drift?"

"No, not really."

Atkins was taken aback but he recovered quickly. His voice thickened. "We like a nice town, Dean. A nice, white town. We like things to be the way they should."

Dean realised what he was saying. He'd just had to pay fifteen hundred pounds to a Romanian to fix the bollocks job Mahmud had left. That was his pay for the month.

"I see you're one of many who've been let down," Atkins said quickly. "Who was it? A taxi driver? A doctor?"

Dean thought for a second. He didn't trust the guy but anything that would help him get back at Mahmud would be welcome. "A builder."

"Yeah? Who?"

Dean wondered whether to say the name but then admitted it: "Mahmud."

"Fucking knew it!" Atkins said, snapping his fingers. "A complete rip-off merchant. If you knew how many people have been had by him…"

Dean wasn't taken in by the patter but he was prepared to go with it. At the very least, a whinge was good for the soul.

"How much he do you for?"

"Thirty grands' worth of work. More or less."

"Patio was it? Extension?"

"Conservatory."

"A conservatory! I tell you. You're not the only one. And it's shit, ain't it? A man serves his country, works overseas to bring back money for his wife and family, works all day and all night, yeah?"

"Yeah, sure."

"A man does the Queen's bidding. And what happens? They come home. They build a conservatory and fucking dickheads like Mahmud go off with their money. It's wrong I tell you. Wrong."

The man had flair, Dean had to admit.

Atkins stepped closer again and tapped Dean on the chest with the back of one hand, lightly enough to feel conspiratorial.

"You know what, Dean? Three times! Three times this year we've come under attack. We, the British people, have come under attack. First was Westminster Bridge, right? A young policeman, unarmed, knifed by a jihadi? Second, Manchester. All those kids, yeah? Third, London Bridge. Last month. Eight people."

The talking irritated Dean but he was saying things people were afraid to.

"And what do you think of that, eh?"

"What do I think of what?" Dean said.

"That all these jihadis were home grown. Raised on British soil. And yet…" He glanced behind him again and tapped Dean on the chest a second time. "And yet, they don't share our values. British values. That's got to be wrong, hasn't it?"

Dean looked into Atkins' dark brown eyes. He thought about reminding him of his former name but Atkins didn't give him the space.

"Look, it's a secret. But I'm connected to a group of people. Special people. We could use men like you. If you wanted work. Money. If you wanted to put your skills to the test."

Dean frowned. Who was this little fuck? "How do you mean?"

Atkins stepped back and opened his arms wide. "Look. I can't say. But they're special people, Dean. People like you and me. Honest, Decent. Hard working. Loyal. Men of integrity. Men with pride. Men prepared to do hard things for the sake of others."

Dean nodded. He was reminded of the quote he'd seen on Facebook. "Like what?"

"How do you mean?"

"Do what hard things?" Dean said, raising his voice.

"Depends. Depends what needs doing." Atkins stepped forward again to tap Dean's torso but this time Dean had tensed his lats.

"I would be prepared to bet that you would do things other people won't. That's what the Paras are for isn't it? The ops other regiments can't handle?"

That was true, to an extent. But Dean was also thinking this man was full of shit. He studied Atkins' face to decide whether to pick him up by the throat or hug him.

"Listen, Dean. I can see you're a man of judgement. I mean, who's this little fucker coming in here and gobbing off. But let me prove I mean what I say."

He pulled a wallet from his back pocket, opened it, and teased out the notes. He then folded the wallet up and put it away one handed.

"Look, here's what? A hundred and fifteen quid, yeah?"

"You going to pull a rabbit from a hat?"

Atkins counted the money again. "A hundred and twenty-five. And it's yours, Dean. If you could do a driving job this weekend?"

Dean knew Michelle hadn't planned anything. He'd promised to take Elizabeth for a drive but that could be any time. That meant gym, match on TV, curry in, and movie with Michelle fast asleep on the sofa as soon as the titles were over.

"Drive what? Where to?"

A hundred quid would go a long way. The day before, Bolton had said something about the drivers' pay being late this month while he sorted the cash flow. Dean had immediately said, no, fuck off. The drivers they had left were reliable. They had mortgages and kids and families. You don't do that. He was shocked that such things could be on Bolton's mind, the devious cunt. He was as bad as Mahmud.

"Cash. I need someone to take a small parcel to an address in London. Finchley. Three hours down, three hours back. No hassle. Drop off, get a receipt, come back. The rest of the day's your own."

"Why don't you do it?"

Atkins extended his hands wide and shrugged. "Reasons, Dean. That's all I can say. But it's easy money if you're up for it. I tell you what. I'll make it a hundred and fifty. That's twenty-five quid an hour. That's like, double the rate ain't it? And I can give you it up front, too. That's how much I trust men like you."

It was this vote of confidence Dean respected. He'd paid Mahmud up front and the man had used it to fund other jobs. As progress on the conservatory faltered Dean realised he had no recourse over Mahmud at all, yet here was Atkins offering him complete faith. But he kept his hands folded.

Atkins continued. "I do know the guy who did you over, Dean. It's Shaky isn't it? Shakir Mahmud."

Dean nodded.

"We've been watching him for a while. I can't say too much. But we think he's in one of them grooming gangs. Based out of a mosque."

It was a common fear in the town. Girls as young as twelve. There'd been cases on the news and like any father, Dean worried for his girls.

"You want me to drive some dosh to Finchley for a ton fifty?"

Atkins nodded.

Dean rubbed his chin with one hand. Who said he couldn't use his initiative? Who said he was wooden?

"I'll do it," he said, pulling the notes from Atkin's hand.

Atkins made an expansive gesture then extended a hand for Dean to shake again. "Mate, you're just the man we need right now," he said.

Malcolm, July 2017

Malcolm spotted his old mucker Mark Simpson sitting at a table outside the pub. He waved as he approached. Mark rose. They shook hands and then embraced.

"Great to see you, mate."

"It's a pleasure, Mark. I couldn't miss the chance while I'm here."

"Well, thanks. I hear you did amazing things on your second tour of Afghan. Congratulations."

There was an element of respect in Mark's voice that Malcolm had not been expecting. He thought Mark's operational experience was the greater from the 2009-2010 tour. And, having seen Mark on TV, he wanted to get to the heart of the matter.

"How are you feeling? After the case? You were fucking screwed."

"Glad it's over. And I got exonerated. Completely exonerated. I have to be honest and say it was a relief when they gave their findings."

Malcolm shook his head then indicated they should sit. It was warm enough to remain outside. "Military justice my fucking arse."

They'd met in Kendal, a tourist town of hotels, walking

shops, art galleries. The pub was empty save for three bearded, booted walkers supping bitter.

"How did you get here?"

"I've got a hire car. I can't go on the lash, sorry."

Mark smiled. "We won't do another Mirabel then?"

Malcolm laughed. "We can. But I'll not drive back. And as for those women…"

Mark picked up the menu, studied it. He watched Malcolm sit.

"You're putting on weight."

Malcolm nodded. "I've had to cut the carbs down."

Mark nodded and returned to his menu.

"But you want to eat?"

"Absolutely. I'm starving. But I need to go back by nine. I've work to do tonight."

"You said. What are you doing now?"

"I work for Delaine, the management consultancy? I run a programme about procurement improvement. I'm at Barrow this week."

"On the submarine base?"

"Yep. Still got my security vetting, see?"

Mark nodded. "Still with Miss Penny Hunter? The fiery redhead from Newcastle, County Down?"

"Yep. She's now Mrs Penny Sewell, the fiery redhead from Newcastle, Tyne and Wear."

Mark laughed as he extended a hand over the top of the menu. "Congratulations, mate. That's awesome. I saw on Facebook you had a kid, too?"

Malcolm nodded. "Yep. Luca. He's a year. Mad as a coked-up rhino. Wide awake twenty-four hours a day."

Mark chuckled. "So you're going to work to get some sleep?"

"Yep."

"Situation no change there, then?"

The two men laughed. Time had not passed. They got beers; a hoppy, amber ale that was 5.2%. Malcolm thought he would have one and the food would soak it up so he could drive.

"Again, mate. I'm really sorry for what happened to you. It's a fucking shambles. The whole thing."

Mark grimaced. Malcolm read in his face the personal embarrassment and the bitterness that the institution he had served and loved should betray him.

"I tell you. If I ever have a few months to live, I'm going to take Kerry Nairac to hell. I'll kill him on his doorstep in front of his wife and kids. And as for Colonel fucking Rawlins…"

The conversation stopped while the waitress took their food order. They were polite but formal with her. Malcolm sipped from the top of his second pint thinking about having another and crashing on Mark's sofa.

"So what's with the pub? You bought a bar?"

Mark nodded. "Always wanted to. A cosy little country pub. Full of *ladies*. Nice looking *ladies* in *lycra*."

He was grinning. The pair had been wing-men in the bars in Colchester and the nightclubs in London. Mark always went for the easy ones. *Go ugly early*, he always said. Malcolm had more patience and higher standards. Unless they were in France. Or Holland.

They talked of families and work, nights out, and doing the Haute Route. They knew they were different from those around them. But the shadow of the army hung over them.

"You know, the army's shot to fuck. There's no *integrity* anymore. There's no *moral courage*."

Malcolm ordered a third beer. It tasted too good and Mark needed him. He would stay over and get up early. He agreed with what Mark was saying.

"I've learned more about leadership outside the army than I did inside it. As a civvy, you have to inspire people. They don't *have* to do what you say. You have to motivate them."

Deciding to leave had been immensely hard for Malcolm even when Penny agreed to marry him. He'd loved it all. But he couldn't spend his entire life commanding platoons on operations.

Malcolm said, "Let's see what the next defence review says. They'll cut the army back again, bet you."

"We couldn't fight another Falklands."

"And we have to face the fact that we lost. In Afghanistan. We didn't stop the drugs. We didn't beat the Taliban. We couldn't even hold Sangin."

Malcolm thought of the men he'd lost. "Was it fucking worth it?" he said.

They were silent for a while, eyes blank, then Mark said, "Yes, it was worth it. Of course it was. You know why we went. And we're the only ones who can do these things. But when you're over, when you're out, you're worth nothing. The machine rolls on."

Kyle, previously

Char got me in to see the doc eventually. The thing about the antidepressants is they make you feel great at first. Proper happy. But after a while it's like seeing yourself through fog. The feeling isn't real. And when I realised the drugs had no effect at all, I was just numb. I felt nothing: no joy, no pain.

But they do mean I can go out. I can go to the shops and meet the guy from SSAFA who got me onto a list and that got me into a flat.

Char and Danny were proper stars. In the end I was screaming all night and this kept everyone awake. Little Dan's face in the morning was so scared I felt terrible. So I had to go. I even said I'd sleep outside for a bit so as not to disturb them. But Danny said don't worry. They told little Dan that I had gone to war and was now having scary dreams about what I saw and little Dan came in and put his arms around me and I'm like trying hard not to cry.

But now I'm in this flat and it's dead nice. No veterans as it's in Shelton where the students live. But it's under two hundred a week and SSAFA have said they can help me if I need it.

It's small: a kitchen and a bedroom, really. Toilet. No living room but there's a bit at the end of the kitchen where there's a sofa on one side and a telly on the wall on the other. I've been here two weeks and it's dead noisy compared to where Char lives but that's fine. It was the same round Mum's and if I have to leather some student for playing shit music at two in the morning then I will.

So I've decided today I don't want to cook. It's my birthday. I've no bread to make a sarnie so think I'll just get some chips from the one by the Uni and this means I'm walking along the road at about the same time the schools finish. The sun's in my face and it's warm but this means I can't see clearly. I'm blinking and have my hand up over my eyes. There are all these students coming in and out of the concrete building and I'm checking my arcs all the time: the windows, the alleyways between the concrete pillars, the back lanes where the bins are kept. There are no cars to speak of but the odd works van, ladder at an angle, mixer tied down with orange nylon rope.

I can see the chip shop ahead and there's this child on a bike coming towards me on the pavement. I can't see his mother so I'm thinking, why is this child out on his own on a bike? Why is he coming this way? Why is he heading towards that crowd of people coming out of the university building?

And that's when I think of Amrut and the market square and this time I don't have the gun. Gaz has the gun and I've got a rifle because of my ankle and Jim Muir is asking questions on the radio about this kid on a bike coming into the market square. We know something's going to kick off. We've been given specialist Int from the phone intercepts. But most we can feel it in the air. The tension. The expectation.

And Jim shouts over to get a bead on the kid on a bike as there's something odd about him. His clothes, maybe, the way he rides. His face. Not happy. Serious. Scared. Like you'd been sent to get your Dad out of the pub. So I kneel and lift the sights and put the arrowhead on the little kid, right in the centre of his chest. I'm looking at his clothing, the shape of it. Looking for anything that might say suicide vest or backpack. But he has nothing. He's just a little kid with a cheeky little face and dimples and dark eyelashes. If he don't smile it's because he's been sent to the market by his mother to get some food. There's a sort of trailer on the back of the bike but I can't see what's in it.

And Jim is shouting at me and I'm looking at this little kid and thinking I'm not going to slot him unless I have to. I'm not going to shoot a child in the middle of his chest.

So I'm tracking him. He's unsteady on the bike. It's old. A woman's bike. No central bar. He's wearing one of those long white shirts but it doesn't get caught in the pedals or the chain. He stops and looks over his shoulder, head turned away. He has one foot on the ground, one on the top pedal as he looks backwards. Black sandals. And then he looks at the crowd and leans forward to push his weight forward. He's only fifty feet from me and I couldn't miss if I tried.

Jim is yelling at me but I don't want to hear what he's saying. I'm just watching the kid. He's not a risk, I think. He's not a threat. So I lift my head to assess the wider situation. The kid is now in the market square. I can see the other patrol among the people. And at that moment there's this blast and smoke and all the birds scatter and the wires on the poles shake and fall. And Jim's shouting and the Sergeant-Major's shouting and Gaz is shouting and I can't hear any of them and I'm limping because the sudden burst of adrenalin has made my boots tight. There's this woman with clawed fingers and I can't hear what she says and there's Captain Wilmott sitting against the wall, his leg blown off, trying to fit a tourniquet below the knee.

And I think, this is all my fault. That kid was the bomb.

And so I'm in College Street and there's this kid coming towards me on his bike. He has a helmet on and a blue coat. He's at the road crossing and he stops. He puts one foot down. And he turns back to look over his shoulder. And I know it's for his mum. I know it. But there's something about the way he does it, the way he moves, the colour of his hair and his cheeks and then I'm face down, one hand on the side of the bin, bent over, throwing my guts up.

Great splurges of it. Yellow. Rasping in the throat. Spattering on the floor, hot, like yellow blood. I lift my head and the mother is looking at me with her hand on the kid's back. Her mouth is a funny shape. I must look like an alky or a druggy and I'm bent over in the street throwing up in a bin. I want to say no, don't worry. But I can't talk. I can hardly walk.

The kid wobbles on his bike across the road. He doesn't look at me. The woman shouts for him to stop at the next junction. She looks at me hard slightly turning her shoulders.

It takes a few minutes before I've got my breathing down. I've got vom on my kegs. I can't walk past all these pretty students in their t-shirts and glasses. So I turn round, get a pint of milk and some corn flakes from the corner shop and leg it home. That'll do for today. I'll text Char not to come.

Dean, August 2017

This time, his fourth run down and back, Dean had got up at four. He'd got to Finchley by seven and parked outside the house where the exchange was made. He was using a different car this time, a work one. If Bolton challenged him about the mileage he would say he was driving round checking on the drivers. He could bluff it. He had always blagged his way out of trouble.

He got out of the car and stretched. A fit girl in grey lycra ran past, ponytail bouncing behind her head. Dean eyed her buttocks as she disappeared round the bend in the road. Nice.

The Spaniard was at the window. Dean raised his hand in recognition then looked carefully up and down the street. He studied the windows on the far side, a long terrace of two-storey brick houses, mostly painted white on the upper floor. Then he studied the cars, one by one, looking for the outline of a person behind the windscreens. He gave a thumbs up.

The Spaniard came down the steps leaving the front door open. He had an orange wheelie bag and Dean opened the boot so he could put it in the car. At the same time, he pulled an envelope from his inside pocket and placed it on the sill of the boot. The Spaniard snatched it up and slid it into the back of his jeans in a single, seamless movement.

Dean closed the boot. The Spaniard sauntered up the steps into the house, long dreads tied behind his head with yellow ribbon. Odd looking on a white man. He hadn't said anything or shook hands. Now Dean had a three-hour drive north. Atkins had given him five hundred for this trip plus another hundred for fuel. Dean didn't ask what was in the case. He wasn't stupid. But he didn't ask, he just drove. Five hundred would go some way to getting a car for Elizabeth if she ever passed her test.

Steve, August 2017

Parking up, Steve felt his heart racing. This was odd as he knew Malcolm before his accident. He'd been the platoon commander before the tour and Steve respected him as a person and an officer. He'd been very fit. The seniors liked him too, men like Swampy Chadwick and Pete McCardle, the Company Sergeant-Major.

So why was he nervous? This wasn't a job interview. It was a meeting to decide if Malcolm was the right person to be Steve's mentor. A mentor was someone who opened doors and would help him get the job he wanted.

Orpheus House had been sandblasted as part of the refurbishment process. The huge beige stone blocks had sharp edges and no sign of weathering. The extension, which housed the ensuite accommodation rooms, was only distinguishable because the stones were the size of breeze blocks and the windows were newer. The bushes round the carpark were supported by wooden stakes and had not yet joined up to form a hedge. Steve nipped through a gap to get to the walkway that led to the paved courtyard, the centrepiece of which was the life-size bronze statue. It showed two men, one blinded with his hand on the shoulder of the one in front. The leader walked on a crutch but was able to see. He had one hand held out as if being guided by someone unseen.

The statue was a physical representation of the *Save Our Heroes* logo. They'd told Steve on one of the courses that it was based on a First World War painting. Steve had never paid it much heed. The blokes on the course, all WIS, had christened the figures *Ant and Dec* because one leaned on the other as if pissed and the front one looked like he was demanding a massive bung.

The statue was popular with civvies though. They loved taking pictures of it and of themselves holding the hand of the figure in front, pulling him along. That's what was happening as Steve crossed the courtyard to the main door. A group of men and women, all middle aged, well dressed, chortling, were taking turns to have their picture taken. They were obviously civvies judging by how they stood. Two men in very slim suits smoked by the main door. They stopped talking as Steve approached. As he got closer one of them stepped out and waved his hand at the automatic sensor. This made Steve laugh.

"Thanks. But I can see out of one eye."

Inside, the building was cool and familiar. Clive was by the cabinet of branded merchandise with a woman in a trouser suit who was buying a teddy bear and a mauve fleece. Steve nodded to Charlie, the guard on the reception desk. It was a Sunday, so it had been an easy drive along the A66. He needed to piss but as he walked towards the toilets by the canteen he saw Malcolm Sewell by the big picture window, sitting on the sofa, talking into his mobile phone. Steve walked quietly to the end of the sofa behind Malcolm's line of vision and waited. He was deep in conversation and spoke only occasionally so Steve left him and went to the loo. When he came back, Malcolm was just putting his phone on the coffee table.

"Hello Sir! I mean, Malcy!"

"Steve! How are you, mate?"

Malcolm rose, spinning on his heels. He extended a hand, realised it was the wrong one, then swapped. Steve shook it firmly. Then, according to an unspoken rule, they changed the grip of their hands and came together for a hug.

When they came apart, Malcolm kept hold of his hand and placed his other on Steve's shoulder. "How are you getting on, Steve?" he said.

"Yeah, alright, Malcy. Good, yeah!" He tried to use his prosthetic to tap Malcolm on the elbow but lifted his shoulder too quickly, making the thing swing like a bludgeon.

Malcom took a good look at it and Steve was comfortable letting him do so. Civvies always shifted their gaze. It took a veteran to know what he was looking for.

"Why's it black?"

Steve chuckled. "Well, there's a story there," he said.

"I bet there is! Look, have a seat. We're just about to be introduced anyway, after lunch." Malcolm nodded to the civvies in the corridor and the gang coming in from outside.

"So you're on a course?"

"Coaching and mentoring. All of us are, from Delaine. It's one of the big four consultancies. Global company. Most of us have been paired with a WIS. After lunch we get to meet them. So if you and I talk now, we are coming in under budget."

He was smiling. He looked no different. Rounder in the face, perhaps, and longer hair. He didn't wear glasses before, not that Steve could recall. But he looked suddenly very sad. "Mate. Before we go on, I'm really sorry about what happened. I heard about the explosion the day after.... All the blokes. And Seb Wilmott, of course..."

Steve nodded. "Yep. Captain Wilmott. He were a good lad, him. But the explosion took his leg below the knee and he bled out. So I heard, after. I didn't see owt. I were unconscious. The bike the kid was on. Handlebars hit me in the head."

Malcolm glanced up at the civvies shuffling towards the canteen. They had noticed him there and Steve sensed this gave Malcolm a power over them. He thought that if Malcolm had been there he would have been killed like Captain Wilmott. He was lucky to get out.

It was often down to luck. A meter here or an inch there decided who died and who lived, who stood on the IED and who had a major blood vessel ripped open by shrapnel.

"Is that what happened?" Malcolm asked.

Steve nodded. "Lifted my hand to protect my face. Automatic, like. But it was travelling so fast it took it off below the elbow."

"And the head injury?"

Steve shook his head. "Don't rightly know. The blast knocked my helmet off. I think I just fell over when I lost consciousness. I were trying to grab Spanner – you know Spencer? – as he was down. Shrapnel got under his body armour. He were killed outright but I didn't know it at the time."

Malcolm looked serious. "So you had lost an arm and you were trying to save Spanner's life?"

"I hadn't lost it. It was hanging on by a bit of skin. But I couldn't use it."

Someone, Clive, called Malcolm's name from by the canteen. Malcolm looked over and waved acknowledgement.

"And you heard about Kyle Hutton? Smiler?"

Steve looked down. "I did, yeah. A great shame, that. Nice lad. Great shame."

A silence fell. Malcolm said, "Look, I should join them for lunch. But we'll meet afterwards. And you can decide if you want me as a mentor."

Steve smiled. Here was his old officer, someone who knew him really well. Of course he'd have Malcolm. The others were just civvies. What did they know about life as a soldier? Or becoming a civvie? Or being WIS?

Malcom stood up and offered his left hand to shake. Steve took it. "Good to see you again, Steve. You've obviously come a long way since your injury."

"Good to see you, too, Sir," Steve said.

"Isn't it your birthday this month?"

Steve's face broke into a wide smile. "Today, actually."

"Very happy birthday, mate." With that, he made a curt nod of his head and bent to pick up his phone and notebook. As he turned to go, he said, "They didn't give you a black man's cock as well, did they?"

Both of them laughed. "I wish," said Steve. "You get bigger things in ashtrays."

Pete, September 2017

Pete stood in front of the gambling machine at the Royal British Legion on Helen Street. There was nothing left of the pile of coins on top and no folding in his wallet. What had started out as a tenner had become thirty, and then he'd won fifty. Over the course of the next hour, he'd lost all that and twenty more, gone to the cashy and returned with a hundred. He now had one spin left.

Pete loved being at war. It was devoid of fussiness, murk, complexity. It was pure adrenalin. It was a contest representing everything that had beaten him down; his mother dying, his father's lonely brutality, his brothers' tacit avoidance of him. In Dundee, aged sixteen, the recruiting sergeant had tried to push him into the Gordon Highlanders but he'd bluntly refused. Why would he want to be based at Fort George? Or join the mob his father was in for National Service?

No. His belly was full of anger and he wanted a regiment where it was acceptable to be violent. That meant one thing and a rail pass to Aldershot. At the depot, he fought all the way through basic training and didn't stop fighting till he passed out, the only recruit in the platoon with no family at the final parade. *The Aldershot Orphan*, they called him.

In battalion, the junior soldiers, *crows*, had to give money to the old-sweats, the Falklands veterans, the tough guys. Pete fought them too, had his jaw broken the first time and his cheekbone the second. But they stopped taking money from him and he found himself posted to the mortar platoon where his aggression could be put to use. *Baseplate Pete*, they called him now.

Then, in 1993, still a junior soldier, he and his mate Dean from the machine guns were attached to C Company during a tour of South Tyrone. On a dark night in November, the two of them were placed at the back of a farmhouse by a young officer while the rest of the platoon prepared to raid the place for weapons. In the following three hours, shivering in the nettles and cow shit, they watched the lights go on and off in the kitchen, the bathroom, the landing. They watched a man come out the back door into the yard, smoke a cigarette, then be summoned back in by a sharp woman's voice. They watched a small car arrive and a suited man get out, look carefully where he placed his feet, and knock on the back door. The woman came out, hugged him and kissed him on the mouth. They held their breath. Once the man was inside, they waited another hour, wondering when the search would begin. The batteries in their radio went flat. The dew started to freeze. The concrete became increasingly uncomfortable underneath their thighs and elbows.

Slowly, carefully, while Dean covered him, Pete knelt up to piss, the liquid steaming as it rolled back towards his knees on the sloping ground. The smell of it made the cattle in the cowshed jumpy. They started lowing louder and louder until a man came out the back door, silhouetted against the yellow light, a long-barrelled weapon in his hands.

The next two hours had been chaos. The woman and children screaming. The cattle stampeding. The officer running. The police torches. The dogs.

Following the tour, they had given Dean a Mentioned in Dispatches for finding weapons in the boot of the car. But because he'd killed O'Hare, the man who'd saved the most atrocious Provos from imprisonment, Pete was promoted. From then on he could do no wrong. He possessed a sharp mind that his officers respected, a political instinct that kept him out of the Regimental Sergeant-Major's bad books, and a reputation for toughness that his peers feared.

Then, as a sergeant, things changed. Where once a soldier would be considered an old-sweat if he'd done two tours of Northern Ireland and had two medals at the end of his service (after all, who really deserved the Long Service and Good Conduct medal?) there came a period where the army was constantly deploying on exciting operations. First it was Bosnia. Then Kosovo. Then Sierra Leone. Then a small intervention by the Gurkha battalions in East Timor. The army patched up flooded rivers in Selby and pulled people from their homes in the freak storms of 2002. They searched the fields round Dover for the missing schoolgirl Millie Dowler. They went back to Belfast as urban reinforcement battalions when the Prods kicked off about their right to march down Catholic streets.

It was in the blizzard of this activity that he met a stunning Russian woman behind the tills in Asda, dated her, married her, and had a daughter with her. The constant absence was good for both of them. It was only when he was home that they argued and by 2008 they were separated and divorced.

And then Iraq. A sweaty, terrifying intermezzo that ended with a statue of Saddam Hussain being tugged off its pedestal by an American tank, the supporting steel poles bending but clinging on. The British army withdrew to its allocated area and hunkered down into the sort of operations it understood: patrolling an area where two factions competed for dominance.

And then Afghanistan. What had once been a quiet training and support operation conducted as a low-key foreign policy intervention for the national army, became a NATO operation with the British Contingent taking a role it neither had the men nor the political will to properly execute. Battalions were deployed at first to interdict the flow of drugs out of the fertile Helmand Valley but ended up fighting a vicious, unpredictable, highly kinetic war with inconsistent domestic support. It was here, as he came to the very end of his career, that Pete felt his joy turn sour leaving him with a sense of dirty dissatisfaction.

He was at Bagram airbase collecting ammunition and mail for the blokes when the siren rang and he knew, instantly, that it was his boys coming in by chopper.

The first Chinook arrived in a whirlwind of dust. The medics ran off with two stretchers trailing the bloody bandages and wrappings of an explosion. One female medic was holding a saline drip high in her hand. Pete watched it empty and the girl refit another on the run. The casualties went straight into the operating theatres followed by bin bags of body parts, some theirs, some belonging to others.

Out of the carnage only one casualty survived although he lost his arm at the elbow and was damaged in the head. Pete watched him arrive on a stretcher, lopsided, caked in blood. How he lived no one would ever know. They cut out a disk from his skull to reduce the pressure on the brain, put him into a medical coma, and flew him back overnight. His heart stopped twice on the twelve-hour journey. But he was alive when they got him to Queen Elizabeth's and it was a source of joy to everyone in the battalion when they heard, finally, that the young man, Steve Reedman, had woken up surrounded by his family. That was two and a half weeks after the bombing in the market square.

An officer was killed that day, bleeding out before the choppers arrived. Two soldiers were killed outright and every year, on the anniversary, Pete posted on Facebook to say he remembered them. They'd been his guys. They'd died on his watch. As Company Sergeant-Major it had been his job to keep them safe. He'd tried to. He'd really tried to. But he'd failed. And his failure dragged on him. It was a vast canopy of inadequacy from which he hung limp and helpless.

Four years after the tour one of the other blokes who'd been in the market square, a young reservist who Pete had stuck in the machine gun platoon because he was big and a bit simple looking, hanged himself at a veterans' hostel in London. He'd died alone, unwatched, unloved, with no one to talk to. No one who could say, "Mate, it's fine. We all go through it."

Pete had failed him too.

That morning, there'd been a call from Regimental Headquarters in Colchester. It was the Regimental Secretary, Ray Paulson. Paulie had been a role model for Pete for more than two decades.

"Hello Sir!"

"Hello Pete, how are you, mate?"

"Well, you know. Civvy, aren't I?"

Paulie laughed. They talked for thirty minutes, mostly about golf and motorbikes. But then Paulie changed the subject.

"Listen, Pete, I need to talk about the O'Hare case. Just want you to know, the regimental charity will cover your expenses if you have to go back to Belfast to make further statements. And we'll ensure you're safe, of course. We'll book you in somewhere. Palace Barracks, maybe. Or Thiepval. You'll be under guard in the Sergeants' Mess."

The call had been intended to reassure. What had once been a heroic act in the furnace of a Tyrone tour was now being treated by the press as another example of military excess, a suspicious muddle of partial truths badly brushed under the carpet of Operation Banner.

"Thanks, Paulie. I appreciate it," Pete said as the call ended. But the subsequent half hour saw him walk out of his door, into town, and directly to the bar in the Legion. He'd given a tenner to Pat behind the bar and asked her to change it.

And that was why he was standing in front of the gambling machine, looking at the buttons, watching the orange lights flash. He knew it wouldn't matter. But for one millisecond, the moment his finger felt the spring give, he was as virile as he had the first time he had thrown himself out of an aeroplane, yelling at the top of his voice: "One thousand, two thousand, three thousand. Check fucking canopy! Ya fucking beazer!"

Alexander, September 2017

From early childhood Alexander was certain that he belonged in power and knew that getting there required, above all else, voter recognition. He revelled in publicity but knew that with premium coverage came those who wanted to constrain his advances and limit his ambition.

Despite everything he did as Mayor for London, a back bench MP, and Foreign Secretary, certain sections of the liberal media only showed him bundling over a boy during a game of touch rugby, dangling from a zipwire waving a Union Jack, or being ridiculed on the TV quiz *Have I Got News For You* for offering to have a journalist beaten up. He overcame these attacks by looking avuncular, bumbling, and chummily laughing off any criticism. This became part of his charm. The attacks did not stop, however. The media were constantly seeking to trip him up, even at great cost to those who were never seeking to be in his, or their, way.

In 2016, a British-Iranian woman, Nazanin Zaghari-Ratcliffe, had been arrested and prevented from returning to her family in the UK. She was a project manager for the Thompson Reuters Foundation, a charity set up to ensure effective news transmission following disasters such as the Rwanda genocide or the Indian Ocean Tsunami. She had been in Iran with her daughter purely to visit her family for Nowruz.

The Iranian government believed Britain had owed it £400 million since the 1970s. This was true. At the time, Britain had agreed to sell Iran a division's worth of main battle tanks because the head of state, the Shah, was very much an anglophile. His removal in the Islamic Revolution of 1979 led to Britain cancelling the order and refusing to refund the money already received. America did the same for a similarly cancelled arms deal. This left Iran, an asset-rich but cash-poor country with powerful enemies on all sides (notably Israel and Saudi Arabia) to pursue its ends through the only means it had available: imprisoning foreign nationals until their cases were escalated to the level of political dialogue.

It took until 2016 for the United States to repay its $400 million in exchange for the release of four Iranian-Americans including a journalist from the Washington Post. Britain, however, did not repay what it owed. As a result, Nazanin Zaghari-Ratcliffe was imprisoned on charges of spying. She was periodically released, reimprisoned, and had her term extended. Her mental health deteriorated, thereby increasing the pressure on the British Government. Her husband, Mark, wanting only for his wife to be released, kept the issue in the public eye.

During his term as Foreign Secretary, Alexander was cornered by the liberal media demanding a comment on her case. Poorly briefed, he replied that it was totally absurd that she should be imprisoned as she had merely been teaching journalism. This statement was unfortunate as it served to legitimise her imprisonment in the eyes of the Iranian government and enabled them to extend her sentence in order to increase the pressure on him.

But he was not one to bow to pressure, either from the media or from foreign powers who acted in such despicable ways. Papers found later at 10 Downing Street dated September 2017 record that:

For Nazanin, dual nationality
Did not prevent her captivity.
The rag-headed Mullahs
Are demanding their moola
But one cannot approve such depravity.

The papers don't record that Nazanin Zaghari-Ratcliffe was finally released in 2022 after Britain repaid Iran the £400 million it owed.

Dean, November 2017

Michelle pulled out a chair to sit at the kitchen table. She placed her mug down and put a hand on Dean's arm. "What are you thinking, love?"

Dean took hold of her hand. She'd taken off her wedding ring to do the dishes and he rubbed her finger lightly with his thumb. The snow in the garden made the light sharp. Her hair, newly bleached, seemed to shimmer. He shook his head and shrugged. "I don't know. Do they both need to go?"

"To university?"

"Yeah..."

He leaned forward with his elbows on the table so his shoulders came up by his ears. He realised the implications of what he'd just said. "I mean, Vics is more clever. Elizabeth could do it, but..."

Michelle knew he was joking. She patted his arm again. "I could go back to work. Full time, I mean, not private clients. In a salon."

Dean thought about it. It wasn't a bad idea but he knew she preferred working independently. She earned nearly fifteen grand as it was.

"Now the girls are grown up, I don't *need* to be at home," she said.

The costs seemed to be mounting. Elizabeth had recently skidded in the snow turning into the drive. She hadn't been going fast but had stamped on the brakes causing the car to lock into a slide. The slope of the road, barely visible if you were walking, was enough for the car to crash through the boundary wall and it was amazing how little speed was required to twist the axle. The car would easily cost two grand, plus VAT, to fix.

"And we'll need another car. The girls will want one each. If we can afford the insurance. Can't we send them out to work?"

Michelle pulled a face, the corner of her mouth tickling into a knowing smile. "Elizabeth's already stacking shelves. Plus she has schoolwork. We just have to cut our cloth, Deano, that's all."

Dean looked at his hands. Both girls had him wrapped round their little fingers. He still had contacts on the circuit and could always get work overseas again. If GR didn't want him, one of the other big players would have him as a country manager. It didn't have to be Iraq. There was always things kicking off somewhere and whenever they did, journalists rushed out in their blue body armour, did a piece to camera, and went home again. And they always needed a CP team.

"I could give Cleggy a call," he mumbled. "He's going to Libya soon."

Michelle scratched her upper lip with an immaculate pink fingernail. "I don't want you going away, Deano. The girls need you."

He was glad she thought so. Though he missed the banter and the rush of it, and he certainly missed the four hundred a day, it was a boring and repetitive life. Long days with nothing to do but porn and weights. And he missed the girls' innocence and joyfulness; their giggling and impenetrable language.

"I could ask Billy if he has more work," he said.

"Billy?"

"The guy I do the driving for."

Her eyes dropped. "Is it legal, Deano? What you're doing?"

Dean didn't answer.

"He was on the news last night, you know. Been charged with racialist hate crime after throwing bottles at this guy outside court. I mean it was right outside the court! With all them cameras!"

Dean smiled. He'd got to know Billy and knew it was a carefully judged publicity stunt. The men he'd thrown a bottle at were all Muslims accused of abusing a white girl.

"Didn't hit them, did he?"

Michelle shook her head. "No, but he could of. And what he did made the case against them go out of court."

"It what?"

"Their lawyer. Said it was unfair so the judge threw the court out. And then Atkins got brought in. Contempt. Or something."

Dean hadn't seen the news but he'd somehow known Billy was up to something.

"Do you really have to work for that guy, Deano? He's…"

"He's what?"

"He's nasty, that's what he is."

Dean sat back in his chair. "No, he's a good bloke. It's just he says what other people think. All those grooming and rape cases? It's never a white man, is it?"

They rarely argued but Michelle's lips were pressed tightly together.

"I'm not saying he's wrong. I'm saying he's…"

"He's what?"

She shook her head, frustrated at being unable to find the words. "Dean, he's only after himself."

There was some truth in that, certainly. Dean had watched Billy at a demo in the town centre, surrounded by others, pointing and jeering at a line of patient police officers. There had been a parade outside the town hall against the level of hate crime. Billy and his gang had jeered the speakers. And the thing that tickled Dean was the fat bloke in the bomber jacket following Billy round, filming him.

"Maybe. But if I say I want work and he's got it, he'll give it me. He trusts me. Trusts me more than others, actually."

"Of course he trusts you, Deano. But that doesn't mean he *trusts* you. It just means the guys who hang around him..."

Ignoring her pleas, Dean picked up his phone and dialled. He had to tell Billy he couldn't get to London this weekend anyway since the car was out of action and he didn't want to use a work vehicle again. He looked at Michelle as the ring tone pulsed in his ear.

"Dean."

"Billy."

"What can I do for you, mate?"

Dean exhaled. "Mate, my car's out of action. One of the girls... it doesn't matter. I can't drive anywhere this weekend. Just thought you should know."

Billy said nothing then spoke with a gentle and very calm voice. "Thanks for letting me know, Dean. Very professional, that's what you are."

Dean looked at his wife. She had heard and looked away.

"So, I was wondering. Have you got anything more local?"

Dean was pleased with his words. It made him sound in control.

Billy was silent for a long time. Then he said, "I think there is something you could help with, Dean. In fact, I think there's something you'd be really good at. I'll call round to the office and talk to you there, ok? Tomorrow, about two?"

"Yes, mate, hundred percent." Dean said. "Fourteen hundred at Bolton's Yard. See you then."

Steve, November 2017

As Steve rounded the canteen at Orpheus House he saw Malcolm sitting at one of the dining tables near the TV. He was writing something with a pencil in a large notebook. He had one of those tablet computers propped open. It looked really cool and important. Steve had bought the latest iPhone with part of his payout – his present to himself to help him find work – but he'd stopped short of an iPad. He wasn't confident on how to use them and thought it would be a waste of money.

Malcolm looked up and immediately rose, extending first his right hand, then his left. "Steve, how are you?"

Steve smiled. In truth, he was a bit confused and uncertain. Although he'd had three interviews, none of them had led to a job offer and he didn't know why.

"I'm alright, yeah!" he said. "Do you want a brew? I'll get them this time."

Malcolm was grateful. He said he'd have a cup of tea and started putting his stuff away in a leather briefcase. Everything about him looked expensive and when Steve came back with the second mug from the counter, he said, "Do you need a driver or owt, Malcolm? I can be your bag carrier."

Malcolm smiled but shook his head. "I've got one," he said. "I've got a team of people, actually. I couldn't take you on even if I wanted to. But I'm here to help you get a job for yourself, Steve, that's what this is about, yeah?"

They traded small talk for a while. Malcolm had stopped off in Darlo on his way home to Newcastle. He'd get the next train and be home by ten. He'd have to work over the weekend because that was expected. "The long-haired general won't be pleased. Again."

"So it's not all slipper city being a civvie, is it?"

"No, Steve, it's not. In fact, I've learned more working for Delaine than I did in my last two years in the army."

Steve smiled as he looked at the floor. His shoulder ached from the driving.

"But we're here to talk about you, mate." Malcolm said. "The last time we spoke you said you wanted to be a case worker here at Orpheus, for *SoH*. We talked about it and we agreed that they were looking for people with a slightly more developed ability to use computers and make contacts in town councils, that sort of thing."

Steve knew Malcolm had spoken to Bronagh and Clive. That was expected. Officers should talk to each other to get to know their blokes and he remembered Malcolm – the blokes called him 'Gland' because he could trap any bird in a pub – as diligent and caring. He always put the blokes first.

But he was strict too. He was pushing Steve to see that he was never going to get a job in Orpheus House.

"I just want to help veterans," Steve said.

"But what is it about helping that matters, Steve? Or what is it about veterans, for that matter?"

Steve thought. "That were a good question," he said, his eyes following the lines of white tiles cross the floor.

Some veterans were worth the effort. Tanner, from the acting course, had become a good mate. And Bridget, who organised long-distance walks, was really cool and as fit as a badger.

But some were wankers, though. Jonny from the room next door would steal anything left unwatched. And Fib had finally been thrown out. They'd given him three chances but caught him lying about where he was and found marks on his arm.

"For example, if you're talking about helping people to grow, or develop, are there other sections of society you would be willing to support?" Malcolm said.

"Like who?"

Malcolm said nothing. He opened a hand in a gesture that passed the question back to Steve. "Do you mean kids? Or the homeless? Or old folk. I couldn't do them."

"I don't blame you," said Malcolm. "It's a particular skillset, that is. How is your mother, by the way. Not that she's elderly. But is she alright?"

Steve chuckled. "Yeah, she's ok thanks for asking. Still working at Lidl. Yeah, she's fine. Not met anyone but I'm in the house now so she's got me to cut the grass and fix stuff."

"So you're the man of the house?"

"I guess so."

The conversation died. Malcolm sat low in his chair, legs extended and arms folded across his body. Steve didn't know what was expected of him. "Are you waiting for me to say something?"

Malcom pulled himself up by pressing with both hands on the seat. "I'm trying to get you to define exactly what it is you want to do in life. Can we get beyond the statement that you want to help veterans?"

"Oh, right, yeah."

"The last time we met, you wanted to be a case worker. But we agreed you lacked the computer skills and you didn't like doing a full eight-hour shift. You got tired after a few hours."

The way Malcolm was talking did not sound insulting and Steve was thankful.

"Then you went for a job interview with the Lansdowne Trust. The place that did biking and canoeing for special needs kids. You got an offer but didn't turn up for work, is that right?"

"Yeah. I phoned them. It were the day before I were due to start. Gary his name were. I phoned him and said look, my mum's taken a turn. I'll be a couple of days late. And he said that was fine, thanks for letting him know. But when I went there, on the Wednesday, they said the job had been given to someone else. They didn't need me anymore."

Malcolm's jaw was clamped tight. "And then we talked about getting work experience with retail companies. Asda, Lidl. Your mother got you an interview?"

"Yeah. But I don't want to work at Lidl. Not if my Mum works there. It's a bit sad, isn't it? A man my age being given a job by his mother. It looks sad, doesn't it?"

He was smiling. He knew it was sad even though his mother said the other women got their kids work, all girls though.

"But what happened with Asda?"

He kept pressing. Steve had hoped he wouldn't keep asking but he did.

"I just don't want to do it, Malcy. I don't want to work in a shop. It's just..."

Malcolm was nodding. "It's just what?"

"It's just shit. It's just about money. And things. It's selling people things. It's not... it's not..."

"Meaningful?"

"Yeah, that's it. Sort of. It's just not important. Not like being a soldier is important."

Malcolm smiled, finally. "Ok, this is good. I'm sorry to labour this but I'm trying to get you to define for yourself what floats your boat. What would you really consider meaningful and ..."

"You know what?" interrupted Steve. "You know what would be meaningful for me, Malcolm?

"No, what's that?"

He sounded doubtful but Steve didn't know why. "I want to tell people my story. I want to be a public speaker."

Malcolm's mouth fell open. He was nodding but there was a hollow look in his eyes. "Ok, that's great, Steve. You want to be a public speaker. That's a great idea. Where did that come from?"

"It were from the acting course in London..."

"The *Best Foot Forward* programme? Was that it?"

"That were it. We did this thing on where we had to tell your story. Five minutes. Inspirational After Dinner Talker, that's what they said we were. Like Bear Grylls, or Fergie from ManU. Or one of them politicians who get paid thousands for just one night."

"So you'd like to be an after-dinner speaker?"

"Yeah, I would. I've a story. I've rehearsed it. Got it down to eight minutes now. It's all about resilience, Malcy. Resilience. That's the key."

Malcom leaned back in his chair and folded his arms. He looked at his watch. "OK. Let's talk about how we can make that work. What skills do you need to be a good after-dinner talker…"

Pete, November 2017

Pete was met off the plane at Belfast City by two plain-clothed PSNI officers who looked at their phones, at his face, and whispered his name. They drove him in an unmarked but armoured Ford to Thiepval Barracks in Lisburn and through the security gates as far as the Sergeants' Mess.

"They've sorted you out in there, mate, so they have. We're to collect you at nine tomorrow and get a statement from you in front of the lawyer at ten. Then we'll get you back to the airport, that ok?"

"I'll not say fuck all," Pete replied.

The driver looked at him in the rear-view mirror, chin lifted. He shook his head.

"I can't advise you on that, mate. All I can say, man to man, is I'm sorry you're here."

Pete looked at him in the mirror. He nodded. He knew this was just the taxi service so he got out, stretched, and watched the car spin round and drive away.

It was cold. The high cloud made the light soft. He watched soldiers and civilians walking from the offices back to their cars as though it was dinner break at a corporate mall. Things were different in his day. There'd been a bomb here in the mid-nineties. He'd known a guy who was injured. The place had looked different back then as this was where the Brigade headquarters had been. He'd been based at Palace Barracks for an entire tour and had done another six months in one of the shitty, high-walled camps in West Belfast. But it was the rural tour of South Tyrone that he remembered most clearly.

He looked at the door to the Mess. No one was there to meet him. He picked up his daysack and went inside, finding the staff were all civilians and no one was at the desk. There was an envelope on the lobby table with 'Donaldson Inquiry #1 night only' written on it. He found the room and sat on the bed, taking in the familiar furniture: the G-plan chair, the chest of drawers with an adjustable mirror, the sink in the corner. His back ached so he lay on the thin carpet tiles to stretch but the room was too narrow to do this easily.

As promised, his escorts met him the following day. He hadn't spoken to anyone throughout dinner, nor at breakfast. He left the key where he'd found it, on the table, but with the words 'Donaldson Inquiry' crossed out and his name and rank written in capital letters: WO2 PETE McCARDLE PARA.

The car took him to the Barrack Street entrance of the police station. He was escorted through security and into the main building where a desk sergeant offered him a coffee. He waited in the corner of an open plan office listening to the clacking of keyboards and ringing phones.

His solicitor finally appeared, flustered and red-faced. "Pete, very good to see you. I just made it. Flight was delayed. If you're ready, we can go now."

Pete rose and followed him to a boxy interview room. In it was a table at which sat a young man and woman. They glared at him and he met their gaze evenly, coldly.

They asked him what happened on that night in November 1993.

"No comment."

They asked him if he had placed a weapon in the deceased's hands.

"No comment."

They asked him if he had shot the victim in the back of the head and mangled the body to disguise an act of murder.

"No comment."

They asked him why he had perjured himself before the Donaldson Inquiry.

"No comment."

They asked him if he thought the British Government would continue to protect him.

"No comment," he said, then, "No comment" again.

Afterwards, he left the room. The man and the woman watched him leave and he felt no pity for them, no respect, no leniency. They were too young to have known what it was like. They were dredging up what should have been left to die. He was having none of it. The same icy hatred was still with him and he wasn't going to give himself up. O'Hare defended known criminals. If that wasn't a corrupt and evil thing to do, what was?

Looking out of the window of the narrow, twin-engined aeroplane, he spotted the giant yellow cranes at the edge of Belfast harbour and admired the shimmer of sunlight on the water.

"Fuck you," he muttered.

Kyle, previously

Char rang to make sure I was up. She knew I had an appointment at the doctors as I missed the last one and she said that was bad. They are only trying to help and if I don't turn up then other people can't have my slot and the doctor's time is wasted. I won't get charged for it but we shouldn't behave like that.

People say all sorts of things to me and it's like my head is in a bucket and all the sound is distorted. There's a constant humming that blocks out most of what people say. I can't concentrate.

So I'm in with the doctor and he tells me to sit down and roll up my sleeve. He takes my blood pressure and pulse and oxygen levels and says that the BP is a little high for my age but within normal range.

He says, "How have you been feeling with the last prescription?" and I say it's fine. It takes away the pain during the day. I'm not hyper.

He says, "And what about the night-time. Are you sleeping?"

I shake my head. No, not really. I get these really fucking vivid dreams.

He's a Paki, or an Indian, but he doesn't flinch when I swear. His face is very dark and thin and serious and he has this put-put-ding-ding accent and a way of shaking his head that's kind of funny.

"What sort of dreams?" he asks.

So I tell him. I dream about the blokes. And this cloud, this thing, this obligation. And everyone is shouting at me but I don't want to do it. But they're shouting at me and I don't know what to do. But this cloud gets nearer, and nearer, and darker, and it's really fucking scary and soon it's going to smother me. And if I don't do something about it it's going to kick off and the blokes are going to get hurt. And if I do it'll be me that gets hurt. And it'll be my fault whatever.

And you know what, right? The dream makes me really fucking angry. I'm trapped and I'm scared and there's nothing I can do to stop this thing, whatever it is. It's just there, coming towards me, day after day, and nothing I can do will stop it. Why me? Why do I have to be the one? Why was I sent there? You asked me to do this. Why don't you sort it out?

I know I volunteered. But that was to fight a war. Not to get told to kill kids or bag up the lacerated meaty red remains of them. What was all that about? We were told it was to stop drugs getting into the supply train. We were told it was to promote democracy. And help women live proper lives not be slaves. But it wasn't about that, was it? It was so politicians could say they was doing something. That they was brave. That they was big men.

I have to stop then as I'm sweating and the doctor's leaning back in his chair. It's not his fault.

I'm not crying when I tell him. Usually when I wake up in the night I am. But this time I'm not. I just tell him because I took the pills this morning and I'm numb.

He types on his computer. I can see by his face he

don't really understand the terror of my dreams and I'm wondering if this is doing any good, whether it would be better if he spends his time helping old ladies or little kids.

But then he says, "I think we need to refer you to a specialist consultant, Mr Hutton. We should get you assessed for PTSD, which is the most likely cause of your symptoms right now. Do you know what PTSD is?"

Of course I fucking do.

He nods. He knows I know. "Well I think you need to see someone who can explain the treatment options we have available through the NHS. There are all sorts of remedies that will help with your attention span issues and your recurring nightmares. A psychologist is best placed to explain what these are."

I think that's a breakthrough and at the same time I'm thinking why has it taken you so long? PTSD? Former soldier? No shit Sherlock.

"Are you working at the moment?" he asks.

I shake my head. Char's managed to get me on Universal Credit. I don't get fuck all from the army, though. But the SSAFA guy has referred me to Save Our Heroes and I spoke to a woman in Catterick, Irish voice. Brona something, who said she would help get me processed.

"If you have a diagnosis, it might help you get a war pension," the doctor says.

I stare at the plastic bit of vertebra on the far end of his desk. There are nerves and blood vessels coming out through the gaps and one is red and the other is blue. In reality they are both shiny, glistening, sticky. The fat around them is white and smells yucky.

Outside it's really hot. I'm sweating as I walk home because I'm wearing a parka, a thick one. It helps me feel safe.

Dean, January 2018

It said in the papers that the number of rough sleepers had doubled due to the government's austerity cuts. Dean shivered in his car. The snow was still falling and now lay four inches deep along the brick wall on the opposite side of the road. If people were choosing to stay out in this weather they must be hard as fuck. Or mental. Or really, really hard up. This was the third time he'd pulled a watch on the backstreet mosque, which Billy was paying him to do. Not much, just fifty quid an hour, but it was work that Billy wanted doing and something Deam found easy to do. This wasn't anything like what he had to do on the recce course. This was just sitting in a car and noting what he saw.

The mosque wasn't a grand building, with towers and domes like the one in the town. It was a terrace house in a quiet residential street. The walls were painted white and there was a sign in English and Arabic above one of the windows. It didn't look like anyone was in.

One advantage of the weather was that the snow was covering the windscreen so that no one could see his outline. But as it piled deeper, the area through which he could see was shrinking. He had lifted the seat upright but very soon it would be fully covered and then he'd have to wipe it off, and that would mean compromising the position. He could drive away and then back, parking somewhere else in the street, but that would be risky, as much from the snow as from people clocking him sitting there.

It would be a shame to move. He had been pleased to get this spot by the allotments opposite the mosque. It gave him an excellent view of the entrance and up the hill along the line of terraces. When he first parked up there had been some comings and goings in the houses. The residents were all Muslims in long-tailed shirts and baggy trousers. But why not, he wondered? It was Saturday night, the 6th of January. They were entitled to celebrate New Year as much as anyone. But he agreed with Billy. There was too many of them.

When he'd tried to take Elizabeth to the doctor after she hit the garden wall, every one of the men in the waiting room was wearing a hat like *Citizen Khan* on the telly, or a pakul like Terry Taliban. The women were veiled, a habit that made Dean intensely suspicious.

Billy had asked him to put a watch in on the mosque for a few nights. Different days, different times. Two hundred quid for a few hours. He said he wanted a feel for who goes in and who comes out. Does anyone live there? What's the security like?

Dean had said, "Sure, no sweat, hundred percent."

He had now been sitting in the car for four hours. His feet were freezing and his exhaled breath was condensing on the inside of the windscreen. It would be hard to make a quick getaway if someone knocked on the window. He would never have made this mistake in Northern Ireland, not after those two corporals got killed.

He shivered and hugged himself. The gritter had been up and down Moseley Road but had not yet turned up this street. That meant any escape would have to be done through four inches of fresh snow. It wouldn't take much to slide into one of the parked cars and set the alarm off.

While he had been watching, no one had gone into or come out of the mosque itself. The lights were off. There were no cameras and the nearest streetlight was out. It had no more security than your average house. And from his previous night's watch there was a bathroom window round the corner, in the alleyway, that might be prised open.

Dean shook his head. Enough for today. No one else in the English Templars would have stayed so long or been as observant.

That was the gang Billy said he ran. *The English Templars*. Under the radar, low-key agitators doing dirty work to keep the town safe, keep it pure.

It was a shit name. No, it was a great name. He just wasn't sure it would live up to the billing. He was a knight. He was a warrior. Were the others?

Back in the day he would have remained watching for another four hours. On that tour of Tyrone, when they'd shot the lawyer, he'd been in a long-term observation post for three days and being a junior soldier at the time he'd been given the shit stags in the middle of the long, freezing nights.

But he wasn't a crow anymore and this wasn't Northern Ireland. It had the feel of Billy thinking up things to keep people busy so he could gob off about them. Up to him, of course. Dean would take his money if he was giving it away. But there was nothing happening right now and he could always swing by in the morning, walking fast with hood pulled down, to see if there were tracks by the doorway.

Alexander, February 2018

The secession negotiations between the European Union and the United Kingdom were complex in both content and process. Almost all UK law reflected European Union legislation at a structural level. It ensured customer protection for everything from the bearings in car wheels to the sugar content of ice cream, from the origin of bananas to the safe routing of air traffic. Leaving the Union forced the British establishment to evaluate not only what the law stated but how laws were made. Were they the prerogative of the government, who represented the electorate, or the courts, who would enforce them?

In January, after a year and a half of wrangling, the British Supreme Court insisted that it was necessary for the government to debate leaving the European Union. Due to the ever more complex implications, the 2016 referendum was not sufficient on its own.

This decision threw Members of Parliament into paroxysms of fear. They would have to decide whether to vote according to their personal consciences or honour the electorates they represented. All the while, the ghost of Jo Cox hovered over them.

Whatever deal was struck with the European Union, it had to apply to the entirety of the UK, including the

Province of Northern Ireland. The issue was that Northern Ireland shared a land border with the Republic of Ireland, a European state. European Union negotiators were adamant that any deal would need to prevent smuggling or the exploitation of national advantage. In short, Britain had to be prevented from exporting lamb through Ireland in case it would disadvantage French farmers.

Even if Alexander did not care about Northern Ireland, the negotiators were painfully aware that politics in the Province was a simmering, tribal affair easily capable of returning to armed conflict. A fundamental pillar of the Anglo-Irish Agreement of 1985 was the tacit acceptance that the border between the North and the South may exist in principle but should not exist in practice. By 2018, all military patrols, police checkpoints, and customs searches were a distant memory. People both north and south of the border moved freely in either direction. The island of Ireland enjoyed all the trappings of a united country but with two administrative systems. As a result, loyalist and republican terrorism faded from the headlines. Investment poured in. Black cabs took tourists to photograph the murals of West Belfast. Weapons were destroyed. And a vast exhibition about the Titanic was erected in the former Harland and Wolff shipyard.

This posed a simple but intractable problem for the British government. Either it accepted the need for a hard border, thereby risking a return to 'The Troubles', or it accepted that Northern Ireland should have different trading rules from the rest of the United Kingdom. The border would be, effectively, in the Irish Sea. The Loyalist community would be abandoned to what they saw as Papistry and foreign meddling of the sort they had fought against since the Battle of the Boyne over 300 years previously.

In short, it was either *Brexit means Brexit*, or the *United Kingdom means the United Kingdom*.

At this point, Alexander's unequalled ability to hold two opposing views at the same time proved essential. He wrote to May stating that Northern Ireland would have to accept border controls and that trade would not be adversely affected. At the same time, he met Arlene Foster, leader of the Democratic Unionist Party, at a country house near Liverpool. There, he swore never to create anything that would, in any way, recognise a difference between Northern Ireland and Great Britain. As always, his charm won her over.

Papers found later at 10 Downing Street dated February 2018 record that:

> Foster is ugly and obstinate. Legs like a billiard table. Voice like an angle grinder honing a plough blade. In ancient times she would have been a Spartan warrior in the front rank at Thermopylae. Which is rather where I wish she were right now. But if I tell her that a border in the Irish Sea is a moral, practical, and theoretical absurdity, she will believe me.

Dean, March 2018

The Albion was on the other side of town from where Dean worked. It was easy to find, a shitty pub on the edge of a shitty estate. The damaged sign was a soldier in a red coat bearing an unfurled Union Jack into battle. It reminded Dean of an *Iron Maiden* album cover. There was also a wind-torn, faded flag hanging from a pole by the front door. Dean was relieved to see it was the right way up.

Billy's delivery van was parked on the unpaved patch of ground to the side. Dean drew up next to him, bouncing over the potholes. Once he'd got out, he looked around, checked the car was locked, checked again, then went inside.

The inner door swung open to a dark, thick beamed room. The floor was noisy and worn. The bar had underlighting behind the optics and hanging glasses. A gambling machine flashed orange and yellow but made no sound. A dart board. No one around.

"Dean."

Billy was round the corner at a small, copper topped table. He had a pint of lager and a cigarette, which looked odd after the smoking ban. "What do you want?"

Dean shook his head. "Driving, mate. I'm on site this afty."

Billy looked tired. There were dark rings under his eyes and his face was puffy. His gold necklace was caught over the neckline of a company sweatshirt.

"You on stag last night at the mosque?"

Billy looked at him with unfocused eyes. "No, mate. Too much else on. Someone was though. One of us. A Templar. I like to keep eyes on the place. The police don't care. They're too scared. Too liberal. They daren't say what needs to be said. These Pakis are a scourge. They're all over town. Running it. Ruining it, mate!" He gathered his breath. "But I do. I care. And men like you care too, Dean, I know you do."

Dean took a stool, folded his arms, and leaned back against the window shutter. It was starting to rain and that wasn't a bad thing. It would wash away the slush and soot-stained ice gathered on the street corners.

He was becoming sceptical. He hadn't met anyone else from the Templars, only Billy. And though Billy was obviously the boss – he'd been interviewed on national radio about crime in the town – Dean still thought he was a dick. He agreed with much of what Billy said but he wasn't the leader he pretended to be. He liked having lackies around him, and lackies made Dean uncertain.

"I can see you're having doubts, Dean."

"Just not sure about what I'm doing," Dean said.

He couldn't quite voice his thoughts. Why should he, a former Colour-Sergeant in Her Majesty's finest, spend his nights watching a backstreet mosque that was no more threatening than a newsagent? Was he there to instil professional capability into Billy's pathetic little gang? Was it to show off? Was it to make a name for himself?

"Dean, Dean. Listen." Billy turned to face him and leaned on his elbows. He lowered his voice. "Listen, mate. We need you. It's nearly time. I've got most of the evidence I need. I just need a couple more bits, then we've got a case."

"For what?"

"A case. A solid case. We can prove that mosque is at the centre of a grooming gang."

"Fuck off."

"Dean. Seriously. Listen. That mosque. Just off Moseley Road? There's girls in there that shouldn't be there. I mean Latvians. Russians. Ukrainians."

Dean frowned.

"Mate. I saw them myself. Saw them go in. Got out of the back of a Luton and got dragged inside, six of them at least. Two men pushing them around. I tell you mate, that place is at the heart of it."

"So why didn't you go to the police?"

Billy shook his head and started drawing shapes on the tabletop with the curved corner of a bar mat. "Mate, I told you. They don't want to know. And if we rang them they'd do a raid and the cover would be blown. All that work. All your work. Those hours, watching. The police would waste all that effort. They're riddled with spies. They have to recruit from the local population, don't they? So they're like, seventy percent Muslim. So no operation is ever secure, is it?"

He tapped Dean's elbow with the back of hand. "You know all about that stuff. Operational security."

"OpSec."

"Exactly! As soon as the police plan anything the boys in the mosque know about it and get the girls out. Spread them about. And they stick together, these Pakis, don't they? They never behave like Englishmen."

Dean thought again of asking Billy about his father's surname but didn't. They guy wanted to pretend, so let him. And there was always the sense that he might suddenly explode. He was one of those tempestuous little fuckers. Though Dean knew he could handle him there was always the possibility of getting a blind punch.

A woman appeared behind the bar, looked over at them both, then turned away when Billy nodded at her, tipping his pint and stubbing out his fag in the glass ashtray.

"Anyway," said Billy. "With the Russians poisoning that geezer in Salisbury the plod are too busy. It's the big stuff they're after, not girls. And you've got girls, haven't you, Dean? How would you like it if one of yours got taken by a Paki?"

He realised immediately he was going too far.

"Mate. Joke. Joke, ok? But listen. I'm sure of it. That mosque is the base and we're going to prove it. Blow it out. So the council can't say they didn't know."

Dean exhaled heavily. "We'll see," he said.

Later that evening Dean got a picture of what Billy had meant. He was on the local news having been charged with contempt for disrupting the court case a few months before. The footage showed him walking into court with a confident swagger and a stern face. Journalists shouted questions at him. He looked calm and composed. Behind him, his gang of heavily built lackies carried a large Union Jack between them, chanting: *"Billy! Billy! Billy!"*

"I hope you're not still involved with that creep," Michelle said, nudging Dean with her elbow.

Dean said nothing. He didn't want to be told what to do. He was a free agent. And where did she think the money was coming from?

Pete, March 2018

Pete sat in the dark living room of his bungalow with the blinds drawn. The cars coming round the corner of the road outside threw beams of light against the window which rose and slid by. He had sold most of the furniture and the space now seemed devoid of purpose. The only things he had retained were his record player and the boxes of vinyl he was keeping for a collector. He nibbled his lips, a habit he knew was getting worse.

Sveta's lawyer had sent a note advising of a restraining order. There were three messages on his phone, all from the loaders on his team asking if he could repay the money they'd lent him.

He'd known it was wrong when he did it. You didn't screw your own blokes. But he was out now and that somehow made it allowable.

There was nothing left in his account. He'd made it to the last week of the month but he'd had to eat at the staff canteen at lunch times, glad that one of the functions of middle age was that he didn't need more than one meal. Unless he started drinking. The bottle of Glen Aldi was on the counter in the kitchen but he hadn't opened it yet.

He'd spent the past half an hour filling in a form on the internet. He knew the key facts were that he had a job and owned a house. That's what they wanted and he bluffed the stuff about his outgoings.

Afterwards, when he'd pressed 'submit', he felt sick. But it wasn't terror. He knew how to control that. And it wasn't the sickness of effort. That was something to be proud of, a sign that he'd worked hard. This was self-hate, an experience he'd never had before.

When the phone rang, his hands shook as he answered it.

"Mr McCardle?"

"Yes."

"Could you confirm your date of birth and post code?"

"30th of March 1971. Delta-delta one-one two bravo-alpha."

The line was silent for a moment. His breath was high in his chest. His heart thumped.

"I'd like to confirm that your loan has been approved. The money should be transferred to your account within the next hour. Is there anything else I can help you with today?"

"No," Pete said. "Cheers very much. Bye."

Kyle, previously

I'm in my flat watching TV. It's about six in the morning and I've been up a long time. I made myself a slice of toast and a brew and sat in the sofa. Thought about cracking one out as it usually helps when I can't sleep or I'm stressed but I can't be bothered.

So I turn on the telly and every channel has the same story. There's this little kid lying face down on a beach in Turkey. He's wearing a red shirt and blue shorts and he's face down in the sand with his bum in the air. At first I thought that kid's crashed something proper. Flaked out. But he's not asleep.

And when I look at him, I wonder why no one has covered his body. Why are the cameras just taking pictures?

There's this red line of writing underneath the picture. It says the boy drowned trying to get from Turkey to Greece in a little boat and there was like, way too many people on board so the boat collapsed and this little kid got swept back onto the beach but he couldn't swim so he drowned.

And I'm thinking why did he try to cross? Why did his family take him across the sea in a fucking dinghy at fucking night? Surely it can't be that bad. Surely it can't be so bad where they live that they take a little kid, his shorts just reaching below his knees, out in a rowing boat like the ones you see at the seaside.

I can't move. I'm in the two-seater sofa at the end of the kitchen. I'm like pinned to the back of it, sitting upright, legs straight out in front of me. I'm pushing the TV away with my feet but it's only the carpet moving. I change the channel but when I do it's the same image only this time it's worse. The camera is closer, or from an angle where you look at the boy's face and you can see his shoulder and the right side of his face are buried in the sand. There's water pooling in front of his chest and by his mouth and his left arm is extended towards his knee as his bum is in the air. The palm faces up and the little fingers are curled.

That could be little Dan. He's chubby and little and has the same colour hair and then the father comes on telly. He's surrounded by people with cameras and he's crying and shouting and ashamed and relieved and afraid and I can see all of this in his face.

Only he knows what happened on that boat. Only he knows how he entered the water. How he tried to save the little boy's life but couldn't. How he tried to save his own life and did.

So I'm saying, no, no, no and there's this banging in my head. So I put my hands over my ears and keep my lips tight shut and still there's this banging. It won't stop. And someone is shouting my name. My name. They're calling for me. It's not the television. It's someone real. And it's not Gaz or Ginge or Stu or Lucky Si.

I'm still then, listening. It starts again and I realise it's the front door. So I get up and go to it and there's the two students from the flat upstairs; an Indian boy who's unshaven, curly hair, black tee-shirt and his girlfriend who's quite pretty but has really bad acne.

The boy is like bent a bit, standing back from the door, arms extended towards me. He says they could hear me shouting. Was I ok? Did I need anything? And I realise I must have been louder than I thought I was. There's blood on my knuckles on the right hand. The left hand is ok but there are splinters of wood in the skin. I look at the boy and the girl and they take another step backwards.

The boy says, "It's ok, we're going now, stay calm, we're going," and he backs away more towards the stairs pushing the girl behind him.

I'm actually really sorry for them. They're nice. Always smiling. I didn't mean to frighten them and I can see I have.

But when I close the door there's this little kid on the telly and I think I put him there. He drowned because of me.

Dean, May 2018

They'd chosen a Wednesday because the place would be empty between the last prayer time and sunrise the following day. They only needed an hour to break in, find evidence, and get out.

Before the raid, Billy sat tense and fidgety in the passenger seat, staring down the road with his eyebrows clamped in a hard frown. He nibbled his lips.

Dean felt at ease. He understood the intensity of waiting, the mental preparation. He sat in the driver's seat, shoulders relaxed, keeping an eye on what was down the road as well as behind using the side mirrors. By zero-two-hundred there'd been no movement except for the last buses and a police car on Moseley Road.

"Ready?" Dean asked.

Billy played with his bottom lip. Dean wondered if he was looking for a way out. This wasn't filming yourself jeering at defenceless libtards. This was criminal.

Billy said, "I don't think the girls are there. Not anymore. But there may be passports. Identity cards. Names. I want to find something…"

He obviously believed what he was saying. Dean was here because he was trusted. The only one he trusted, given they were alone and that was enough for Dean to see the truth of it. Billy's little gang, The English Templars, were a bunch of fat, clumsy, and dipstick stupid wankers. Dean was the only one with the nerve and skills to do this.

Billy said nothing as he picked up the crowbar from by his feet and got out. In the cold air, Dean pulled down the peak of his cap and drew the string of his hood tight under his chin. They wore gloves and Dean also strapped on knee pads while they were in the car. Billy had looked at them, frowning.

"You'll find out why," Dean said.

In the silent night they walked side by side down the pavement, keeping their faces hidden. They'd parked a good distance up the hill so the number plate would not be picked up by any cameras in the immediate area. Dean had left his phone at home and hoped Billy had too. They didn't speak and Dean took an occasional glance behind feeling like he was on patrol in West Belfast.

A fox nimbly leaped a low garden wall, looked at up them, and sauntered away with its nose to the ground and thin legs padding quickly. Dean liked foxes and had often watched them in the desert, all ears and big feet. They brought luck.

Some way off, a police siren seemed to be coming their way but went quiet. A light came on in a top floor window across the street. Dean kept walking. He was enjoying the excitement of being on an arrest operation again. His heart thumped and he breathed deeply into his stomach.

The mosque comprised the end two properties of a brick terrace. There was a wide parking area to the side of the building onto which a single ground floor window looked out. He had been right about luck coming with the fox. A delivery van parked near the wall provided good cover.

Billy muttered to himself, "Paki cunts."

Dean said nothing. With a glance down the side street opposite the mosque, and a quick check behind, he nipped into the parking area, pulling Billy with him.

The window was locked on the inside. Billy pulled the crowbar from his jacket and handed it to Dean. Dean felt along the edges of the window for any weak points. It was a modern, double glazed unit with mottled glass. There would be the toilet inside but they just needed to get in and open the main door.

He felt no tension, just eagerness. Billy, too short to reach the window, stood gawping behind him. Dean flicked his head towards the street. Billy nodded, realising what Dean wanted him to do. He went to the front of the van and keep look out, glancing up and down the street.

Dean shook his head. Too obvious, too visible, his clothing standing out against the white wall. Fuckwit.

But he had his own role to play. The window was a good one, that was certain. A black rubber seal was pressed between the window and the frame. There would be lever locks inside the uprights. The only real way to do this was to tease out the beading round the glass panel but the crowbar was too thick for the job. They needed a stripping knife, or a Stanley. Dean thought of the contents of his tool kit in the shed. Nothing he had with him would provide enough leverage.

He clicked his tongue. Billy didn't turn round so he did it again. He still didn't turn round, so Dean hissed through his teeth. Billy turned, one elbow raised.

"What?"

Dean put a finger over his lips. He mimed leveraging out the window with the crowbar and waggled his finger. Billy seemed to be following.

With a frown of frustration Dean took hold of the crowbar with both hands. Bracing his feet on the tarmac, he smacked the curved end as hard as he dare against the bottom of the window. The bar bounced back with a force that took him by surprise. It jarred his shoulder. He inspected the glass but it was completely unmarked. The sound of the strike hung in the darkness like a bell tolling.

Dean shook his head at Billy. They weren't getting in this way. Billy nodded and reached inside his jacket to pull out a tin of spray paint. In rushed letters he wrote RAPING SCUM on the wall between the window and the corner. The paint smelled of alcohol and Billy coughed before covering his mouth with his arm.

"What is the meaning of this?"

An old man in a brown shalwar kameez stood on the pavement. He raised both hands in the air and dropped them against his thighs before raising them again. His beard was grey and untidy. He looked upset more than angry.

"What are you doing?" he demanded. "What do you think you are doing?"

Dean and Billy looked at each other. Billy hurled the paint can at the old man, who raised his elbows to protect his face. Dean darted round the parked van. When he came level with the road, Billy had the old man by the shirt, punching him on the side of the head. The old man's legs buckled.

"Oh my God! Oh no!"

Billy hit him again on the cheek. The man whimpered and rolled on his back. A leather slipper fell off one foot.

Dean crossed the road glancing left and right. They couldn't return straight to his car as that would draw attention to it. Instead, he ran down the side road to the next street. He could hear Billy's footsteps behind him but kept going, increasing the pace.

He was angry. There was no need to hit the old man. They should just have legged it.

At the end of the side street he turned uphill along a parallel road. He could hear Billy laughing behind him. He was a liability, Dean thought. Got high on the blood rush.

As the hill steepened, Dean slowed and stopped by a streetlight. Behind him Billy had one hand on his chest.

Dean smirked. When Billy got to him, he grabbed his arm and pulled him along. "Keep moving. Just walk."

Billy's breathing was fast and shallow. Dean felt fine although drenched in sweat. His feet swept along at a fast, even pace. At the sound of a siren he looked behind. A small car sped by on Mosely Road followed by a police car. That was good. The cops were busy with other things.

"If we turn right here, we should be back at the car. We'll drive off as though nothing's happened. When we pass the mosque, don't look in."

Billy nodded. He leaned forward to put his hands on his knees but Dean pushed him onwards. "Keep moving."

There was no one at the car. No lights, no movement. Dean slipped quickly in the driver's side and started the engine. Billy fell into the passenger seat lifting his legs in one by one. They looked at each other. Dean turned to put the crowbar on the floor behind Billy. If they were stopped he didn't want that found. He was angry but didn't know how to express it. He should have known Billy would do something like that.

"What's the matter?" Billy was smiling and nervous at the same time.

"I'll tell you later."

Dean said nothing more. He drove off quietly, keeping the speed down. The way out took them past the mosque so he said, "Don't look," Dean repeated but Billy did anyway.

"Nobody there. But a light's on inside," Billy said in a high, excited voice.

Dean turned left onto Moseley Road. He took the next right and then drove in a vague way towards the motorway before returning via the country roads to the Albion. Billy coughed into his hand and sat straight in his chair with his head tilted back. His breathing was laboured.

"You having a heart attack?"

"Asthma."

Dean said nothing but drove carefully, watching the speed limit. A hundred meters from the pub he pulled into the side and put the car out of gear.

"We should do a hot debrief on that," he said. He thought they'd been unprepared, undrilled, uncoordinated. Amateurs. Why did Billy have to batter the old man? What was a minor affray was now GBH. This wasn't professional. This was shit stupid.

But Billy had regained his breath. He grinned with a cruel edge to his voice. "That was fucking great, wasn't it!" he said.

Alexander, June 2018

As the negotiations between the United Kingdom and the European Union stumbled over the intractable problem of the Irish border, the Office for National Statistics published a forecast that the country would face the worst growth since records began. In ten years, the country would be £500 billion worse off. Growth had declined by 8% on the previous year. Interest had risen to 5%, putting millions of domestic mortgages under increased pressure. The *British Medical Journal* stated that the government's austerity policy had led to 120,000 unnecessary deaths. The facilities management company Carillion, responsible for a host of public sector contracts, collapsed with debts of £1.5m.

Wanting to push the European negotiators towards a favourable deal, Alexander had to play his trump card. He floated the idea of a 'Hard Brexit' in which the United Kingdom would leave without a deal and refuse to pay for anything. This caused immense concern to businesses on all sides of the debate. How could they plan cash flows, investments, contracts, or supply chains if they didn't know the rules under which they would be operating?

Alexander was unconcerned. This was a matter of principle and his steel had to shine through. Responding to media questions about the impact of Brexit on corporations, he replied: "Fuck business".

Dean, July 2018

"It looks like Mount Longdon up here, doesn't it, with all the rocks?" said Dean, standing on the limestone pavement and scanning round in all directions. To the north, rocky gullies gave way to expansive grassy moorland that dropped into a deep ravine. To all other sides the land fell away from the outcrop to bogs of bracken and baby-head tussock grass. A curlew whistled as it rode the wind. The sky was clouding over and it would rain soon. "This is about as much cover as we'll find. We could camp here."

They had trudged up from Malham, round the cove and along the valley to the Tarn. Keeping north, they left the tourist walks to strike out across the limestone pavement even though it was slippery and awkward, then north-east past a farm and a disused barn draped with verdant, spongy moss. Finally on the high ground, they'd found a well in a limestone outcrop and hunkered down. They'd made good time at first, easily passing the civvies and fogeys, but then they'd slowed into a steady walking pace and stopped for a brew.

Out of the wind, Pete was completely at ease, sitting on a roll mat, leaning against his old bergen. He was using a gas cooker to boil water in an oblong, military issue mess tin. He said, "You know, I went Down South once, with B Company. When I was a platoon sergeant. Fucking amazing battlefield tour."

For both men, the Falklands had been instrumental in making them want to join. Most of their careers had been spent hoping for the chance to prove themselves equal to the men who fought there. And then Afghan happened and everyone got as much war as they could wish for.

Dean stepped carefully down from the polished rocks using his hand for balance. There had been several weeks of hot, dry, airless days so it was typical that it should rain on the one day they had fixed to go camping. "If it ain't raining, it ain't training. We could go down into the next valley for better cover. There's a forestry block about an hour away."

Pete crossed his feet and looked up at the sky. "I'm happy here," he said.

Dean sat against a block of limestone. "Me too. And it's a good walk out in the morning. Down through Gordale."

Pete nodded. While the water heated, he bent one leg and pressed the knee down to the side, forcing his thumbs deep into the muscle tissue.

"Hips?" said Dean.

Pete nodded. "Agony, pal. Fucking agony."

Dean said nothing as he pulled his food bag out of his rucksack. Unlike Pete still using his military bergen, Dean had a fitted, light blue rucksack with lots of straps and buckles. The nylon fabric was thin but strong and he liked the way the drinking tube could be fed over the shoulder strap. He sucked at the teat then closed the top cover and placed it behind his back. Since he had a box of them in the garage, he'd brought an issued hexamine stove rather than a gas cooker.

Pete chuckled. "How many have you got left?"

"About fifty. Do you want one?"

Pete shook his head, laughing. "No. I'm cooking on gas the now. No so much weight. And the smell, you know?"

Dean nodded, grinning. There was nothing so evocative of living in the field as the smell of hexamine and nothing so redolent of barracks as the smell of burning polish when the blokes were bulling their boots for a parade.

"I saw you in the paper again," Dean said after a while. "Well, Michelle did, actually. There was all this royal wedding, Harry and Megan stuff, and then there's you. You in court again?"

Pete dropped a teabag into a brushed aluminium mug. "It's never ending, pal. They've sold me down the swanny. One minute they promote you and the next you're a pawn in the peace process. I'm sick of it."

Dean met his eyes. "If you want me to say something, I will. You know that..."

Pete waved him to silence. "No. It'd only make things worse."

His water started bubbling. He watched the bubbles rise for a while then lifted the mess tin in a gloved hand to pour the water out of the corner into the mug, his actions practised, fluid. He touched the cooker lightly to test how hot it was, disconnected the canister, then folded everything away into the mess tin, padding it out with a stained bar mat to stop it rattling.

With the brew kit stowed, he picked up his tea and rested it on his thigh. "It's like those fires. In Manchester. Some stupid fucker has a barby, sets the peat ablaze, and legs it. The fire service do what they can. They're in full kit with the wagons and choppers and everything. But their union won't allow them to work more than eight hours, so they go home and just leave the fire blazing. So who do they call to put the fires out?"

"The army," Dean replied.

Pete nodded. "No kit. Wearing combats. No masks. A 1940s green goddess fire engine. Days on end. Some poor fucking private from the local infantry unit smashing the heather with a bit of rubber tyre on a broom handle. It's shit."

Dean had had the same thought. At first, he'd felt admiration that the army was once again stepping up to the plate. But then he felt it was not being used so much as abused. The wildfires had continued to spread across Saddleworth, Ilkley, Bangor. The news showed tumescent plumes of dense smoke billowing over scorched gorse. The images made people think of war and the fact that the army had been brought in, just as it had with Foot and Mouth, the flooding, and the Olympics, emphasised the idea.

"So are you going back to court?"

Pete shrugged. "Don't know. My lawyer lets me know if I'm needed. I'll say fuck all. They'll only use it against me."

Dean agreed. As he put his cooking equipment away a Swaledale ewe appeared on the rocks above him and bleated loudly, making him jump. He knocked his mug over spilling boiling water on his shin.

"Jesus!" he said, then "Ow! Bastard!"

The animal bleated again, ragged tufts of grey wool hanging off its shoulders. It watched the men with an unwavering glare, then bent its back legs to piss.

"Fuck off," Dean shouted.

Pete laughed, leaning back on his bergen with one hand on his belly.

Dean picked up his mug and put it to the side, then heaved himself up to standing. The ewe stamped its forefoot then turned and ran across the rocks, the ragged fleece trailing.

"Twat," Dean said as he brushed his leg down.

As he sat again, Pete was still chuckling. "So what's this about you joining the Rotherham black shirts?"

Dean glanced at him as he settled back down in the same place.

"Mate, I'm Rotherham born and bred, you know that. It's not about racism. It's about the crime. It's always the Muslims, mate. Always. Car theft, rape, grooming. Driving. And I'm doing something about it, that's all."

Pete studied him but said nothing more. They'd known each other so long, and been through so much, they didn't have to talk.

"Be careful, Swampy. If you get arrested, they'll crucify you. *Ex-PARA joins neo-Nazis?* Doesn't matter if it's not true. That's what it'll look like. Trust me."

Dean didn't look up. Pete had always been politically astute. That's why he'd been awarded the Queen's Warrant while Dean only made it to Colour-man. Of the two of them, he was always the first to start punching.

"My town, mate. It's my town. Just me and Billy's doing things about it."

"Billy Atkins?"

"Yep. Known him since school. Used to follow me round like a little puppy."

"The guy on the telly? Always yakking on about Pakis and Arabs."

"Yeah, him."

Pete shook his head. "Swampy, you've been taking too many juicing pills. He'll get you fucking jailed."

Dean stared at the rocks. He was disappointed Pete didn't get it. A protruding fern wafted in the breeze. The scent of sheep piss reminded him of cheese.

"It's not that bad, alright? It's men doing shit about crime in their hometown. A good town. A white, working-class town. Or it was…"

His face flushed. Pete said nothing, leaning against his bergen. "Just be careful, mate. They'll use you, these 'Templars'. You got to see that."

"I'm not stupid mate. And it's not me giving all my money to the gaming machines. And all Sveta's as well."

He had retorted out of anger and immediately regretted it. He knew there was truth in what Pete said. He growled deep in his throat and took a long sip of tea. It was colder than he liked it. The sun was dropping and very soon they would start cooking dinner. They had passed a pile of fence posts about a hundred yards back that would make a fire.

"Mate, just yanking your chain," Pete said.

Dean grumbled a reply but didn't say anything more. He didn't want to drop Billy. Even if he was a tawdry little fuck, he wasn't afraid to say things other people were thinking. Plus he always seemed to be loaded. In a few weeks they were going to Stoke as Billy was talking at a rally. But Dean had made a plan. If he ever got screwed he'd know what to do. He'd blagged his way out of worse situations than this.

"Do you remember the time I got caught once in the block with a bird, Pete? Slapper from downtown. Redhead. Been through most of the platoon. Well I brought her in through the back gate. Young officer knocks on my bunk – I was a Lance-jack at the time – the bird's on her knees giving me a nosh, and the officer says, 'Shit sorry,' and backs out. Lassie doesn't stop, just keeps going. Later on, Looey – can't remember his name – calls me in and says. 'Corporal Chadwick. You know the rules. Women are not allowed in the block. I'm going to report you to the Company Commander.' So I says, 'Look, Sir. She's the wife of Jimmy Mann. Killed on the last tour of NI. I was comforting her. She was finding it hard, that's all. Lost her quarter. Child aged two.'"

"Jimmy wasn't married. Didn't have any kids," Pete said.

"I know that. But Lieutenant Snodgrass didn't, did he? So I was all, I was just looking out for her, helping out. We put money in for the kiddie for Christmas. But one thing led to another..."

"And then what?"

Dean chuckled. He'd never understood how he got away with this one. "So the next thing is, Looey gets out his wallet and gives me a fiver. He's like fresh out of Sandhurst trying to make friends. The Platoon Sergeant was Boiler. Boiler Kitson. He was away on a course. The screws were off on a recce so it was just me and the platoon commander. He couldn't afford to fall out with me, could he? So he backs off and gives me some money while he's at it. 'Well, sounds like a jolly good cause…'"

"Did you give it to her?"

"The money?"

"Aye, Swampy, the money. I know you *gave* it to her."

Dean laughed, shaking his head. "Course not. Spent it in the Corporals' Mess."

The pair laughed long and loud at the camaraderie, the banter, the sheer absurdity of it all. Finally, as the reality of his situation settled in his mind, and as the sky turned from a sharp to a pastel shade of blue, he turned to Pete and said, "Punching out is hard, mate, isn't it? I miss those times."

Pete, July 2018

Midge smiled. She was now an elderly woman, bent at the waist, the skin on her arms loose and wrinkled. She had worked at the factory ever since Pete could remember.

She'd started as a stable hand with the donkeys, and then been on the floor as a stirrer. She'd been in accounts, in operations, and was now the personal secretary to his brother Sandy, the Managing Director. She was called Midge because of her height. She had a kind face and always wanted to know how Pete was feeling.

"Have you any more news on the court case, eh?"

"No, and I've stopped answering my phone. I just get journalists. I only answer numbers I know."

He put his hands in his pockets. He wanted to appear as though the pressure mounting up was within his ability to cope. Midge was like his grandmother. That she cared about him, as a devout Catholic, really mattered.

"But thanks for asking, Midge, I really appreciate it."

Sandy was on the phone. He looked up when Pete entered but didn't stop talking.

Pete said, "I need four hundred from petty cash to pay the contractors for doing the grass along the bank."

His brother patted the pockets of his tweed jacket while continuing to listen to what was being said on the phone. "I see. It's like that. Oh dear." He found the keys and threw them awkwardly at Pete. They fell short, skidding across the floor. "Sorry, sorry. No, I'm listening. Go on..."

Pete picked up the keys and took them outside to the safe, which was locked in a store cupboard next to Midge's desk. It was well known that only Sandy and sometimes James would ever get past her. Pete turned the keys over one by one until he found the one he needed. He opened the cupboard and then the safe, Midge watching his every move.

The safe was a large iron affair built into the wall. The key unlocked the door, which then had to be pulled open, effectively enclosing him in the cupboard. Petty cash was on the shelf.

"You'll fill in wir book, won't you, Peter?" Midge said.

"I will, Midge, don't worry."

He did so, then shut and locked the door, the cash scrunched in his hand. He locked the cupboard and carefully opened the door to his brother's office to drop the keys on the corner of his desk. Sandy mouthed his thanks. Pete took the money back to his cabin and paid the contractor in cash, shaking hands afterwards.

The following Sunday, Pete found a reason to visit Sandy at home and took the keys from his brother's work jacket while he was away to the Kirk with his wife and children. He then went to the factory, took a thousand from petty cash but didn't register it in the book. He returned the keys just as Sandy and his family were returning home and, when pressed, stayed for lunch.

On Monday, he placed a bet on England to beat Croatia in the semi-finals of the world cup, certain in his mind that England would win against an insignificant Balkan nation. They were the favourites but not by so much as to make a bet purposeless. The money he expected to win would replace what he'd taken and cover his payday loan.

When England lost, he sat immobile on the floor of his house and finished the bottle of whisky. He knew it was now only a matter of time.

Malcolm, July 2018

Outside MOD Main Building, getting out of the taxi, Malcolm glanced at the statue of Field Marshall the Viscount Slim. There was something about the figure – feet wide apart, binoculars grasped in both hands, slouch hat – that reminded him of a former Brigadier.

Inside the entrance hall he put his briefcase and suitcase on the conveyor belt for the scanner and patted his pockets for his security pass. As he was collecting the bag on the far side someone called his name.

"Malcolm Sewell? As I live and breathe, it is!" The tall and big chested lieutenant colonel was jovial and flushed as though just out of the shower.

Malcolm smiled. "Gordon! Long time no see! What the devil?"

He stepped out of the throng coming through security to shake Gordon's hand. The last time they met, at the rugby in Twickenham, Gordon had been a captain. He held a tammy in his hands, the hackle a blood-red plume. Malcolm shuggled the rank slide on the front of Gordon's shirt. "What's this? That's amazing."

Gordon's face reddened even more. "Yes, well, you know. I got lucky. I tell you though, being a half-colonel here is like being a lance-corporal back in the Forty-Twa. The place is rammed with brigadiers and generals. I just make tea!"

"You must have picked up on first look at the promotion list. Congratulations, mate. Very well deserved."

Gordon was in the Royal Regiment of Scotland, the battalion once called the Black Watch. They'd been at Sandhurst together, and Warminster, then Catterick during their respective careers. He was affable and charming, a great raconteur. But was he really Commanding Officer material?

Gordon said, "What are you doing here? Don't tell me... you work for one of those hugely expensive consultancies that are crawling over everything we do?"

Malcolm grinned. "Yep. I'm running Project Firefly for Delaine. Procurement Improvement."

Gordon opened his hands wide. "Not my area, sorry. I'm G1, Personnel. But G4 is a target rich environment! It's like *Jurassic Park*, this place. My laptop still has *XP*. And the dynamic between the military and the civil service...oh my god!"

Malcolm was conscious of time and knew Gordon would be too. "Fancy a beer after work?"

Gordon started to back towards the exit. He gestured with his tammy.

"Yes. I'm in a flat on the South Bank. Marvellous, I know! All at the public expense! But hey! Who am I to complain?"

"So you're about?"

"Not this week. Next week, certainly. Well, maybe. This week I'm in Glasgow. A court martial."

Malcolm folded his arms. "You weren't involved with the Mark Simpson case were you?"

Gordon pulled a face and glanced up at a group of senior officers climbing the marble stairs. He came close to whisper.

"Shocking wasn't it! All that time and effort. And the poor bloke. We were at Glenalmond together. He was properly screwed. Deserves every penny he gets in compensation."

"Will he get some?"

"I should think so. I mean, the case ruined his career. He left, didn't he? And he could have been a CO. He was such a lovely man."

Malcolm didn't think of Mark Simpson as lovely. He thought of him naked in a brothel in Holland, one of only a few other officers with a regimental tattoo.

Gordon seemed to realise this was the only moment they would have. Life would move on after they separated. "But listen. You got out. And it's going well? Penny ok? It was Penny, wasn't it? There were a few…"

Malcolm put his hands in his pockets. Gordon was always so disarming. "Yes, mate. It's going well. When you decide to go, it's time to go. And if you stay, that's good too. I'd run my course."

Gordon patted him on the chest with his tammy and leaned in to whisper.

"Well you did the right thing, chum. I tell you. Morale is low. They've halved our pensions. I mean, we're the ones who fought all those wars. From Bosnia to Kosovo to all those little places your boys did so well. And then eight years in Iraq and twelve in Afghanistan. And all those people who died or got maimed. And they cut our pensions! I mean, that's low isn't it?"

He looked round.

"But no one above the rank of Brigadier was impacted. Not one. It's limited to officers and soldiers between certain years of birth. Which means it's the ones who did all the fighting."

Gordon never swore. He always looked clubbable but was actually teetotal. So when he scowled Malcolm knew how angry he was.

"That's shocking, mate."

Gordon jammed his tammy onto his head and poked his thumbs into his stable belt. Malcolm thought about making a joke about how large he had got but knew he was no one to talk. Hello pot, this is kettle, over?

"It's jolly good to see you, Malcolm. Really. It has made my day. I find it a bit depressing when I see the good ones leaving. What does that say about me, eh, left with the dregs."

"You'll always do well, Gordon, no matter where you are. But don't just stay for the Boarding School Allowance."

Malcolm tried to be effusive but he couldn't carry it off as well as Lieutenant Colonel Gordon Halford-MacLean. His joke fell flat. They patted each other on the shoulder.

"See you at Twickers! Or, even better, Murrayfield! We'll give you a good run next year!"

"Will you fuck, mate. But see you."

Alexander, July 2018

Seeking to facilitate a way through the cacophony of Brexit demands, Teresa May summoned her Senior Ministers to Chequers, her country estate. She intended to define a mutually agreeable policy for leaving the European Union, which was due to happen in under a year.

The result, after three days of intense effort, was a proposal for a Free Trade Area. This would mean Britain adhering to a set of common rules but be otherwise free to make its own decisions. The import and export of goods would follow European Union laws but Britain would only partially agree to the other freedoms that underpinned the Union: the movement of people, services, and capital. Inevitably, the proposal was seen by European Union negotiators as cherry picking the conditions Britain wished to comply with and they worried that one of the largest economies leaving the Union would prompt others to do the same. They refused the deal.

With her Proposal rejected by the British media, the European Union, and key politicians, many of whom had been in the room with her, it became apparent that her days were numbered.

Alexander could no longer be associated with her weakness. It shamed him that a British Prime Minister should be so enfeebled. Papers found later at 10 Downing Street dated July 2018 record that:

> I resigned today as Foreign Secretary. I will blame the withdrawal deal to cast myself as the brave romantic, a modern Miltiades holding the plain of Marathon against the invading hordes even though the cowardly Spartans had refused to fight. I now have the opportunity to make a speech in the House. What I'm penning will make Churchill sound like a sozzled bone hawker and Cicero a rasping cicada.

Pete, July 2018

Whenever he was under pressure, Pete buried himself in work. He went in at six to heave the swill cans onto the flatbed for the drivers to take away when they came in at eight. His hips ached but he ignored the pain and kept lifting. He cleared the accounts and made sure they added up, then took a hard copy printout to his brother's office, leaving it with Midge. He rode his bike all the way down to Dunfermline to speak to the distribution agent about the issues they were having, asking them, as a personal favour, to keep the pallets moving.

The following morning, Midge handed him another letter from the MoD. He knew she'd concealed it from his brother and he thanked her as he slipped it into the inside pocket of his jacket.

"Thanks, Midge."

"You take care the now, Peter. I'll see you after, eh?"

There was a note in her voice that worried him. He noticed her avoidance of looking him in the face. No one had mentioned the petty cash and he was beginning to wonder if he'd got away with it.

Back in his portacabin, he sliced open the envelope. The letter said two things. Firstly, that he was to face trial for the murder of Seamus O'Hare. Secondly, that his name and address had been leaked and was known to republican sympathisers. He was now a target for dissident Irish Republican Terrorists and it was highly recommended that he move house.

The next thing he did was phone Swampy Chadwick. At that moment, what Pete needed was a mate, a bottle of Jack, and cold wind in his face.

Steve, August 2018

Steve had never been important. He was shorter than average and always in the bottom set at school. In basic training he'd been happy to just get through. The second time round, when he'd re-joined, he'd had the basic infantry skills but had to work on his fitness to join the Paras. The training weeded out anyone who wasn't committed and he had to throw himself into it knowing the instructors would have been happy to see him fail. In their eyes, he was an ordinary infantry soldier.

Standing in the assembly hall of a primary school in Carlisle, surrounded by little children, he was enormous. The room was spacious and lit by tall windows on both sides. The floor was tiled with dark wood in a herringbone formation. The walls were decorated with interfaith images and posters titled 'British Values.' The children, about forty of them, sat on the floor in neat rows. The white girls wore long white socks, grey tartan skirts, green pullovers. The brown girls wore longer skirts and had their heads covered with blue shawls, faces exposed. Three of the boys had a blue bandana covering knots of hair. There was one white boy.

Things had been quite different as a kid in Bootle. He had a mate, George, whose father was Ugandan and mother white. He'd been in the cross-country team and got into the Grammar School. He'd been the only coloured kid at St Mark's and there were no coloured kids at all in Carlisle.

The headmistress, Amina, herself wearing a headscarf, clapped her hands and called the room to order.

"Children, good morning. We have with us today a young man who has an amazing story to tell. A story of courage through adversity. Of resilience. Of belief in the self. Mr Reedman comes from Carlisle. He was a soldier in the army and injured in Afghanistan."

It was the way she said it that made him glance at her, the guttural stress on the vowel. *Afghonnistan*. She smiled. Her eyes, a very pale green, were stunning with the black line around them. When she'd finished her introduction, she clapped her hands softly, one hand patting the heel of the other. The children joined in.

They looked up at him expectantly. He took the glove off his prosthetic, pulling the fingers one by one. There was a girl in the third row, a white one, who was sitting cross-legged in such a way that he could almost see her knickers.

He put the glove down on the lectern and took off his fleece. The front row leaned forward to study him.

"I chose this one because it's more comfortable than the one I had," he said. "The other was white. But it rubbed on my stump and it were quite painful at times. This one's dead comfy and it's lighter. But they didn't have it in my colour."

The children giggled. He didn't know why. He chuckled with them. If they found it funny, that was good. He glanced at Amina to see if she was happy and she nodded, smiling.

"My name's Steve. I've come here to tell you my story. It's not very long but I'd like you to listen and I'll take questions at the end."

He'd done the basic methods of instruction course as a soldier before being promoted to Lance-jack. Once he'd joined the Paras they made him do it again although he never got promoted. Leaving the army and then re-joining had set him back by several years but he wasn't bothered. It was all he ever wanted.

Or so he'd thought.

Talking to the kids, he knew not to look at the whiteboard that had his name written at the top. He knew to cast his eyes round the room and he knew not to be drawn towards the girl sitting cross-legged. She was only about nine anyway.

"... so I joined because there was no work where I lived. Not for someone without qualifications. So my message to you is to study. Passing your exams is important. But anyway, I joined up because I wanted to travel and see the world..."

One of the boys was wearing a decorated cap like a Pashtun, embroidered round the sides and a slit up the front. The boy next to him had a white lace cap that clung tightly to his skull. His hair was clipped short.

"...then, after Iraq, my regiment were told that we have to go to Afghan. Does anyone know where it is?"

Half the children put up their hands. He picked a girl with a shawl over her head.

"Yourself."

She answered clearly, "Afghanistan is a country between Iran and Pakistan. The capital is Kabul. The President is Mr Ashraf Ghani. He is a Pashtun and is supported by the Americans but is opposed by the Taliban and the Islamic State."

Other children tittered.

He glanced at the headmistress. She nodded slowly.

"Correct. That's very good, that. Very good." He paused for a while, then started again. "Anyway, we were told that we were going to Afghan..."

The kids were smiling at the girl's answer but he just kept talking, letting the story flow.

"I woke in hospital. In Birmingham. My mother was at the bottom of the bed and she were crying. The first thing I said was where's my weapon? Where's Spanner, my best mate? Or Bilge? She had to tell me they didn't make it..."

The teachers were studying the class. He'd been told to make it age appropriate but he didn't know how to change it. The story was the story. But the kids didn't seem scared and he hadn't mentioned the little boy's head bouncing along the ground or the woman's entrails, the last things he saw before the second explosion knocked him out.

"It took four months before I could walk. And another four before I could pick up a cup of tea. I had to learn to use my shoulder not the biceps..."

He looked at the boys in bandanas. One was frowning but attentive.

"My accident happened in 2012. It's taken me six year to get to this point. The things that matter, what kept me going when I were really low, this were after my girlfriend left me..."

He realised too late that he probably shouldn't have said that but it just came out. The teachers would probably have to do the birds and the bees later on. But they covered all that nowadays, didn't they? Relationships and cooking.

"It's all about resilience. Bouncing back. Having the confidence to say I can do it."

He'd learned to pause. Malcolm had taught him to count to ten in his head.

"Well, that's what I came to tell you. Thank you all for listening. I hope it's been interesting. Has anyone got any questions?"

On the methods of instruction course they taught him to ask questions to confirm understanding. But that wasn't necessary here. Amina was clapping rapidly. She stood up, and the other staff members did the same. One of them wiped her eye.

Steve blushed. He didn't know where to look but a rose of pure joy blossomed within him. People valued him.

A girl put her hand up, the same one who'd answered the question earlier. Amina pointed at her. "Yes, Hannah. What question do you have for Mr Reedman?"

The girl had a round face. The veil framed it. She looked kind. "Do you think that we look like letterboxes if we wear the niqab?" she said.

The children fell totally silent and looked at him. Steve processed the question. Had he said something wrong? Who would imagine that a girl looked like a letterbox? Wrong colour for a start.

Amina said, "Mr Reedman, I think what Hannah is referring to is an article written by Mr Johnson, the Prime Minister, in which he said that Muslim women dressed in full rights, when only the eyes are visible, look like letter boxes. I think Hannah was asking if you had any advice for young people growing up with such attitudes around them?"

She was good. The girl had been provoking him. But he wasn't one to rise. The staff sat down again.

"Well, I don't know what Boris said. I'm sorry. I watch the news on telly but I don't read much 'cos of my eye. But what I can say is I grew up in Liverpool as a little kiddie. I supported Everton. And all around me was Liverpool supporters..."

There was a whistle of disapproval from one of the boys, picked up by others. Then laughter as the headmistress's eyes settled round the room. "Children!"

"I were chased home after school every day. Once, they got me as I had my hand on the gate. Dragged me back behind the hedge and gave me a good slapping. Took my sweets."

In the fourth row, the white boy's mouth fell open.

"I mean, I could have changed sides, couldn't I? I could have got mysen a red shirt and a red scarf. But thing is, my dad were blue and he took me to the matches. It were what we did. Before he took off, but that's another story..."

He gathered himself. "You see, what matters is that you can be yoursen, no matter what. Everything I done is about believing in yoursen. Everything. That's where my resilience comes from. That belief. That and my boxing skills..."

The last sentence slipped out but the kids spluttered to laughter. The headmistress sprung back to her feet, clapping her hands high in the air.

"Thank you, Mr Reedman. That was absolutely inspirational," she said in a choked voice.

Pete, August 2018

At eight-fifty-five on Friday morning Pete watched as both his brothers strode towards his office across the carpark. Both of them were wearing the white coats and trilby hats of the early morning shift. Pete was still in his leathers, sipping coffee, looking out of the window. The loaders wished the two brothers good morning but they walked past without responding.

Pete knew his time was up.

There was a brief knock on the door and Sandy entered, followed by James. They stood side by side, Sandy a head taller, chin high, James shorter and scrofulous.

"Morning," Pete said, taking his coffee behind the security of his desk. "What can I do for you both?"

Sandy had an envelope held against his chest. He stared at it then stepped forward to place it in the in-tray.

"I suspect you know why we're here, Peter. I don't expect any dingies from you at this stage. We are deficient in petty cash to the tune of one thousand two hundred and forty pounds. We know you took it and we know why."

James stood beside him like a guardsman on parade, eyes unfocused, but then looked down with his arms opening in a gesture of incomprehension. "Why did you no come for help? We could have done something. Why d'ye no ask?"

Sandy glanced at him with a disdainful scowl. Pete thought they must have been preparing to confront him for some time. Though he could have had fun at their expense he knew this was the chance he needed to be free of his debts. Carefully, he put the coffee mug down on the desk, placed his boots against the edge, and rocked his chair back on two legs. He interlaced his fingers on top of his head and stared at the strip light, listening to its quiet hum.

His brothers watched him.

"Father always said you were better off in the army, Peter. It was the best place for you."

Pete didn't respond.

James said, "We'll no desert you. We know what you must be going through. You can sell your house. Clear your debts. And we'll find you a place somewhere safe. We'll not leave you to the wolves. Nor the Roman…"

Pete smiled to himself, a hard ironic smile. He dropped his weight forward so that all four legs of the chair were on the floor. He stared at his brothers, the elder boys who hadn't protected him when it mattered, the ones who'd stood by and watched him getting leathered by their father.

As a sergeant-major it had been his job to bollock soldiers for being late on parade, or fighting, or generally fucking up. They were marched into his office at double time, slammed their tabs in, stood to attention. They called him *Sir*.

On operations he was the one they trusted, the one they looked to, the one they modelled themselves on, the one they feared. The one the company commander whispered to for advice. The one the toms came to when they'd split with their wives, lost a child, felt their minds warping.

Now he was being dismissed by Laurel and Hardy, two men standing in front of him with all the charisma of a pair of marionettes. He felt ashamed that he'd taken the money and frittered away his self-respect. Briefly, he thought of Midge. But most of all he felt shame that of all the people who should be in this position, it should be Warrant Officer Class Two Peter McCardle, Company Sergeant-Major, Support Company.

Sandy said, "We will say that you have chosen to seek new challenges."

Pete looked from one to the other.

"And it goes without saying that you have our continued love and respect. If the IRA come for you…"

Pete tutted. "What the fuck could you two do? You couldn't protect me from a terrorist attack any more than he could from the rain." He swallowed. "Or dad." The sneer on his face hardened. He waved his brothers away with a flick of his hand. "Both of you. Fuck away off."

They stood for a moment with their mouths open.

"Make any arrangements you need," said Sandy in a fluster. "But perhaps you could be clear of the factory by midday."

When his brothers had left, Pete found his hands were shaking. He interlocked the fingers to force them to stop but he couldn't. After half an hour a huge sob of relief swept through him. He wiped his nose and stood up to pull a hanky from his pocket, wrestling with his leathers to get it. He blew his nose and coughed, hawking up an unpleasant gob of phlegm.

And then the anger rose.

Malcolm, September 2018

Malcolm sat at the hot desks on the third floor. He didn't know the people either side of him but didn't need to. There was an unspoken expectation of silence.

Following Brexit, the credit rating agency Moody's had dropped the UK's score from AA1 to AA2. The cost of capital was increasing therefore long-term procurement projects such as submarines and warships would become significantly more expensive. Malcolm was trying to construct a discounted cash flow forecast on an excel spreadsheet. He was not confident with the numbers and worked slowly. He should have asked Veerle to do this but wanted to prove to himself that he could.

His phone buzzed. He looked at the screen and swiped to accept the call, whispering.

"Alicia."

"Malcolm, good afternoon. Are you on client site?"

"No. In the office. Do you need me?"

He looked over to the lifts.

"I wanted to know where you have got to with the next

Executive Steering Group. I'd like to see the pack before you send it to the client."

"I'm finishing the cash flow slide. Then there's the key messages to add. I want to get it out by tomorrow evening so they have time to digest it. I've done the prepositioning. If I send it to you tonight can you turn it round by tomorrow lunchtime?"

He liked the speed at which Delaine worked and that he didn't have to be deferential to a partner. It was so much more efficient than in the army.

Alicia said, "I knew you'd be on top of the game. I'd be happy to work to that deadline. I'm sure there'll only be minor points of feedback."

Malcolm knew there wouldn't be just minor points. He would have to rewrite the entire pack which was why he wanted it turned round quickly. He had fallen in love with PowerPoint; the economic simplicity of a headline, an image, a box of text; how one page could convey so much information. He felt he was mastering the art of sewing difficult messages into the image. The simple fact was that the MOD allowed military officers to make procurement decisions. They were rewarded in their careers for changing things. But submarines took twenty years to design and build. What the suppliers needed was a consistent and reliable brief rather than a constantly iterating set of demands.

Alicia continued: "If you continue like this you could be looking at a very high score in your annual appraisal this year. You could even be considered for an Executive Consultant role."

He knew she was dangling a career carrot in front of his nose. Why couldn't she just say 'thanks, good job'?

"Shall I meet you at the coffee shop, as before?"

"Yes, let's do that. And how is young Jerome getting on? I hear he is excelling."

Malcolm wanted to ask who she had heard that from. Jerome, himself, he suspected. The day before, he had challenged Jerome on his hotel expenses. The invoice had included a line for 'Communication services' which Malcolm thought would be a paid-for movie. In other words, porn.

Jerome swore he hadn't claimed for something he shouldn't have. Malcolm looked him in the eye. "Stop bullshitting me. You know the rules."

"It was a wifi connection…"

"I'm not a fucking idiot. Take it off."

The boy had slunk off, red faced. "Ok fine. I'll pay it myself."

"He has potential. But I have concerns. I can discuss them face to face when we meet. It's an integrity thing."

The line was quiet for a while, which was a surprise. Malcolm heard his own words in his head and was happy with them.

"I see," Alicia said.

Pete, September 2018

Pete stopped part way up the back stairs of the block of flats and rested. Someone on the middle floor was playing a radio and he hated the tinny pop music. The femur of his right leg was grinding into the bone of the hip socket. It burned. Since the lift wasn't working again he had to carry his shopping up all four flights of concrete steps to his flat at the far end of the third floor. He looked up the next flight and braced himself, then bent, picked up the shopping, and pushed through the pain.

"One, two, three, four…"

At the top, he turned along the walkway. Mrs Clarke, his Jamaican next-door neighbour, was leaning on a mop to scoop up a dog shit into a freezer bag. She saw him when she straightened.

"How are you today, Mr McCardle?"

Pete grimaced and puffed as he put the bags down. She made a delicious spiced rum which she said was good for the joints. Her two sons were further along the walkway, leaning on the balustrade, looking at him over their shoulders.

"Why are you picking that up, Mrs Clarke? Can she not do it herself?" Pete nodded to Mrs Nielson's flat on the other side of the stairs. It was her Yorkshire terrier that shat everywhere.

Mrs Clarke broke into joyful giggles, her white teeth expansive against her skin. Pete loved the odd mix of Scots and Jamaican in her accent.

"You know, Mr McCardle, how difficult it is for her. It's no bother to me, sure it isn't."

She knotted the bag and dropped it into the binbag at her feet. She'd swept the walkway to the steps. By mutual agreement, Auld Alan did the other side. His flat got just enough sunlight to grow pots of late summer flowers by his door so the far end was always the more colourful.

"You're a darlin'," Pete smiled.

"Oh, 'tis only what God asks of us, to care for others as we would oursel'."

When he'd first moved in, Pete thought her boys would be a problem. He quickly realised they were gentle souls more afraid of the world than the world was afraid of them. They spent most of the time on their phones, thumbs constantly moving. But they provided effective sentries. No one could enter the building without them noticing. He wasn't armed but had a riot baton hanging from a leather thong by his door if he needed it.

"You want my boys to take one of those bags Mr McCardle?"

"No, I'm fine. Just a bit stiff in the cold."

She was short, stout, and would not be hurried. The eastern side of the top floor was her kingdom and Pete was happy that was the case.

"You hear back from the council?" she asked as they got close to her door.

"Not yet. It's only been a week. But there's no way we need a fire warden for a three-storey building. It's bollocks."

She glanced at him, smiling nervously.

"Excuse my French. They're just panicking after the Grenfell thing in London."

At her door, she put the binbag down and held the mop handle in both hands. He was always fascinated by the way she slid her flipflops along the floor. He thought her feet must be made of rubber since the concrete was so cold.

"We lucky to have you is all I say," she said. "Nobody in council listen to the likes of us. But they listen to you, Mr McCardle. I say to Grace, we so lucky God sent you. Ain't no way we can affor' fire warden. How can we do that, eh?"

Even though she was angry her face showed a broad and open smile. Pete sensed in her something he had never known: a way of being that was totally different to anything he had known but not necessarily worse. She was a second-generation immigrant, a single mother, and had probably lived on benefits most of her life. Her boys had made little of school and were stopped by the police whenever they went into Dundee town centre. But she was accepting of her place and happy. He found that touching.

"If I don't hear, I'll call them in a few days," he said. "I'll not let them f... do us."

Her eyes were wide. "You know how to do these things! It's a wonder we have you. Such a wonder!"

Pete didn't think he'd done that much when he suggested the residents meet to discuss the letters they'd all received from the council and the housing company. His most striking observation was that all the other residents were on social housing. He'd asked them to gather on the ground floor. They'd gassed for a while, introduced themselves, and then he'd clapped his hands and called for order. They'd looked at him with the same scared, unchallenging faces of week-one recruits.

At first he'd been scornful of their intransigence. He thought they were lazy and inconsequential and wondered why he'd fought for people like them. But over the following few weeks, and having been to see the twat in Asset Management at Dundee Council, he realised they were neither incapable nor disinterested. They were unheard. No one ever listened to them and they had become, by steps, cynical, distant, and unresponsive.

"You can't let people like that dictate your life," Pete said.

She leaned the mop against the window and went inside her flat, kicking off her flipflops as she entered the doorway. She reappeared a minute later with a quarter bottle in one hand. It said vodka on the label but the mixture was a deep marmalade colour.

"This new brew," she said. "You tell me what you think now, eh?"

The boys were watching. He nodded to them. "Gentlemen," he said.

They said nothing but turned to look out over the playpark and the school beyond. The sound of children screaming rose above the pop music from the floor below. He thanked Mrs Clarke for her kindness and carried his bags to his door. Inside, he put a tenner in the meter and turned on the heating. It was the first week of the month so he'd got himself a bottle of gin. He knew he couldn't keep accepting Mrs Clarke's rum. He'd got enough food for the week and was already twenty quid over budget from his pension and the stipend his brothers had agreed to. He'd claw that back somehow though he wasn't sure how.

He put the tins in the cupboard and the dairy in the fridge. He filled the kettle through the spout and put it on. He checked the radiator in the living room and rubbed his hands, then used his sleeve to wipe away the condensation on the window. Back in the kitchen, he got a glass down from the cupboard. The yellow door hung lopsided on the hinges.

"Fuck," he said, realising he had neither tonic for the gin nor coke for the rum. That meant another trip to the corner shop and back up the steps, which he wasn't ready for. He'd get some after his GA meeting in the morning. For now, he'd take the rum neat.

The glass half full, he went back to the living room and sat in the big chair looking out through the damp windows across the blue-grey city. It looked dismal. Two gas rigs were anchored at the docks, their legs cranked up and deck lights blazing. The rail bridge slid out from the city like a shiny black eel, cutting across the river in a dash for the far bank. The aluminium windows rattled in the wind. The pulse of pop music came up through the floor.

Once upon a time he'd worn a crown on his arm. Now, he'd come to this.

Alexander, September 2018

When Alexander returned to the back benches, the media knew it would only be a matter of time before he challenged May for the Premiership. Attention on him grew to unprecedented levels. Although he declared publicly against their intrusion into his private life, the constant attention enabled him to air a numbers of aspects that, had he concealed them, might damage his future leadership bid. This was a no-holds-barred contest and he was unafraid of the fight.

Like many charismatic and powerful men, Alexander knew he was irresistible to women. They were drawn to him and he to them. He and his wife declared they were to divorce. At the same time, he ended an affair with Jennifer Arcuri, an American technology entrepreneur who had founded a long list of businesses, councils, and forums. Her extensive interests had brought her into Alexander's orbit while he was Mayor of London. She had been a regular visitor to his flat and he had awarded her thousands of pounds in funding grants and invitations to trade delegations.

As their relationship ended, he started another with Carrie Symonds, a woman twenty-four years his junior who worked in his press office. Her great skill, which she shared with only one other person, Alexader's strategy advisor Dominic Cummings, was to help him see complex issues clearly so he could make a decision.

Papers found later at 10 Downing Street dated September 2018 record that:

> If Berlusconi can have his bunga-bunga parties at seventy, I'm sure I can at fifty odd. Carrie is like Psyche to my Cupid. I have to steal to her in the night and be gone by morning. Unless I summon her at midday for a strategy meeting.

Malcolm, October 2018

Malcolm had been thinking about it all day. As he bent to put dishes in the washer, he imagined himself lying on top of Penny, the voluptuousness of her breasts, the softness of her belly, how her pubic mound and its clipped hair rose to meet his groin. He liked the smell of her neck after she had showered and the sounds she made when he entered her. Although he didn't resent being faithful, the enforced rarity of sex was uncomfortable.

When he was serving he would go out in London or Colchester, usually pull and usually get a shag. On the whole he'd found women boring and treated them with disdain. But then he'd met Penny at a wedding at which she'd been a bridesmaid. They'd shagged that night and he'd known immediately she was his equal, both sexually and intellectually.

That morning, when they woke, she'd said later, after the boy was asleep, she wanted him to give her a good servicing. He'd chuckled as he watched her pull on the bathrobe, her hips broad and breasts heavy. He had played with ideas all day, thinking up things to do.

Now, after putting the dishwasher on, he sat in the living room listening to Penny put the boy to sleep on the monitor. She sang a lullaby. She had a lovely voice and the thought of imminent sex made him hard.

When she stopped singing, he listened to her close the door and take heavy steps into the bedroom. He waited for her call. It was getting late and he hoped she would not be too long. *The Great Escape* was just starting on Film4 but he didn't have the energy to watch it even though he really identified with the Steve McQueen character. He would never tire of watching the bike jumping the wire.

Softly, his cock thickening in his pyjama trousers, he walked barefoot to the bottom of the stairs. Bonkers was on his bed by the TV. He raised his head to look at him then dropped it and didn't move again. Malcolm couldn't hear Penny. The monitor pulsed with the child's innocent breathing.

She'd fallen asleep.

He thought about being angry but knew how exhausting it was to look after the boy. He was away much of the week and didn't do a fair share. Penny had quaint, old-fashioned ideas about gender roles. She expected him to earn so that she could mother. It worked for him too.

Back on the sofa, he watched the News at Ten and made a mental note to ask what the latest CBI figures would mean for his client.

Turning off the telly, he listened to the house. The dishwasher hummed in the kitchen. The blue monitor lights pulsed up and down. Penny coughed once from the bedroom and was silent.

He wondered if she was waiting for him. He crept up to see but she was asleep in her clothes on the bed. He was now wide awake and knew what he needed, the only thing that would break the busy chattering of his mind.

His tablet was in the briefcase, unmoved since Friday. He slipped it out, wondering if there was enough power left. He turned it on and watched the screen go through the startup routine, waiting for the picture of the three of them to appear.

There was nothing to prop the tablet against so he lay on the sofa, feet towards the stairs. He found the site he used when he was away and scrolled through the categories: *Amateur, Cheating, Big Tits*.

In the search box, he typed 'Dutch' and 'skinny'. The page loaded a new set of videos and he scrolled through them, looking at the thumbnail pictures for a girl he liked the look of.

There was noise upstairs. He dropped the tablet flat against his chest, his fingers fumbling for the volume button. The sound increased, a high-pitched rhythmic panting. He frantically pressed a different button until there was silence. He listened to the house once more: the dishwasher, the bedrooms. From where he was lying he could see the landing light against the wall where the stairs turned the corner. If anyone was on the landing, there'd be a shadow.

He waited a while, enjoying the anticipation, then lifted the tablet and put the film back to the beginning. The format was familiar. The girl gave the man a blowjob and then they fucked. She had long blonde hair which he held behind her ear so her face was visible to the camera. She looked like she was enjoying it and that mattered to him.

Malcolm's cock pushed against the fabric of his pyjamas. He stroked himself, slowly at first, then faster. He thought of Veerle, imagined her sucking him. He imagined her beneath him, her boniness and small breasts. As the film reached its climax, so did he, spurting into the pyjama fabric thick and plentiful.

Spent, he lay back, breathing deeply, sweating. There was dampness in his pubic hair and stickiness on his fingers. He wiped his hand on his bottoms and turned the tablet off.

As he put his stuff away, he thought of lying on his cot in the Operating Base in Sangin, listening to Dean Chadwick banging one out in the cot next door, the urgent thumping of his fist against the dossbag. When he'd finished, Malcolm had glanced across and caught his eye. Both of them had burst out laughing.

"Gotta do it," Dean said.

Kyle, November 2015

I had to leave the flat in Stoke because the other tenants complained. And the landlord said there was damage to a door and the wall. I don't know what I did to upset them. They were just snowflakes. I was inside most of the day. What was bothering them?

But the Irish woman from Save Our Heroes *said she could help and they have this place in Tidworth, right in the garrison, and there's a lot of veterans like me there. Did I want to try it? I said yes, that's what I want to do.*

Char said she didn't think it was a good idea. But Danny said they couldn't provide what I need, it would be better if I went. He and Char couldn't cope with the level of shit, basically, that I was going through. I needed professional help. And he was right. I knew he was right.

Char was crying on his chest and I looked round for little Dan but he wasn't there and they said he'd gone to visit Danny's sister's kids for the weekend. It was a party and he'd been invited and they might have been telling the truth.

So I'm in Tidworth, which is an army garrison full of gunners and mechanics and all these people I never really came across. There's this big house owned by Save Our Heroes *and I have a room by myself. My bunk is neat and tidy. There's a locker but I don't have many clothes. I keep my kit in my bergen so I can deploy at a moment's notice. I'm always ready. Ready for anything.*

The locker door's open. There's a jacket on a hanger. It's my jacket. I need to stand up and put it on and then pin my medal on the lapel. It's Remembrance Day and we're going to march down to the parade. It's at the Legion and all the units will be there, plus the padre, plus the scouts and families. The war memorial is this statue of an infantry soldier in First World War uniform with a kit bag dragging on the floor. At first I thought it was a body bag and this poor guy had been told to clear up the market square but it's just a kit bag.

We've been told to be on parade at the Legion at 10.30. That means we will leave here at 10.15. It's not far but they want us to be in the right place before the Minute's Silence. The staff are trying not to tell us to form up outside and march down but if they asked us to do it, we would. Easy.

It's beautiful. The leaves are falling and they're all red and yellow and the sky is clear.

But it's ten now and I'm thinking do I put the jacket on and then fit the medal, or do I fit the medal and then put the jacket on. I can see really good reasons why both are correct and really good reasons why they are stupid and actually dangerous.

Someone shouts my name, knocks on my door. He says five minutes outside and do I need any help? I'm on my grot with my head against the wall looking into the open locker. I say no. I can manage.

Steve, November 2018

Des, the Branch Secretary of the Royal British Legion had asked Steve to lay a wreath on Remembrance Day. Steve had thought about it. He'd talked to his mother. He'd even thought about calling Malcolm to see what he thought. But in the end, he said no, he was just a Lance-jack. In fact, he was a tom. He'd lost an arm but there were others who'd lost far more and he didn't feel worthy.

Des said, "That's a shame. You're a local lad. You were in t'Paras. Served in Iraq and Afghanistan…"

But when his decision was made, Steve stuck to his guns. "Sorry, Des, it's not for me. I'll be there, in the crowd. But I'll not do owt fancy. It's just not me."

For the parade, he wore the big coat his Mum had bought him. It was knee-length, black, wool, from Marks. It was smart like the ones the politicians wore on the telly and though he didn't like it, at least he could bury his arm in the pocket and no-one would look at him funny.

He wore his para beret. He'd thought about wearing the Duke of Lancaster's one but decided that the maroon one was better. There'd be fewer of them in the crowd. His medals had been court mounted and his mother had polished them but he kept them partially hidden underneath the coat. He liked them that way, poking out if you looked at him from a certain angle. If anyone asked, he could explain what they were. But he didn't feel comfortable having the full rack on open display, just the poppy in the lapel hole.

In town, the castle had been done up like the one in London. A flood of red poppies poured over the wall and down into the field below. It was really powerful. Each poppy represented a life lost, the fallen. Steve and his mum had their picture taken against it, shoulder to shoulder, smiling. She was in a black hat with a veil and held on to his good arm, afraid to slip on the wet brick paving. During the ceremony he watched the old men laying the wreaths and felt it right that they be doing it.

There were no major units on parade which he thought a bit disappointing. There was a small squad of RAF from the station at Spadeadam but they were all chubby and the women couldn't keep step. He liked the cadets though. He'd been a cadet and it was that experience that started him on the journey.

After the parade, his mother went home because her ankles were swollen and she was on shift at the supermarket later. Steve kissed her on the cheek saying he'd be home for tea. He just wanted to be among other veterans for the moment. He didn't drink but wandered from tent to tent talking to the older men about their time in Northern Ireland, or Bosnia. One guy, from the Lancs, had been in the first Gulf war in ninety-three. Of all those he met, Steve didn't know anyone. All his school friends had long since left the town, or grown up, or just weren't here. By early afternoon he was getting tired and thought it was time to go home. It had been a good day and he should finish on a high. He thought he'd watch *The Great Escape* on DVD and go to bed early. He liked the Charles Bronson character best, how he had to overcome his claustrophobia to dig the tunnel and he was one of only three who got away.

Steve could have walked home but chose instead to get the bus. It was starting to rain again so he flipped his collar up, awkwardly reaching over his head with his good hand to set it on his right side. The bus shelter was crowded but he didn't mind standing in the rain. There was something timeless about feeling his beret swell with water till it dripped off the peak. He thought of range days and Norwegian containers of all-in-stew, passing a mug around, sharing fags. He thought of advances to contact across the Brecon hillsides. He thought of Bilge, smiling, and the fat girl sucking him off. That was in Arnhem, the year before they went out to Afghan when Bilge and Spanner were killed.

He thought of Kyle. Why had he not asked for help, the silly bastard?

People in the bus stop glanced at him, their faces unreadable. There was an old woman and some teenagers, one of whom was an extremely pretty girl. He was starting to think about getting a cab – he had money after all – but then a double-decker finally appeared out of the station and crossed the junction towards them. He thought the teenagers would barge past the old woman but they waited respectfully for her to climb aboard before they scrabbled up, paid, and climbed the stairs to the top floor. He went to pay himself but the driver waved at him from behind his plastic screen.

"What's the matter?"

He had glasses and thin hair that was too long on top. He wore a green company tie. "Are you a veteran?" he said.

Steve nodded.

"No fare, not today," the driver said, and this made Steve smile.

"Oh, thanks!"

Elated, he climbed the steps to the top deck. At least someone appreciated veterans, on this of all days.

The bus started moving just as he got to the top floor. He snatched for the upright and absorbed the movement in his legs. The teenagers had spread themselves across the four seats behind the steps. He didn't want to push through them with the bus in motion but he didn't want to sit in front of them either. He thought they might tease him but he couldn't now descend the stairs as that would be cowardice. So he plumped himself down in the nearest seat and adjusted his coat. In the corner mirror he could see the bald patch on the driver's head. He could feel the teenagers looking at him but sat still, waiting to see what they would do. It crossed his mind to take his false hand out of his pocket so they'd know he was injured, but he didn't.

"Mate? Excuse me, mate?"

Steve looked round. One of them, a guy with pale skin and a trimmed beard, was talking to him.

"You after me?"

"Yes, I am. I wonder if you wouldn't mind helping me?"

The boy was polite and the pretty girl was right next to him. She had large, round eyes and long curly hair. She had a soft face and her eyebrows were natural rather than plucked. Steve liked girls who looked natural.

"You are in the army, yeah?"

"I were. I'm discharged," Steve replied.

"But you were in the army?"

"Ten years, all counted. Why?" It should have been obvious. He was wearing a beret and his medals were under his coat. The boy could see them.

"I wanted to know what you thought of British foreign policy in Afghanistan, that's all. Do you think we did the right thing?"

He had to be a student, asking questions like that. The others had the same innocent, naïve faces. Clever, no doubt, but no idea of the realities of life. Steve had a feeling he was going to ask that question all civvies asked.

"We went there to make the place better," Steve said. "They were killing women with stones in the football stadium. Hanging people for listening to music. And exporting heroin. You know, from poppies?"

The girl glanced up at him but didn't hold his gaze. Her lips were taut. She turned to look out of the window. The bus came to a halt and there was the sound of disembarkation below.

"But do you think we are making matters worse by creating a culture of aid dependency?"

The boy was serious. Steve didn't know how to answer it. Were the Afghans dependent on them? To some degree, certainly. The National Army were a shambles. The Police, the ANCOP, were as corrupt as they come. You never bought an Afghan, only rented one. But there were one or two units, the ones trained by the Brits, who fought the Taliban like lions. For every British soldier killed, ten Afghans had died.

"I wouldn't know," Steve said. "It's not an easy question that."

The girl was looking at him. He wanted her to keep doing so. There was something amazing in her face. It was pity, he realised. She saw him as damaged.

Another boy spoke. "Were you at the parade?" he asked.

"Of course. Why would I not be?"

This one had curly hair brushed upwards. He was busy rolling a cigarette as he spoke, the pouch of tobacco on his leg.

"I just wondered why you'd want to celebrate mass slaughter?"

He had a curl to his lip Steve didn't like. If he'd had both hands he would have given him a good clip. But they were just civvies. Kids, really.

The bus was moving quickly. They were parallel to the motorway. The roof scraped under the branches of tall trees.

Steve looked at the boy with calm eyes. Words appeared in his mouth from deep within him. "What I want you to appreciate, youth, is they gave their tomorrows so you have your today. Think on that," he said, and turned round to look out of the window.

Dean, November 2018

It was Remembrance Day, exactly one hundred years since the Armistice. On the eleventh day of the eleventh month, and a little past the ninth hour, Dean climbed the steps out of the Underground, the shoulder of his jacket brushing the nicotine-coloured tiles. He felt the sunlight, warm and hopeful. He had wanted to get close to the Cenotaph but was surprised by how busy it was already. Not that it mattered. These were his people.

Traffic barriers lined the pavements. A policeman was posted facing the crowd every fifty yards or so, and a pair of Special Branch men walked quietly through the throng, Heckler and Koch rifles holstered across their chests in a way Dean would never have done.

Behind the barriers the veterans were already five deep. Some wore new suits, slim cut, their jackets hanging open to expose regimental ties. Some wore cream trousers with brass-buttoned blazers, cap-badges on the breast pocket. Some wore jeans, dark glasses, biker jackets, their faces bearded and weather beaten. All wore berets.

Dean scanned the landscape of headdress on display. There were black berets for the tankies, cavalry, scaleybacks, loggies, medics, and sappers. There were dark green ones for the Light Infantry and the Green Jackets. There was olive green for the Adjutant General's Corp and pea green for the Intelligence Corps, though these were harder to spot since Int Corps people tended to be short, runty types.

There was that muddy colour of the Guards Regiments and a small gaggle of light blue, the finest chopper pilots in the world. There was that jungle-at-night-time green for the Bootnecks. That made Dean smile. He liked Marines, saw them as equals. He'd known a lot of them on the security circuit and learned they could handle themselves in a situation.

The jocks were there too, in glengarries with red and white side panels, or tammies tugged forward to hang jauntily over one eye. Some had red hackles, some blue, some green, some white. Some had grouse feathers arching outwards. A huge man with the craggy features of a lock forward and a dark walrus moustache wore a caubeen, half beret half doss bag, pulled down low over one ear. He had an old-style UDR cap badge and Dean thought he looked proper Ulster, East Belfast through and through. He noticed Dean looking at him and stared back without changing his expression. His face was as angular as the pillars of the Giant's Causeway. With huge hands, he adjusted his caubeen and looked back to the road. He had to be six foot eight if he was an inch.

There were dark blue berets for the navy and grey-blue for the crabs. There were women in plastic bowler hats tied on with elastic. There were old men wearing homburgs, and even older men in wheelchairs wearing brand new berets bought for the day. They wore them awkwardly, misshapen, the cap-badges unevenly fixed. But what did it matter if you had a rack of medals like that? One old boy had the Burma Star, the Defence Medal, a Military Cross. Dean was surrounded by heroes though not one of them would see himself as such.

But there, to his right, Dean saw what he wanted. A clot of maroon: dense, impenetrable, select, elite. It was clear from the way they stood that they were special. The berets of other colours drifted round them, like leaves in fast water. He shouldered through the crowd. "Coming through."

The first guy in the pack he did not recognise. He must have been from one of the other battalions. But behind him was Johno and Dinger, Dusty, and a guy he hadn't seen in years. They'd done Juniors together, or Seniors, in Brecon. Or was it the patrols course? Either way, it didn't matter.

And then there was Cleggy, his weight unevenly supported on one leg.

"Nice to see you, Swampy," Cleggy said, bending to pull a can of wife beater from a plastic bag at his feet. "Get that down you."

Dean had left behind his wife, the girls, his work, and all that stuff Billy wanted him to do. This was about honouring the fallen and being with his mates. Billy had suggested Dean join him on the parade in Rotherham but Dean refused outright. He knew Billy would turn it into something it wasn't meant to be. This was a celebration of the sacrifice of others, an honouring of the fighting man. It was the nation accepting the debt it owed to those who had served. And within that, it was about those who served knowing they were valued.

"Swampy, did you hear? Merkel's on the parade in France."

Dean frowned. "What's she doing that for?"

As the crowd thickened, Dean could see that he'd lose his place if he needed a piss, so he stopped drinking. There would be plenty of time afterwards. There were so many faces Dean hadn't seen in ages he was as giddy as a kid at Christmas. By ten-thirty no one could move and Dean had to crane to see the squads of sailors and soldiers marching into position. He could just see the top of the Cenotaph but wasn't going to see the Queen.

One thing he really wanted was to get a picture of himself against the poppies pouring out of the Tower of London. He'd seen the pictures others had taken on Facebook, how the window looked like a gunshot wound with the blood of England flowing down the wall and across the grass in a wide scarlet pool. A poppy for every man killed. The scale of it seemed daunting. How many had they lost in the Falklands? In Ireland? Even in Iraq or Afghan? Nothing by comparison.

As the hour approached, a reverential silence seeped along the crowd like a dark mist. One by one, each man and woman put their heels together, braced their arms beside the body, and pushed their thumbs down the seams of their trousers. They pulled back their shoulders and felt for the neck in the back of the collar. Chins lifted, eyes forward, they stood as only soldiers can.

And faintly, floating, the bugle came, as ethereal as victory, calling them to remember. As if any of them could forget.

Pete, November 2018

For the parade, Pete went back to Arbroath because he didn't want to be involved in the big thing at Dundee High School. He wanted to be somewhere low-key where he could hide in the crowd and wouldn't have to explain his position, either personal or legal, to anyone. He'd dosed himself up with naproxen and paracetamol and ridden up on his bike in the rain.

He was in his leathers for the parade. He pulled his beret from the inside pocket of his jacket and fitted it using the Greggs window as a mirror. Others had their medals on display but he had sold his on eBay for cash.

The parade was sombre in the dreich weather. The Legion and the cadets put on a reasonable show and the churchgoers and other veterans were marshalled into an untidy hollow square round the great stone block of the war memorial.

He wasn't far from his old bungalow. He wondered if Sandy had sold it or retained it as a rental. Either way, Sandy had cleared his debts and bought him the flat in Dundee.

After the parade, as the cadets and the piper marched off, Pete felt lonely and unfulfilled. He shrugged his shoulders against the wind and thought about riding back to Dundee. On the way up, he'd skidded in a deep puddle and was, for once, cautious about the conditions. He followed the ambling crowd down the slope to the main road thinking it might be better to sit in the supermarket diner until the rain eased. The front of the crowd halted at the traffic lights and waited to cross. The rain had seeped down the back of his neck and he stamped his feet to get the blood going. He thought about jumping the queue by nipping round on the wet grass but was conscious that he might skid and fall over. Then he became angry at himself for being such a ponce and cut across the grass in a purposeful manner.

"Pete McCardle! Airborne!"

A man wearing a Sunday suit and a Gordon Highlanders glengarry was calling him. It was Hammy, the Social Secretary from the Legion. He waved. Pete could not pretend he hadn't seen him. He was, after all, the only one wearing a maroon beret.

"Hammy, how are you?"

Pete shook his hand and smiled. He was still a member at the Legion but since leaving Arbroath had not been in touch. If the club was wealthy it was partly due to the fortune he'd poured into the betting machine.

"You'll be coming for a drink?" Hammy said. "We've no seen you for a while, though we've seen you in the papers. The boys have been asking after you."

Pete didn't want to get into details. He'd been told that another solicitor had been appointed which didn't fill him full of joy. He couldn't afford any personal legal advice and had lost confidence in the bloke he had before.

"I just... stay low, move fast, you know?"

Hammy was tall and affable, red faced in the cold. He had his hands in his pockets and his wife stood behind him, smiling.

"Hi Pete."

"Hi Jean."

Hammy said, "Look. There's no pressure. You'd be very welcome. I know things are tough for you right now. So come for a drink. Watch the London thing. We've a big screen up, so we have. And there's a buffet. You can be my guest."

The free food persuaded him. His hips were not as sore as they might be due to the drugs but the muscles in his lower back were stiff from standing. He patted Hammy on the arm.

"I'll come, thank you, but I'll only stay for one as I'm on my bike."

"You've got the Tiger?"

Pete smiled. "Yes. Haven't sold that yet. Sold everything else, but not the bike. I'll see you there in ten."

Nipping through the traffic Pete felt lighter than before the parade. Being with others was a good thing, he realised. It made him feel less burdened. He rode round to the Legion and heaved the heavy bike onto its stand against the wall. Hammy and a couple of smokers were by the door as he pulled off his helmet.

"Pete! Good man, get yourself in."

Hammy stood out of the way to allow him to enter and stamp his boots on the vestibule carpet.

"It's like a range day in Otterburn," Pete quipped.

"Aye. Glencourse on a good day, eh?"

He shook the rain off his jacket and hung it with the other coats then placed his helmet on the floor next to a brolly stand. He was wearing leather trousers, a black regimental sweatshirt stained with paint, and a red snood. He'd shaved that morning but his hair was wet and unkempt from the helmet.

Hamish followed him in. "It's good you're here. Come in the now."

Pete allowed himself to be guided. The Legion had a welcoming feel. The hallway was dark, thickly carpeted, the walls decorated with regimental plaques and photos. This led through to the bar, a bright space with pine cladding and high windows. At the far end of the room Pete noticed the gambling machines had been removed. Hamish saw him looking but said nothing. He placed an arm round Pete's shoulder.

There were about forty men and women in the room, of all ages from their twenties through to the elderly. They stood or sat in small groups with paper plates and a drink in their hands. The women were wearing long dresses, dark jackets, wide brimmed hats. The men, regimental blazers or kilts. Anyone who had served wore medals and regimental headdress, mostly tammies with a red hackle or the same glengarry as Hammy.

Pete felt underdressed. He went back into the hallway to get his beret from his jacket. Having fitted it, he returned to the bar. The London parade was on television and the newsreader's sonorous, Welsh voice droned on through the protocols as the units paraded past the Cenotaph. At the bar he stood awkwardly between attention and at-ease and apologised to the room in general.

"Excuse my dress, ladies and gentlemen, I've…"

He couldn't think of a reason why he hadn't come dressed correctly. He could have brought something to change into and it was the sort of misjudgement a Lance-jack would make. Hammy was quick to ensure he was comfortable. He walked over and put his arm round his shoulders again.

"Everyone! Most of you know Pete. If you don't, he's here as my guest. We'll not give him too much grief for running off to join an English regiment but we'll all make him welcome."

There was a smattering of claps from various people. He had never told anyone who he was but they seemed to know. He leaned against the bar by the brass bell and glanced at his watch.

Hammy said, "You can crash, if you want. We often have people dossing on the benches on Burns night."

Pete was disconcerted by his kindness. He didn't know why he was being looked after like this. He had never really engaged with Hammy before apart from the formalities of annual subs and paying his bar bill.

The young man behind the bar was dressed in black. He was lean faced, dark haired, tall. He was staring at Pete between the beer pulls.

"Are you... Trooper P?" he asked.

Hammy interjected, "Jon, I said we were no to..."

Pete silenced Hammy with a hand on his arm. Looking the boy in the eyes he saw an inquisitive, active mind. "Yes. I am."

The boy blinked, smiled, and immediately started pouring a Tennent's. "Well, this one's on me."

Pete watched the golden liquid fill the tilted glass, the smooth skin on the boy's fingers. "Thank you, Jon," Pete said, and turned outwards to watch the TV.

As he did so he realised that the men in the room were coming towards him. They were led by a bent old man in an ill-fitting Royal Marine's beret walking with a stick in one hand. He had a Korea medal on his blazer, and an MM.

"Like I said, Pete," Hammy explained. "You're among friends here. We follow your case and we think it's disgusting the way you've been treated."

The old man inched towards him, head craned back, eyes rheumy but determined. Watching them approach from all angles, Pete thought he was on a set of *The Walking Dead*.

Hammy introduced the old man. "Now this here's Iain. He's a Marine as you can see. But I'm not expecting the two of you to start fighting, that understood?"

Iain craned his head sideways to look at Hammy and smiled. He swapped the stick and extended a curled, sinewy hand to shake Pete's.

"Iain Johnstone. Formerly of Her Majesty's Royal Marines. You're Peter McCardle, I understand. The one they call 'Trooper P' in the papers?"

"That's me."

Iain didn't let go. His grip was as cold and firm as an iron vice. "It's shocking what they've done to you. It's truly shocking. You should be lauded as a hero not tried as a murderer. I'm ashamed, so I am. Ashamed!"

Others stood nodding.

"We're with you, all the way," someone said.

"Whatever you need," said another.

Pete didn't know where to look. He felt a frog rise in his throat and his cheeks began to flush. "I'm really... look, thanks..."

The boy behind the bar passed him his beer nudging his shoulder with the glass. Pete was glad of the excuse to take a long swig. When he'd done so he wasn't sure if he had regained control of himself.

"There's no need to say anything," Hammy said quietly. "You're with your aen here. You needn't hide. We're all veterans and we all look after each other."

The frog returned to his throat. He felt like a newly promoted sergeant having to tell a joke to the Seniors gathered in the Mess to welcome him.

Iain poked him with a stiff finger. Pete bent down to hear him.

"Get yourself some food. And then let's chat. I have something that you may find useful."

Malcolm, November 2018

Malcolm was never going to go to the parade in London. Since he spent all week down there he didn't want to go back on one of his few days off. Penny had suggested he go to the one in town, or at least to the local church, but he didn't want to miss time with Luca.

She took the boy from him, straining under the weight. "Oh my God. Aren't you the big boy? Why don't you watch it on telly at least?"

Malcolm lay slouched on the sofa. He checked his shirt for dribble. "I'll do that. I don't need to go anywhere. It's with me all the time."

The boy gurgled and Penny bobbed up and down to shush him. Malcolm had never learned the technique and watched her carry him to the kitchen. She closed the door behind her and this brought into view the picture he was given by the Officers' Mess when he left the battalion. It was of a Hercules, the heavy-lift transport aeroplane he once jumped from. There was a small figure in the side door about to make his exit into the windy dawn.

Malcolm thought: *one thousand, two thousand, three thousand, check canopy*. What a way to go to work! He wished he had done more jumps. Once he'd qualified at Brize Norton he never did any during all eight years of his service. With Afghanistan, there were never any aircraft for non-operational activity.

The picture was the only memento Penny allowed in the house and it was on a wall usually hidden by the open kitchen door. The rest were in boxes at his parents' place. He once smuggled a small bronze statue onto the hearth by the fireplace. His dogtags hung round the neck on long loops of plug chain but after Luca was born the statue was put back in a box. It was upstairs, at the back of his bottom drawer, along with his stable belt, beret, and his rack of three medals.

At five to eleven, he turned the television on. The presenter had a sombre Welsh accent. A bass drum thumped out slow time. There was a high-level shot of the crowd, a contingent of Guards already in position. He turned the volume down and stood up. His feet were in socks, not shoes. He felt both silly and sad at the same time.

He brought his heels in and lifted his chin. Then he moved his left foot out and brought his hands together in front of him, bowing his head, preferring this position to being at attention. He recited the poem. It was only four lines. He felt the weight of the words, the duty to remember. He was proud to have served and had enjoyed every second of it. He felt he was giving back now with what he did for Steve Reedman but he knew, too, that he didn't do enough.

If he had not left, if he had gone on that tour, would he have been killed like Seb Wilmott? Or would he have made different decisions and saved the lives of his men? The sense that he let them down, that it was his fault, dragged on him like a parachute underwater. The guilt drowned him.

In the kitchen, the boy started to cry. He lifted his head, turned off the telly, and went through to help.

Steve, December 2018

Steve was elated as he held the phone to his ear. "They paid me! They paid my expenses. That's good isn't it?"

Malcolm sounded pleased. "It's brilliant, mate. Congratulations. This is really working out for you, isn't it?"

While he was talking, Steve had the sound turned down on the telly. The news had been pretty boring, just stuff about companies going bust. This time it was HMV, the record shop. Steve didn't care as he'd never really been into music.

"So what happens next?" said Malcolm. "How can you build on this?"

Steve had known Malcolm would ask something like that. He had a habit of asking probing questions and Steve had come prepared.

"Well. I've been thinking," he said. "You know I get on well with the kiddies. They like to hear my story. And I get on well with the staff at these schools I go to. They always stand and clap for me when I've finished."

"Go on?"

"Well, I've been thinking. I'd really like to be a teacher, Malcolm. I'd really like to teach kiddies."

Malcolm was silent on the phone. Steve's feet were on the small coffee table in the middle of the living room. He waggled his feet and could see the reflection of his socks in the blank TV screen. "Well, what do you think?"

"I think...."

He was drawing out his response which meant he wasn't as pleased as Steve thought he would be.

"What makes you think... I mean, how could you... Start again. What qualifications do you need to be a teacher?"

This made Steve think.

"Well, I've had my DBS check. And I've done the methods of instruction course. And drill and duties. So I know about basic leadership. And I've done all the courses *Save Our Heroes* offer, all of them. What else would I need?"

Malcolm sounded like he was sucking his teeth. "Have you looked it up? You might find you need a degree."

"A degree? I haven't got one of them. What would I need one of them for? It's just little kids? Do you know what I mean?"

"I do, Steve, I do. But I think you might want to check whether you're qualified to be a teacher before you set your heart on the idea. Even primary teachers are highly educated…"

"Where would I start? How do you find out stuff like that? Do you know anyone?"

Malcolm sounded distant. "I'm afraid I don't, Steve. I don't know any teachers. But you've got a phone. Have you tried googling it? Try typing in something like 'how to become a teacher.' Will you try that?"

"Can you help me with it?"

The line was silent for a while, then Malcolm spoke. "I think you really need to look at this yourself. This isn't about me telling you what you can or can't do. It's about you finding out what you want to do and working towards it."

"I want to be a teacher, Malcolm."

"Yes, I get it. That's great. But what do you *need* to be a teacher. How do you get the qualifications?"

"Oh," said Steve. "I see."

Malcolm, December 2018

Malcolm got to the meeting room two minutes before the session was due to start. There were people inside and they didn't seem to be finishing. Using his height, he stared at them over the frosted band along the glass wall. They noticed him and folded their laptops. Alicia appeared from the lifts just as they were vacating the room.

"Sorry," they said to her.

"Thank you," she replied.

The room was on the fourth floor. The high cloud, the city, the river, the traffic on the road below were all shades of grey fading to the horizon, blocks of different sizes, angular and hard edged. A line of planes descended slowly overhead towards the airport. The room had pale curtains half pulled across the windows. In the corner was a flipchart stand with two black pens on the tray.

Alicia was expensively dressed in a white suit with pearl earrings. The emerald wedding ring stood out on her finger. Knowing what he had paid for Penny's, Malcolm recognised the cost of what she was wearing and knew she liked him noticing.

He pulled out a chair for her at the end of the table and sat across the corner. Since he wasn't on client site he had eschewed the company uniform of a dark suit, white shirt, and blue tie. He wore cavalry twill trousers, a pink shirt open to the first button, his green regimental cufflinks, and a sports jacket with a thin blue box check.

"You look very country," Alicia said.

"Polo club," Malcolm quipped but her face told him she didn't know if he was joking or not. "Well, anyway, thanks for making time. You wanted to go through my assessments ahead of the Appraisal Review?"

"I did. You won't have done one before so I thought it worth preparing. Plus, I'd like to know how you have graded everyone. It's my job, or one of my jobs, to ensure continuity and balance across the teams. So there's no grade inflation laterally or longitudinally, over time."

She placed her elbows on the table and played with the pearl that hung round her neck on a gold chain. She smelled floral.

"I've prepared appraisals for four of them: Jenny, Timur, Jerome, and Gabriel. The other two I'll do next week. I haven't done Veerle as she's going back to the Paris office."

Alicia dismissed Veerle with a wave of the hand. "She won't be discussed. But those four will. Jenny and Timur are Graduates seeking to be Consultants, and Jerome and Gabriel are both Consultants looking to be Seniors, is that correct?"

Malcolm sat back, hands in pockets, nodding. She already knew. He looked her in the eyes. "My headline is Jenny and Gabriel are ready, the other two are not."

Alicia let go of the pearl and leaned forward. "Well, let's have the conversation. Who should we start with?"

Malcolm opened his A4 notebook. He pulled out a single sheet of A4 paper with four columns containing his notes: what each of the four were good at and what each needed to improve. He had wanted to write 'weaknesses' but Delaine discouraged such language. They had strengths and *learning opportunities*. He span the sheet so it was orientated towards her. She studied it.

"Excuse my writing. Let's start with Jerome, shall we?"

Her face was implacable. She nodded.

"His strengths are that he has strong client relationships at the middle manager level. He's structured in his messaging. He works to time and completes his deliverables to a high standard. He is very good. There's no doubt about that."

She looked at him out of the corner of her eye. She knew that he knew she was interested in Jerome for personal reasons. It was the Delaine way. Patronage was encouraged. The successful had a string of people behind them. Promotion engendered loyalty and loyalty encouraged performance.

"But..." Malcolm said, hoping she was ready to hear him and conscious of the bead of sweat above his ear.

"You should say 'and'. Otherwise people don't hear what you say in praise."

He shook his head. "*But* there is something about him I find caustic. He is self-serving. And extremely immature."

"There's nothing wrong with ambition," Alicia said. "In fact, it's a requirement. We used to have an 'up or out' culture. It really was intense. Thank goodness things have moved on. But you should realise that advancement is expected by both the company and the employee. Your job is to ensure it's done efficiently."

It was somehow his fault that Jerome was immature.

"It's the maturity and integrity that bother me more than anything."

"Say more?"

Malcolm exhaled. He wondered how much to tell her about Jerome's expenses and the way he responded to feedback.

Alicia placed a manicured hand flat on the table then lifted it, hinging at the wrist. "What you need to realise is that turnover in this industry is close to twenty-eight percent. I'm sure you get the head-hunters calling. I've lost count of how many times IMV have tried to poach me to be their Operations Director. Young Jerome has a lot of potential. He was at the top of his peer group on the GDP and will continue to grow. We need to help him do so and holding him back is not the way."

"Well, I'm glad we're getting to the heart of the issue. I struggle with him. Writing his appraisal was difficult."

Malcolm thought of why he didn't like him. The clash of cultures. The stylistic differences. He thought of what Jerome would be like as an officer. He lacked the clarity that defined a leader. He certainly didn't have the integrity or the internal steel. Men like Dean Chadwick or Pete McCardle would simply wave him off as an irrelevance. Dean would knock the smarmy grin off his face within a few minutes.

Malcolm shook his head. "If you promote him, you are reinforcing his way of carrying himself. He's good, in front of the client. I have no issues there. But his personal attributes are not those of a Senior Consultant. By our own capabilities model. He does not meet the expectations in the *personal attributes* box."

Alicia nodded. "But he does meet expectations in the other three: delivery, sales, teamwork?"

She had him there. He couldn't put his finger on what it was he didn't like. "I told him I would not be recommending him for promotion."

"You shouldn't have done that."

"Why not? I wanted to say it face to face so his expectations were set prior to the Review."

Malcolm feared he had done himself harm. He had been relying on experience and suddenly realised that Alicia had called this meeting because Jerome had complained to her.

"He started crying when I told him, which proves my point. This isn't personal. I just don't think he's ready. Holding him back a year will force him to mature. And if he flounces off to IMV, the change will encourage him to grow."

He could see her mind working. "But what I'm hearing you say is that he scores highly on three of the boxes of the balanced score card and on the other, personal attributes, your concern centres around maturity."

Malcolm corrected her. "Maturity *and* integrity."

"But these are attributes he will learn. If he's put on a new project, for example. Or has a different team leader."

Malcolm sensed the subtext. He wouldn't be sorry if Jerome was taken off his team.

"I don't think they are learnable skills, Alicia. I think they are innate. You either have integrity or you don't. He doesn't. People will not trust him in a leadership position."

Alicia looked at her watch. It was twenty-five past eleven. They had covered one of the four but both knew that if they had him correct, the others would follow.

Alicia patted the table again. The ring clattered. "My take is Jenny, yes, absolutely. Gabriel, yes. Jerome, yes, definitely. Timur, I agree with you, is not yet ready. In fact, we should put him on a Personal Improvement Plan."

The gradings suddenly made sense to Malcolm. He saw as Alicia saw, as Delaine saw. He could place himself in the same scale and understood where he fitted.

"As you wish, Alicia. I can triangulate from there and will redraft the cards."

She nodded, smiling.

"But it remains my view that you are making a mistake. You will find he will not be respected as a Senior."

Her face soured. "I hear you, Malcolm. And I understand the values that underpin your opinions. But this is the Delaine way."

Malcolm felt imprisoned. He was out of his depth and angry that she was not hearing him.

She read his face. "Malcolm, I really appreciate the effort you have gone to in developing your team. It is very noticeable. No one else works so hard for their team."

"Jerome won't. I'll tell you that for nothing."

She frowned. It now looked personal. Someone knocked on the glass wall.

"Thank you, Malcolm. Now, if you'll excuse me I have to be on the fifth floor for a strategy review with the other Heads. Please send the revised cards by tomorrow."

The meeting was over.

Alexander, December 2018

Much to his chagrin, Alexander did not enjoy the support of the entirety of the Party Membership for his bid to be the Party Leader and Prime Minister. A few Members of the back benches possessed a dim view of him as a man, a Member, and an exponent of Brexit. One of these was the former army officer Tom Tugendhat.

In Parliament, challenging Alexander's intention not to pay the legal bill required by any Brexit agreement, Tugendhat asked, sarcastically, if Alexander had also persuaded the Russians to return Crimea to Ukraine.

Courageous and principled though he may have been, Tugendhat could not compete with Alexander's brazen rhetorical abilities. In the brilliant Hansard response to Tugendhat's question, Alexander thundered that black was white, the questioner an ill-informed coward, that a nuanced change in policy towards the Northern Irish border was required but that in no manner should he be responsible for working out the details. And he did all this on his feet in under three-hundred words while simultaneously casting himself as the sole and tenacious champion of the British interest:

'My honourable Friend, from a sedentary position, compares the European Union to Lavrov and Russia. I think that that is an entirely inapposite comparison. These are our friends. These are our partners. To compare them to Russia today is quite extraordinary.

'We should say that we appreciate the good work that is being done to protect the rights of citizens on either side of the Channel but we must be clear that we will not accept the backstop. It is nonsensical to claim that it is somehow essential to further progress in the negotiations. The question of the Irish border is for the future partnership, not the withdrawal agreement. It was always absurd that it should be imported into this section of the negotiations.

'We should use the implementation period to negotiate that future partnership, which is what I believe the Government themselves envisage—and, by the way, we should withhold at least half that £39 billion until the negotiation on the new partnership is concluded.'

Kyle, previously

After three weeksmove. Other veterans room.
Want stay. But no. Can't do it.
London. Got dossbag so parks after dark.
Gucci kit. Cushty.
Parky locks gate but stay low move fast. No bother from drunks.
Day time keep askingcard with number 25096767 please help. Some do some don't.

Keep moving. Cash machines good but have to fight with gypsies.

Always moving. Always safe.

Under bridges train rattle. People look down. No dog but card. Alleys smell piss but darkies got gear. Need to nick.

Corner shops too careful. Too many. But Lidl Aldi good. Lidl Aldi good.

Aldi walk in. Green light doors open. Sarnies. Take one, long. Walk quick. Look at milk and put sarnie in coat. Don't look up. Don't look for cameras. Just act.

Woman with kids watches me and pushes trolley. I'm sideways through tills. Walk tall. Be scary baseball cap.

Outside doors close. Big guy high-vis grabs me. Twist punch but too quick. Ouch down ouch hard gravel. Radio.

Surrender, sorry mate, sorry, sorry.

Drags me roller door. Beating coming, cover face.

Let's go. Lift. Unzip jacket.

"Listen mate. I saw you take it. I'm not going to smash you. I can see you're a veteran. Your tee-shirt. Here's a tenner. Go and get some food. I was fifteen years in the bootnecks."

Back to wall. Look down shame.

Two sarnies now plus a tenner.

"Just screw the nut and don't come back."

Want to sorry but go. Starving scoff. Gear tenner.

Gear smashed no dreams.

Please no dreams.

Malcolm, January 2019

The Ulster light had a quality Malcolm could not quite define. He felt its warmth even in the depths of winter. He thumped his chest to quell the heartburn. The food and wine over Christmas and his birthday were punishing him and he had another night to go with Penny's parents before the flight back to Newcastle.

Penny's father was driving. He was a huge man, taller than Malcolm and with a chest few could put their arms round. They were taking the coast road from Newry having collected a prescription for Luca and a pack of sausage meat from one of the few butchers Penny's mother patronised.

"Do you know where you are?" William asked.

Malcolm looked at the road, the trees, the narrow stretch of river. The green hills on the far side. They passed a squat castle with stone walls but no roof.

"Is that the Republic of Ireland over there?"

"Tis, aye. So d'you know where you are?"

Malcolm shook his head and burped into his hand.

"Wait till I show ye."

They came to a roundabout. William indicated and pulled into the outside lane then followed the roundabout all the way round and back the way they had come. Very soon, on the left, there was a narrow strip of trees beyond which William slowed and stopped. They were a hundred metres short of the square-sided castle. Malcolm looked out of his window. A row of red military wreaths and wooden remembrance crosses were tacked to a wooden fence by the roadside.

"Have a look," William said as he unbuckled his seatbelt.

Malcolm joined him, glad of the fresh sea air. He had tried to keep up with him but couldn't. He will blame having to work or needing to sleep. Anything so he didn't have to drink all night.

He read the handwritten notices on the wreaths wondering why they were on this stretch of road. A wooden cross had written on it, 'Narrow Point Massacre, 1979'.

"Is this... Warrenpoint?" he said.

"Tis, aye. This here is where the first bomb went off. Killed a truck load of your boys. Paratroopers. Then the IRA opened fire from across yonder. They set off the secondary by that there castle when the casualties were being evacuated. Killed the CO of the Highlanders. Eighteen men all up."

Malcolm looked at the terrain with an experienced eye. He knew how to set an ambush and what it was like when one had been set for him. "They knew what they were doing," he said.

"Oh, they did, aye. Brilliant, tactically. Cannot fault it. Revenge for Bloody Sunday, so it was."

Malcolm was dredging the depths of his regimental history. He didn't want to look a fool and sensed that William cherished the past in the same way all his people did.

"You think it'll come back?"

"What?"

"Terrorism. With Brexit, I mean. They're talking about a hard border. Customs checks and all that."

William folded his arms across his enormous chest. It was only just above freezing but he was in a short-sleeved white polo shirt with the knitted tank-top he got for Christmas. He looked across the narrow waterway. Someone in a canoe was floating down the central stream on the outgoing tide using the paddle to steer at the stern.

"Tell you, Malachi, those boys in London, Boris and what have ye, they don't understand a jot about this place, so they don't."

He looked upriver, shaking his head. "We've had peace here, or a sort of it, since the late nineties. And for why? Because both sides could say they won. The republicans had the island of Ireland. They can drive north and south and east and west and no one gives a monkeys. And the loyalists, they can say they have both Stormont and a seat at Westminster."

"So it's the best of both worlds?"

He tried to sound wise but sensed depths he could plumb but not swim. William was hoping he would dip his toes and try to understand.

"If there's a hard border, and we go back to the nineteen-seventies, the republicans will break away from the Good Friday Agreement and collapse the Assembly. Stormont.

They'll walk out. So we'll have no functioning government, no one deciding the things of the day. Who gets what, you understand?"

Malcolm nodded as he looked up the river.

"The DUP will say they cannot function without Sinn Féin and will take away their bat and ball. They know that's what Sinn Féin wants but they'll do it anyway."

"But that doesn't mean anyone will take up arms."

"No, not in itself. But they will, Malachi, they will. You see it was all about drugs. Who controlled what. The IRA, Slab's little gang, they controlled supply in Tyrone and Londonderry. But the prods controlled Belfast and the university. And all those wee students, you know, toking away. But it's different now. Different drugs. Different supply. It'll be a bloodbath for a few years, so it will."

William shook his head and narrowed his eyes in the low sunlight. Malcolm knew he was lucky to be alive after a bombing and that he still checked under his car every morning. His pale eyes watered in the cold air.

"What we'll lose is the cooperation. I ran a border station for twenty years. We never had any conversation with the Guards in all that time. But see now, we work together."

He held out his hand, first two fingers crossed.

"Car crime is down. Smuggling is down. Joy riding's gone away because there's work for the young and they only did it for recreational violence. The Assembly talks to the Dáil. PSNI talks to the Gardaí. Our Ports Authority talks to theirs. You get the picture. This isn't a big place. You marry a girl from the mountain and you marry the mountain. As you know, Malachi. So cutting it in half again will do a world of hurt, so it will. Shameful. It's shameful."

He put his hands in his pockets. The thick red hair on his arms caught the light.

"And it's not just us, you know? We voted against Brexit and so did Scotland. They had a referendum and said they'd stay. But if the jobs dry up, or if there's more austerity, you wait. The Scots will up again, wanting independence. And that'll be the end of the United Kingdom."

Malcolm shook his head.

"You didn't vote for Brexit did you, Malachi?"

"God no."

He thought of what to say. William had always been so welcoming to him, so proud that his daughter should marry him.

"I voted conservative all my life. It was natural, you know. But I look at them now and I think, is that what we've come to? Do these people represent me?"

William stood facing the river, arms folded, looking over his shoulder at Malcolm. "Difficult for you, so it is. Who else do you vote for in England? Corbyn? Not a hope. And the liberals are a waste of oxygen."

Malcolm saw where Penny got her brains from. He stayed silent.

William said, laughing, "Easier here, in a lot of ways. You just vote for your favourite football team, you know? Green or Blue!"

He chuckled, his great shoulders shaking.

"Anyway. Thought you'd like to see this place." He nodded to the car. "Come on ahead. Let's get home and have a swifty before dinner. She's making a pork roast, so she is. You like pork, don't you, Malachi?"

Malcolm swallowed. "Love it," he said.

Dean, February 2019

Dean was tidying up the kitchen after their Sunday fish and chips. Michelle and the girls had gone through to the living room to watch the recording of *They Shall Not Grow Old*, a movie made of black and white films that had been colourised by the same bloke who did *Lord of the Rings*. Dean had watched it when it first came out but called to them to say he'd be through as soon as he'd done the dishes.

The best thing about fish and chips was that he could stack the trays and push them all into a bin bag. The ketchup went back in the fridge, as did the mayo. He knew he'd have to train hard to work off the fat he'd been gaining since Christmas. His jeans were getting tight round the waist and thighs.

Throughout dinner the girls had been teasing him. Victoria clearly knew something about Elizabeth but the older one kept telling her to shut up in an increasingly angry manner. It was obviously about a boy. Perhaps Michelle knew something but her face didn't give anything away. In fact, she had avoided eye contact. Dean had said nothing. The last thing he wanted was all three women ganging up on him.

Standing at the sink he washed the metal knives and forks under a running tap, scratching the crusty fish batter off with firm strokes of his thumbnail. The kitchen window now looked into the newly completed conservatory and Dean was grateful that Michelle had found Jakub, someone reliable, hard-working, and professional. It was a splendid job and had been done for a very reasonable price. Even his old man had been happy at Christmas, smoking away, his thin legs crossed, Mr T on a mat at his feet.

The conservatory was dark. A thick layer of snow covered the roof. Dean was wearing slippers so stepped quickly through the snow to drop the bin bag in the wheelie bin, cracking the frozen hinges as he lifted the lid.

Back in the house he heard his phone ringing. Michelle shouted that they were waiting for him but he shouted back for them to start. He picked up the phone from the kitchen table and saw that he'd missed a call from Billy. It was about time they talked.

"Go on. I'll be there in a minute."

He pressed the redial button. It had been several weeks since they'd spoken. He wanted Michelle to think he'd distanced himself since Billy had been given a suspended sentence for contempt of court. When she had seen it on the news she had slapped her knee with one hand. "Good!" she said. "Nasty piece of work, that man."

But Dean needed more training pills and Billy was his go-to supplier.

"Billy. You rang me?"

"Dean. Just the man. Got a minute?"

"Yes, mate. You been good?"

Billy kept a heavy silence, then inhaled. "I was keeping low, Dean. Like you said. *Stay low, move fast,* yeah?"

"Good. That work?"

"Yeah, I guess. Bound over, wasn't I? But that's it, isn't it? You tell those in power what they don't want to hear and they get you, don't they?"

Dean didn't want to get into that. "So what can I do for you?" he said.

There was silence on the line.

"Billy?"

With a quick glance into the living room Dean opened the French door into the conservatory and sat in the darkness. With the phone in his hand he looked at his reflection in the window opposite.

"We're going again, Dean," Billy said. "But we're getting in this time."

"Going where?"

"The same target. We're going again but this time..."

"You fucking mad?" Dean said. "After you got..."

"It's the principle, mate. I saw it with my own eyes. The girls. The van. I saw it, Dean. I watched them being pushed into the place. And sometimes you have to put the country before yourself, yeah? You have to take risks. This is not about me, it's about Rotherham. My town. Your town, Dean. We've got to do something."

"Like what? Spray graffiti and batter old men? Come on, Billy."

He wasn't sure if Billy would explode but didn't much care. He wouldn't take much handling one to one but he did have a gang. And people like Billy could make life difficult if they wanted.

238

"That was unfortunate, Dean. Really unfortunate. I mean you couldn't get the window open, could you? Not that it was your fault. I mean it was locked, wasn't it. No one could have got in. Not that way. And we got rumbled, didn't we? They heard us. Sent their boys out..."

Dean didn't remember boys. Just an old man in brown pyjamas with cracked skin round his heels. An old man more disappointed than a threat.

"I don't know, Billy..."

"You losing your bottle? Don't care about the town? 'Cos, if that's the case, we're fucked. Might as well let them take over. So decent men, local men, get shunted. No place to live. No access to doctors. No nothing."

"Who said I was losing my bottle?" Dean said.

"Well are you?"

"Course not. But that doesn't mean I'm going to break into someone's house does it?"

"Not a house. It's a crime scene. I tell you. There's women in there and I can prove it. But this time there'll be three of us. Three, Dean. You me and one other guy I think you'll like. Ex military. A patriot. A thinker. And well up for a fight. I've recruited him. He's just back from working in security. Like you. Middle East. Knows his stuff. You'll get on great. And this time we've got a better plan..."

Dean wanted Billy to know he needed to be convinced. "And what's that then?"

"I'll tell you when I see you. But let's say that our friend has a key. Useful to know people who work at the shop where the doors were made, yeah?"

Dean said nothing. He could see Michelle through the kitchen window. She was getting another cup of tea.

"Alright mate, we'll chat later, yeah? Gotta go. Bye. Bye."

He pressed the red button and pushed the phone into his trouser pocket just as Michelle came to the French doors and leaned against the side. "Who was that? Everything alright?"

Dean nodded. "Yeah, just some work Bolton wants me to sort."

"Bolton? What's he want on a Sunday?"

Dean pushed himself up from the deep sofa. "It's fine. How's the movie?"

"It's fantastic what they've done. Are you coming or what?"

He patted her belly as he went past her into the kitchen. "I'm coming. Get me a Peroni from the fridge. I'll see you in there."

Although he wasn't sure about Billy, he wanted to feel he was free to do what he wanted. It was his world and he'd live by his rules.

Kyle, previously

Thinking Charlotte lots. Close, I know, but no, not here.

Army Recruitment Office, Pimlico. Walk by and there was this Guards sergeant at the door. Proper shiny brown boots. Big chest. Slashed peak. Green and black cap band: Welsh Guards.

He looked down. Proper down over nose.

I wanted to say I was one of you. I was there. But didn't. Cover veteran's badge with hand.

Looking down pond life.

Lay in park. So shit. Crying, crying, crying.

"Never do that to me again, Kyle,"

Sorry Dad. Too hard. Just a STAB. Blokes won't help me, not like this. Why would they? Vagabond. Less than craphat. Panfat. And they're in America anyway. I can see that on Facebook.But at least came off gear. Bad shit bad.

Newspaper in bin. Chips. Yes, cushty.

Taliban take Amrut. Kabul bombing.

And I'm like what? You fucking wanker! I lost three mates taking and holding that shithole. Two shot. One IED. And then two others injured.

And what for? What's the fucking point?

Pete, March 2019

The old Marine turned out to have something more than useful. It was glorious. The caravan was on a hillside on the edge of Kielder Forrest, just over the border in England, surrounded by a one-acre copse of pine trees. The nearest house was a mile down the dirt track and the nearest village was a mile beyond that, on the other side of the A68. The caravan was old and stained from top to bottom but structurally sound. The tyres had long since rotted so it sat on logs and piles of stones. All this made Pete extremely happy.

The cooker worked. He bought a large gas bottle and one in reserve. He parked his bike between two trees and sheltered it underneath his old basher. At first he slept in his old dossbag but then found sheets and a duvet in a charity shop in Hawick and started to make himself at home. He bought an axe and a bow saw, then a small diesel generator and some pans.

He found a blue, two-hundred litre feed bin by the side of the road and appropriated it, carrying it to his camp as dark was falling. He cleaned out the grain and tested the locking mechanism on the lid. Then he bought a battery powered drill and an assortment of bits and cut a hole to fit a tap.

A farmer rode up the lane on a quadbike with an alert collie on the back. Pete told him who he was and that he had Iain's permission to be there. The man nodded, went away, and came back later in a vast tractor with some pallets on the bale spike. Pete took these and built a platform for his feed container which was now his water supply. He bought thirty yards of hose and ran it from the burn trickling down through the peat into his new water tank. Naked to the waist, he sucked on the hose until the brackish water trickled through. He cheered. It took a day to fill the bin but once full it was easy to keep topped up.

The ground behind the caravan became compressed from use. Pete bought a shovel and levelled the earth.

Bucket by bucket, he stole gravel from a pile by the side of the main road at the entrance to the village. He laid it as a pathway from the caravan to the water tap and wished he'd thought more about what to put where. But it was too late now, the caravan being fixed and the water tank being too heavy to lift. So he bought a camping shower from an outdoor shop and strung it from the trees behind the water tank. Naked, he washed himself in the freezing water, his body milk white save for his face and hands.

After three weeks there, a car drove up the track, weaving between the potholes. Pete had grown a beard that sprang richly from his face, grey at the tips. He waited for the car to come, hands on his hips. The only weapon he had was a replacement shaft for the axe. He studied the number plate and recognised it.

The car stopped short. It was James. He got out, looking round at the open moorland and the forestry blocks, and shivered.

Pete walked down to him and they embraced.

"Bring any food?"

James nodded nervously, indicating the boot.

"I did. And some letters that were in the flat."

Pete didn't see a need to respond. He stood, hands in pockets, watching his brother's face.

"We're worried about you," James said. "You just left. The gas got turned off. Your neighbours were... are you alright?"

"Couldn't be better," Pete replied.

James was the first person he'd spoken to in six days. His voice sounded odd, he thought. He felt belligerent.

"Sandy bought that flat for you, Peter."

"No he didn't. He bought it for himself. To save face when you sacked me."

James' mouth dropped open. His jaw worked in circles as he considered what to say. "Look, do you no think I could come in? It's cold."

Pete thought of asking what for but relented. He took his brother inside and shook the kettle to gauge the water level.

"Do you have matches?"

"There's the lighter in the car..."

Pete patted his pockets. "No, I've got one."

James sat on the small bed, knees pressed together. He hadn't taken off his coat. Pete lit the gas and held the grey button in to make sure it caught.

"Now, what can I do for you, James?" he said, leaning towards him. "Why'd you come all this way?"

His brother looked nervous. "I... I thought you'd welcome company. You haven't answered..."

Pete shook his head. "There's no signal here."

"So you haven't heard..."

"Heard what?"

"You haven't read your letters?"

"Why should I? Bastards do nothing for me. They just want to kick me about like a fucking football?"

James' mouth hung open. Pete was glad it was him rather than Sandy. "Have they let me off? Have they thrown the case out?"

James shook his head. "No. But I think you should appreciate the public support you have."

"The what?"

James got out his phone and started pressing the screen.

"There's no signal. If you want Wi-Fi you'll have to go to the pub down in the village."

James nodded, his throat wobbling. Pete wondered why the three of them were so different. Sandy had been too old for his father's anger. James was too timid to attract attention. It had always been Pete, the rebel, he picked on.

"Alright, let's go take a look. You can buy me dinner while we're there."

Steve, April 2019

Steve was low. Nothing was working. He'd met a girl from Penrith on two occasions but she'd stopped responding to his texts and now she'd blocked him and the frustrating thing was that he didn't know why. He wasn't a lunatic or a rapist. Why did she have to run away like that? Why didn't she just say he wasn't for her?

He was in the living room with his feet on the coffee table. He couldn't even be bothered to watch the London marathon. How bad was it that a thirty-two-year-old man was living with his mother?

The school talks had dried up. He'd registered with an agency and been impressed by the people on their books: a former England rugby captain with cauliflower ears and dark hair, politicians he didn't know, the guy who lived in the wild and ate berries. But no work had come out of it even though he'd already paid a grand for them to promote him. He'd even left a message to say he would cover his own costs if that would help.

Most of all, though, he wanted to be a teacher. Help little kiddies learn about the world, be streetwise, be resilient. When Malcom rang he was lost in daydreams of saving a child's life from a car crash, his prosthetic arm being crushed under the wheels.

"Steve, how's it going?"

"Hello Malcolm. How are you?"

"I'm good, mate. Did you watch the race? That little Kenyan is amazing. He'll break two hours, bet you anything."

Steve chuckled. "What's his name again. Ketchup? Chipotle?"

Malcolm laughed. "Kipchoge. Eliud Kipchoge."

"That's it. Kipchoge. Funny name isn't it?"

"It is, mate, it is. But listen, sorry to disturb you on a Sunday but I'm back at work tomorrow. I haven't called because I've been away."

"Where've you been? Anywhere good?"

"Not really. I've been working in a submarine factory. But it's high security so they take your phone off you."

"The one in Barrow? That's just down the road from me that is. You should come in for a brew. Have a chat."

"I'd like that very much, Steve. But the working week is quite long, you know. Fourteen-hour days. So I'm usually knackered by the time I'm finished. That's the only reason I haven't rung."

"I know you're busy, Malcolm. I know you have commitments. I appreciate everything you do for me. I do. I really do."

Malcolm sounded relieved. He exhaled heavily. "So how are you getting on at the moment? Did you get anywhere finding out what you need to be a teacher?"

Steve didn't answer. The weight of finding out was too daunting for him and he feared rejection.

"What have you managed to do?" said Malcolm when Steve didn't respond.

He still didn't answer. The question felt like a bayonet thrust. He didn't know which way to turn.

"Is it something you can help me with, Malcolm? I'd appreciate it if you can help me find out. I don't know where to start."

It was Malcolm's turn to be silent now.

"I know you've always been there for the blokes, Malcolm. I'd appreciate a bit of help if you have the time. I know you're busy. But I don't know…"

Malcolm said, "Alright. Alright. I'll do a quick search and see what I come up with. But this should really be you doing it, Steve, not me. You need to take ownership of your life. It's not for me. I'm not your platoon commander."

Steve nodded. On the TV screen he watched the reflection of his feet as he parted them and slapped them together. The undersides of his socks were dirty.

"I know. But you do it much quicker than me and you make it make sense. I get lost in all these pages you get on t'internet."

"I know mate. You do have to wade through it all to find the information you want."

His voice had changed. Steve knew he'd won the debate.

"Look," Malcolm said. "I'll send you some links tonight. I'm away again tomorrow morning, early, but we should catch up in a week or so. As well as being a teacher I think you might want to consider just working in a school."

"How do you mean?"

"Just being in the school. Admin staff. Groundsman...."

"Do you mean a cleaner?"

He didn't reply for a while then spoke softly. "Would that be a problem for you?"

Steve didn't know how to respond. He'd cleaned the block. Cleaning things was part of being a soldier. Or painting them white.

"You see, Steve, what's on my mind, and I'm just going to say it straight, is you may not be qualified to be a teacher. But if you worked in a school, and they get to know you, they might find things for you to do that are really fulfilling."

"Like what?"

"I don't know, Steve. We won't know till we get there will we?"

He sounded frustrated. His voice was rising. The idea had merit but Steve had his heart set on being a teacher. He liked the way they looked up at him, the innocence of their faces, the feeling of responsibility.

"Have a think about it, mate. We'll talk in a bit."

"Alright. Will do. Bye."

Malcolm, April 2019

"Hello, is that Malcolm?"

The voice was soft and romantically Irish. "Yes, Malcolm Sewell."

"Hello, my name's Bronagh. Bronagh McDaid. I'm a case worker for *Save Our Heroes*?"

"Ah! You're calling about Steve Reedman?"

Malcolm thought quickly. The project had recently got very busy so he hadn't called Steve in a while and felt guilty about it. He also felt bitter that Steve was so dependent on him. But if it wasn't him who else would it be?

"Bronagh, I know your name. Steve talks about you with great fondness."

He looked at his watch. The others round the table were glancing at him so he got up, phone to his ear, and went into the corridor.

"Is this a good time?"

"I have ten minutes. I'm at work. Er... what do you need to talk about?"

"We've just had a review of our post-recovery cases. Steve's name came up as we don't know how he's been doing."

"I've sent in the paperwork. Whenever I've called him or seen him."

He wanted to make it sound like he'd seen Steve but, in truth, he hadn't for some months. He had called though, both times hoping Steve wouldn't answer. It was never a short call when they talked.

"And how's he doing? Is he in work yet?" Bronagh asked.

"He set himself up as a public speaker. I helped him find schools to talk to."

"A lot of WIS do that," Bronagh said. "It's good for them. Makes them feel valued."

"I'm sure. We all need that. And his talk is good, he delivers it well."

"That's great. How sustainable do you think that is? Will he be able to keep doing it?"

Malcolm sucked his teeth. "Mmm. On a scale of one to ten, one? It's me that finds the schools. And he keeps changing his mind. He says he wants to be a public speaker one week and the next week he wants to be a climbing instructor. Or an astronaut."

Bronagh laughed. "He was always like that, sure. He never settles. It's always been one thing, then the next, then the next."

"A function of his brain injury, I suspect."

Malcolm held the phone close. It felt conspiratorial but she was on the same side.

"That's it. He doesn't seem to know what he can't do," Bronagh said.

Malcolm liked this turn of phrase. Was that not true for all of them?

Later, talking to Penny by phone for their midweek chat, he told her about the conversation.

"I didn't say I wanted to finish. Just I wanted to know what finishing looks like."

"How do you mean?"

"On the course at Catterick they said that a coaching relationship is successful if you make any positive change to someone's life."

"Have you not done that? He's better off now, surely?"

"Yes, he is. He's stable, anyway. And doing something he enjoys. But it's not going to last forever."

"No. But it's not your job to look after him forever is it?"

"I hope not," Malcolm said. "But I don't know who'll do it if I don't."

Alexander, May 2019

By the middle of the year, an ever more diminished Teresa May had presented three possible versions of her withdrawal deal to Parliament. On all three occasions they were rejected. Her position became untenable.

Following her sour, tearful resignation, Alexander confirmed he would run for the leadership. He had played a masterful game: he had championed the Leave campaign to put himself in the public eye knowing that economic growth was an essential pillar of the national interest. He had stepped back to allow Teresa May to be crushed by the intractable dilemma of the Northern Ireland border while simultaneously confounding and confusing the issue with all those involved. He had trumpeted the threat of a hard Brexit, undoubtedly ruinous to millions of businesses, while simultaneously braying that the government should do everything in its power to avoid such an outcome. He had warned of 'the catastrophic consequences for voter trust in politics' while simultaneously deceiving nearly everyone he came into contact with. He pushed for the UK to leave the Union while simultaneously suggesting that it should not have to pay for doing so.

Papers found later at 10 Downing Street dated May 2019 record that:

> I have the shield of Heracles on my arm. It is wrought with fine inscriptions and the visages of Kydoimos, Palioxis, and Eris surround the face of Phobos. Confusion, flight, and strife arising from fear.
> The shield rebuffs those who attack me.
> I am invincible.

Dean, June 2019

It was still light but they didn't intend to be long. The plan was simple: park the van on the street opposite the mosque. The driver, Frenchy, would keep watch with the engine running. Dean and Billy would enter using the key Frenchy had got from work. Inside, they'd split and search the building, Dean upstairs and Billy the ground floor. If they found girls, they'd take them out. If not, they'd grab laptops, hard drives, computers. Evidence. In and out in five, tops.

Billy was sweating and pale. He was dressed completely in black, even to the polo shirt Dean suspected he had bought especially. Dean was in his work wear, the same trousers and boots he used at Bolton's, a non-descript hoodie on top. He would pull the snood over his nose before they went in.

Frenchy stuck carefully to the speed limit. This was the first time Dean had met another English Templar. When Dean had got in the van through the side door Frenchy had kept his hood up and face hidden. He didn't speak and Dean didn't get a chance to look at him. There was no rear-view mirror so he studied him from behind. He looked muscular and had a full beard that appeared gingerish in the streetlight. He was wearing dark glasses and a baseball cap under his hood. There was something familiar about him. Was he one of those people who had tried to join the Paras but failed?

It didn't matter. They turned the final corner and the van slowed. Dean knelt, thankful for the knee pads. He pulled the snood over his nose and ears and put a hand on the inside handle of the door.

"Get ready lads," Frenchy hissed over his shoulder.

Billy twisted down behind Dean and gripped his shoulder hard. Dean stopped himself from shaking his head. He didn't understand why people should feel nervous when they were crossing the Start Line. It interfered with focus. This was a simple operation. Speed and momentum. Same as boxing, same as rugby. He adjusted the snood, tugged his hood forward, and drew the strings tight at his neck. He then pushed his hands into his gloves, extending and waggling the fingers.

The van mounted the kerb making it tilt one way and then the other. It straightened and crept forward before coming to rest. Billy thumped Dean on the back but he didn't move.

"Frenchy, see anything?"

"No."

"Behind?"

"Clear. Go, go, go!"

That was good enough. With a tug at the handle he pulled the door release and slid it slowly to keep the low rumble quiet. He stepped out, looked left and right, then walked purposefully towards the mosque. His shoulder didn't hurt as he'd strapped it. The van's lights were on but Frenchy knocked them off as he passed the cab. Behind him, Billy pushed the sliding door so that it was almost but not fully closed.

At the corner, directly opposite the mosque, Dean glanced up and down the street. He paused in the shadows, feeling his heart. This was like NI arrest op back in the day: bang the door, upstairs, whip back the bedding, crack to the shin with a baton, grab them by the balls and out they come as compliant as a lamb.

The fox was not there this time.

Because of his strength, all his life he'd been the first one through the door after the grenade went off. It was what he liked being: the shock and awe guy. He felt free.

After crossing the road he pressed the metal lever on the gate and eased it open. The hinges squeaked. He held it for Billy, who took hold of it as if it was a young baby, turning to close it behind them.

The key worked. One turn, then two, and the handle dropped under pressure from his hand. He shouldered gently against the door to see if there was an internal chain but it opened into a narrow hallway with one door off to the right and a set of carpeted stairs in front.

He went up, light on his toes. There might be people in bed and he didn't want women and kids screaming. Placing his gloved hands softly on the banister, he peeked round to examine the landing. There was a window high above the corner of the stairs and he knew from watching the house where it was on the outside wall. The layout of the drains and downpipes told him which doorway led to the bathroom and which ones were likely to be bedrooms. He checked them off mentally and listened out to the noises of the house as he stepped round the corner.

A red light came on: a camera in the corner. There was no time to hang about. Billy was downstairs clattering around like Michelle with a hangover.

Four doors. He didn't bother with the bathroom on the right. The next one, underneath the camera, was a small, front facing bedroom. Lace curtains, bedding rolls stacked vertically against the wall. Billy was right. There could have been people staying, although they weren't there now. He took a picture on his phone.

The second room was also front facing. An office desk stood in the middle of the carpeted floor with a chair behind it. There were two metal filing cabinets against the far wall but both were locked. There was some Arabic scripture in a thin frame on the wall reflecting the light from the window. On the ceiling, what he thought was a recessed smoke detector was actually an arrow pointing towards the corner. There was Arabic writing on it but he didn't have time to guess what it was. The desk drawers were unlocked but empty. He tried the filing cabinets again then felt along the edges of the room and into the corners of the windows. He found a brass radiator bleed key but nothing that would open the cabinets. He moved on.

The last room contained books, all in Arabic. Qurans. Others that looked like prayer books. Books with a faded picture of a minaret on the cover.

On a shelf against the wall was a large black and gold box on a marble base, a model of the thing in Saudi. Gold lines ran round the box horizontally. There were little carved curtains along three sides. It was very beautiful and Dean wondered if it was gold. He picked it up and a coin rattled inside it.

He took one more look round the room. No bomb making equipment. No manuals. No girls. He left, pulling the door closed.

With fast steps he descended the stairs, ducking to avoid hitting his head. Billy was in the prayer room on the ground floor. It was set at an odd angle for the layout of the building. He had a book in his hands, which he was fanning out to look for anything hidden in the pages. There being nothing, he flung it away.

Dean clicked his tongue, nodding towards the door. Billy took one more look round and followed. Backing out, Dean closed and locked the front door, keeping the key in his gloved hand. Both of them stepped over the low wall rather than use the gate and Billy could not help breaking into a run as they crossed the road.

The van's lights came on. There was still nothing up the road and nothing on Moseley. Billy was about to pull his balaclava off but Dean hissed, "Stay covered!"

As soon as they had pulled the door closed, Frenchy pulled out towards the mosque then left up the hill.

Billy started laughing. He pulled his headcover off. His face was red with sweat and his hair ruffled. "That was excellent, men. Excellent."

Dean said nothing. He was on his feet, rolling with the corners, braced against the door. Through the front window, he studied the empty streets, the parked cars, the deserted parks. He was happy but not excited. All in all, it had been a non-event. They'd broken into someone's place of worship, nosed around, and come out empty handed. He didn't know what it meant. Would he stay with this crew or tell them to fuck off? Was Billy the voice of his generation or just a small man with a small dick?

They drove eastwards, then north, then round the ring road to bring them to the Albion. The van pulled into the carpark, splashing through the ruts. Both Dean and Billy had left their cars. Frenchy would take the van away and replace the number plates. He seemed a good egg and Dean patted him on the shoulder when he got out.

In the cold night air Dean pulled down his snood but kept the cap low. As agreed, Frenchy turned round and sped off.

Billy was still flushed and giggling to himself as they walked back to their cars. The night was totally silent.

"Fucking good job that!"

Dean nodded. "Tell me about Frenchy," he said as they stopped by their cars. "Is that his name?"

Billy shook his head. "No mate. I protect you all, yeah? I keep your identities safe."

"But his name is *French*, yeah? He's not a Frog, is he?"

Billy shook his head as he felt in his trouser pockets for his keys. "No mate. But like I said, he's ex-army. You thought I meant British Army, didn't you? But he wasn't, see? He's a top bloke and when the time is right, I'll get you together. You served in the Paras. He was in the Legion. The Deuxieme REP. So, Frenchy, see?"

Dean felt a punch to his belly. Yep. They had met before. Saying nothing, he got into his car and drove off. He should have recognised him. Was that beard part of a disguise? Did he know who Dean was?

If he was now relying on the likes of that cunt he was in trouble.

Malcolm, June 2019

Dressed in black tie, Malcolm stood with his back to the bar watching the consultants mingle prior to dinner. There were forty of them in the Public Sector Transformation team and all of them were accommodated in this spa hotel, the best in Wiltshire, for both Friday and Saturday nights. He added up the cost in his head: inclusive rooms, meeting areas, the conference hall, dinner, the free bar and disco, the prizes. It easily came to a hundred grand.

The event had included an intense programme of work which Malcolm helped organise. His training module had focused on team building, which a lot of Senior and Managing Consultants attended. But the main event was the dinner. Alicia would soon invite everyone to the dance floor so they could listen to her 'view from the bridge', a summary of how the business was performing and their targets for the year ahead. She would announce promotions for the coming year and award prizes to those whose professional behaviours were above and beyond the level expected of their grade.

Quietly, Malcolm wondered if he might get a prize. He had been promoted after his first year but had also sold on four times, matching the sales target of an Executive Consultant. He had run a joint client and consultant team and guided the Chief Executive to a solution she was implementing across all her procurement lines. He was proud of what he'd done and hoped he could now move on to a new project.

The hotel staff moved silently and swiftly between the ball gowns and the dinner jackets. The men in his team kept calling them 'tuxedos'. He corrected them and had to show them all how to tie a bow tie. He knew they called him names. Command was a lonely place and he was comfortable in it. He liked the name *Austin Powers* but was less keen on *Eau de Tiger Balm*, which he used often on his knee.

"Hi Malcolm," Jenny said.

She was delicate, hunched, pale skinned. She wore a green velvet dress and a thin gold necklace with a heart pendant. She had recently got engaged.

"You look absolutely wonderful. May I get you a drink?"

The others in his team joined them and he ordered for them too. "It's on Delaine, so I'm getting you a double."

Their laughter was genuine but thin. They seemed shy, as though meeting for the first time. Malcolm felt he had to calm their nerves, charm them. It was like being a young officer hosting the brigadier's wife. He often wondered how these people could be so professionally brilliant and yet so personally insecure.

Jerome loomed into the circle. He had already had too much to drink and his breath smelled.

"I got promoted, didn't I? Despite everything you said."

The others looked down. Malcolm dropped his chin. One hand was in the pocket of his trews playing with his room key. The other held a gin and tonic.

"Not the place, Jerome. Not the time."

"It is the place. It is the time. I got promoted. Alicia told me."

Malcolm was conscious of Jenny. She would also want to know. "Yes. You have been promoted. As have a number of others. You deserve it."

"But you said I wasn't ready. You said I was immature."

Jenny looked from him to Jerome, as did Timur. She took a small step sideways sucking at the straw in her orange juice. Timur stood gawping.

Malcolm thought about walking away. Instead, he smiled, patted Jerome on the shoulder. "I was wrong, Jerome. You were absolutely ready for promotion and you deserve it fully. My hearty congratulations. Now, please excuse me."

He started to move away. The praise flummoxed Jerome. He blinked dumbly. Jenny turned away too and Malcolm glanced at her and winked. She smiled at him with innocent blue eyes. She had plaited her hair and he suspected her of testing how it looked.

"It suits you," he said.

"Thank you," she replied and was about to say more when Jerome shouldered her aside, one finger extended from his pint glass.

"I got promoted. I got it."

Malcolm drew his left hand from the pocket. He pointed at Jerome with all fingers extended. The Brecon forearm. His voice was loud, curt, and forceful. "Stop there. You just barged Jenny out of the way. Sober up or go to bed. Do you understand?"

People were looking.

"You can't talk to me like that…"

Malcolm snapped. He pointed his hand directly at Jerome's face.

"Yes I can and yes I fucking will, you little cunt. You got promoted. But you have a lot of ground to cover before you're ready for the next grade. You're making yourself look a fool. Grow up or fuck off."

Jerome blinked, mouth open. His weight was on his heels. Malcolm wanted to deck him but stopped himself.

Jerome's face reddened. He made a 'gawf' sound as though sobbing.

Jenny and Timur were looking at Malcolm with wide, frightened eyes. They had never seen him so angry. He pulled a hanky from his trews to wipe his lips.

"Jerome, drink some water and have something to eat."

With that, he turned away and looked over the crowd to where Alicia was lifting the microphone. He glanced down at Jenny.

"You ok?"

She nodded but said nothing.

"Sorry, I didn't mean to scare you."

It made him angry that he had upset her. That Jerome had got to him. He knew then that Delaine was no longer the place for him.

The people around them who had watched him give Jerome a bollocking were pretending it hadn't happened and started talking about work. They avoided his eye. He checked again on Jenny. Her eyes were still wide and he thought her idea of him had just changed radically. He looked round and Jerome was at the bar, wiping his cheeks with shaking fingers.

He knew he was right. He also knew Delaine wouldn't agree. Jerome would complain to Alicia, crying like a baby. He'd go to HR and say Malcolm was a bully.

Malcolm knew what he had to do.

He straightened his jacket and adjusted his tie. He was charming and charismatic all evening. He danced by himself on the empty dance floor when the ska came on. He danced like no one was looking even though they were filming him on their phones. He was the last to bed. He gave them something to remember him by, something that emphasised the essential difference between them. They might be brilliantly academic. They might be willing to work themselves to death. They might even be commercially astute and wonderfully persuasive. But the fact was he had something they didn't have and never would.

In the morning, after a bacon sandwich and a large bloody mary, he found Alicia and asked, in a somewhat hoarse voice, if he might have a quick chat.

Alexander, June 2019

During the leadership campaign, Alexander visited his girlfriend, Carrie Symonds, at her London flat. The media joyfully reported that a neighbour, never identified, was disturbed by them having a noisy fight and called the police. The neighbour was quoted as saying they heard Symonds shout for Alexander to 'get off me,' thereby positioning him as abusive and predatory.

Following the incident, Alexander's former editor at the *Daily Telegraph*, Sir Max Hastings, wrote in *The Guardian* that:

> 'He is unfit for national office, because it seems he cares for no interest save his own fame and gratification… He would not recognise the truth, whether about his private or political life, if confronted by it in an identity parade.'

Papers found later at 10 Downing Street dated June 2019 record the following short anecdote:

> Sunny day. Great sex.

Dean, July 2019

Billy was flapping like a ten-ton budgie. One of his mates, a guy from Leeds called Tommy, had been jailed for streaming himself live on Facebook jeering at Muslims by the Crown Court. The Muslims were being charged with abusing young girls. The case was ongoing and the judge had no option but to protect the accused.

"That's exactly what I did! Tommy copies me, he does. He does everything I do. So listen. I might end up going to prison. And they're full of Pakis, mate. Seventy percent, Wakefield. One of my boys is a warden. One of the Templars."

They were in the Albion, Billy pacing the worn wooden floor from the juke box to the bar and back again. There was no one else there and Dean had come to understand why Billy wanted to keep him apart from the other Templars. He was the only person of any real capability. So it suited him to be untarnished by others. He was increasingly sceptical of what this angry little man and his lackies could really do.

"Listen mate. I know. I know what we have to do. I need to go to ground for a while. Stay low, yeah? And that means... that means, Dean, I need you to do all the London runs. I need it to be you, mate. Usual rates, yeah?"

Dean shook his head. "Can't, Billy, not this weekend. The car's in for an MOT."

Actually, there was nothing wrong with his car, he just didn't want to put more miles on it and the drive was becoming boring. He had high professional standards and using the same car again and again was a risk.

Billy stopped in the middle of the floor and rubbed his chin. He was wearing a crisp white Fred Perry shirt, blue jeans with the bottoms rolled up, and ox-blood Doctor Martens. "Can you take the train? What's wrong with the train?"

Dean hadn't thought of it. "I don't want to get lifted if the coppers have a dog..."

He was silent for a while and Billy paced again. Then he stopped. "I'll get the Spaniard to meet you at King's Cross. Straight down, straight back. Same train. No need to hang around. You can see the coppers a mile off. Just avoid them. He'll meet you by the Harry Potter thing. Be thirty quid each way. Less than fuel, actually. You got a rail card? You're a veteran. Do they do railcards for veterans?"

Dean shook his head.

"That's shocking. State of this country, Dean, isn't it? They give houses to fucking immigrants and all the while there's our boys on the streets…"

"I know, Billy. I know."

Billy went back to pacing, his boots heavy and rhythmic. Someone was changing the barrels in the basement. The smell of beer came up through the floor in waves. Billy strode to the table.

"You use pills, right? For training? Do these runs for us and I'll get you some. The proper Anabolics. For proper training, mate, proper hard training, like what you do." He put his hands round Dean's arm, gripped hard. His lips were flecked with spittle.

Dean looked at him without moving. He didn't even tense his biceps. "Alright. I'll do it. But I'll pick the time and I'll let you know, ok? You have him there waiting. If he's not, I'm not staying."

"Good man, Dean. Fucking good man. Always knew you could be trusted. Always knew. I'll get you a stash of Trenbolone. That do you? That do you, big man, eh?"

Billy flicked his shoulder a couple of times. Dean nodded. "Yes, mate. That'll do. Plus the ticket price. Plus six hundred."

Later that day, Dean booked a train for the Thursday. When the time came he finished work, got a lift to the station and jumped on the next train to London. It was a sultry, hot afternoon and the carriage was boisterous and busy. He hadn't booked a seat and was lucky to find a place on a table of four. He sat quietly, keeping his legs in close so the little girl opposite didn't kick his knees.

Her mother was hot but Dean didn't make eye contact. He allowed himself to be forgettable, the grey man. He had no bag, which made him feel conspicuous, but he knew he would return with an orange wheelie one that he'd collect at the crusty baguette shop. The train was thirty minutes late arriving into Doncaster so he hoped the Spaniard wouldn't lose his nerve. He had no way of calling him except via Billy.

He was there, long-limbed and dirty looking, dreads tied behind his head with a bandana. He had a kind face. They nodded at each other and walked round the block of shops to swap ownership of the bag. Having done so, he tapped Dean on the arm and disappeared down the steps to the tube station. Dean hurried back across the concourse towards the barriers.

The train he'd come down on was from Leeds. The next train back was cancelled due to some signalling problem. The tannoy was telling everyone to wait but there was no way Dean was going to hang about. The train to Edinburgh was boarding at platform four. That went through Doncaster so Dean joined the throng of anxious travellers pushing through the gates.

He didn't want to risk putting his ticket in the machine in case it rejected him so he nimbly skipped through the double gates after a woman with a pram, lifting the orange bag over the barrier as it closed. He walked quickly, looking ahead. He was just another work-away traveller. It was Thursday and he was going home.

"Dean Chadwick!"

He ignored the shout. The platform was just ahead on the left and he pressed on past men in suits and an old woman with white hair. There were people checking tickets some way down the platform and Dean quickly rehearsed in his mind what he would say. When he got there, the guard in a high-vis jacket stopped the woman in front of him. Dean swerved round them and kept walking.

A voice behind him had a light Geordie accent. "Keep moving! The gestapo are watching."

Dean sniggered. He knew the voice immediately and impersonating a line from *The Great Escape* was exactly his style. He turned around, grinning. "Captain Sewell, Sir! How the devil?"

He swapped hands on the bag so he could extend one to shake. They could move faster than most people and were heading for the front. They looked in the windows of each carriage they passed but they were all chaotic, crowded, unsettled. It was a replacement train and one of the older ones.

"I hate London. Let's get on this one," Malcom said.

Dean thought Malcolm had been a good platoon commander. He'd punched out before the 2012 tour and that was a shame. He'd been replaced by – what was his name? It didn't matter. Ineffectual, anyway. Lost a leg in a suicide bombing and bled out on the way home. Shame but there you go. Malcolm was different. Dean was pleased to see him but was also conscious of the bag.

The pair clambered up into the carriage but there was no point pushing through to get a seat. People were lifting their bags up to the rack, edging past each other, apologising. There was an air of resigned panic. An elderly woman with a handbag on a long strap shifted her weight from side to side. The internal door tried to close but she was standing on the pressure pad and it kept slapping open. In the vestibule, Malcolm leaned against the wall. They were on the train and that was all that mattered. The toilet door swung open to reveal a wet floor and an unpleasant smell.

Malcolm had a small wheelie bag with a long handle. He pressed it down so he could sit on it. "It won't thin out till York. Best just chill for now."

A gang of four young men climbed into the carriage but turned round when they saw how busy it was. "Next one," the front one said.

Dean and Malcom looked at each other. They recognised the tone, the quick decision making. They smiled at each other.

"Where you going?" Malcolm asked.

Dean retracted the handle on his bag, lay it on its side, and squatted down beside him. At least the bag was being useful. "Donnie," he said. "Then Rotherham."

Malcolm clicked his tongue. "That's it, Rotherham. But you're out now, right? You got out after that tour?"

He still had that calm air of command. Dean remembered him as assertive, loyal, dutiful. He was a good soldier, too. Very fit. He was also a good laugh. When they'd taken him downtown, the SNCOs out with their officer, he scored with more women than even Dean.

On the platform, a train guard in a red jacket had a whistle in his lips and a white paddle in his hand. He shut the door from the outside. With the old people now taking their seats a sense of calm descended.

"Yeah, I'm out. I got extended, 'VEng' you call it. But punched out at twenty-four. Did a few years on the circuit. But now I'm home. Transport manager. What about you, Boss? Made a million?"

Malcolm shook his head. "Sadly, no. I went into financial services but hated it. Money-grabbing wankers up their own arse. Not one of them I would trust. So I left and went into consulting. I work for Delaine. One of the big ones? Or I did until recently. I've just handed in my notice."

Dean hadn't heard of Delaine but wasn't surprised. Malcolm was educated. Of course he would be working in a suit and carrying a briefcase.

"So what you going to do next?"

"Don't know. I specialised in leadership development. You wouldn't believe how bad civvies are at leading teams. So I know there'll be work for me somewhere."

The guard on the platform blew his whistle. The train jerked. The platform slid by through the window and a passing train going in the opposite direction distorted Dean's perspective.

"Were you with Global Risks? On the circuit?" Malcolm asked. There was a note of jealousy in his voice. People always thought it was something it wasn't.

"I was, yeah. But two years was enough."

Malcolm nodded. "I heard about John Clegg getting shot in the foot by a new guy."

"How'd you hear?"

Malcolm shrugged. "I've got mates at GR too. Plus I work in London so I see people all the time. I thought about it, you know? Going on the circuit."

"But...?"

He pursed his lips and shrugged. "I can earn more doing what I do. The numbers look good at first. But actually, if you're month on month off, it's only six months' pay."

He was right. And though Dean hated working at Bolton's it was steady income and he was home every evening. The stuff he did for Billy was extra for the girls.

He told Malcolm about the journalists he'd driven around Iraq and about how hard it was to train up the Iraqis in anything. He felt easy talking even though it had been three years since they last saw each other. He also knew Malcolm had been close to Pete McCardle, the Company Sergeant-Major.

"Tell you what. Let's get a selfie. Send it to Pete. He'll be pissed off to see us together."

Malcolm started laughing. "Tell him we saw Clapton at Wembley. Or Rush. Genesis. Any of those prog-rock bands he's into."

Dean took the photo with Malcolm leaning in and grinning. "It'll go when it connects. The WIFI's down."

Malcolm's voice changed. He became sombre. "Send him my best. He was a great Sergeant-Major. I don't know what I can do for him but if he needs anything he just needs to ask."

He was silent then, jaws clamped.

"I will, boss. He's ok. It's shit what he's going through but he's as hard as it gets."

"Tell me if you go see him. I'd like to see him again."

Dean nodded. "I will."

At Peterborough people got out and the train staff stopped anyone else getting on. They said there was another train in ten minutes. As they pulled out, the ticket inspector appeared out of the crowded carriage and looked at the two of them sitting on their suitcases, one in jeans and the other in a suit.

"Tickets please, gents." He was obviously from the northeast. He looked drawn and Dean suspected there'd been trouble earlier.

Holding Malcolm's ticket the Inspector said, "Sir, this is a first-class ticket, you do realise that?"

Malcolm nodded. "It was rammed so I legged it for the front. Then I met an old friend. It's ok, isn't it?"

Dean glanced across. Malcolm had chosen to stay with him.

The Inspector had a puzzled expression. "Of course. But we can't give you a refund if you choose to sit in Standard Class."

Malcolm shrugged and waggled his finger. "I know. And I'll have a look again after Doncaster, when my friend gets off. This happens every week."

The Inspector handed his ticket back. "Sadly it does, bonny lad. But London's crazy this week."

"It's Trump's visit," said Malcolm, smothering a snigger. "There's a parade."

The Inspector nodded. "That'll be it then," and took Dean's ticket. He drew a squiggle on it with a biro and handed it back. "Just make sure you don't block the exits, ok gents?"

Dean said they wouldn't and the Inspector moved on.

"Donald Trump, eh?" Dean said. "There's a man!"

Malcolm's face clouded. "Think so?"

Dean did. "Yeah, Boss, I do. He shakes things up. He's not afraid to take on the elite."

His voice trailed off. He became conscious that Malcolm was, or could be, one of those elites. "You're not one of those metrosexual hipster libtards are you, Boss? All beard no bollocks? You vote conservative, right?"

Malcolm didn't respond. He bent his leg in to hook an arm round his knee. "Used to," he said.

There was something he wasn't saying. Dean knew what it was but didn't want to discuss it. Brexit divided everyone.

"How's Michelle? The girls?" Malcolm said to change the subject.

It impressed Dean that Malcolm should remember his wife so easily. "Oh, mate. They're good, thanks. Still getting away with it, know what I mean?"

Malcolm smiled and shook his head. "You're one lucky bastard, Dean. You could blag your way out of anything."

Dean clicked his tongue as he made an apologetic gesture with his hands. "You know me, Boss. Many years of practice, yeah?"

Malcolm nodded. "Yes. I remember."

Steve, July 2019

Steve thought about wearing a jacket and regimental tie but his mother said it would be better if he dressed down. The job was to be a school general assistant and support worker, which meant he should look relaxed and unthreatening, like someone the children could go to. He was at his most relaxed in a polo shirt and jeans, so that's what he should wear.

He hadn't argued though he felt underdressed as he waited in the corridor to be called for interview. It was a sweltering day and the sun blazed down through the window behind him throwing long shadows across the linoleum. He passed the time by making shapes with his good hand.

He'd arrived much earlier than he'd been told. The secretary, a warm lady called Imogen, got him a coffee. Two people had been in for interview while he waited, both middle-aged women. They made him wonder if he was in the right place.

"How was it?" he asked the second one.

She looked at him with a quizzical expression. She stood bent slightly forward at the waist.

"Was it hard? Did they ask you difficult questions?"

She looked like she didn't know what to say. Eventually, she said, "It was very fair. Are you being interviewed for the role too?"

Steve nodded, wondering whether he should stand up. "Yes. The care assistant. I think I'd be good with the kiddies," he said.

"I think we called them *students*, nowadays," she said, "or *children*. We don't tend to use the term 'kiddies' anymore."

"Oh, thank you," Steve said, afraid he'd done something awful. But the woman turned to Imogen who said they'd be in touch when the interviews were completed. The woman waddled off with her anorak over her arm.

"Mr Reedman, please."

The woman standing in the doorway was slim and dressed in a pastel green skirt, blouse, and cardigan. Steve went straight towards her and extended his left hand to shake, which she took with a grip so weak he could barely feel it.

"Oh, I see!" she said, looking at his prosthetic. "Yes, of course. Come in, Mr Reedman."

"Steve, please," he said as he edged round her.

The blue sign on the door said 'Staff Room' in white letters. The room itself was barely larger than a cupboard and had low, faux leather chairs around all the walls except one, which had cupboards and a sink. A thin man with grey hair and a narrow face sat facing him. He didn't stand. The woman in green indicated a chair on the opposite wall and Steve sat down and crossed, then uncrossed his feet.

"Bet it gets tight in here," he said. "At breaks, I mean."

The woman smiled as she sat next to the man. They both had clipboards and pens. "I'm Abi Hewson, the Head Teacher, and this is my Deputy, Mr Snowden," she said in an accent he couldn't place. "We are interviewing you for the role of a care assistant and general support, it that correct?"

"Yes, I believe so," Steve replied. He was sitting upright on the edge of the chair. He wanted to shimmer backwards so that he looked more relaxed but, since he'd now set his position, he thought it would look odd if he moved. As if he was fidgeting.

Mr Snowden had a reedy voice and lifted his chin as he spoke. His adam's apple was pointy and moved energetically in his throat. "Mr Reedman, I see from your CV that you served in the armed forces and have been injured. I also see that you have been a public speaker for a year. Would you tell me a bit more about that? What skills did you develop and why do you want to move on?"

Steve frowned. That was two questions, both of which required thought.

"What skills? Well, let me think." He put his good hand over his mouth as he looked at the cupboards above the sink. Realising he never did this in real life, he put it down. "It were about confidence, really. The confidence to realise I had a story that kiddies, I mean students, children, wanted to hear. I told them what I've been through. It's about resilience. It's about getting up when you're down. Bouncing back. It's about believing in yourself..."

Snowden interjected. "Yes, I understand that's what you have learned from your life experiences. But could you tell me what you learned from this particular role? From the act of speaking?"

Steve frowned. He had been doing just that, hadn't he? "How do you mean?" he said.

Snowden lifted and readjusted his legs. "Let me put it another way. It says here that you were a public speaker in the education sector for eleven months. Could you tell me how many talks you gave per week?"

Steve nodded. "Four. I gave four."

"You gave four talks per week...."

"No. I gave four talks. One to a school in Carlisle, where I live. And another to an interfaith school in Penrith which I could drive to. And another to St Martin's, which is also in Carlisle but the other side of town..."

"And these were at secondary level?"

"No. Little ones. Primary. They were all to primary schools."

"Primary. You gave lectures on warfare to primary level children?"

Snowden's head was tilted back. His adam's apple slid up and down. Steve opened his mouth and closed it again.

Abi straightened in her chair. "Mr Reedman, I understand you have had your developed DBS check and you have excellent references from the staff at *Save Our Heroes* in Catterick and from your former commanding officer, Captain Sewell."

Steve smiled. He'd been pleased with what Bronagh and Malcolm had written. It showed him in a really good light. He wanted to say Malcolm was his platoon commander, not the Commanding Officer. Civvies never understood the difference.

"We are an equal opportunities employer. In fact, we agreed to interview you because you have been injured. I understand from what you've said that you delivered four public talks in the past year and that you have a... that you lost... that you have some issues with your primary hand..."

She kept staring at the matt, realistic skin. Steve wanted to make a joke about the colour, how it contrasted with the rest of him, how long it took to learn to write, shave, and masturbate with his other hand. But he didn't.

"I'm interested to know what... how do you...."

Snowden chipped in. "Could you tell us, please, Mr Reedman, what experience you have working with slightly older children? Beyond the talks you delivered?"

Steve thought. There'd been that advance by the Taliban in the fourth month of the tour. The families of the other tribes had fled north through the Amrut valley. They'd come into the town like refugees, begging for protection from the British. The company commander had said they should set up a reception centre in the market square.

They used two shipping containers flown in by Chinook and a Hesco barrier to establish a protected holding area against the town wall. They surrounded it with barbed wire leaving only a small gap to stop people clambering over the containers. One panic-stricken woman had lifted her child up over the wire ignoring the cuts to her flesh. Captain Wilmott had grabbed the child. The woman's face was turned almost skyward, wailing. He'd shouted at Steve to let her through, into the compound. He'd held the child under one arm, his rifle in the other. He'd looked scared. Then all the women started holding out their babies, crying out, the blood running down their arms.

That had been the week before the bombing.

"Mr Reedman?"

"I don't know what to say, really," he said. "I'm not a teacher. You know that. But I have my DBS check and I'm a good team player and I learn quickly. It says so in one of them letters, the one from Bronagh, my case worker. I think I'd be good..."

"Would you tell me the extent of your injuries, Mr Reedman?" Abi said. "How impaired are you?"

This was a question he could answer. "I have lost my right forearm from the elbow joint downwards. I had a craniectomy in the field hospital after the market square bombing, the same incident that took away my arm. I also have damage to the right optic nerve and some loss of sight in my right eye. I have to take some medications for the injuries to my brain. Apart from that, I'm fine. I can drive and..."

Both Abi and Snowden spoke at the same time.

"Do you have PTSD?"

"You said there was a bombing..."

There was a pause. They looked at each other, then at their clipboards. Steve didn't know which question to answer. Eventually, Abi straightened her skirt over her knees, pinching the fabric between thumb and forefinger. "I'm sorry. You must understand that we have the welfare of the children to consider. Would you tell us a bit more about your mental health? Is that ever an issue for you?"

Steve shook his head. "No. I don't believe so. There are days when you get low mood but everyone feels like that, don't they? It's just one of them things. But I don't feel my mental health is an issue, thank you for asking."

Abi looked sad. Snowden's head was tilted to the side.

"Were there any questions you had for us?" Abi said. "Is there anything you'd like to know about the role?"

Steve thought for a moment then shook his head. "No, the brief was pretty clear," he said. "When can I start?"

The two of them started to laugh. Steve laughed with them in long, deep chuckles.

"You are not the last person we're seeing, Mr Reedman, and then we have to review and discuss the options. We'll let you know in the next few days. Is that ok?"

Steve nodded. "Yes, thank you." He stood and extended his good hand for Abi to shake. This time she managed to make a reasonable grasp of his finger ends. Snowden seemed unwilling to shake hands but Steve kept his extended until he did so.

"Will you let Bronagh know? And Malcolm Sewell?" he said at the door.

Abi's mouth changed shape. She seemed to want to laugh. "We'll let you know first. We think it's probably best if you let your referees know our decision in your own time."

Steve nodded. "Makes sense. Thank you."

He closed the door behind him and thanked Imogen for her help.

"Goodbye, Steve, good luck," she said as he walked away.

Alexander, July 2019

On 24 July, Her Majesty the Queen accepted Teresa May's resignation and appointed a jubilant Alexander as Prime Minister. Papers found later at 10 Downing Street dated July 2019 record that:

I've appointed Cummings as Special Advisor. I'll leave the details to him, oily tyke that he is. Carrie also has much to say on a full host of issues. The two of them bicker like Crisis and Phocus. But that does not concern. Canis caninam non est.

Finally in the seat of power where he deserved to be, Alexander instructed the House of Commons that it was his intention for the United Kingdom to leave the European Union at the end of October 2019. This was a mere three months hence and was to happen with or without a structured deal. It was therefore the responsibility of the European Union negotiators to decide which.

He demanded of them that any preconditions about the Northern Irish border be removed from the agenda. He argued that the clever use of technology, or trusted trader schemes, would slice through the Gordian Knot of European legislation with a pragmatic British sword.

The legislators did not agree. They were obliged to demand customs checks and it was really not their concern if terrorism returned to Northern Ireland, especially if the Province was no longer within their bailiwick.

This created the sort of impasse that Alexander revelled in. He duly repeated his tactic of brinkmanship, pitting himself against Donald Tusk, the former Polish conservative Prime Minister and then Chairman of the European Council. Papers found later at 10 Downing Street record the level of determination Alexander possessed:

> The problem with the likes of Tusker is that he is an essentially honest follow who plays with a straight bat – if the Poles ever mastered cricket. I don't think he understands the extent to which I will go.

Steve, August 2019

Steve was low. He was certain he had that job and didn't understand why Abi had blocked him.

Malcolm sounded loud on the phone. "So what did you do?"

"I looked her up on Facebook. She seemed really nice and I just wanted to be friends."

"She'll be your boss, Steve. You don't normally send friend requests to your boss."

"You were my boss and we're friends. Aren't we, Boss?"

"That's different. We wouldn't be LinkedIn if we were still serving. Or friends on Facebook. She told me you were stalking her."

Steve didn't know what to say.

"Look, Steve, I'm really sorry you got knocked back. I told her they missed a real gem in not hiring you."

Sitting on the sofa in his living room, feet crossed on the coffee table, Steve stared glumly at his socks. A band of light from the window fell over his ankles making them look distorted and lopsided.

"All I wanted is a job, Malcolm. A job I can do. I thought it would be perfect for me, that. Helping those little kiddies. Children, I mean. I don't even know what to say nowadays. It's a minefield, Malcolm."

"It is, mate, it is. And you're going to have to accept that people say they want to hire a veteran, and they honestly imagine they do, but they don't know what that means...."

Malcolm's voice trailed off.

"How'd you mean?"

"I mean people think they want to employ a veteran. Particularly an injured one like yourself. But they have no experience of meeting us. So they imagine we're all fucked in the head."

Steve nodded. "They did say that..."

"Said what...?"

"How's my mental health? Do I suffer from PTSD?"

"They didn't!"

"They did. It were the man what said it. Snowden, you call him. He were the Deputy Headmist... Deputy Headmaster. He asked, so I told him. I've got no issues with my mental health. Just like I don't have issues with my hand. It's just one of those things you got to get over isn't it?"

Malcolm said nothing.

"Did I do something wrong?"

"No, Steve, you didn't. I'm just considering what to do. I can't really call them again and argue your case. I'm thinking about writing... but she said you'd been waving at her? Poking her? What's that about?"

"It's a thing you can do on Facebook. You can send someone a friend request, which I thought would be wrong since she would be my boss. Or you can poke them. It's like waving. It wasn't meant to be..."

"It doesn't matter, Steve. It doesn't matter. But I wouldn't do it anymore, ok? Civvies think differently about these things. You're just going to have to get used to that."

Steve could hear his mother in the hallway. She'd been fussing around since the letter arrived. It had been her idea to give Malcolm a call. He'd texted, knowing Malcolm rarely had time nowadays but he'd rung back after an hour.

"So did I fuck up or what, Boss?"

"You didn't fuck anything up, Steve. Be yourself, that's all you've got to do."

So what was it? Be yourself or not be yourself? He was being himself when he poked her. He thought it would be fun. He poked her and wanted her to poke him back. Then they'd chat about when he could start. Everything he did seemed to crumble between his fingers.

"Steve?"

"It's alright, Boss. It's fine. I just need to think about it that's all. Bye..."

"Steve listen, it's fine..."

"Bye."

Alexander, August to September 2019

As the arid, unforgiving summer dragged on, the national legislators continued to bicker in the House of

Commons over both principles and details. They did so nervously, uncertain where their true duty lay. They did so passionately, hoping others would understand their fear. They did so tenaciously, hoping their voices would not go unheard in their constituencies.

They knew the debate really mattered. This was not about the depth of tyre treads or accessing the housing market. This was about the identity of Britain as a nation, as a state, and as the unequal and yet functioning bundle of countries it had been for several hundred years.

British Steel, one of the last bastions of heavy manufacturing, went bankrupt with the loss of several thousand jobs in one of the most deprived regions of the country. The economy continued to shrink. TV pundits explained the dreary implications for house buyers, lenders, and low-income earners.

The British ambassador to the United States of America, Sir Kim Darroch, became embroiled in an unseemly row after emails from him to the UK government were leaked. He described President Trump as inept, insecure, and dysfunctional. He concluded that his term could 'end in disgrace'. This proved to be true but that did not stop the story causing intense embarrassment to the government. In the end, Darroch had no alternative but to resign.

Darroch had been appointed by Teressa May. His cables were leaked by a Brexit supporting civil servant to a freelance Brexiteer journalist. Leavers such as Nigel Farage argued for his removal. Donald Trump tweeted in response that Farage would make an excellent ambassador to the United States, publishing a picture of the two of them against the gaudy opulence of one of Trump's lift lobbies.

The incident mirrored the Brexit process in miniature. Critical insight and long experience became subjugated by vanity and social media debate.

And then it started raining. It rained constantly and heavily day upon day. A month's rain fell in a week. The baked earth couldn't absorb the water. The ground shifted and the antiquated, heavy-gauge, cast-iron sewage pipes split open at their junctions. Fields flooded. People had to be evacuated from low-lying properties. Rivers rose and burst their banks. Cars floated round carparks. People left vulnerable homes to stay with relatives or shored up their gateways with sandbags. The rivers rose yet more and still it continued to rain through the tired night and into the morning.

Ignoring the rain, huge numbers congregated in London to demand a second Brexit referendum. This could have been a plausible lifeline for Alexander. Agreeing to a confirmatory referendum would have allowed time for the debate to cool. If the Remainers won, he could argue that he saved the nation from the brink of certain peril. If the Leavers won again, there would be a clear mandate.

But he didn't take the lifeline.

In the midst of the environmental and political tumult he found himself utterly unable to make a decision. His special advisor, Cummings, was telling him one thing. His media-minded girlfriend another. He was not a man of detail. He was a global stateman who need only make big-picture analogies. Yet his position as Prime Minister required the comprehension of fiendish detail and the conceptualisation of their strategic implications.

Access to the European markets was necessary for the British car industry to survive and support the thousands of jobs in Middlesborough, Luton, Redcar, and Cleethorpes. Therefore the reams of European Union legislation about foot pedals and exhaust emissions were important.

Such concerns were not the only order of business the government was unable to address. With the entire chamber absorbed in matters of process and principle about Brexit, exhausted Members were unable to answer even basic domestic concerns. As a result, pensioners died on hospital waiting lists, farmers couldn't sell their milk and lost their meagre reserves, and tour operators couldn't book for the following year, meaning they started running at a loss.

Alexander's brother, Jo, also a Member of Parliament, resigned from government citing the conflict between family and the national interest. As the pressure increased and the government still proved incapable of agreeing what to do, others followed. Phillip Lee crossed the floor to the Liberal Democrats, a party of Remain, thereby removing the conservative majority.

The Labour Party tabled motions to unblock the impasse but it was no longer a matter of left versus right but Remainer versus Leaver. Both factions existed at all points across the political spectrum. The way the nation perceived itself was changing. It became impossible for any motion to achieve the support required to move the debate forward.

Traditional, noblesse-oblige conservatives, some with service dating back to Margaret Thatcher, found they had no alternative but to back Labour initiatives. Their brand of conservatism recognised the importance of international alliances. They knew it had been France's agreement, in May 1982, not to supply Argentina with replacement warheads for their Exocet missiles that had saved much of the British navy anchored in what was known as Bomb Alley, the narrow waterway between the two Falkland Islands. Alexander sacked eleven of them for failing to follow the Party whip. Then, when the weight of his action became apparent, he reinstated them. This led to his Work and Pensions Secretary, Amber Rudd, resigning from government. She described the treatment of her colleagues as an 'assault on decency and democracy'.

Seeking to limit the possibility of the House uniting against him, Alexander used an archaic instrument, prorogation, to freeze Commons business. By not allowing Parliament to sit he sought to reduce the available debating time, thereby forcing it to accept his plans.

He got this wrong. The public became so frustrated by the government's inability to reach consensus that cities around the country rose in uproar. Increasingly violent parades nearly became riots and then global news. Members were so ashamed at being denied the opportunity to do their jobs that they sat in the Commons anyway. People took the government to court about the legality of Brexit, the legality of the Brexit process, the legality of the legal process. The courts ruled that Brexit would not have a negative effect on the economy. They ruled that it would. They ruled that a no deal Brexit was legal and that it wasn't. They ruled that rules were meant to be broken. And then, on 24 September, the Supreme Court stated that prorogation was illegal and that government should sit.

Papers found later at 10 Downing Street dated from this period showed nothing but scribbles and jottings, page after page. On one, a spurting phallus. On another, black triangles reinforced and emphasised, again and again. Then, on a Friday, *Defututum est*. And some pages later in scratchy black ink:

Colei canis est. I know what to do. I'll fuck them all.

Kyle, previously

Under the motorway it's dry and warm if you get a place on the sand not the concrete. Most nights I have to get the knife out: My dossbag, fuck off.

Got soup and a roll from a church hall. Most low-life with dogs on string. Some proper wet pants, fly undone, tongue out, humming. They look bad but it's to keep people away.

There are veterans here. We know each other at first glance. Same eyes. We nod but don't talk. What would we say? We were soldiers once, now scum?

I'm hungry so think about begging. Just a few more days and I'll sort myself out.

There's a bus going round the roundabout. Purple. Toad faced man on the back. Big yellow letters: TAKE BACK CONTROL.

I'm trying motherfucker. I'm fucking trying.

In dossbag. Headtorch. Knife. Red line. Thin at first then down through the layers to the yellow fat. Bleeding down thigh drips on the inside of the dossbag.
Just one drop good, sharp pain beautiful.
Red line. Close the wound. No pain. Control.

Dean, September 2019

"When are they ever going to get this fucking thing done, Chel, eh?" Dean grumbled as they sat on the sofa watching the news. "The *remoaners* are blocking it. This isn't democracy. And the fucking BBC..."

He didn't need to go on. His family knew his position and teased him about it. Much to the girls' amusement he kept saying 'porogue' instead of 'prorogue' so they kept asking questions to make him say it. When he did, they doubled up in that cruel, high-pitched giggle of theirs.

He shook his head, dismissing their jibes as immaturity. He struggled to understand why it was taking so long. They'd triggered Article 50 ages ago but now there was a bill to prevent Brexit happening without a deal.

"Why do we even need a deal? Come on, Boris. Sort these fuckers out. It was us bailed them out in the First World War. And the Second..."

Michelle said nothing. She had her feet crossed and was leaning slightly against him. She was conveying a coldness he knew meant she was angry. He was glad she shared his bitterness. The government should do their job.

It was Thirsty Thursday, meaning Dean was allowed a beer. When the local news had come on, the girls left the room and went upstairs. They would come back down when dinner was ready.

The picture on the TV changed. It was almost as if the BBC had got bored of Brexit and needed something else to spread their lies about. The anchor man said something about increased inter-racial tensions. Then there was a man with a microphone standing outside a white terrace building. There was something about the light that made

Dean realise where it was. He snapped his fingers and pointed.

"That's... that's the mosque on..."

Michelle turned to look at him with a frown. He stopped talking. He hoped he'd got away with it and was pleased to quickly think up a reason why he knew the place.

The journalist had a grave, professional voice: "...and this Mosque in Rotherham was broken into only a few days ago. Although nothing was stolen, the prayer hall and washroom were desecrated. Police found human DNA on the walls and floor and have taken away samples for testing..."

Dean tensed and knew immediately Michelle felt him do so.

Billy, the fucking idiot, he thought. He'd pissed on the floor, hadn't he? Surely he couldn't have been so stupid?

His mouth was open. Michelle shifted round on the sofa to face him, one knee pressing on his leg. He took a drink of lager and looked at her. It was going to be one of those chats.

"I ran into your friend Shaky today," she said, blinking.

"Mahmud? How's he my friend?"

"Mahmud. That's it. Horrible man."

"Absolute cunt. Lying bastard. What did you say to him?"

She looked at the telly. "Ran into him in Asda, the big one. He was coming out and I was going in."

"Did he say something?"

"He said 'Hello Michelle. How are you,' and I didn't recognise him so I just said hello, smiled like. It was only then I remembered who he was."

"Then what?"

She put her hand on her chest. "So I said, why do you think I want to talk to you? Frankly, I think you're a lying, dishonest man."

Dean could picture the scene. She had this way of saying such things that Dean had never mastered. If he said them he'd get punched.

"Do you know what he said?"

Dean shook his head. "No, what?"

"He said..." she nodded at the television. "He said his mosque was desiccated by someone. Two men, possibly three."

"Did he?"

"Yeah. And he wanted to know if you were in the country."

"He what?"

"He said. 'Is your Dean in the country?' So I said yes, why? What business is it of yours? You owe us twenty grand. If you want to come round I'm sure my Dean would love to talk to you. Come round any time."

She was smiling to herself, proud of the man he was.

"Yeah?"

"Well, then he said it had happened before. In the mosque like. The vicar, the what do you call it? The Imran. He was beaten up. At night. So they put cameras in. Film cameras. And he wanted to know where you were on Sunday..."

"What fucking business is it of his?" Dean said, leaning forward to put the beer on the coffee table. The drink swirled inside it. "Who does he think he is asking my wife..."

His voice was too high pitched and he knew it sounded like he was lying. He got out his phone and started scrolling through his contacts, flicking the list up and up and up again. "I'll fucking kill him."

Michelle leaned forward to place her mug down on the coffee table. She then interlaced her fingers round one knee.

"It wasn't you, was it, Deano?"

Dean looked up.

She looked at her knee between her hands. Then she stood up. She picked up her mug and his beer glass and stepped over Dean's legs.

"I haven't finished that," Dean said.

"Come into the kitchen a moment will you, love?"

He was being kitchened. It hadn't happened since Pete had stayed and somehow there was a puddle on the carpet at the top of the stairs. Dean reached for the remote, killed the TV, and followed her through.

In his socks the vinyl floor was cold. The incessant rain drummed heavily on the conservatory roof. Michelle put his beer on the kitchen table. He went to pick it up. She stepped deftly behind him and closed the door to the living room.

"Dean, tell me you were not involved with that mosque."

"I wasn't involved with that mosque."

She folded her arms. Then she unfolded them and put her hands on her hips. He had once watched a TV documentary about elephants. It wasn't when they put their ears out that they were about to charge it was when they folded them back in again.

"Dean, why do you think Elizabeth doesn't bring a boyfriend home?"

Dean shrugged. "Don't know."

"Do you know she has one?"

Dean shifted his weight between his feet. This was like being grilled by the RSM and he didn't like it. His shoulder ached. He rubbed it with the other hand.

"Does she? Should I have a chat?"

"No, Dean, you shouldn't."

It was Dean, not Deano. The charge was coming. The best thing he could do was go on the offensive.

"Look, Michelle, what's this about?"

He put a coarse edge to his voice. He never did this, not to her. He knew the consequences. They'd been married since he was a Full-Screw. All those years, thick and thin. All those tours. All that worry and fretting. The awful quarters on the Pads' estates. He'd always been safe, mind you. He'd never brought anything home. He knew how lucky he was. God he knew.

"Your daughter is dating a young man who wants to join the police," Michelle said. "If he doesn't get into the police he wants to join the army."

Dean smiled. "Sounds like a good lad."

"He is. He wants to serve his community, Dean. He wants to do good for the world. He told me and I think he's great."

"That's great, love, but what's his…"

Her face was fierce, her lips a tight line.

"And Elizabeth really likes him. She told me. And I could tell that she really, really likes him."

"Is this about…"

"No, Dean. You're not listening to me."

Not knowing what else to do, he put his hands into the pockets of his jeans.

"I do not want your daughter to be ashamed of her father," Michelle said. "You have always put them first, I know that. But lately you have…"

"I've what? What do you mean…"

"I do not want you to lose your daughter, Dean Chadwick. And you will, if you are not careful."

She raised a finger to him. Not only did he not understand what was being said, he didn't know why it was his fault.

"The reason you don't know that your daughter has a boyfriend is because she doesn't want you to know."

He started blustering. "Well, how do I…"

"And the reason she doesn't want you to know… She actually sat in that chair in tears, Dean…" She nodded at the kitchen table. "Last night. Begging me not to tell you."

"Tell me what?"

"His name's Mohammed."

Steve, September 2019

The man sounded upbeat. He called himself the *Clerk of Works*. His voice had a familiar ring, like a Company Sergeant-Major's. His name was James Snowden and he was the brother of the man with the bouncing adam's apple. Steve knew he owed the other Snowden a big debt of thanks for passing on his name.

Snowden said, "You won't be teaching the children but you will come across them. You will interact with them."

Steve said, "So it's to be a handyman?"

"Yes," Snowden said. "We call it the Estate Manager. You'll look after everything in the grounds but nothing inside the buildings. That falls to the House Manager. But given your background we might find a role for you with the Combined Cadet Force if we think you're right for it."

"The cadets? I were a cadet."

"I'm sure. Army cadets are where a lot of boys start their journey into the army. We have a Combined Cadet Force. CCF as opposed to ACF. The CCF tends to generate future officers."

"And you want me to what?"

"Don't know yet. But when we get a feel for what you like to do we might find something you can do. You can shoot, for example?"

"Yeah. Marksman, me. And GPMG trained."

"That's great, Steve. We don't get issued the General Purpose Machine Gun but we do allow the boys to shoot a .22 conversion on an indoor range. You were a JNCO at one point?"

"Yeah, a Lance-jack."

"Good. So you'll know how to coach people to shoot."

Steve got up from the sofa and walked to the window. The living room was on the top floor as his mother had changed the house round when he first moved in and the nurses needed access through the night. His bedroom was still on the ground floor. In the street, the sunlight was warm and kind. Mrs Hartigan was in a shirt as she laboured up the hill with her shopping. He'd go help her but he couldn't take both bags at the same time.

"Just to be clear, Steve, you can drive, can't you? Your injury is not a limitation?"

"I have a licence, Mr Snowden. My car's been adapted but I can drive owt else. Lawn mowers. Tractors."

"And you would be happy to take on this role? We are a very prestigious school. We count a number of famous names among our alumni."

"I just want a job," Steve said. "I want a job that makes me feel useful to society. I were useful, once. But I'm not being useful at the moment if you know what I mean."

"I do, Steve. I know exactly what you mean. So why don't we think about a three-month trial? There's no need for an interview. I will take you on my brother's recommendation. You can move into a tied flat, too. It's not very big but you're single. And we're not that far from home anyway. If we offer you this post, when could you start?"

Steve beamed. "Friday," he said. "Day after tomorrow."

Pete, September 2019

Very quickly, Pete came to enjoy the walk down to the village. As a Sunday routine it punctuated his week and he found he had become one of the local oddities, the hermit from the woods, the old man with a secret. Far from being shunned, or exposed, the locals protected his privacy. He was among others who sought the isolation found at the fringes of maps. He didn't tell anyone who he was but neither did he hide it. They guessed, and some of them guessed correctly but kept their counsel. The sporty couple who ran the Inn agreed to take his post. The farmer gave him odd bits of cash work and with weekly access to the internet he found a way to order anti-inflammatory drugs for his hips while ensuring that he couldn't spend any time on the gambling sites. In the end, he realised that gambling was just thrill seeking and he started to imagine his life changing into something new. He wanted to be pure, free from rules, free of incumbents, free from dependents, unattached to anything. The world carried no meaning, and he rejected it.

After placing his beer on the table by the window he plugged two chargers into the socket by the radiator, one for his phone and the other for the battery for his drill. The bar was full of walkers with tired legs, dogs unused to sitting under the tables, cyclists in lycra, farm hands in coveralls. He turned his phone on and prepared for his weekly insight into the world outside.

He liked Facebook more now than before. He understood how it worked and liked the functionality. He enjoyed reaching out to his friends to wish them happy birthday, to praise the achievements of their children, or encourage them as they fell to cancer, arthritis, bike crashes. It made him feel connected to them and to his past, a point in his life where he worked with the most reliable men he'd ever known.

Having been in the news a good deal, in the past two months he'd acquired over six hundred friends. Some of them he knew personally, men he served with and respected. Others were people they knew, a second tier. He accepted their invitations on the basis that the first tier must have vetted them and he thought he could probably use as many supporters as possible. He wanted to feel he was right. Killing the lawyer had been a good thing. Being charged with murder was not.

To protect himself, his account had only vague details about his age and background. The profile picture was his bike. If anyone really knew him they'd recognise it. Who else had a Triumph Tiger?

When he'd sat at this table the week before he'd posted a meme about the clocks going back. It was a picture of two spitfires, one behind the other, surging up over the white cliffs of Dover. The superimposed text read: *When the clocks go back, I'll set mine to 1939 when this country had some balls*.

"Wake up, people!" he'd added as a comment to the post.

This week, he scrolled through the responses people had left:

> "@TriumphTiger, exactly right mate. F*** libtards have screwed us. Hope your well mate. Fucking keep going."

"@TriumphTiger, smash it mate. We're with you. The people spoke!"

"@TriumphTiger, Get it fucking done."

Pete smiled to himself and nodded. If anyone thought he would bend over and take it up the arse they were wrong.

His anger burned. He'd never give up.

Yes, he'd admitted to killing a man. But there was no way he was being imprisoned for it. If they wanted him they'd have to find him. The whole country needed shaking up. The whole fucking lot.

Dean, October 2019

Dean didn't speak as he drove. He'd decided to go cross country which meant the driving required more attention than on the motorway. Billy didn't seem to mind. He sat in the back in a green Harrington jacket, elbows wide, looking out the side window, saying nothing. He looked small on the back seat.

He hadn't told Michelle he was on this job and hadn't told Billy what Michelle had told him. The police had not been in touch and Dean was trying to recall if they would have his DNA profile. He had never been arrested as an adult. Not as a civvy, anyway. And in the chaotic aftermath of the shooting he couldn't remember if the RUC took his blood or not. Why would they, when Pete got the kill?

Billy leaned forward to tap him on the shoulder.

"I appreciate you doing this, Dean."

"No problem," Dean replied automatically but added nothing more. He knew that he was being used to make Billy look like a Commanding Officer with a staff car.

Billy had hired the Skoda from one of the big chains. He had wanted a sports car, a Lambo or a Maserati, but Dean had said no. They were what Pakis hired for weddings. They were like skinny jeans. They looked good but weren't made for real men.

The Skoda, however, was solid. A Passat, really. Same engine, same chassis. Dean liked it and made a mental note for when he could give the Mondeo to the girls.

The thought of Elizabeth not being able to talk to him needled his intestines. Was he that unapproachable?

There had been a few Sergeant-Majors you didn't go near, of course. But the best ones were those whose door was always open, those who nurtured their platoon sergeants. If there was a problem with a corporal, or even a platoon commander, it was these men who fixed things, kept the company running. He thought of Chris, Kev, Abs. Gordon and Dave C. Pete. Over the years, these men had helped him grow. It was them he emulated when he made Colour-man. He would have followed them anywhere.

Was he wrong? Was it acceptable for the Pakis to drive without insurance? To teach their jihadi shit at faith schools? To raise their boys as spoiled brats and their girls to hide behind a towel? He'd seen it all in Iraq and Afghan. This was England. And the English didn't do that shit.

The grooming gangs were real, that was certain. They'd been on the news and mainly because Billy made sure the media couldn't hide the fact. If it wasn't a racialist issue, why was every face brown?

He shook his head. He didn't know what to do. He just didn't want another bollocking from his wife.

But as he drove into Stoke through narrow lanes of brick houses and litter-strewn, empty shops, Dean worried that he was wrong in being there. He couldn't trust Billy, and certainly not the others. Direct action was one thing. Punching old men to the ground another.

Civvies were cunts, all of them.

Billy leaned forward. The parade wasn't licensed so was being made to look like an informal gathering. The plan was to march from the cemetery to King's Hall, all of a hundred yards away, where there would be speakers. Billy seemed to think he was the headline act. He wanted to be seen getting out of the car. Dean would have to find somewhere prominent.

"I had a look on google," Dean said. "Time spent in reconnaissance is never wasted. I'll park up near King's Hall and roll round when you're called. What time you on?"

"I don't know. They just want me ready. There's people saying things about Tommy Robinson. Then someone about immigrants in Stoke. Then me."

Dean's fingers flexed round the wheel. "You're not going to say anything about the mosque?"

"Don't be stupid. Course not."

Billy tapped Dean's shoulder with the back of his hand. "But it was good, wasn't it? You and me? Straight in, straight out?"

"Didn't find anything, though, did we?"

"Yeah we did. You found those mattresses, yeah? Evidence, Dean. Ev-id-ence! I told you I saw it with my own eyes."

He was warming up. The colour was back in his cheeks but Dean had heard it all before. He nodded curtly.

"Tell you what, drop me at King's Hall and go find somewhere to park. Shopping centre. Then come find me on the platform. I want you there."

Dean didn't want to look like Billy's close protection. He certainly didn't want to be on the news. He formed a plan. He'd drop Billy off, find a supermarket and chill out for an hour or so, then pretend he'd got caught in road works. He could always blag his way out of trouble.

In town, the drop off worked perfectly. As he came off the dual carriageway, following the road round the civic hall, he recognised the buildings. Opposite the church, the road was constricted by scaffolding and a skip. Three TV vans were already parked beyond. Journalists were setting up long-legged tripods. Young reporters with bags of cables and microphones brushed their hair in the van windows. A loose crowd was forming at the church. A pair of policemen stood patiently by the roadside talking into their radios.

Dean pulled in beyond a TV van. He put on his desert glasses and pushed the door open with his foot. He looked round, grim faced, then stepped carefully round to open the offside door. Billy got out, straightened his jacket, and cut through the crowd. The gathering was mostly men, mostly middle aged, mostly fat. Someone was shouting through a loud hailer. People at the back clapped loudly.

A policewoman with slim hips was coming towards him so Dean got back in the car. He was on a one-way street, double yellows. He pulled out and followed the lane round the civic quarter and out through dingy suburbs to wide access roads and industrial estates bordered by sharp green fencing. This was the lengthy diversion he needed.

At the next junction he turned left thinking he would box round to the dual carriageway. He was now travelling north, judging by the shadows. A mile down the road he saw the starburst B&M sign. He turned in and parked a long way from the entrance where he could see what was coming. Dropping his seat back, he closed his eyes. He thought he would wait there and work his way back when the time was right. He could go for a piss in the shops if he wanted. There was a tool station next door so there'd be a burger van somewhere. The area had the masculine feel of bacon baps with brown sauce.

A woman was pushing an overloaded shopping trolley towards a grey Micra parked on its own. One wheel kept sticking so the woman had to keep wrestling it into line. She was small and mouse like, quite pretty. There was something about her he recognised but he couldn't place what it was.

He spotted the boys on bikes as soon as they appeared through the narrow strip of planting that separated the carpark from the pavement. They rode with limbs straight, their weight forward on the handlebars. They followed the woman and span round in a wide arc to circle behind her.

The woman pushed her trolley against a kerbstone that marked the parking line. She was tired and flushed. The boys wheeled closer, eyeing the hand bag on top of her trolley.

Dean booted his door open and marched briskly towards them. The closest one immediately turned the handlebars and cycled away, innocently looking back over his shoulder. The second one followed.

The woman was transfixed. Dean pointed at the boys wondering if she even knew they were there.

"Dean?"

She knew his name.

"It is Dean, isn't it?"

He studied her face. She had a nice smile. She tilted her head in a way that made her hair fall to the side. "Yes?" he replied, not knowing quite what to say next.

"It's Charlotte Moran. My brother, Kyle..."

Dean snapped his fingers. Smiler's sister. She'd been at his Passing Out Parade in Catterick because his mother couldn't travel. He took two paces forward and awkwardly extended his hand. She took it lightly but didn't let go.

He could have offered more. After the parade, when the newly qualified soldiers were having their formal pictures taken, he'd been mingling with the families in the dining hall and she'd come to talk to him.

"You will look after Kyle, won't you?" she'd said.

"He won't need mothering," he'd replied.

Thin waisted, small breasted, she'd looked up at him with pale blue eyes. Dean knew instinctively what that meant. "Come with me," he'd said.

She'd brushed flakes of sausage roll off her lip and looked for somewhere to put the paper plate. Five minutes later, in the Stores, he was standing stiffly upright in his Number-2 dress uniform while she knelt before him and undid the zip of his trousers.

But that was back then. This was now, in a supermarket carpark. "I'm really sorry," he said, "About Kyle..."

She put a hand under her nose and looked away, blinking.

He placed his hand on her elbow. "He was a great soldier…"

Her chin puckered. He dropped his hand thinking he was making it worse.

"I'm sorry…" she said, making a sucking intake of breath. Her whole body shook. Tears ran down her cheeks. Delving into the handbag on top of the shopping, she pulled out a packet of tissues and teased one from the wrapping.

"You were an inspiration to him," she sniffed. "He told us, me and Mum."

She turned away to gather herself. Dean checked on his car. He walked back to close the driver's door then returned to stand closer. He took hold of her elbow again. "We never forget," he said.

Her chin was still puckering, pink and unsteady. She swallowed. "He said… he wanted to be like you, Sergeant Chadwick."

She swallowed again and this time her voice sounded normal. "He said that if he ever went to war, he wanted to be cool under pressure. Like you. He said you always did the right thing no matter how hard it was."

She blew her nose and folded the tissue into a square. The rims of her eyes were red. Her teeth stuck on her lower lip, pushing it outwards. She looked at him with an even, unfaltering gaze. "He was so glad when you went back to the battalion. That you were on the tour with him. He wrote and told us so."

Dean blushed. Had he really looked after the boy? Did he really do the right thing? Then, maybe. Life was easier then. Now, he wasn't so sure.

Alexander, October 2019

Now clear in his mind on what to do, Alexander met his counterpart, Leo Varadkar, the Taoiseach of Ireland, that October. Between them, they hammered out a protocol recognising that Northern Ireland sat outside the European Union but, since the Union's export rules could be applied, goods could move unimpeded and unchecked from South to North and on to the mainland. Goods could not, however, move unchecked in the other direction. Thus, they agreed to construct a customs border in the Irish Sea.

Alexander did not understand the details of the protocol but with magnificent chutzpah he persuaded Arlene Foster, leader of the Democratic Unionist Party and First Minister of Northern Ireland, that it was in the interest of the people of Northern Ireland. There would be no border between the North and South so terrorism would not rear its ugly head.

Foster accepted the argument. She had succeeded in creating a voter base unable to distinguish between EU membership and Catholic rule from Rome. She also knew her Party was at risk of losing core voters to other protestant parties, notably the Traditional Unionists. She was trapped. Failing to back Alexander's Withdrawal Agreement would leave her exposed to a charge of reneging on Brexit while supporting it could be interpreted as tacit support for a customs border between Northern Ireland and the mainland. So she followed a well-established trope for pro-union politicians in regard to the Tory Party. She publicly backed the Agreement then immediately declared Alexander to be a treacherous snake.

But Alexander ignored her moans. She had already handed him the keys of the castle and the advantage he needed. He now had a Roman Catholic European Union leader and a Protestant First Minister accepting a common position in respect of their mutual border. The European Council had to oblige with everything else he had demanded. It was a masterstroke.

Others in Parliament with far longer memories of the hard-won battle against both loyalist and republican terrorism, and a far better understanding of the issues, made it very clear that his proposal was not going to be workable. Arlene Foster's Party did not represent the majority of Protestants in Northern Ireland, let alone the majority of people. Peace depended on trust, and trust was unlikely in a world where politicians reneged on previous agreements, such as the Good Friday Agreement of 1998 and the Joint Declaration of 2017.

But Alexander dismissed these irritations. He imagined this to be his finest hour. Papers found later at 10 Downing Street dated October 2019 record:

> Fine use of epistrophe in the House today. I was challenged by both Lady Hermon and Hilary Benn to the effect that I did not understand the matter. Untrue, I said. I must remind the Honourable Gentleman, that the risks of border controls are untrue; the Honourable Lady, that I wish to abandon the Good Friday Agreement is utterly untrue. That violence must return is untrue. That what they say is untrue. Untrue, I tell you, untrue!
>
> I have them now. I have the border. I have the deal. Now, as Cummings keeps saying, let's get this done.

Kyle, previously

Tugging at the bottom of the dossbag.

Bloke says, "Hi mate. Could I have a word?"

I tell him to fuck off. This is my dossbag and I'll kill him if he touches it again. He's silent for a moment but I know he's there. I unzip the hood, poke my face out and give it who the fuck are you?

"My name's Barry. Are you a veteran?"

Welsh voice. Musical. The question surprises me. He laughs. Friendly, kind face. Grey hair, quite old. Chubby. Couldn't pass a BFT but right now I'm hungry and I wonder if he has money.

"It's the sleeping bag. Dead giveaway. Could I ask your name and regimental service number?"

I tell him. Why does he need that?

"So we can be certain you're a veteran. Therefore eligible."

I sit up. I must look like the hungry caterpillar. I give it: Listen mate. I'm really fucking famished. If you've got some scoff give me it or fuck off.

He fills in the form on his clipboard. Doesn't respond to what I said.

"Listen, Kyle. I work for The Hero's Hospice. We've a shelter in Shepherd's Bush. It's not much, but we have a spare bed tonight and can provide you with food and access to support. Are you interested? You would have to be clean and remain so."

I say not on it. Bad fucking nightmares.

"So would you like to come? I can take you now if you want?"

Fucking wind up.

He laughs again, tuneful. "Seriously. This is gen." *Then he sits down next to me looking down the slope towards the roundabout. He's not afraid to get his jeans dirty.*

"I was in the Welsh Guards, Down South. I was one of the lucky ones who got off the Sir Galahad on the first wave. Before it sank. When I got home after the war I was homeless for a period of time. So I know what you're going through. Come with me and at least I can get you a chip supper?"

I don't say Dad was Welsh Guards. But there's something about him I like, soft but strong. I feel embarrassed. I stink so bad even I can smell it.

"Don't worry, mate. I did four-week patrols in Belize. You could smell me from Airport Camp. Even the ladies in the Rose Garden wouldn't go near me. We can get you a shower if you want, even dhobi your kit."

He laughs as he talks. I climb out of the dossbag and stuff it in my bergen. He looks at my desert boots, my tee-shirt.

"So you were..."

I nod.

"Thought so. You're not the only one who's been under this flyover. Were you on the 2012 Herrick tour?"

I nod.

"Must have been a real bastard." He sucks his teeth and indicates the way down to the gap in the fence. If I leave someone will take my place.

"Let them have it, Kyle. I'm going to take you to the shelter. You'll get a bunk in a dry room. A bed. And we can get chips on the way. And if you don't like it I'll bring you back."

I'm wondering why me? Why now? But I follow him. He's not afraid. Even as night falls he's in a polo shirt, military watch on display. Blue-red-blue strap. No one else dares come here except the rozzers.

Then we're at the shelter. Full belly is painful. So warm. My teeth hurt from the fight I had two nights ago. Barry guides me into this entrance hall: bright, noticeboards with plastic signs. Men cutting about, coming in, going out. They don't make eye contact but you know they're veterans.

Behind a window with a sliding glass panel is Mark. Mark says to Barry, is he clean?

Barry says, "Yes, he's not on it. Could we put him up for a night?"

Mark bends down to look at me through the window. He slides it shut then comes out of the office through the door. He's very tall, dark hair. I'm standing with my bergen over one shoulder, leaning forward, holding the arm strap with both hands.

The floor is hard rubber matting. Little patterns repeating. It's like the Guard Room. In front of the sliding window is a table. On it there's a book to sign out and in and a pen on a string with Sellotape.

Mark sits on the edge of the table, one foot on the floor, the other at an angle. I put my bergen down. He asks me lots of questions and tells me the rules. Long list of don'ts. I'm properly tired.

"Have you ever had suicidal thoughts, Kyle?"

I look at his belt buckle, how his belly hangs out. No one here could pass a BFT let alone a CFT. But I'm so ashamed. Neither can I. Why am I here? I'm no hero. How did I get to be this person?

"Look, I'm going to put you in a twin room with Fib over there. You'll get along fine. He was Rifles so you'll have a lot in common, you gravel-belly infantry types. *He nods at a bloke sitting on a chair in the corner, same chairs you get in the Naafi. Proper weaselly looking bloke I wouldn't have spoken to in battalion. But we're all equal here and there's no fighting.*

"Fib, could you take Kyle upstairs please? He's going to be with you."

The bloke gets off his arse and as he's about to lead me through the double doors and up the stairs when Mark whispers something in his shell-like.

Fib nods. "No worries, Mark," *then,* "Follow me, mate," *and I do.*

The stairs are hard. Four flights. Sucking air from Guildford. Out of shape but maybe this place will get me back on my feet. There's that smell. The floor, the heavy gloss paint, the banging of doors, the stamping of feet, the laughter. Neon lights humming. It's clean. It's dry. It's warm.

The room has two bunks. Green piss-proof mattresses like in battalion. I think of Dean, Sergeant Chadwick. He was known as Swampy by his mates because he'd piss himself when he was minging. But if the blokes called him that they'd get leathered. Small bloke. He took me through training in Catterick because there weren't enough proper officers. He's the reason I got through.

Fib says, "That's your bunk, mate. I'll get you some sheets. You might want to take a shower. Mark will give you some clean kit while yours gets dhobied. You don't snore do you? Last one I had, fuck me!"

I'm afraid he'll nick stuff so lock everything in the locker. I take a shower. Blokes see my tattoo. Yes mate. The best.

At night, Fib won't stop talking. Scars on his arms. Toes. Still using. One of his eyes droops as though he's been hit by a hook. Makes him look stupid. He says it was surgery to help with PTSD.

"You got any gear, mate?"

I shake my head. Sorry.

"You got any money?"

I shake my head again. Sorry. Skint.

"You don't?"

I shrug. Just don't.

"How do you cope with the nightmares?"

I just don't sleep. I'm as thin as a cigarette paper and hollow. I'm not the best, am I? I'm not a romping-stomping, death-from-above, steely-eyed airborne warrior.

I'm scum in a hostel.

Dean, November 2019

"It's not you, Dean Chadwick," Michelle said. "That's not who you are."

Elizabeth was running upstairs, crying. She slammed her bedroom door and her feet stamped heavily above his head.

She'd called him a stupid pig. "It's *racist*, Dad. Not *racialist*. God you're so *dumb*."

He'd slapped her. How dare she say such things.

Now it was Michelle's turn to knock him about and what he found most difficult was that she was not even shouting. She was sitting at the kitchen table as cold and calm as ice.

"You're a better man than your father, Dean Chadwick. You don't need to compete with him. He's a miserable old shit. You've always set an example to the girls, which he never did."

"Easy tiger..."

"Well he wasn't there when you were a lad was he? He was away pretending to be someone else entirely, conning people..."

"Ok. Fucking stop. Unload…"

Her voice rose. "No, Dean. You fucking stop and unload. You just hit your daughter."

She pushed the chair back to stand. It fell over. She placed her hands flat on the kitchen table. The blood vessel on the side of her head started to protrude.

"Dean you can't behave like that. You can't go round…"

"Alright. Alright!"

He lifted his hands then put them down. He had to raise his voice to quieten her. The nonstop barrage was winding him up. He could feel tension building in his shoulder. The police had said on the news they knew who they were looking for but hadn't mentioned a name. That meant they had DNA evidence and that meant it was only a matter of time before they took Billy in. If they did that, it was only a matter of time before there would be a policeman outside his door.

He'd admitted to Michelle what he'd done. Elizabeth had overheard from the living room. The thought of being arrested didn't bother him but he was very aware of how it might look to his girls. His face reddened and he looked at the floor. He brushed a piece of the dog's food to the side with his socked foot.

Michelle folded her arms, lifted her chin. Mr T got off his mat by the freezer and waddled into the living room. Dean opened his mouth to say something but Michelle didn't move. She was looking at him with what he took to be pity.

"What are you going to do?" she said.

Dean shook his head. "I don't know."

Michelle said, "Well, Elizabeth knows. So her sister will soon. You need to think quickly, Dean. I would like the girls to have their father here at Christmas. I will not come and visit you in prison."

He felt suddenly nauseous. There was a real risk that could happen. But her anger constrained him, hemmed him in. He would give anything to be out of the kitchen.

But with his trepidation came clarity, a certainty that had been eluding him since he got back from Iraq.

He interlocked his fingers. He hadn't felt this bad since he got bust down to Lance-jack for punching that officer. He'd always been able to blag his way out of trouble with a smile, a wink, or a saucy joke. But this time he had nowhere to turn. The endless possibilities were terrifying.

"I need to make some calls," he said.

"To who?"

"The police," he mumbled. He looked up. "Then I need to ring Malcy."

"Who?"

"Malcolm Sewell. An officer I know. The one I ran into on the train. Had a first-class ticket."

"What will he do?"

"He'll give me a character reference if it goes to court."

Alexander, November 2019

In a field in Kent, a farmer used a seven-furrow plough to inscribe the message 'Britain now wants to remain' into the meadow grass of his largest field. It had become obvious to the agricultural sector that Britain relied too heavily on imported labour and foreign markets to profit outside the European Union.

In Parliament, the government was forced to delay Brexit a third time, on this occasion to the end of January 2020. But by now the Leavers, and Alexander, knew the end was in sight. With the Irish Border solved by the draft Protocol, and the European Union negotiators struggling to find other things to object to, it was only a matter of time.

Papers found later at 10 Downing Street dated November 2019 record:

> I'm calling an election. Get Brexit Done. This is my moment. The country will be with me. It's mine.

Steve, November 2019

Steve's shed was in the far corner of the cricket pitch tucked into a recess in the strip of tall oak trees. It was made of corrugated steel sheets bolted to a wooden frame and painted a glossy dark green. Steve liked it. The wriggly tin reminded him of defence exercises on Salisbury Plain. The front wall was partially covered in ivy, which wove round the single, dusty window and threatened to block out the light. In the wet weather the entrance became a pool of mud. The grass needed cutting along the bank but it hadn't stopped raining so he couldn't get the strimmer out.

Inside, the shed smelled of chain oil and turpentine. The tractor mower was on its side as he had removed the blades to sharpen them with a rasp. He was tightening the screws on the vice when the football whacked against the outside wall. It made him start. His mug of tea jumped on the bench, spilling over the side.

The ball hit a second time. The kids were winding him up. He put the rasp down and crept out the side door but instead of going clockwise round the building into the open, he went the other way, round the bank of brambles and rusting slip cradle. Two of the boys were by the corner, glancing round towards the pitch. They hadn't heard him. The other kid was out of sight, kicking the rugby ball in the air and running to catch it.

"Where's Groundsman Wullie?" the far one said. His voice was posh, southern.

The nearest boy had a single, bent cigarette hidden in the palm of his hand. He put it to his lips and nudged the third lad for a lighter.

Steve walked up silently behind them. "What's going on here?" he demanded, his voice hard and sharp.

The boys jumped. The one with the fag put his hands behind his back. They stood awkwardly, unsure whether to be cocky to the groundsman or respectful to a member of staff. The one with the cigarette had fresh skin and long, permed hair. The other had his hair cut short and dyed blonde. He didn't know the one on the right but the one on the left was in the cadet force, a Junior Under Officer. Steve thought he'd make a good officer one day.

He laughed. "Got you there, didn't I, Smith?" he said. "Now put the fags away and get off back to your house. You need to work on your sentry skills if you're going to command men on operations."

Malcolm, November 2019

Malcolm sat on the sofa reading the jobs section of the Financial Times. Penny hoovered the floor, her belly distended in loose-fitting dungarees. The thrusting motion of her hips made Malcolm smile.

"You want to break free, Freddy? Shall I do the rest?"

Penny chuckled but shook her head. She pressed the pedal with her foot and the hoover died.

"Dog hair. It gets everywhere so it does. Find anything?"

"No. Well, yes, but they want someone with more commercial experience than I have. One or two transformation leadership roles but they're at my old client and I can't apply to them for six months."

Penny restarted the hoover and rammed the skirting boards below the bend in the stairs with the dog bed pulled aside. Malcolm watched the expanse of her bottom where the fabric had worn pale. He wondered if she would take him when they went to bed. He had decided he liked the lusciousness of her hips, her thighs. His tastes had changed. And he'd seen her clean the house like this before, every surface and corner. It was shortly before she told him she was pregnant with Luca and the idea of a second child made his ears glow.

Luca was on the sofa next to him. He was trying not to fall asleep after their afternoon walk. Thick ankles poked beyond the cushions, the strap of one shoe open. He smelled of skin cream. Malcolm tousled his hair as his head lolled forward.

"Should we put him to bed?"

"No. Keep him awake. It'll be easier later."

Malcolm nodded. He was not in control and was happy not to be. He enjoyed being home.

When he left the army, he panicked. He rushed from agent to interview as if on a military campaign. He had a spreadsheet, an expected salary, a list of names. This time he felt relaxed. Delaine paid him so well that he didn't have to work for three months. That would be enough. There was always work and Brexit actually offered opportunities for someone with his skillset.

"Do you know what you're looking for?"

Malcolm shook his head, shrugged. "Not really. I just know what I don't. I don't want something turgid and structured. I don't want something where money is the only motivator. Delaine was a fantastic learning experience. I cannot fault them for that. But do you know what their profit margin was?"

"Tell me."

"Seventy-five percent."

"You're joking me!"

"Gen. Anything less had to be signed off by a partner. I was charged out at nearly two grand a day."

Penny shook her head. "Aye. You told me."

They were silent then. The boy dozed but neither of them woke him. Bonkers had sloped halfway up the stairs to watch over them through the banister, his ears dangling and ragged. Penny coiled the hoover tube and carried the machine upstairs, one hand pulling on the banister.

"Out of the way. Move."

The dog ran back down now that his bed was back in its place. Malcolm circled an advert with a pencil. He had two interviews lined up in the next week and a third on the week following. He liked the idea of a water company. He thought the job would suit him.

Daydreaming, the pencil rubber resting on his lower lip, he considered taking his family away. They could go skiing if they could find a deal, before crossing the borders became impossible.

Radio Four was on in the kitchen. The voices were friendly and informative. Malcolm got up to make supper for Luca. As he opened the cupboard doors the news came on. The headlines were punctuated by the thick, decisive chimes of Big Ben.

"The Home Secretary denies Brexit is responsible for a dramatic increase in hate crime."

"Torrential rain has continued to fall across England causing extensive flooding."

"As the economy continues to shrink, unemployment hits new levels. Good evening. I'm Charlotte Green..."

Malcolm stood with a piece of bread in each hand. He put them in the toaster but didn't depress the lever. He shook his head angrily.

Penny was upstairs hoovering the bedroom. The sound was low and muffled. Malcolm shuffled the tins to find the beans with a ring-pull top.

"Luca? You like beans or spaghetti?" he shouted over his shoulder.

He opened the tin before the boy answered and knew immediately he had made a mistake. Luca said something from the living room. He went through.

"What was that? Beans?"

"Naw. Spuggi."

"Beans? Yum yum! Beans!"

He had the open tin in his hands. He was making a joke of it but knew the boy was capable of refusing food he didn't want. He had a pugnacious gene Malcolm thought was pure Ulster. He was never like that as a child.

His phone rang. He went through to the kitchen and was amazed to see it was Dean. He put the phone to his ear and stood with the open can in one hand, a spoon sticking out of it, the smell of sauce in his nostrils.

"Dean! What's up, mate. Something wrong?"

Dean sounded nervous.

"Boss. I need a favour."

Malcolm put the tin on the counter. He feared he was going to be asked for money. "What do you need, mate? Got caught this time?"

"No. I'm handing myself in."

Malcolm had been joking. He spluttered. "You'd better tell me the full story."

He sat, one finger in his open ear. In the background he could hear the radio. When Dean talked, he put both voices together.

"You ransacked that place in Rotherham."

There was silence on the line. He turned the radio off.

"Boss, look, I'm ringing to ask a favour. Not be put on orders."

Malcolm exhaled. He smiled to himself. It was legendary what Dean got away with. He'd been arrested by the RMPs naked in the Hospital Officers' Mess. He'd somehow come across ten jerrycans of red diesel in Friday Woods while walking his dog. The vertical dent in his car had nothing to do with the leaning lamppost discovered after a dinner night.

Malcolm chuckled then shook his head. "Mate, I'm not judging."

Dean told him what he needed. Malcolm said, "Alright mate, let me have a think. I'll ring you back during the week. And get a lawyer. Don't say anything until you have one."

Penny appeared leading Luca by the hand as Malcolm put the phone down on the table.

"Who was that?"

"Dean Chadwick. My old Colour-man. Needed some advice."

"The guy who wanted to go undercover..."

"Him."

He picked up the beans and lifted a heavy-based milk pan from the hooks on the wall. Penny put Luca into his chair and strapped him in.

"So what does he want, Dean I mean?"

Malcolm shrugged as he spooned beans into the pan. "He's been a silly boy. Needs a character reference if something goes to court."

His voice was tired. Why did it fall to him to sort this shit out? He was not serving any more. He was a fat civvy.

Penny opened the drawer and rifled through the cutlery looking for the spoon with the thick green handle. Malcolm depressed the lever on the toaster. He'd need to let the toast cool or the boy would burn himself.

"Five minutes. Sorry, mate. Bad Daddy," he said.

"You don't want to do it?"

"I don't know. I don't know why I feel so heavy about it. It's just the news, I guess. Not the rain. But the austerity. Brexit. I find it depressing."

He stirred the beans, listened to the hiss as the rim bubbled. Penny put her arms round him and rested her head against his shoulder.

"But don't you think it's amazing? After all this time, they still come to you?"

Malcolm, December 2019

Malcolm sat at the kitchen table staring at the postal voting form. There were four candidates for Newcastle East and, though he could discount the Greens, he was still agonising about what to do.

The incumbent was a Labour MP he recognised. He thought of him as hard working and loyal. He wasn't a local lad but he'd been in the area since the eighties.

Malcolm couldn't vote Labour as that would mean Corbyn, a joke candidate from the Looney Left. If his army mates ever found out, when Corbyn had shared a platform with the leaders of the IRA, he would be pilloried.

The Conservative candidate had come round knocking on the doors. He had a Welsh name. But Malcolm couldn't bring himself to vote Conservative either. That would mean supporting Boris and Brexit and it wasn't something Malcolm agreed with.

The Liberal Democrat was a woman. Penny said she'd vote for her above all of them but Malcolm knew it would be a waste.

Sitting at the kitchen table, pondering what to do, he became angry at the choices. He had been a servant of the crown, a public sector employee, for the first part of his working life. He had never imagined himself as a consultant. That happened because he left the army and he did that because he had grown tired and sceptical, if he was honest with himself, of what they were doing in Afghanistan. The needless cost. The needless death. All that blood and treasure wasted in the sand. And now he was looking at a piece of paper that asked him to decide which fuckwit should be allowed to send the army into the next war, or the next.

This was a time when the world most needed statesmen. Not dividers. Not the war mongers who used the rhetoric of conflict. Not the venal, the entitled, the self-serving. But the one who would to unite, to unify, to bridge. The one who could take a small seed of human commonality and build it into coherent policy, a guiderail that even the weak and the stupid could grasp. But there was no one like that listed on the piece of paper on the table.

When he thought back to his time at Sandhurst and the list of leadership principles they'd all been forced to learn, he didn't see any political leader demonstrating any of them. Service? Moral courage? Not a hope. Integrity? They were a bunch of self-serving wankers.

Penny and Luca were watching television. Malcolm stared at the sheet on the table. *Put an X in the box opposite the candidate's name. Vote for one candidate only.*

He flattened the form against the table and stood to get a pen from the blue and white milk jug.

"Fucking hell," he muttered.

Dean, December 2019

There had been no snow in the run up to Christmas. In fact, it was quite warm for the time of year. A heavy morning mist clung to the beech trees behind the Albion and the general feeling of winter had made the roads thick with slow, uncertain drivers. The world seemed laden.

This was about the girls, Dean told himself. Sitting in the car, he recalled playing Victoria at *Angry Birds* on the Xbox the night before. She'd won and had done a cartwheel on the spot, her limbs as flexible as willow. Elizabeth had demanded a go and he'd offered to let her play her sister but she'd insisted. "No Dad, you! You!"

They were trying to forgive him. The thought made him so, so sad.

He stared at the pub door. It was fifty yards away. The car lights were off and he was parked on the right side against the grey railings. It was unlikely anyone would see him. He would wait until Billy arrived, give him a minute, then join him. Hopefully he would have brought Frenchy as well. Two birds with one stone.

Was this what deep cover felt like? The uncertainty, the shifting sands, the betrayal? He was happier knowing where he stood, the comfortable stability of rules.

The phone rang, loud and bright. He fumbled, answering in a panic. He thought it might be Billy but it was Pete.

"You celebrating?"

"Am I what?"

"Are you celebrating? It's going to happen."

"What is?"

"Brexit, you fucking eejit. Have you no been watching the news? Johnson's in. It's gonna happen. End of January."

Dean tried to laugh. "Yes, mate, yes, I know. Great, eh? But look. I'll call you back, ok? I've other things on. Talk later. Bye."

He put the phone down quickly to hide the light from the screen. At the police station, after meeting the Inspector, he'd come away with his hands shaking. How could he get out of this. But sitting in the car, his daughters' laughter in his mind, he felt coldly certain. His spine was as hard as a girder.

Pete texted. "Swampy, we still on for New Years? You, me, and Malcy Sewell?"

Dean texted back: *Yes. Laters.*

A car was approaching from round the corner, lights blurred by the fog. It wasn't Billy's works van as he'd lost that job. It was too far away to see clearly but who else would be outside the Albion in this weather at this time? It parked up by the pub. The lights died. Two men got out and walked round to the door, silhouetted against the walls.

This was great. Billy had been in hiding. Frenchy had vanished. The police wanted to speak to both of them.

Dean shook his head. Fucking amateurs.

Billy and Frenchy unlocked the pub door and went inside. It shut with a slam that hung in the dead air. Dean slid the phone in the door pocket and pulled on a pair of NI gloves, flexing his fingers under the padded knuckles.

It was time.

Kyle, previously

I'm on my bunk with my feet on the edge of Fib's and my head against the wall. My locker's open. Fib had a key. No surprise there. He's been here ages so worked out how to play it.

He's taken my dossbag. He'll sell it under the flyover, get a deal.

But that's ok. It doesn't matter anymore.

I go downstairs to get myself a brew. The stairway is lit by a skylight. Shafts of warm orange sunlight angle down the walls between the flights. It's warm on my skin.

Mark is coming upstairs. Hair is untidy. He looks up: "Morning Kyle. How are you today?"

"I'm great, Mark, really great, thanks."

He's surprised and stops to look at me. "Good, mate. I'm really glad to hear that. How are you and Fib getting along?"

"He's out at the moment. But I'm sure he'll be back later."

Mark nods. He looks like he wants to say something but doesn't. You can see the way of him. Sergeant-Major for sure. Gunners maybe. Engineers. He starts to climb the stairs again but then turns. "Kyle, we tried that number and the local police. We haven't found your sister yet, but we will. We have people looking."

I say, "Thanks, Mark. I really appreciate it."

Truth is, when they asked for my next of kin I gave them my mother's old landline in Foley Street. I don't want Charlotte or little Dan knowing I'm here. She'll be thinking of me, sure. It's my birthday in two days. But there's something I want to do and I don't want her to talk me out of it.

Right now I feel weightless. The blokes smile at me. They can tell I've made up my mind. And I love them all.

Alexander, December 2019

On 12 December, Britain went to the polls for the fifth time in ten years. To the relief of many of the electorate, Alexander won. He immediately announced the UK would leave the European Union at the end of January 2020, one month hence.

The Leave electorate were ecstatic, seeing in the election a return to the glory days when men were made of iron and ships were made of wood. The Conservative Party, especially those to the right of it, were ebullient. They were looking at election returns not known since the Thatcher era and the collapse of Labour dominance in the North of England.

The Remain electorate retired to their drawing rooms to sulk that being able to say 'I told you so' was not going to be useful when the time came.

Arlene Foster was replaced a year later as Party Leader and First Minister of Northern Ireland. The Northern Ireland Protocol continued to prove problematic. Although border controls were not enforced, the inherent paranoia of the Northern Ireland Protestant population was exacerbated. The distancing from the rest of the United Kingdom left them feeling isolated and having to recognise that Ireland was an island and that they may be better off looking south rather than east for their identity. Consequently, the threat of terrorism continued to rise and by 2024 had reached the same level of severity that was a permanent feature of the 1980s.

Dominic Cummings, Alexander's political strategist and the architect of the Leave campaign, enjoyed a brief period in the spotlight when a film was made about his role. Within a year of the 2019 General Election he was ejected from Number 10 Downing Street following a decision allegedly orchestrated by Carrie Johnson (née Symonds). He scurried from the building with his possessions in a cardboard box to spend the next years plotting revenge.

Alexander would remain as Prime Minister for two and a half years.

Kyle, previously

Fib won't be back till he's dry and that won't be till morning. I have the room to myself.

It's quiet in the corridor. Everyone's in bed as there's no noise after twenty-two hundred.

High up on the wall there's a little air vent. It slaps when the wind changes and you can smell the cooking downstairs. In front of the reinforced glass there's a single iron bar across the width of it bolted to the wall. I get the chair. If I stand on the back I can reach.

My laces are white paracord. I pull them through the gillie ties on my desert boots. I always keep the laces long to do a turn round the leg. Two laces, reef knot.

I put the chair to the wall leaving enough space for my toes. I can't take my weight on the arch of my feet; the bar is too sharp. So I climb down and put my boots back on without the laces.

That's better. I can hold the iron bar on the window while I tie another reef knot. It's just long enough.

No point thinking more. I push my head through the loop then slowly turn, one foot then the other. The loop is under my chin and my ears. It'll cut the blood off quickly. My heels are against the wall. I'm holding the iron bar with two fingers on each hand but this is just for balance. Once I kick the chair away, I won't be able to hold my weight and my feet won't reach the bed.

For a second I think of being in the door of a C130. It was the best thing I ever done, jumping, apart from war.

If you're number one in the door you look out at the pointy back of the fuel tank on the end of the wing. You can see the fields, the hedges, trees, little cars. Your weight changes as the plane rises and dips. You've got your bergen, plus the parachute, plus the machine gun and all the ammo, plus the reserve. Two hundred pounds, easy. You just want to get out to get the weight off your shoulders.

The red light comes on and the loadie yells in your ear. You snap your hand off the stanchion and slap it onto the other wrist. Be strong. Be fearless. Be airborne.

Green on. Go!

Step out into the slipstream. That beautiful release.

Then you're falling free in clear bright air.

One thousand. Two thousand. Three thousand. Check…

Brothers in Arms I – January 2020

After eating at the Inn in the village, they left their cars and staggered up the hill to Pete's caravan. Malcolm shouldered his bergen. Dean carried his over one shoulder like a binbag, the padded strap small in his huge hand. They'd had several pints and the journey took longer than expected. They stopped to piss against an electric fence and laughed uncontrollably when Dean got shocked.

"Aw, you fucker. Didn't think it was on."

"Swampy, you're a spanner. Listen to the ticking."

At the back of the caravan, the fire had died down. Pete placed logs in a ring, fencing in the grey embers, then two large ones across the middle. Very soon, they caught and the flames rose. He pulled some old folding chairs out from under the caravan. At first, Malcolm sat apart making the circle egg-shaped. The fire blazed, scattering flicks of light against the caravan. Wet logs created a pillar of smoke that got in their eyes. The stars were a resplendent splatter across the sky.

Malcolm's walking boots were warm through the sole but the rest of him was cold. He took off his jacket and pulled on the thick woollen jumper he'd bought years before from the regimental shop. Norwegian army issue with a tab of green Velcro on the neck. He then zipped his jacket back on and edged his chair nearer the fire. He leaned forward to rub his knee in the heat, pushing deep into the tendons with his thumbs.

"They didn't tell you about the arthritis when you joined, did they?" said Pete.

"Nor the tinnitus," said Dean.

"Say again?" the other two responded, and all three laughed. They took sips of their drinks. Malcolm had a box of wine and the other two had beer.

"But you would do it all again in a heartbeat," Pete said wistfully.

"I might not punch that officer," Dean said.

"I wish I had punched that CO," Malcolm replied knowing they'd know which one he meant. "That would have been a good reason to resign."

The other two nodded, smiling. He had told them about leaving Delaine. They didn't fully understand what working for such an organisation was like but were astute enough to know that if he said he had to leave, it was his affair. In effect, he'd done something honourable with the Mess Webley.

"How come you get knee pain, Boss?" Dean quizzed him as he cracked another can.

Malcolm knew there was a ribbing coming because Dean had nudged Pete with the back of his hand. Pete lit a cigarette and hawked up a cough, clouds of smoke expanding in the freezing air. Bonkers sat on the frozen ground, shivering, staring down the dirt track. He made occasional whining sounds as he looked round.

"Bit sore is it?" Dean and Pete were both chuckling.

"Alright, what have I done?" Malcolm asked.

Their laughter was infectious and Malcolm's shoulders shook even though he knew he was the butt of their joke.

"You can't have knee pain. You just can't."

"Why the fuck not?"

"You only did eight fucking jumps."

The pair burst out laughing. Malcolm pulled a face of shameful recognition.

"Ok, so I'm the crow. And you two old sweats have more right to be injured?" He continued rubbing his knee albeit with a wide smile on his lips.

The two soldiers continued laughing. Malcolm thought of a counter. "So, your Dad was undercover, is that what you said?"

Dean nodded.

"And he was away a lot when you were young."

"Yeah, that's it."

"And he investigated animal rights activists."

"Yeah."

Malcolm took his time. His lips twitched and he threw a glance at Pete. He winked.

"But it's not why you're called Swampy?"

Dean thought that was the punchline. He shook his head. "No. I was called Swampy because I splashed when I'd been on the piss. Slept in the bath after a dinner night if I had any sense."

He cracked up again, knocked back a swill of beer.

Malcolm said, "Just wondering. At Christmas, did you get a card from your Dad's other family?"

Dean fell silent, staring dumbly at him across the fire. Malcolm knew the joke was low but they were soldiers and nothing was sacrosanct. Pete started to laugh. Smoke ballooned out between his teeth as his body convulsed. It clouded round him, the smell welcome over the sharpness of the air. He wafted it away with wide sweeps of one hand.

Dean's mouth twitched. The officer had ribbed him and he knew it was a good one. He was trying not to react. Malcolm sputtered with laughter. He couldn't gloat at Dean's expense as there was always a risk of him losing it. But Pete laughed so much he descended into a hacking cough. "He got you there, mate. You were snapping."

"I wasn't."

"You fucking were. He had you."

The laughter subsided but the levity continued to bounce in Malcolm's chest. He was one of few officers with a regimental tattoo on his arm. In the lore of the soldier, the junior tom could only get a tattoo when the senior tom said so. At the end of his last tour, his platoon had held a council and told him, after a half-hour trial in the Forward Operating Base in Sangin, that he was allowed to get one. In fact, he was ordered to do so since it was discouraged for officers.

And here he was, with two old soldiers who'd asked him to join them despite his rank. They hadn't even discussed Brexit, or Boris, out of sympathy to his politics. They respected him as a man and there could be no greater honour than that.

They both looked at him across the fire and raised their cans.

"And happy birthday, Boss. Belated, I know. But happy birthday."

Malcolm reddened.

"Thanks, lads."

Brothers in Arms II

Dean got up to piss along the fence beyond the trees and returned pulling up his zip and adjusting himself.

"My nob still fucking hurts."

He smiled at Pete and winked at Malcolm. "That was a good one, Boss," he said.

Malcolm looked down at the flames. He looked content and sleepy in the low chair, head pulled into his neck. They had already agreed who would sleep where. Malcolm had chosen a spot behind Pete's bike in a gully between the trees. It was soft and padded by moss. Dean had said he would sleep on the floor of the caravan but Pete said no fucking way: "You're staying outside in case you splash."

They all laughed then fell silent for a while, watching the flames. Malcolm's dog sniffed Dean's hand and he patted its head. Bonkers circled round by Dean's chair then settled with a grumbling noise, wrapping round himself. He placed his head on his paws in such a way that he could see Malcolm.

"Good boy."

"So what's happening Dean?" Malcolm asked. "What do you need if your case goes to court?"

Dean cracked another beer. He was three ahead of Pete and even more ahead of the captain who had long since stopped, the box of wine on its side by his chair.

"I've pulled another blinder, gentlemen. My biggest blag yet."

Pete's teeth started to show as his mouth widened into a smile. "What have you done now, Swampy?"

Dean sat forward watching the bubbles settle in the sip hole. He took a long swig and burped, thumping his chest with his fist.

"What you need to appreciate, gentlemen, is that I always watch my back. It's what you do, isn't it, as a civvy. Since no fucker watches it for you."

The other two saw there was a story coming. Their eyes smiled.

"So, it was like this, right? I told Billy Atkins I wanted a meet. Told him to bring his sidekick, too. And what you don't know is his sidekick is a walt. Claimed to be 2REP, French Foreign Legion. Didn't think I recognised him but I did. He was the twat who shot Cleggy when I was with Global Risks."

"And he didn't recognise you?" Malcom said.

"Might have done. But he'd grown a beard and I was with Billy when we did the mosque. He was driving. Never really saw him."

Pete glanced at Malcolm. They both pulled faces. Dean hurried to the good bits.

"So, anyway. I told Atkins I wanted a meet and to bring this Frenchy with him. So I goes into the bar. The Albion it's called. Proper little shithole… but anyway, Frenchy's name is actually Maddison. Sean Maddison. Calls himself Mad Dog. I go in the door and he knows I'm going to do him. He takes a swing with a barstool so I drop him. Out cold. Great fucking punch. 'That's for Cleggy, you cunt'. I then look round and there's Atkins behind the table, pleading. 'No Dean, please Dean'. So I slap him round the side of the face. He tries to leg it as Frenchy comes round but I stand on his ankle till it snaps. Regular cry-baby. So I plasticuff them both to the radiators, hands out like Jesus, and call the cops from Atkins' phone. I leave it on the table, the watchkeeper talking all the time, and just leg it."

Malcolm and Pete splutter into laughter, heads back, feet kicking up and down at the edges of the fire.

"Atkins shouts all sorts of shit. 'I'll do your wife. I'll do your daughters'. So I went back in and smacked him out cold too. Got out just as the cops were coming up the hill."

Malcolm shook his head. "But what makes you think you got away with it? Do the police not want to interview you?"

Dean sat back in his chair and crossed his feet. He took another drink of beer. "Give us one of them fags, Pete?"

After he'd lit up, he continued.

"You see, the week before, I went to see my Dad's old mate. I told him I was a concerned citizen, right-wing groups ruining my good town. All shit like that. And he just sits there nodding like Churchill. Oh yes. Oh yes. And this is the guy who said I wasn't good enough to join the police. Said I was thick. Lacked initiative."

He paused. Took a drag of the fag, inhaled through his nose and exhaled as if he used to smoke.

"Then what?"

"I didn't tell him I was in the mosque. But I said I'd infiltrated one of the gangs. I was in deep cover. If they wanted the pair who did the mosque, I could make it happen."

"And..."

"So I did. I gave them the pair that did the mosque. Turns out they'd been caught on a door camera doing a recce the day before. Tried the doorhandle even. There was already evidence. Fucking idiots. Police just needed the bodies."

Malcolm and Pete look at each other, mouths open.

"What happens if they drag you in when it goes to court? If they name you as an accomplice?"

Dean looked at Malcolm out of the corner of his eyes, the cigarette dangling from his lip. He blinked through the smoke.

"They won't," he said. "Turns out Frenchy was wanted for aggravated burglary. He was on the DNA database. Been on the run for ten tears. They owe me."

"You fucking jammy bastard," said Malcolm.

Brothers in Arms III

By two in the morning the stars were hidden by high cloud. Snow would come by daybreak. Pete went inside to make a brew and cheese toasties for them all, something to soak up the beer. Dean stayed outside, staring into the fire, smiling. Malcolm's dog sneaked into the caravan and onto the bed, head low. His eyes were red.

"Tired, aren't you," Pete said. "You stay there. We'll put your boss to bed soon."

Pete pulled aside the thin curtain to see if Malcolm was still asleep in his chair. Seeing he was, he pulled a blanket out from under the dog and took it outside to place round the officer's body.

As he went back inside Dean got up and followed him. He lay on the bed, pushing the dog aside.

"You haven't told him, have you?" Dean said after a while.

"No. You?"

"No. I've told no one. Ever. Not even Michelle."

Malcolm appeared at the door, sleepy headed, drunk, the blanket round his shoulders like a refugee. He shut the door behind him. Now all of them were hunched in the little caravan waiting for the kettle to boil.

"Haven't told Michelle what?" mumbled Malcolm.

Pete looked at him. "It wasn't me shot O'Hare," he said.

Malcolm's face changed as he saw the gravity of the statement. All the court cases. The inquiries. All the stories. The medals. The career paths.

"Who did?"

"Me," said Dean.

Malcolm looked from one to the other. Pete had a wooden spatula in his hand. Dean lay on the bed looking content.

"Do I want to know this?"

Dean sniggered. "I opened fire. That's all there is to tell."

Pete turned to explain, waving the spatula. "No. I knelt up to piss, which set the cattle off. So this bastard comes out with a shotgun shouting *who's there, who's fucking there?* They must have thought it was kids or something. Or the INLA after their weapons. But he was armed. And raging."

"Did you shout a warning?"

Dean and Pete exchanged glances. Both shook their heads.

"No time. I fired a round at the wall to shut him up but the ricochet kills him stone dead...."

"Next thing we know, all hell breaks out round the front. It's that very moment when the lead call sign goes in the front door."

Pete and Dean looked at each other. They had never told anyone before and Malcolm sensed they needed to.

Dean said, "I wanted to go for Special Duties selection, you see? I wanted to join the Det, 14 Intelligence Company. They wouldn't have me if my mug was splashed all over *An Phoblacht* for killing a provo lawyer."

Pete continued, "So we legged it to the car and there were a stack of weapons in the boot, all bagged up, including the SA80 that the jocks had lost."

Dean started laughing. "But bigfoot here thought he'd disarm the body, didn't I. So I kicked the shotgun out of his hands but his finger was still round the trigger. Fucking thing went off, straight into the cowshed. Hit this fuck-off great bull in the foot and that started the bastard stampede. They broke through the gate and the two of us legged it out of the way back behind the fence. The cows go running round the yard kicking up everything and trample the lawyer's body to bits. Nearly trampled the platoon commander, this young looey who'd come round to see what we'd done..."

Pete said, "So we legged it back behind the plough in the nettles and there was me, the senior one of us, going 'Contact, rounds fired, wait out...' into a dead radio..."

Dean said, "But he never knew, the platoon commander. He was too busy running from a herd of fucking..."

The two descended in laughter, their eyes watering.

"Then the woman came out of the house and saw the body of the lawyer. Flung herself on it. The cows had already trampled all over him. And that's when one of the boys appeared out the back door and dragged her inside by the hair. I tell you, she was like the black witch of hell after that. Took two blokes to hold her down. Spoony had to hit her in the head with a rifle butt. I think she was shagging that lawyer."

"Yeah, I do. The man they caught in the house was a right little retard. Kept saying it wasn't me, it wasn't me. He was just a farmer. Turns out he didn't want to store the weapons. It was her that was the sympathiser. The lawyer obviously used her."

"Yeah. She'd also stashed a ton of Semtex in the shit tank underneath the cow barn. The dog teams found it the next day. If we hadn't got the cows out they would never have seen it."

They went silent then, their bodies occasionally convulsing with the aftershocks of laughter. Pete turned to flip a sandwich in the frying pan. Malcolm frowned.

"But you haven't done anything wrong. It was all legit."

Pete turned, the spatula in his hand. "Oh yeah. We were clean. We had every right to open fire. Rule 556, wasn't it? But Swampy said to me they'd never have him on Special Duties now. He'd go to court and his face would be seen."

Malcolm looked down at Dean who'd swung his feet onto the floor. He had one hand on Bonkers' back.

"It was all I ever wanted to do. Undercover work. And I knew killing the lawyer was the end to a... to a dream."

Malcolm imagined them fidgeting angrily in a bunch of nettles, the cold concrete under their legs, having just killed a known IRA lawyer and found a stash of weapons but wanting things to be different.

"So that's when Pete said he'd take the hit. He'd say it was him. We'd switch what we did. He got the kill and the shotgun went off when he tried to pull it from O'Hare's hands. I got the find."

Malcolm looked from Dean to Pete. Pete shrugged, pulling the sides of his mouth down.

"You did that for Dean, so he could stay in the shadows?"

"Yep. Course."

"And so all that trouble..."

Dean and Pete looked at each other. The credit for the killing had got Pete on a career path that earned him his crown. Dean had never made it through Special Duties selection but at least he'd had the chance to try.

"There's things you do for a brother," Pete said quietly. "So we switched rifles, cos mine hadn't been fired, and that's when Paulie Paulson came out the back door and called us in. He was the platoon sergeant."

"Paulie. From RHQ, Paulie? Ray Paulson?"

"Yep. Him. Asked us what happened. We told him. Except we switched roles. Pete got the kill. Paulie looked from him to me. He knew something was up but didn't know what. And so he said, stick to that. Don't ever change it. No matter what happens, if it goes to court, or whatever, just stick to that. So that's what we done."

"And we've never told a soul otherwise," Pete said.

Both of them turned to look at Malcolm. Malcolm looked from one to the other. He saw their fierce fraternity and recognised he was being invited to share in something special, a small ball of unity that no one else would ever know.

He drew a zip across his lips with one hand. The officer part of him knew that he was now party to something, if not a crime, then something very wrong. But the soldier part of him knew he wouldn't ever say anything. How could he?

"That kettle ready yet?" he said.

Brothers in arms IV

It was ten-hundred and time they were on their way. The men embraced and held each other firmly by the elbows. They did so easily, without hierarchy, as equals.

"See you soon, mate."

"You too, buddy. Any time."

Malcolm bent to hoist his bergen onto one shoulder and whistled for Bonkers. The dog was snuffling in the fire pit. Some of the embers were still orange underneath the crust.

"Away. Back away."

Pete nodded to him and he nodded back. "Let me know if there's anything you need."

"I will. See you, Boss."

Then Malcolm and Dean started downhill towards the pub where their cars were parked. They walked silently, side by side. Both had thick heads, Malcolm especially. Dean was pleased his trousers had been dry when he woke. He felt exposed too, that Malcolm knew something, but he couldn't think what. He would remember in good time.

After a hundred yards, the dog shat against the fence, his back legs high in a tussock of grass. Malcolm couldn't face picking it up. He turned to measure the distance from the caravan and reckoned it was far enough to leave. A cold wind blew across the moor, tumbling over itself, splashing flurries of snow in the corners of fields then whipping them up again. The heather bent to its will. The valley felt desolate and empty as if they were alone. There were no cars on the road. The block of pine trees on the far side was dark and unwelcoming. The sky above them was white and unreachable. The two of them were minute figures, footnotes to a distant glacial passing.

But for all their smallness they stood taller than other men. A civvy would never understand what it meant to be them.

Pete was sitting on a chair by the caravan watching the two of them off. He had a Tilly hat on and they could see him nod and raise his hand.

"Fucking shit, isn't it, what they've done to him?" Dean said.

Malcolm glanced at him. He didn't notice. "It is, Dean," he replied.

They turned and walked on before the cold began to hurt. The track had become skiddy. The puddles were solid uncracked ice. Some of the rocks had frozen to each other. Malcolm wanted to get home before the roads became difficult. Dean had even further to go.

At the corner, they turned and waved one last time. Pete waved back, then pushed himself upright and walked round the caravan out of sight.

ENDEX

Author's Note

My previous novels in this series examine the impact of military service on a small group of individuals: *In the Shadow of the Mountain* (2013), *Sunrise in the Valley* (2016), and *Along the Swift River* (2019) concern, respectively, the experience of learning how to lead within the context of Northern Ireland, the relationship between the media and the military within the context of the Balkans, and moral collapse within the context of Afghanistan. To some degree they also map the rise, maturity, and decline of the New Labour government (1997 to 2010).

These stories leave a question hanging: *what happens next?* The investigation at the heart of this novel is to capture the experience of five soldiers who left the army after the Iraq and Afghanistan wars. What did they find easy and what did they find hard? What helped them adapt? Why did some people do well and some not? I wrote this book so that service leavers could anticipate the challenges of military to civil transition (MCT) and prepare themselves for it.

The work is the main output from my PhD research at the University of Keele. My findings were that there is a common flow the experience of MCT although individual lives remain unique. What makes one person's experience differ from another's is their background, the nature of their service, the presence of any complicating factors, and how they apply five key principles, what I refer to as 'critical pillars'.

Background issues

- Stability of the childhood home
- Early exposure to violence
- Parental absence
- Trauma in early life
- Being in care
- Educational achievement
- Level of employment experience prior to enlistment

Military experience

- Level of enculturation on joining
- Level of absorption of military identity: drilling, mission command, trust
- Discharge and demobilisation experience
- Overall positivity or negativity of military experience
- Operational exposure to trauma
- Operational exposure to morally challenging situations

Transitional Challenges

- Ability to construct a civilian identity
- Ability to modify a military identity: status, wealth, purpose
- Ease of translating personal skills into meaningful work
- Ease of finding how to prosper as a civilian
- Ease of finding affordable housing
- Strength of supportive personal relationships
- Civilian supportiveness at the local level
- Levels of ownership and choice at discharge
- Rank and organisational knowledge
- Age and organisational influence
- Access to supporting networks (having someone to talk to)
- Willingness to seek help
- Coping with ambiguity and paradox
- Coping with memorialisation

Critical Pillars

- Having support from a spouse and/or young family
- Finding a sense of place
- Finding a job that provides an acceptable civilian identity
- Maintaining a support network
- Being willing to learn and adapt

Outcomes for all service leavers

- A new identity: status, income, sense of belonging
- Adapted ideas of patriotism and masculinity
- Understanding the need to find equivalent trust and kinship
- Having a sense of superiority over civilians
- Having a need to help other veterans
- Finding outlets for military humour or learning to adapt without it
- Learning to adapt to civilian norms and leadership styles
- Coping with boredom and a slower pace of life
- Coping with ageing: weight gain, deafness, arthritis, libido decline

Possible additional unsuccessful outcomes

- A sense shame and stigma
- The inability to resolve new identity
- Issues amplified by limb loss
- Addiction
- Homelessness
- Self-harm and suicide
- Problems with the law
- Mental health breakdown
- Social exclusion

Complicating Factors

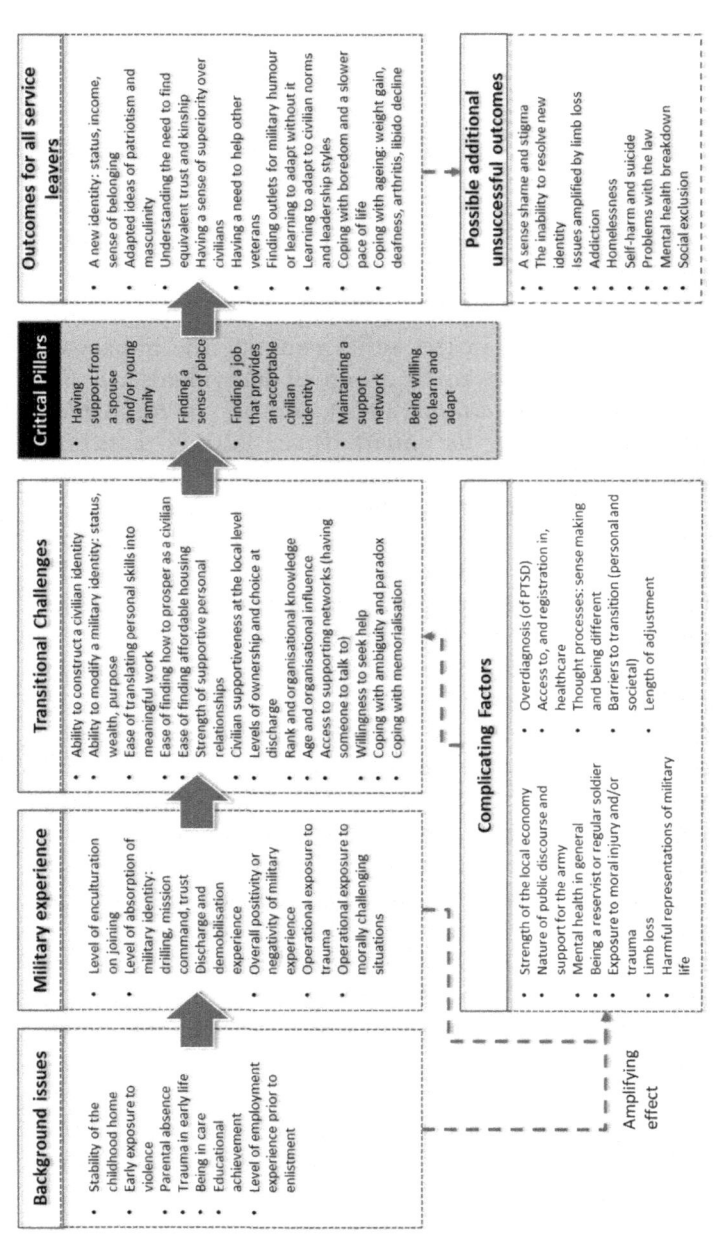

- Strength of the local economy
- Nature of public discourse and support for the army
- Mental health in general
- Being a reservist or regular soldier
- Exposure to moral injury and/or trauma
- Limb loss
- Harmful representations of military life

- Overdiagnosis (of PTSD)
- Access to, and registration in, healthcare
- Thought processes: sense making and being different
- Barriers to transition (personal and societal)
- Length of adjustment

Amplifying effect

A through life military-civil transition process map showing critical pillars and the spectrum of possible inputs and outcomes.

These critical pillars, listed in the model above, explain the full range of possible outcomes. This is not to say they are deterministic. It is possible to adapt very well to being a civilian despite being divorced, say, or having to undergo non-elective limb loss. But, in general, the more veterans have these critical pillars in place the easier their MCT journey is.

The narrative of this novel, what each of the five characters go through, is structured to show how they apply the critical pillars against real-life problems that veterans face: the excitement and terror of enjoying enormous freedom of action; having to adapt to new understandings of leadership; toning down the soldier's sense of humour; coming to terms with new understandings of patriotism or masculinity; the difficulty in making civilian friends; and coping with a lack of moral purpose.

I note that there are many national and regional initiatives in place to assist veterans in their MCT journeys, notably the *Armed Forces Covenant* of 2020. Laudable though these are in concept, I fear they answer the wrong question and in the wrong way. *The Covenant* is an enduring commitment by the Crown spurring the nation to ensure that serving soldiers, veterans, and their families "should face no disadvantage compared to other citizens in the provision of public and commercial services". As such, it makes a demand of civil society but expresses itself as an evasive double negative: that there be *no disadvantage*. The covenant makes no demands of the veteran nor provides any pragmatic guidance. As such, I fear it is meaningless. I consider MCT to be a personal, through-life journey undertaken by the individual veteran. Although society and the military undoubtedly have a role to play, it can only be experienced by the veteran and therefore they must take accountability for it.

In addition, the way soldiers are represented in films, TV shows, and novels has always interested me. My observation is that veterans are represented as either mad, bad, or sad and this is lazy plotting. Just because someone is a veteran does not mean they have PTSD. In fact, the percentage of veterans who do very well in their second career is extremely high, about 97%. So this novel is an attempt to show veterans as they really are: dedicated to what excites them, politically aware, funny, loyal, and, above all else, characterful.

Any comments on the novel would be gratefully received at books@headsailbooks.com.

For their support in the development of this novel, I would like to thank my supervisors, Professors Helen Parr and Tim Lustig, and my viva panellists, Rachel Seiffert (whose work is an inspiration) and Professors Mark Featherstone and Jon Shears.

Most importantly, however, I would like to thank everyone who contributed to my research. Nearly all my subjects came from my personal network and were forthcoming and unashamedly honest in their responses to my questions. Furthermore, I am hugely grateful to Daz, Neil, Troy, Steve, Graham, and Martin for the time and effort they put into being interviewed. Though I knew many of them from my period as an officer in the 1990s, they did not owe me anything and gave their time, hospitality, and opinions freely and without agenda. As a young platoon commander I was always told that an officer should 'know your men better than their own mothers do'. Although I thought at the time I did, the interviews made me realise that I was merely scratching the surface. Each of their life stories was richer, more varied, and more dramatic than I could have imagined. Listening to them was a truly humbling experience and one for which I will remain ever grateful. Thank you, and *Utrinque Paratus*.

Lastly, may I also thank my writing colleagues who have continued to comment and shape my work: Rachel Sargeant, Peter Garrett, and my dear wife, Joanne.

As a final note, this is a work of fiction. The main characters are inventions and any similarity to real people or events is coincidental. This is not true of the political characters. Some of the details in the Alexander sections are real and drawn from newspapers, Hansard, or the internet. Other sections are complete fabrications. I leave it to the reader to decide which ones are which.

Fergus Smith
March 2025